# CHRISTMAS BELLS

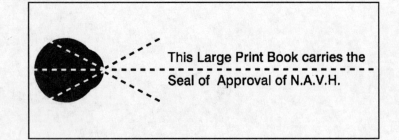

This Large Print Book carries the
Seal of Approval of N.A.V.H.

# CHRISTMAS BELLS

## JENNIFER CHIAVERINI

**THORNDIKE PRESS**

*A part of Gale, Cengage Learning*

GALE
CENGAGE Learning·

Farmington Hills, Mich • San Francisco • New York • Waterville, Maine
Meriden, Conn • Mason, Ohio • Chicago

## GALE
CENGAGE Learning®

LIBRARY OF CONGRESS CATALOGING-IN-PUBLICATION DATA

Chiaverini, Jennifer.
    Christmas bells / by Jennifer Chiaverini. — Large print edition.
      pages cm. — (Thorndike Press large print core)
    ISBN 978-1-4104-8190-0 (hardcover) — ISBN 1-4104-8190-5 (hardcover)
    1. Longfellow, Henry Wadsworth, 1807-1882—Fiction. 2. Large type books.
3. Women teachers—Fiction. 4. Christmas stories. I. Longfellow, Henry
Wadsworth, 1807-1882. Christmas bells. II. Title.
PS3553.H473C47 2016
813'.54—dc23                                                    2015035703

Published in 2015 by arrangement with Dutton, an imprint of Penguin Publishing Group, a division of Penguin Random House LLC

Printed in the United States of America
1 2 3 4 5 6 7 19 18 17 16 15

*To Marty, Nicholas, and Michael,*
*who make every Christmas merrier.*

# CHRISTMAS BELLS
## BY
## HENRY WADSWORTH LONGFELLOW

I heard the bells on Christmas Day
Their old, familiar carols play,
   And wild and sweet
   The words repeat
Of peace on earth, good-will to men!

And thought how, as the day had come,
The belfries of all Christendom
   Had rolled along
   The unbroken song
Of peace on earth, good-will to men!

Till ringing, singing on its way,
The world revolved from night to day,
   A voice, a chime,
   A chant sublime
Of peace on earth, good-will to men!

Then from each black, accursed mouth
The cannon thundered in the South,
   And with the sound
   The carols drowned
Of peace on earth, good-will to men!

It was as if an earthquake rent
The hearth-stones of a continent,

And made forlorn
The households born
Of peace on earth, good-will to men!

And in despair I bowed my head;
"There is no peace on earth," I said;
"For hate is strong,
And mocks the song
Of peace on earth, good-will to men!"

Then pealed the bells more loud and deep:
"God is not dead, nor doth He sleep;
The Wrong shall fail,
The Right prevail,
With peace on earth, good-will to men."

# CHAPTER ONE:
# THE MUSIC TEACHER'S TALE

Only the most jaded of critics would deny that the Winter Holiday Concert had been an artistic triumph, and as far as Sophia could tell as the audience filed from the auditorium to meet the young performers in the cafeteria for juice and cookies, no one fitting that description had attended. Granted, the fourth-grade recorders might have been a little shrill on "Frosty the Snowman," and perhaps half of the second grade had mumbled all but the chorus of "I Have a Little Dreidel," and Sophia should have known better than to assign a treble solo to a boy who had started the semester as a sweet-voiced cherub but now looked as if Santa might need to bring him a shaving kit for Christmas. But despite those few glitches, the children had performed beautifully. Certainly the rapturous smiles and the crash of applause that met their curtain calls proved that the audience had been well pleased.

With the assistance of the school custodian and a few helpful fifth-grade girls, Sophia soon had the costumes packed away, the cardboard sets dismantled, and the stage put in order, or at least as orderly as it could be, given the loose floorboards, the threadbare curtain, and the empty sockets they had insufficient lightbulbs to fill. Sophia knew they were lucky to have a theater at all, considering that decades of overcrowding had forced other local schools to convert performance spaces into classrooms. Sophia shared her music room with the art teacher, Yolanda, who served three different schools in the district and came to Peleg Wadsworth Elementary only twice a week. Yolanda had to haul most of her supplies from school to school, packing them into her fourteen-year-old compact car like pieces of a puzzle designed by Escher. Although she was by nature cheerfully optimistic, Yolanda looked perpetually harried and distracted as she pushed her overloaded plastic cart from parking lot to classroom and back, and she had developed a habit of constantly checking her watch and glancing at calendars to make sure she was at the right school on the right day. "Artists must suffer," she joked whenever Sophia asked how she was doing. "I've never felt more artistic."

Sophia and her stage crew finished tidying up in time to join the reception in its final minutes. Empty bottles of apple juice filled the cafeteria's recycling bin, and only a few broken cookies remained of the plates of treats donated by the performers' families. Sophia savored each delicious bite of the last gingerbread reindeer, modestly accepting praise and congratulations from parents, grandparents, and staff. As the crowd dwindled, Sophia returned to her classroom to pack up her things, gifts from her students, and projects to grade over the winter break. Her stomach growled; she could have used a second cookie and a strong cup of coffee. If she hurried, she might have time to grab something on the way from school to choir practice at St. Margaret's Catholic Church, where she volunteered as the children's music director.

She had just wrapped herself in a scarf and was slipping into her black wool coat when Linda, the principal's thin, gray-haired secretary, appeared in the classroom doorway. "Oh, good, Sophia. I caught you." She peered over the rim of her bifocals at the overstuffed satchel on Sophia's desk, so full of little handmade gifts, cards, and carefully wrapped sweets that it could not close.

11

"Impressive. You brought in quite a haul this year."

Sophia smiled as she buttoned her coat. "Yes, I should be fully stocked with fudge and peppermint through Epiphany."

Linda laughed, but her amusement swiftly faded. "Janine would like to see you in her office before you leave."

Sophia felt a flutter of nerves. "Did she say why?"

"You should talk to her." Linda edged out of the doorway looking pained. "Have a nice winter break. Merry Christmas."

"Merry Christmas," Sophia replied as Linda hurried away.

Sophia's certainty that something was amiss rose as she entered the administration offices and the dean of students wished her happy holidays in a voice usually reserved for offering condolences.

She found Janine standing behind her desk in her private office, frowning thoughtfully as she examined papers in a file. "Sophia," she said, glancing up, warmly professional as she gestured to a chair on the opposite side. "Thank you for coming. Please, have a seat."

"It never gets easier," Sophia said lightly as she set her bag on the floor, loosened her scarf, and took her seat. "Being called to the principal's office, I mean, whether you're a student or a teacher."

Janine Washington had been the principal of Peleg Wadsworth Elementary for eight years, and under her direction attendance had soared, test scores had risen, and suspensions had plummeted so low that the faculty dared hope they had become a thing of the past. Sophia had arrived on the scene three years into Janine's tenure, a student teacher full of idealism and grand plans to find a well-paying job with a prestigious music program in an affluent district as soon as she graduated. Instead, she had fallen in love with the children of Watertown and with Janine's vision of how to give them the excellent education they deserved, the kind their more fortunate peers in Beacon Hill and the Back Bay took for granted.

"The concert was excellent," Janine said. "I think it was the children's best yet — and yours. Congratulations."

"Thank you." Spiritedly, Sophia added, "I'm very proud of the students. Each and every one of them did their very best."

"I agree. That makes what I have to tell you all the more difficult." Janine regarded her sympathetically. "You're aware, I'm sure, that the measure to raise the tax levy to increase the education budget failed to pass in last month's election."

"Of course." For weeks, every conversation in the teachers' lounge had circled back to the ballot measure. In the days leading up to the election, Sophia had passed out leaflets encouraging citizens to vote yes, and, lacking a car, she had placed a bumper sticker in the window of her apartment. It was still there, a memorial to the failed measure, a reprimand to those who had supported the cause but had neglected to go to the polls, and a promise to herself to fight harder next time. "But the district will draw on emergency funds to make up the difference, right? I read that there's enough for the rest of this academic year and the next. By that time the measure will be on the ballot again."

"I'm afraid those estimates were overly optimistic," said Janine. "They didn't take into account the mold problem at the high school, or the dip in interest rates. The district's reserves have been dealt quite a blow. I've been informed that at their next meeting, the school board plans to introduce new austerity measures."

"Austerity measures?" Sophia echoed. "You mean budget cuts."

"Emergency budget cuts."

"I see." Sophia sat back in her chair, dismayed. It was no secret which programs were the first to be sacrificed in an emergency. "Janine, children need music in their lives. Most of our students aren't likely to get any arts education if they don't get it here."

"I understand that."

"It's been proven scientifically that music lessons help children's brain development and result in higher test scores, especially in math, and significantly fewer discipline problems. Students without education in the arts are five times more likely to drop out of school. Five times!"

"I know." Janine raised a hand to calm her. "I've read the reports. I've helped write many of them. However, when deciding whether to fund fifth-grade chorus or keep the furnaces going, most people, including those in charge of our budget, see only one logical choice."

"What does this mean for me?" Sophia asked, fighting to keep her voice from quavering. "Will I have to travel from school to school like Yolanda, spending a few days here and a few days there?"

"Someone will," said Janine gently. "But I'm afraid that won't be you. The two other music teachers in the district have seniority.

15

They'll drop to half time and share the single position that will remain. Sophia, I'm afraid you're going to be laid off."

Sophia stared at her, scarcely able to breathe. "Going to be?"

"Yes. At the end of the school year."

"Oh, thank God. I thought you meant I was done, finished, today, without having the chance to say goodbye to anyone —"

"Of course not. That would be a shameful way to repay you for the five years of exemplary service you've offered our school."

Sophia forced a wan smile. "Would you be willing to put that in a letter of recommendation?"

"Certainly. That's why I'm telling you now, even at the risk of losing you halfway through next semester, to give you time to find another position." Janine leaned forward and folded her arms on her desk, her expression full of regret and compassion. "I know you were considering a move to Chicago, and that you had several promising leads there. Perhaps it's time to follow up on them."

"Oh, that's . . . not really an option. I'm not moving to Chicago."

"I thought your fiancé had accepted a job there. I hear things in passing through the teachers' lounge, but perhaps I misunderstood."

"Brandon did take that job in Chicago, but he's not my fiancé anymore." Not since October, when Sophia realized that she couldn't bear to leave her family — and her job and her students and her choir at St. Margaret's — to follow him. She *could* have, but she didn't *want* to — which forced her to admit that marrying Brandon would be a mistake even if he weren't moving away.

"I see," said Janine. "My apologies. I wasn't aware."

"It's not your fault. I announced the engagement, but not the end of it."

"I still regret bringing up an unhappy subject and making a difficult conversation even worse." Janine rose and came around her desk to rest her hand on Sophia's shoulder, a motherly gesture that brought tears to Sophia's eyes. "We can talk more after winter break. I'll see you in January."

Sophia stammered out a perfunctory reply and hurried from the office, keeping her head down as she left the school rather than be drawn into a conversation with any concerned coworkers she might encounter along the way. Outside, a capricious wind drove a burst of snow crystals into her face, startling her so that she gasped, but when

17

the shock faded, she settled into an unexpected sense of calm. She had lost her job, but Janine had given her six months' notice. She would finish out the year as if nothing had changed, and surely she could find a new teaching position sometime before Labor Day.

She wrapped her scarf more securely about her neck — her eldest sister had knit it for her out of the softest cashmere, and it was as warm as it was elegant — adjusted the strap of her overstuffed bag to shift the weight to a more comfortable position, and set off on foot for St. Margaret's Catholic Church.

She dreaded breaking the news to her parents, who were, as ever, fraught with concern for her over the broken engagement and other disappointments. When Sophia was much younger, her parents had encouraged her dreams to become a renowned opera singer, their faith scarcely wavering even when she was not accepted at Juilliard or Oberlin. By the end of her first year as a voice major at Boston College, after many inspiring and humbling months learning and performing with other eager young students — all of whom, like her, had been the best singer in their high school choirs and had won every lead in drama club —

she began to realize that she was talented, but perhaps not talented enough. Suffering a crisis of confidence, she had poured out her heart to her kind but pragmatic academic advisor. He had encouraged her to continue to study music, since it was her passion, but also to expand her repertoire to teaching, the better to share that passion with others.

It proved to be excellent advice. Sophia had not long been a teacher when she realized that she was privileged and blessed to be able to pursue that calling, and now she could not imagine a more enriching or meaningful career. That made it easier to forgive her parents' unspoken disappointment that she had settled for less than her potential had promised, easier to endure the disdain of strangers who dismissed her as "only a teacher."

She would figure it out, she told herself firmly as she strode along, chin buried in her scarf, hands tucked into her pockets, shoulders braced against the flurry in the wind.

She left Belmont and Mount Auburn streets behind and, quickening her pace, lamenting the impossibility of stopping for coffee, she eventually reached Brattle Street. Even though she was running late, she paused on the sidewalk before the stately Georgian mansion that had inspired one of her selections for St. Margaret's Christmas Eve concert.

Although Boston was rich with history, the former residence known as Longfellow House captivated her imagination as much as any of the city's more famous locales, as did the great poet who had once called it home. Henry Wadsworth Longfellow had known great love and success, but also terrible heartbreak. Sophia would never forget how moved she had been when she learned the origin of a Longfellow poem she particularly loved, written one Christmas Day during the Civil War. After suffering tremendous personal loss and enduring along with the rest of the divided nation the hardships of a terrible war, Longfellow had been inspired to compose one of his most beloved and faith-affirming poems — and yet most people, even as they sang the carol his poem had become, had no idea he had written it.

A distant bell tolled the quarter hour. *"I heard the bells on Christmas Day, their old familiar carols play,"* Sophia sang softly, gazing at the house, at the window to the room where, perhaps, Henry Wadsworth Longfellow had written the poem. *"And wild and sweet the words repeat of peace on earth, good-will to men."* And women too, she added silently, smiling wistfully. She could have used a little peace and goodwill right about then.

Mindful of the time, Sophia hurried on her way. The wind had picked up while she had stood lost in reverie in front of the historic residence, whisking snowflakes in graceful swirls and eddies on the sidewalk.

Soon thereafter, about a half hour after setting out from school, Sophia arrived outside St. Margaret's Catholic Church. She went around to the side door, which was always left unlocked on choir rehearsal nights, and had just placed her hand on the latch when the door swung open and a tall figure stepped forth. "There you are," said Father Ryan, relieved. He caught the door before it swung shut and held it open for her. "Lucas was getting worried, so he sent me out to search for you."

Sophia quickly stepped into the warmth of the little foyer. "I'm not late, am I? I should've taken the bus."

"No, you're right on time, but you're usually early, and that was cause enough for worry." Father Ryan was around thirty-five, with an athlete's build, thick strawberry-blond hair, and a dimple in his right cheek

21

that deepened when he smiled, which was often. Sophia had heard more than one parishioner sigh mournfully that his handsome face was wasted on a priest. "Lucas cares about you, you know."

Sophia laughed and shrugged out of her coat. "He just doesn't want to be left alone with that pack of wild hooligans."

"That's not fair," Father Ryan protested, grinning. "Not to the kids and not to Lucas. He's great with them and you know it. He's leading them in warm-ups as we speak."

Then she was even later than she feared. Thanking the priest for his concern, Sophia stamped the snow off her boots on the mat, draped her coat over her arm, and hurried up the staircase and through the side entrance to the nave. Behind the altar in the choir loft stood forty children clad in a colorful array of sweatshirts and sweaters to ward off the chill, warming up with scales and solfège in rounds, accompanied by Lucas on piano. He wore his dark brown hair long, and his eyes were serious and kind and the color of comfortably faded denim.

As she quietly set down her bag and coat and scarf on a front pew, several of the children noticed her and grinned — ginger-haired Alex even broke form to wave, earn-ing him a look of shocked reproach from his elder sister, Charlotte — but with his back to her, Lucas was unaware she had arrived.

For all of her teasing, Sophia admired Lucas's patience with the boys and girls, his manifest kindness, his sudden flashes of humor that never failed to bring the young singers' wandering attention back to the music. Lucas was a brilliant pianist, a graduate student at Harvard, steadily booked for paying engagements, and not particularly religious, which made his unwavering commitment to his volunteer gig at the church a bit baffling, or so Sophia had thought when they first met. It was not long, however, until she concluded that he obviously loved playing the piano, he enjoyed the challenges and rewards of working with children, and the acoustics in the church were excellent. What other reason did he need to spend two evenings a week, most of his Sunday mornings, and one Saturday afternoon a month at St. Margaret's?

Sophia and Lucas were not alone in enjoying the children's rehearsals. Sister Winifred smiled and nodded in time with the music as she quietly walked the aisles, raising kneelers and replacing hymnals and missals.

A few parents were scattered among the pews, some in pairs chatting in whispers, others alone, frowning at laptops or tapping on smartphones. Charlotte and Alex's mother was there too, a perky red beret pulled over her long blond hair, her gaze fixed on the young singers, her expression incongruously bleak. Ever since her husband, Jason, had been deployed overseas with his National Guard unit, Laurie had become markedly tense and unhappy, but at that moment she looked more stricken and upset than Sophia had ever seen her. Concerned, Sophia was just about to approach her when her attention was abruptly pulled away by the muffled boom of one of the tall, heavy doors at the back of the church falling shut. A woman in her early sixties had entered, her short, dark hair neatly coiffed, a black handbag dangling from the crook of her arm. Her eyes met Sophia's; she smiled apologetically, unbuttoned her long coat to reveal a well-tailored red tweed suit and a double strand of lustrous pearls, and settled into the back pew.

At that moment the warm-ups concluded. "Well done, kids," Lucas said, rising from the piano bench. "As soon as Miss Sophia arrives —"

"She's over there," Alex interrupted, pointing. Lucas gave a start and turned, evoking a smattering a giggles from the sopranos.

"We're all here now, so let's continue," Sophia replied, crossing the transept and joining Lucas at the piano. "Let's begin with 'I Heard the Bells on Christmas Day.' " As the children turned to the proper page in their binders, Sophia sniffed the air, sighed, and said to Lucas in an undertone, "Some very lucky person nearby has coffee."

"Yes, you." Busily arranging his sheet music, Lucas nodded to the floor beside his bench, where she discovered a travel mug and a small brown paper bag. "I figured your concert would run late and you wouldn't have time to stop. There's a cranberry scone in the bag if you're hungry."

"Lucas, you didn't," she exclaimed, picking up the cup and bag. "You're a lifesaver, a saint, an angel."

"Not really. Just a guy who walked past a coffee shop on his way here." He spared a glance for the children, who were becoming cheerfully restless. "How was the concert?"

"The concert was great, but —" To her horror, a sob burst from her throat. "I lost my job. Or I'm going to. In June."

"You're not going to teach us anymore?"

protested Alex shrilly. "Father Ryan fired you? He can't do that! We like you too much."

"No, no, Father Ryan didn't fire me," Sophia quickly assured him, and the other children too, for they all were regarding her with alarm. "I meant my other job. I'm not leaving St. Margaret's." As the anxious looks faded from the children's faces, she murmured to Lucas, "Curse his sharp young ears. I didn't mean for him to hear that."

"It's okay," said Lucas, his brow furrowing. "Take a deep breath. Have some coffee. We can talk about it afterward."

Cradling the mug in her hands, Sophia nodded, not trusting herself to speak. She closed her eyes and took a long, sustaining drink of coffee — still hot, comfortingly delicious, exactly the way she liked it. Lucas could deny it all he liked, but he was a saint.

The children were waiting.

"Trebles, let's hear from you first," she said, straightening her shoulders, mustering a smile. "Remember the eighth rest before you come in. Lucas, if you will?"

He nodded, his gaze full of concern and kindness as he placed his hands — strong, long-fingered, elegant — upon the keys.

She raised her baton, the children came promptly to attention, and the music began.

## Chapter Two: December 1860

On Christmas morning as the Longfellow family walked home from church, bells pealed gloriously overhead until all of Cambridge resounded in exultant euphony. Harness bells chimed in, light and cheerful, as horse-drawn sleighs glided swiftly down Brattle Street, their laughing passengers bundled warmly in blankets against the nip in the air. The sky was a flawless azure redolent of Iberian seas with nary a cloud, the sun shone with golden morning light, and a soft, downy blanket of snow covered the earth. Everywhere friends and neighbors called out greetings, and even strangers wished one another a Merry Christmas and courteously made room to pass on the sidewalks. With the promise of a Yule log burning on the hearth at home, a sumptuous feast to come, a good bottle of wine at the table, and friends gathered round to share it, Henry could almost believe that the tidings of that holy day could turn even the angriest hearts to reconciliation.

Yet even as the gospel reading told the story of the birth of the Prince of Peace, Henry had overheard murmurs in the pews, troubling reports from South Carolina. After the service, as the worshippers filed from the church, conversations quickly turned from the exchange of holiday greetings to the rising enmity between North and South. The slave states had been threatening to leave the Union for more than forty years, but ever since Abraham Lincoln had won the presidential election in early November, tensions had soared and calls for secession in the Southern press had become even more frenzied and furious. Equally troubling, foreboding letters from Henry's closest friend, Charles Sumner, the senior senator from Massachusetts, told of rising animosity within both chambers of Congress. Henry trusted Sumner's judgment, for purely as a matter of self-preservation, his friend had become a careful observer of the temper of the Senate. More than four years earlier, Sumner had been beaten nearly to death in the Senate chamber by Representative Preston Brooks of South Carolina, who had taken great offense to one of Sumner's more vitriolic speeches condemning slavery. Sumner's head trauma and psychic wounds had been so severe that he had not resumed his Senate duties for three years.

Through the post, Henry and Sumner debated the likelihood that South Carolina would make good on her threats and leave the Union. "What I am afraid of," Henry confided to his friend, "is not that they will go, but that the North will yield. The tone of the Boston papers — the *Atlas* only excepted — is very weak and spiritless."

In conversations with his wife — his dear, beloved Fanny — Henry tried to be more optimistic. "Nothing will come of this bluster and outrage," he had assured her only a few weeks before Christmas. "The Southern firebrands will settle down after Mr. Lincoln's inauguration, just as they always have."

"Do you really think so?" asked Fanny, her large, dark eyes full of worry and doubt. "Their anger seems different this time. The Southern aristocrats seem inflamed by a particular hatred for Mr. Lincoln, and a desperate fear that he'll take away their slaves with a stroke of a pen on his first day in office."

"If only it were that easy," said Henry ruefully. "Even with Mr. Lincoln as president I believe the abolition of slavery will take time, and it'll come only after the usual squabbling and deal-making in Washington City."

"Then you don't believe war is inevitable?"

"No, my dearest, I don't, not war and not secession." He smiled and kissed her. "I'll believe that South Carolina truly intends to leave the Union when she leaves it and not before."

Fanny had seemed reassured, and Henry too had allowed himself to hope, but then, only a few days before Christmas, at a state convention at St. Andrew's Hall in Charleston, the delegates of South Carolina had voted unanimously to secede from the Union. The stock market roiled, politicians debated what to do, and citizens North and South wondered — some in trepidation, others eagerly — which states would follow South Carolina into rebellion.

With the Christmas bells ringing joyfully and his beloved Fanny on his arm, smiling warmly up at him from beneath the blue woolen hood of her cloak, it seemed to Henry almost unfathomable that anywhere thoughts could be troubled or hearts twisted in anger. He patted Fanny's hand where it rested in the crook of his elbow and felt a

familiar surge of wonder and happiness when she squeezed his arm tenderly and briefly rested her cheek against his shoulder. For all his poetical gifts, he could scarcely put into words what an inexpressible delight Fanny was to him, always and in all things. Although they had been married more than seventeen years, he still never caught a glimpse of her without a thrill of pleasure; she never entered a room where he was without his heart quickening, nor departed without feeling that some of the light went with her.

Henry and Fanny had first met more than twenty-four years before, not in Boston though they lived but five miles from each other, but while traveling in the Bernese Alps — Henry, alone and grieving the recent loss of his first wife in childbirth; Fanny on a European tour with her father, elder brother, sister, and cousin. At nineteen, Frances Appleton had known her own share of heartbreak, and knew more yet awaited her; her mother had died of consumption three years before, a brother a year later, and the same disease afflicted her dear cousin William, who was among the traveling party, seeking respite from his illness in the crisp mountain air.

Upon discovering that members of one of

Boston's most respected families were staying at his hotel in Thun, Henry had sent up his card to Fanny's father, Nathan Appleton, a prominent member of the Whig Party and a prosperous businessman who had built a fortune developing New England's textile industry. The Appletons were out at the time, but several days later, when they all had moved on to Interlaken, they finally met.

Drawn together by their sympathetic understanding of each other's loss, Henry and Fanny became fast friends. For nearly three weeks, amid the sublime beauty of the snow-capped Swiss mountains rising above pure, crystal lakes, they passed many pleasant hours together, strolling, reading, discussing art and literature, boating, sketching, and translating German poetry. Henry enjoyed the company of the rest of her family too, especially her elder brother Thomas — witty, irrepressible, and artistic — and her cousin William, whose fragile health and undaunted spirits evoked Henry's respect and sympathy.

All too soon duty summoned Henry elsewhere, but he parted from Fanny and her family in the consolation of knowing that they would meet again in Boston in a year's time, after their grand tour concluded.

Although Henry was by then an accomplished poet and a respected professor of modern European languages at Harvard, he realized that a significant disparity in social rank separated him from the Appletons. Yet he had been confident that the Appletons were too good, too noble-hearted a family, to let that impede their burgeoning friendship.

What he had not anticipated in the midst of mourning for his lost wife and unborn child was that, over time, his feelings for Fanny would grow beyond friendship. More than a year after they met, Henry declared his love for Fanny, only to be clearly and decisively told that she did not return it. Humbled, he withdrew for a time to recover from the sting of her rejection, but the Appletons remained fond of him, and eventually friendship won out over pride and he resumed calling at their gracious townhome at 39 Beacon Street. He tried to conceal his enduring admiration for Fanny, but failed badly enough that he regularly found himself the object of amiable teasing within Boston society.

Then, two years after Fanny spurned him, his infatuation and his pen conspired to ruin any chance for even friendship between them.

In August of 1839, his philosophical travel novel, *Hyperion: A Romance,* was published to perhaps more puzzlement than acclaim. The story told of a young American, Paul Flemming, who fell in love with an English-woman, Mary Ashburton, while both were traveling in Germany. Mary, whom Paul described to a fictional friend as "not beautiful, but very intellectual," refused him as a suitor despite his many excellent quali-ties. *Hyperion* was widely read, with sales invigorated by American readers' eagerness to learn about German culture, but within Boston society it provoked intrigue for entirely different reasons. No matter how often and how emphatically Henry pro-tested that his book was a novel, a work of fiction, every mutual acquaintance insisted on believing that Mary and Paul were thinly veiled renditions of a certain young heiress and a hapless, lovelorn professor. Within days of the novel's publication, a chill — no, a veritable arctic whirlwind blowing down from the heights of Beacon Hill — descended upon their association.

This second, sterner, seemingly irrevoca-ble rejection plunged Henry deep into melancholy. Writing offered him some solace, but teaching none, so he eventually requested a leave of absence from Harvard

and traveled to Germany in hopes of recovering his health. After several weeks partaking of the regimen at Marienberg on the Rhine — morning sweats, four cold baths a day, vigorous walks, a simple, healthful diet — he felt restored enough to befriend some of the other patients and even to compose some poetry. Yet his longing for Fanny did not ease in proportion to his dawning resignation that she would never have him.

In the autumn of 1842 he returned to America, and soon thereafter he published several poems on slavery he had written during the tempestuous Atlantic crossing. He knew he risked damaging his professional reputation by expressing his abolitionist sentiments, not to mention jeopardizing friendships with acquaintances whose livelihoods in the textile industry depended upon Southern cotton — including the Appletons.

His radical position could not have offended Fanny too much, for she spoke to him kindly and cordially whenever they met in society. And then, months later and wholly unexpectedly, as they chatted at a party in the spring of 1843, Fanny mentioned that her brother would be leaving soon for Europe, and that she would want company in his absence.

Henry was not about to let even the wisp of a chance to renew their friendship elude him. Soon thereafter, he called on Fanny at home, and was received with such warmth that he dared write to her afterward and tell her that time and distance and discouragement had not altered his affections.

To his great joy, she replied that her feelings about him had changed utterly.

In July, seven years after they had found solace in their sympathetic companionship in Switzerland, and at least a year after Henry had abandoned all hope that Fanny would ever love him, they were wed before a joyful company of fifty friends and family in the parlor of the Appleton home. The bride, at thirty years of age, was radiant in a rich yet simple gown of muslin trimmed with splendid thread lace, the tunic gathered on either side of the skirt with orange blossoms, a delicate lace veil cascading from a wreath of orange blossoms upon her head to gently brush the floor. The groom, quietly rejoicing, kissed his bride tenderly and, after the celebration ended, he took her home to Craigie House beneath the soft light of a full moon, resolving never to be parted from her.

He had taken her home to rented rooms, but soon thereafter, Fanny's father purchased the mansion for the newlyweds from the Widow Craigie, and at last Henry felt he had a home worthy of his most excellent wife.

As they approached the residence still known to all as Craigie House, he shook his head in affectionate exasperation as he watched their two sons hurry on ahead of the rest of the family. Flush with the freedom of their release from the solemnity of church, they grinned and teased and jostled each other, until Charley — still playful and impulsive at sixteen — accidentally knocked Ernest's hat from his head and into the street, where a horse nearly trampled it — and Charley too, in snatching it out of the way.

"Do be careful, boys," Fanny called out to them, alarmed.

"Sorry, Mother," said Charley, and his younger brother quickly chimed in the same as he brushed snow from his cap and replaced it jauntily upon his thick brown locks.

"Charley's recklessness will take years off my life," Fanny murmured to Henry.

She had lowered her voice, but not enough. "Will it really, Mama?" asked ten-year-old Alice anxiously. She and her two younger sisters, arms linked and hands tucked into fur muffs, followed behind their parents with far greater decorum than their elder brothers preceding them.

"Of course not." Smiling, Fanny turned to look reassuringly at solemn Alice and golden-haired Edith, all of seven years, and to kiss the rosy cheek of Allegra Anne, who at five was the baby of the family. "It's just something people say." As she straightened and turned, she caught Henry's eye and, unseen by their daughters, cast her gaze to heaven with a look of such comic sufferance that he laughed.

The family arrived home without further incident or injury, and as soon as they crossed the threshold, the delicious smells of roast goose and plum pudding enveloped them. Charley and Ernest began conspiring to charm the cook into allowing them a taste before the feast was served, but Fanny overheard and promptly forbade it. "We have much to do before we can celebrate properly," she reminded them, and assigned each a task or two that they hurried off to complete, the sooner to begin their fun. Henry too was given an assignment, and an easy, welcome task it was — to withdraw to his study and choose an appropriate Christmas story to read to the children later that evening. Fanny promised to summon him when their guests arrived.

A newly built fire crackled on the grate as he entered the familiar room, which smelled of woodsmoke and fine old books and furniture polish. Although he had written many of his most acclaimed poems there, either bent over the desk by the south window or seated in the chair by the fireplace writing in pencil to spare his tired eyes, the study was no dignified retreat where he toiled in isolation but rather a pleasant, welcoming nexus of domestic activity. Charley could burst in at any time of the day to play with his canary and chatter on about friends' antics or dogs or sports or ships newly come to Boston Harbor. Ernest kept his crayons and paper and paints scattered upon a central oval table, and would often sketch scenes from memory or imagination while Henry wrote nearby, two artists companionably at work. The girls darted in and out, safe in knowing that their father would not rebuke them if they interrupted his train of thought with hugs and kisses and requests to mend broken toys or cut them new paper dolls. Quite to the contrary, he delighted in their innocent antics so much that he was inspired to compose a poem, "The Children's Hour," to capture forever the merriment of his daughters' evening ritual of bursting into his office at twilight for hugs and good-night kisses.

He turned around in place, patting his pockets absently as if searching for something mislaid, until he remembered his errand. The newspapers stacked neatly on the desk he ignored, reluctant to allow reports of new threats from rebellious South Carolina to cast melancholy shadows upon the day. The most recent report he had heard, that the rebellious state's newly appointed leaders had announced that the three federal forts within its borders no longer belonged to the United States but to their fledging separatist republic, surely diminished the likelihood that South Carolina would be swiftly restored to the Union through negotiation. At least Henry hoped such efforts were ongoing, and with increasing urgency; considering how President Buchanan had dithered and equivocated throughout the escalating crisis, Henry would not be surprised to hear that he was doing little more than staring at the calendar and counting the days until he could leave office and pass the problem on to Mr. Lincoln.

With an effort, Henry pushed thoughts of political matters aside and went to the nearest bookcase to scan the titles for a story that suited the holiday, something that would entertain the children and improve his mood. He had just taken Clement C. Moore's book of poems from the shelf and was turning to "A Visit from St. Nicholas" when Allegra Anne — his dear little Annie — ran in, her brown curls bouncing, held back from her face by a ribbon of red velvet. "Mama says you're wanted," Annie announced, her sweet, piping voice ringing with authority.

"Then I'm duty bound to come," he said, bowing as he tucked the book beneath his arm. Beaming, Annie seized his hand and led him off to the foyer just as the brass knocker rapped twice to announce the arrival of their first guests.

Soon Craigie House was filled with friends and family, and the very walls seemed to resonate in harmony with their love and mirth and happiness. As the eldest, Charley led the boys' games, merrily boisterous but full of fun and gentle with the younger lads. Alice and her favorite cousin quickly had the girls performing songs and reciting poems for an indulgent audience of parents and neighbors, warmed by the companionship of dear friends as much as by the Yule log blazing on the hearth. A Christmas tree stood in the corner of the drawing room, its evergreen boughs prettily adorned with candles, strings of popcorn, sugared fruits, and small trinkets wrapped in colored paper, gifts for their guests. A side table was laden with so many presents for the children — sent from loving aunts and uncles or left by affectionate friends who had called throughout the week — that it almost seemed to bow beneath the weight.

Then came time for the feast — roast goose, boiled ham, smoked fish, oysters, mince pies, potatoes with chestnuts, cranberries in jelly, and excellent Italian wines for the adults. No one wanted to talk about the secession fever sweeping from Charleston through the South, but as the wineglasses were refilled and the guests began feeling ever more merry and bright, the topic shifted from reminiscences of Christmases past to beloved Christmas stories from favorite authors. Before Henry could forestall it, a general clamor went up that he too should write a great Christmas tale, one to rival those of Clement Moore and Charles Dickens.

From the head of the table Henry caught Fanny's eye, which sparkled with mischievous amusement; unnoticed by the others, she pressed her fingers to her lips to suppress laughter and raised her glass in a small

42

toast to her husband. He was forever being told by well-meaning friends, admirers, and critics alike what he ought to write, and she knew how it vexed him.

As even the children chimed in with suggestions for the proposed Christmas tale, Henry threw Fanny a helpless look, pleading for intercession. Ever loyal, she rose to the occasion. "Don't offer him too much inspiration," she said, her voice carrying above the clamor, "or he'll hurry off to his study to begin writing immediately, and we won't see him again until the New Year."

"We mustn't allow that," protested Henry's good friend Louis Agassiz, a Swiss who had come to America in 1847 to join the Harvard faculty as a professor of zoology and geology. Since then he had become one of the most famous scientists in the world, and his startling theory that much of the Earth had once been covered in glaciers fascinated Henry. "It's Christmas. This is not a day for labor, but for revelry."

"And reverence," added Frances Lowell, the wife of another close friend in attendance, the professor, editor, and poet James Russell Lowell.

"Yes, indeed," declared Henry's brother-in-law, Tom Appleton. "Let's not forget that Henry must also continue to play host to us, his friends and relations. All told, I count three very good reasons he should not write today. Fanny," he said, turning to his sister, "you must insist that he forbear composing any new verses until tomorrow."

"I agree," she replied, and to Henry, added, "Darling, I insist you postpone commencing this grand Christmas epic until January, at the earliest."

"Very well, my dear." Henry spread his hands and looked around the table, shaking his head and feigning regret. "I apologize, friends, but I must decline your most . . . interesting suggestion."

Everyone gathered around the table, save the youngest children, burst out laughing, revealing that they had all been in on the joke.

As dessert was served — plum pudding, which had steamed enticingly upon the sideboard for what seemed like many fragrant and tempting hours, accompanied by a rich, velvety custard flavored with anise — Fanny said, "Henry will have another poem published very soon, which you may enjoy almost as much as a Christmas tale."

Several friends nodded knowingly, for Henry had shown them drafts of the work in progress, but others turned inquiring looks upon their host. "Will it be another

44

'Evangeline' or 'Hiawatha'?" asked Elizabeth Agassiz, Louis's wife, an intellectual, well-spoken woman who had founded a school for girls in Boston. "Another stirring epic tale with an unlikely hero at its center?"

"I wouldn't say unlikely," said Henry. "I call the poem 'Paul Revere's Ride,' and it will appear in the January edition of *The Atlantic.*"

"Who's Paul Revere?" asked Alice, for children were not required to be seen and not heard within the Longfellow household — in fact, they were encouraged to question, to speak, to compose.

"He was a Boston silversmith and a patriot of the Revolution," said Henry. "My grandfather, Peleg Wadsworth — your great-grandfather, children — was his commander in the Penobscot Expedition of seventeen seventy-nine. My poem, however, tells of the night Revere courageously risked his life and liberty to warn the colonials of an invasion by the British."

"Sounds intriguing," said Mrs. Agassiz. "I look forward to reading it."

Henry inclined his head to thank her for the compliment. "I was inspired to write the poem after visiting the Old North Church last April. I climbed its tower, looked out upon the landscape, and contemplated the troubles our forefathers confronted in the early days of the republic and those we face now. I began writing the next day." Then honesty compelled him to add, "I admit I took some liberties with historical fact —"

"As a poet must, for the sake of his art," declared Tom, looking around the table for affirming nods.

"There were three riders, not one, for example," said Henry, "and Revere's role was to warn Samuel Adams and John Hancock that the Redcoats were marching upon Lexington to arrest them and seize their armories in Concord. I think — I trust — that my readers know the story well enough to understand that I altered facts for dramatic effect."

"If they don't, they should," said Fanny stoutly.

"I only hope they see the whole poem," Henry added, almost to himself. "Earlier this month, the *Evening Transcript* ran a version they said they took from *The Atlantic*'s advance sheets. Six lines were omitted — six rather essential lines."

"Mr. Fields won't make that mistake," Fanny said soothingly. "The poem will be printed in its entirety, and the people will love it. Your Paul Revere is a hero for our own troubled times as well as the past."

"Our generation too longs for a great man to save the nation," said James Lowell, frowning slightly as he studied his wineglass. "Only instead of oppression from a foreign king, we confront secession. Instead of red-coated British regulars, we contend with Southern firebrands and slaveholders."

"Perhaps Mr. Lincoln will be the hero for our times," said Fanny. "Mr. Buchanan has availed us nothing, but if God wills it, his successor may yet heal the breach and preserve the Union."

"Hear, hear," said Tom, raising his glass.

They all joined in on a solemn toast that the New Year would bring reconciliation and peace, although Henry suspected not one of them, for all their vaunted intellect, could predict how that might come about.

When the feast was over, the older children pulled on their coats and mittens and raced outside to throw snowballs and tow sleds around the yard in the dwindling twilight while the adults settled in the drawing room to talk and reminisce, and to smile over the younger children as they played with the new toys Santa Claus had left in their stockings the night before.

They were warming themselves with hot coffee and amusing riddles when the children trooped back in, rosy-cheeked and exuberant. Once they were out of their wraps and comfortably settled by the fire with sugared plums and cups of hot tea, Henry read aloud "A Visit from St. Nicholas." The younger children gazed up at him with rapt attention as the story of the jolly old elf's visit unfolded, and from across the room, Fanny regarded him with such warmth and fondness, so much obvious enjoyment of the sound of his voice, that Henry could not imagine feeling any more blessed than he did at that moment on that holy day. The inevitable, trifling frustrations of daily life, the heavy responsibility of raising children, the onerous troubles facing the country — all fell away in the firelight. He marveled to realize that everything that truly mattered to him was represented in that gathering — family, friends, love, faith, hope. It seemed miraculous that one room could contain so much — but if a humble manger could hold the Divine, anything was possible.

The youngest children were dozing in their parents' arms by the time the guests departed, the light of their lanterns and the music of sleigh bells fading as the horses carried them home and away. The Longfellow children were soon tucked into their beds with warm quilts and tender kisses. Shortly after midnight, their father and mother too retired for the night, tired but content.

"It was a very merry Christmas, wasn't it, darling?" said Fanny as she plaited her hair into one long braid and tucked it beneath her cap.

"It was." Henry yawned as she climbed into bed beside him, then he tucked the quilts around them both and kissed her. "One of the merriest in memory. May the New Year be as full of happiness and peace and friendship."

"May it indeed," Fanny replied drowsily, snuggling up close beside him.

Their hopes were short-lived, dashed by shocking developments in Charleston.

While the city slept on the night of December 26, Union Major Robert Anderson, acting without orders from his superiors, stealthily moved his troops from their vulnerable position at Fort Moultrie on the mainland to the incomplete but more strategically located Fort Sumter in Charleston Harbor. The next day, South Carolina militia seized Fort Moultrie and another federal stronghold, Castle Pinckney, and demanded that Major Anderson surrender.

Instead, Major Anderson and his men

resolutely held their position, and the South Carolina militia settled in for the siege.

# CHAPTER THREE:
# THE ACCOMPANIST'S TALE

"You should tell Sophia how you feel," Father Ryan had urged Lucas on more than one occasion, but even the priest acknowledged that the timing had never been right. And then it was too late: Sophia was engaged to marry Brandon, a decent-enough guy, well-meaning but clueless, reliable but lacking in imagination, and definitely not good enough for Sophia. Not that Lucas was biased or anything.

Sophia and Brandon had been dating only a short while when Lucas first met her, and ever afterward he tortured himself with the knowledge that if only he had sat down at the piano at St. Margaret's three weeks earlier, everything might have turned out differently.

On the last Friday before Christmas — which was also Sophia's last day of school before Winter Break — Lucas stopped at a coffee shop on his way to St. Margaret's, and as he stood in line, he remembered the student concert. He figured Sophia would need coffee, so he ordered two cups to go, hers in an insulated travel mug. "How fresh are those scones?" he asked the barista, gesturing to the bakery case.

"Came out of the oven twenty minutes ago."

"One blueberry and one cranberry, please."

Lucas paid, moved down the counter to collect his order, and added milk and sugar to Sophia's cup before heading outside and on his way. The wind had picked up while he was inside, sending icy crystals of snow into graceful swirls and eddies on the sidewalk, reminding him with painful intensity of a night in late November two years before, when an unexpected early snowstorm had compelled Sophia to end rehearsal early. Lucas had walked her back to her apartment, but any hope that she might invite him in to wait out the storm had been immediately quashed when he spotted Brandon's SUV in the parking lot. Some things had changed in the two years since that snowy night, others not so much. Brandon was gone; Sophia still had no idea how Lucas felt about her. But what could he do? She had just broken off an engagement. She needed a friend, and he did not want to be the rebound guy. He had waited for her too long for that.

The realization brought him to an abrupt halt on the sidewalk. That was exactly what he had been doing for the past three years, though he hated to admit it: He had been waiting for her.

Maybe it was time to either tell her the truth or move on.

"What do I have to lose?" he muttered as he continued down the sidewalk, a cup of coffee in each hand, his messenger bag full of sheet music slung over his shoulder. What did he have to lose except his self-respect, his friendship with Sophia, and his volunteer gig with the choir? He would miss the kids, so goofy and smart in unexpected ways and often unintentionally hilarious. No matter how stressful or exhausting or frustrating his day might have been, a couple of hours with the young singers never failed to lift his mood, to put everything else in perspective. Why risk losing all that to confess the truth to Sophia, when she had never — once or twice, tops — in the past three years shown him even a flicker of romantic interest?

"Get over it," he told himself loudly, angrily, as he passed before St. Margaret's on his way to the side entrance.

"Get over what?"

Startled, Lucas turned and discovered Father Ryan at the top of the stone staircase, bundled in a black pea coat and a black-and-gold Bruins tuque, sweeping snow off the landing in front of the tall, ornate double doors marking the front entrance. For a moment Lucas groped for a plausible answer, but he had been raised Catholic and could not bring himself to lie to a priest on the steps of his own church. "You know," he said, deflated.

"Oh, that." Father Ryan nodded and resumed sweeping. "You should ask her out."

"Are you kidding? Less than two months ago she broke up with her fiancé."

"Which means she's single."

"It's too soon."

Father Ryan rested his hands on the end of the broom handle, mulled it over, and shook his head. "I think I would've heard if there was an official mourning period."

"Sophia doesn't think of me as anything more than a friend."

"Only because you've never given her reason to think of you as anything else."

That irked him, because he knew it was true. "Father," he said wearily, "no offense, but I'm a little skeptical about taking romantic advice from a priest."

"Fair enough." Sighing, mildly exasperated, Father Ryan gestured for Lucas to climb the stairs. "The front door's unlocked. Save yourself the walk around the side."

"Thanks." Lucas took the stairs two at a time and entered the warm vestibule as the priest held open a door. "You must really feel sorry for me."

The nave was warm and softly lit, and his footsteps echoed as he made his way to the piano, a magnificent Shigeru Kawai grand donated to the church by a wealthy parishioner. The same anonymous benefactor paid to have it regularly tuned by the most qualified expert in Boston, and its tone was astonishingly clear, rich, and harmonic, with excellent power and projection enhanced by the church's superb acoustics. Lucas had never played a finer instrument, and it almost made him wish he had chosen to pursue music rather than civil engineering, except that urban planning and design was an equal, if less romantic, passion. Father Ryan might even say it was Lucas's calling.

As a kid he had drawn maps of imaginary cities with skyscrapers of apartments separated by wide swaths of land where residents could plant crops. As he had grown older, he had learned that those maps needed to include affordable housing for lower-income residents, and that his avenues of farmland displaced roads, which would be a hard sell before any planning committee. In college he had started out in architecture but switched to civil engineering when he saw how it brought together his two compelling ideals, sustainability and social justice.

"Most people think those are mutually exclusive and competing paradigms, but they don't have to be," Lucas had told Sophia over Indian takeout one evening to celebrate a successful Easter Vigil Children's Mass performance. "Granted, they're still two separate movements, but they share enough goals in common that one day they may converge, and in the meantime, the tension between the two can be very productive."

He had stopped abruptly there, having reached the point where most people's eyes glazed over, but Sophia had surprised him. "How so?" she asked, with apparently genuine interest.

"Well, they can come together to improve neighborhoods in ways as complex as designing the layout of an entire city block or as simple as turning a vacant lot into a community garden." For the next twenty minutes, as they sat on a park bench eating chicken tikka masala and aloo gobi from paper cartons, he had given her more specific examples, ambitious projects he had heard of and admired, others that had failed spectacularly, some that he had worked on during school breaks, a few that existed only on paper or in his head but which he hoped to launch someday. He had also told her about his volunteer work with Habitat for Humanity, and his absolute belief in the radical notion that everyone deserved a safe place to live.

Eventually he had realized that he'd been holding an empty takeout container and that Sophia had set hers aside long ago, and that she had been sitting beside him, her legs curled up beside her on the bench, watching him with interest and not saying a word.

"Sorry about that," he had said, embarrassed. "I think I just gave you my entire doctoral thesis."

"Really? What a wasted opportunity." She had shook her head, feigning dismay. "We should've recorded this. That would've saved you so much work. You could've just played it back and typed it in."

He had managed a laugh. "Thank you for not falling asleep."

"Why would I? I think your work is fascinating."

"You do?"

She had smiled, amused. "Your surprise isn't selling it very well at the moment, but yes, I do. It's relevant and important. I never really thought about the social issues that go into — or *should* go into — planning a city. I'll never look at a vacant lot the same way."

He had studied her appraisingly. "I'm never completely sure when you're joking and when you're being serious."

She had bent close to his ear and lowered her voice to a conspiratorial whisper. "The real trick is to do both at the same time."

She had straightened, smiling, and had begun gathering up their takeout trash, but for a long moment he had only sat watching her. She had brushed her hand against his leg when she had leaned toward him, and he still felt it, the pressure and the warmth. At that moment he'd realized, with a curious mixture of exultation and alarm, that even though he had a girlfriend and she had a boyfriend, he was coming dangerously close to falling for her.

They had met only a few weeks before, not long after Professor Callaghan had assigned

Lucas's History and Theory of Historic Preservation class a research paper on a local building of historical significance and its role in the community. Lucas chose St. Margaret's from the list of options because it was reasonably near his apartment, and he admired the architecture whenever he passed it. He called to arrange a site visit, and after the chipper little nun on the other end of the line assured him that he was welcome anytime, he stopped by on a Tuesday afternoon on his way to meet his girlfriend for a quick supper during the brief interval she allowed herself to emerge from the law library.

The vestibule was empty, but as he passed through another set of doors to the nave, he spotted an older, well-dressed couple sitting in a pew near the back. Their heads were bowed and they sat closely together, the man leaning slightly against the woman as if she bore him up. Something about them seemed familiar, but rather than intrude upon their privacy, he quickly glanced away and continued up the center aisle. He had almost reached the front pew when he spotted it — the gleaming, ebony grand piano near the rows of choir seats behind the altar.

He halted, his gaze fixed on the piano in stark admiration. From off to his right came the soft, muffled boom of a heavy door falling shut; a moment later, a short, stoop-shouldered elderly woman in a plain gray dress and white wimple walked stiffly but briskly in. "Ah," she exclaimed when she caught sight of him. "Admiring our lovely piano, I see."

He recognized the cheerful, quavering voice from the phone call. "Yes, I am. It's a beauty."

She put her head to one side and peered at him with friendly curiosity through horn-rimmed glasses fastened about her neck with a silver chain. "Do you want to try it out?"

"I'd love to." He glanced at the couple seated in the back of the church, their faces indiscernible in the dim light. "But I don't want to disturb anyone."

"It wouldn't be a disturbance, not at all." The nun glanced back at the couple too, then returned her gaze to Lucas, smiling. "He loves to hear people play his piano."

Puzzled, Lucas lowered his voice and indicated the older man with a subtle tilt of the head. "The piano belongs to him?"

"Of course not." The nun clasped her hands together at her waist, lifting her chin proudly. "It belongs to the church."

"Oh, okay." A moment later, Lucas figured

it out. He had not detected the capital H in "his"; she apparently meant that it was God's piano, or Jesus's. "Sure, I'd love to play it."

She beamed and gestured for him to proceed, and as he sat down at the piano, she settled into the front pew and watched him expectantly. He began with a Chopin étude, then played a Bach sinfonia, thinking it suited the setting and the nun might like it. He had just begun the Christmas Sonatina by Carl Reinecke when he realized that someone else had joined the audience, standing in the aisle near the nun, her hand resting on the back of the pew. A surreptitious glance revealed a young woman so beautiful, so radiant and rapt, that he stumbled over the rest of the measure and came to an abrupt halt.

"Don't stop," she protested. "You play beautifully."

"Yes, that piano has never sounded better." The nun gave a little start and glanced to the back of the church, where the couple sat utterly still, either watching them or lost in thought, Lucas could not tell. "Or rather, it's *rarely* sounded better."

The younger woman dropped her bag on the front pew with a solid thunk and joined him at the piano. "Please tell me you're

61

Sister Joanne's replacement."

"Who?"

"Sister Joanne. She was our accompanist for years, but ever since she retired last month, I've been on my own at choir practice. I can play, but not as well as she does." The young woman regarded him with such candid admiration that he was more than a little flattered. "And definitely not anywhere near as well as you."

"Thank you." He rose and stepped away from the piano, and the sense that he was making a terrible mistake did not prevent him from adding, "But I'm not an accompanist."

Her smile faded. "You mean you weren't responding to the notice in the church bulletin?"

"Sorry, I wasn't." He realized then that he actually was sorry. "I'm here on a research assignment. I'm not a member of this parish."

"That's not a requirement for the job," the nun piped up.

Just then, a side door opened and a dark-haired boy of about ten strolled in, followed by a girl of around nine with a younger boy, their ginger hair so alike in color and curl that they had to be brother and sister.

"How well do you sight read?" inquired

the nun as more children filed in and took their places in the choir seats.

Lucas hesitated, reluctant to deceive the nun or to diminish himself in the eyes of the pretty choir director. "I'm not bad," he admitted, and before he knew it he was seated at the piano again, running through scales as the children warmed up, and accompanying them as they sang a few pieces of sacred music suitable for Holy Week. He had expected the children to be all over the staff with their pitch, but they were actually quite good, and Sophia proved to be an energetic and effective teacher, drawing the best out of each young singer.

He forgot about his research project and his dinner date until a few minutes before six, when parents began drifting into the church to pick up their children. Rehearsal ended promptly on the hour, and as the young singers closed their binders, thanked Miss Sophia, and darted off to join their parents, Lucas hastily rose and closed the lid to the keyboard. If he hurried, he could still meet Brynn for supper. He would have to defer his tour of St. Margaret's to another day.

Sophia approached him as he slung the strap of his messenger bag over his shoulder. "Well?" she asked, her expression tentative but hopeful. "What did you think?"

"That was actually a lot of fun," he admitted.

"The job's yours if you want it. We rehearse on Tuesdays and Fridays from four thirty until six, and we sing at the nine o'clock Mass every Sunday morning, and at the afternoon vigil Mass the first Saturday of the month. We also have a few concerts throughout the year for holidays — Christmas, Easter, the usual."

He knew he was too busy and ought to refuse, but Sophia's smile was fading, telling him he had hesitated too long. "Sure, why not?" he heard himself say. He couldn't bear to turn her down and watch her smile disappear entirely. "I'll see you Tuesday."

"See you Tuesday," she echoed, and for a moment he stood there grinning back before he remembered with a jolt that he was expected elsewhere.

He hurried to the law library, composing apologies and inventing excuses for his tardiness. Fortunately, he needed none of them. When he found Brynn at her usual table — laptop open, books spread around, long, fine blond hair tucked behind her ears as she fixed her gaze alternately upon page and screen — he discovered that she had been so focused on her studies that she had not missed him.

Over supper, he amused Brynn with the story of how he had been coerced into performing for the choir rehearsal, entirely neglecting his research in the process. Without deliberately meaning to do so, he made Sister Winifred the clever mastermind and Sophia a secondary character, scarcely more than the nun's sidekick.

"I can't picture it," said Brynn, slipping her hand into his as they left the restaurant. "You, playing hymns in a church with a bunch of kids."

Bewildered, Lucas halted in the middle of the sidewalk. "I love kids. I have four nieces and two nephews, and I'm crazy about them. I think I'm going to enjoy working with the ones at the church."

"You didn't agree to do it."

"I did, actually."

"You can't," she protested. "Your schedule is much too full to squeeze in a regular commitment like that. Anything that doesn't directly contribute to finishing your degree is a waste of time."

"I don't agree, and I can manage my schedule." When Brynn sighed and shook her head, he added, "They need an accompanist, and some of us —" He squeezed her hand and raised it to his lips. "Some of us actually enjoy a break from work now and then. You'll laugh, but I feel like I'd be giving something back to the community."

She did laugh, but then she kissed him. "You're such a bleeding heart. It's adorable."

He invited her to their performances, but she always declined, citing dozens of other obligations. He accepted that. The choir was his thing, not hers, and third-year law students were notoriously busy. Then one Friday in September she surprised him by suggesting that they meet at St. Margaret's after rehearsal and go out to dinner and a concert. He half expected her to cancel at the last minute, but she surprised him anew by arriving in time to observe the last half hour of rehearsal from the third row.

Brynn looked beautiful in a light flowered dress and a little sweater, her long hair held back from her face by a complicated-looking clip and flowing like gold down to her shoulder blades. Lucas proudly introduced her to Father Ryan, Sister Winifred, a few of the kids who were brave and curious enough to want to meet her on their way out, and, of course, Sophia. Everyone was kind and welcoming, but they could not resist embarrassing Lucas by praising his playing well out of proportion to his talent and thanking Brynn for sharing him with them. Brynn endured it with her usual grace and poise, so well that they were halfway to the restaurant before he realized she was upset.

"You never mentioned that Sophia was gorgeous," Brynn said tightly as they waited at a crosswalk for the light to change.

"Is she?"

The light changed, and she began briskly crossing the street. "You also never mentioned she was young."

"She's our age, twenty-eight, maybe a year or two younger."

"Yes, I know that now. You made her sound like she was ready for the geriatric ward." They reached the opposite curb, where Brynn halted, planted a fist on one hip, and frowned up at him. "I thought she was a nun."

"Why did you think that?" He might have omitted certain significant details, but he never would have described Sophia that way. "I talked about *Father* Ryan, *Sister* Winifred, and Sophia. I never called her *Sister* Sophia."

She said nothing for a long moment. "Lucas, should I be jealous?"

"Of course not." He reached for her hand, but she would not let him take it. "Sophia has a boyfriend."

Brynn's long, golden hair spun out in a fan as she turned and strode quickly down the sidewalk away from him. After a moment, he hurried to catch up with her. "I'm sorry," he said. "Sophia's a friend and a colleague. That's all. That's not just her choice. It's mine too."

They walked along side by side in silence for another block before Brynn sighed and somewhat grudgingly took his hand.

A few weeks later, Lucas realized that Brynn's birthday was approaching, and that it fell on a Friday. "I thought I'd skip choir practice so we could go out," he told her over the phone on Tuesday morning as he walked to class. He had wanted to discuss plans for the evening in person, but they had not seen each other in more than a week.

"You don't need to do that."

"It's okay. They can survive without me for one rehearsal."

"Maybe, but —" Brynn was silent so long he thought the call had dropped. "You don't have to. I have other plans. I'm going out with my roommate and some friends."

"Oh." Vaguely reluctant, he asked, "Do you want to go out Saturday night instead?"

"I have to study." She sighed. "Look,

that's not all. I don't think we should see each other unless and until you get over this thing with that choir director."

"What thing? What do you mean?"

"Are you serious? All you ever talk about is Sophia this, Sophia that. Sophia the goddess of music, the passionate teacher, blah, blah, blah. I'm so sick of it."

Lucas felt a sting of anger. "Sophia's my friend. She's never done anything to hurt you."

"Nothing except constantly distract you."

"Brynn, whatever you think —" He had no idea what to say that would not make everything worse. "Listen. I haven't cheated on you."

"Then let's quit while we're ahead, before you're tempted."

So it was that he had spent Brynn's birthday at St. Margaret's with Sophia and the choir, and he had not missed a Friday rehearsal since. Neither had Sophia, but after he finished warming up at the piano and as the choir filled the risers, Lucas began to think that for the first time, she might.

"I'll be right back," he called over the din, rising from the piano bench and crossing to the side entrance. In the stairwell he found Father Ryan, just taking off his coat and hat. "It's almost four thirty. Have you seen Sophia?"

The priest regarded him skeptically. "You're worried she might have gotten stuck in a snowdrift somewhere between here and school?"

Lucas shrugged, feeling foolish. "You never know."

Looking as if he were struggling not to laugh, Father Ryan pulled his coat on again. "You stay here and start rehearsal. I'll keep watch for Sophia."

"Thanks, Father."

The children were a bit puzzled when he announced that they were going to begin and that Miss Sophia would join them soon, but they complied, warming up their voices and filling the church with do-re-mis. Where was she? In the three, almost four, years Lucas had known her, half past four on a Friday afternoon found her at St. Margaret's without fail. He had not felt so sick and helpless since — he didn't need to search his memory, for he knew exactly when. Since Sophia had announced her engagement, on Christmas Eve the year before.

For weeks they had been preparing the choir for their most important performance of the year, the concert before the Children's Mass on Christmas Eve. The choir also sang during the liturgy, so Sophia and Lucas faced the additional challenge of choosing a program that served the spiritual needs of the parish, celebrated the reverence and joy of the occasion, and allowed the young singers to shine without taxing their stamina.

Christmas Eve fell on a Monday that year, and after their last Friday-evening rehearsal before it, Sophia and Lucas had stayed late at the church discussing the children's preparedness and making final decisions about the program and the assignment of solos. They were both tired and stressed from the week, for reasons having nothing to do with the choir, and so when Sophia suggested they move their meeting down the street to a café that served hot coffee and excellent pie, Lucas readily agreed.

The change of scene relaxed them both, and they worked out the final details of the concert and mass well before they finished dessert. When conversation turned to their plans for the holidays, Sophia grew quiet and pensive, until Lucas was compelled to ask her what was wrong.

She hesitated. "It's probably nothing."

"If it's bothering you, it's not nothing."

"Okay, but don't tell Brandon."

Lucas traced an *X* over his heart with his finger. "Promise."

"A few days ago, we were at the jewelry store. I was helping him pick out a Christmas gift for his mother." Her expression was troubled, with an undertone of embarrassment. "We were browsing, looking at the rings and bracelets and necklaces displayed in the cases, when suddenly I saw something that I thought would be the perfect gift for Brandon. You know, to show him how I feel."

When she fell silent, Lucas prompted, "A gold-plated calculator?"

She smiled wanly. "No, silly. That's what I got him last year."

"You're kidding."

"Yes, I am." She took a deep breath. "So I called him over, and I took his hand, and I said, 'This is what I would want to give you, even if I had to sell my hair to buy it.' And I showed him —"

"A fob chain."

Her eyes widened. "Yes. *Yes,* exactly. It was even made of platinum. So you get it?"

"Of course I get it. 'The Gift of the Magi,' one of the greatest Christmas stories ever written. The wife sells her beautiful hair to earn enough money to buy her husband a fob chain for his most prized possession, a gold watch that had been in the family for generations. What she didn't know was that her husband had sold the watch so he could buy her a set of combs for her beautiful hair."

"So it's not a completely obscure reference, especially at Christmas." Suddenly her air of vindication vanished, and she looked utterly miserable. "I felt so stupid. I still do."

"Why would you feel stupid? It was a very nice thing to say." It was more than nice, but that was the best Lucas could manage while forcing back his jealousy.

"Because Brandon didn't understand at all. He just gave me this blank look and said that he didn't own a pocket watch, he didn't know anyone who did, and he was surprised that the jeweler would carry a fob chain for something no one used anymore."

"Oh." Lucas inhaled deeply and ran a hand over his jaw. "Wow. Well, maybe he isn't a fan of O. Henry."

"Evidently not, but even after I explained the story to him, he still just shook his head, completely bewildered. He couldn't understand that the point of the story is that Della and Jim loved each other so much that each sacrificed their greatest treasure for the other."

73

"Right, because the other person's happiness was more important than their own. The other person's happiness was *essential* to their own."

"Yes, exactly." Sophia reached across the table and squeezed his hand. "Thank you for confirming that I'm not crazy."

He held his hand perfectly still, unwilling to do anything that might encourage her to move hers. "You're not crazy. You just . . . have a better grasp of literature than Brandon." He forced himself to add, "That doesn't make him a bad guy."

"No, of course not, but I was really disappointed when —" Sophia sat back, cupped her hands around her coffee mug, and frowned into it.

Lucas could not resist. "When what?"

"When he said that the entire problem could have been avoided if they had just taken the precautionary measure of exchanging Christmas lists."

"Precautionary measure?"

"That's an exact quote. When I tried to explain that their gifts were a symbol of their profound love for each other, he got this panicked look on his face and asked me not to cut my hair, because he prefers it long." She shook her head, and for a moment Lucas thought he glimpsed tears in her eyes. "Then, as we were leaving the store, he said that the wife came out ahead in the deal, because her hair would grow back, but the husband's watch was long gone."

"Sophia, I —" Lucas sat back in his chair, shaking his head. "I'm really sorry. I'm sorry he didn't understand, but you shouldn't feel stupid."

"And yet I do," she said, forlorn. "To top it all off, we were so busy arguing that Brandon forgot to buy his mother's present, so the entire trip was a waste of time."

"I'm sorry," Lucas said again.

"You know something?" Sophia brushed her long hair away from her face and studied him. "Sometimes I wish Brandon could be more like you."

Pained, Lucas managed a shrug. "That's not really fair to Brandon. It's taken me years to achieve this level of awesomeness."

She smiled then, and he felt both rewarded and profoundly sad.

It wasn't until much later, after he had seen her home and had returned to his own apartment, strewn with his books and papers and maps and models, that his churning thoughts settled upon one irrefutable fact: He loved Sophia, and he was tired of her not knowing. He would never deliber-

75

ately create a rift between her and Brandon, but evidently one already existed. Nothing prevented him from telling her the truth. Lucas would tell Sophia how he felt and let her decide if instead of wishing her boyfriend were more like him, she would choose him to be her boyfriend.

His Christmas gift would speak for him, would say all he had been unable to say for far too long. He would buy Sophia a set of exquisite combs with jeweled rims, like those Jim had given Della in the story. Sophia would understand what it meant.

It took some searching, but Lucas was determined, and two days before Christmas he found the perfect combs in a boutique on Brattle Street. On Christmas Eve he wrapped them carefully and wrote out a card, a simple message of love and friendship. Determined not to lose his nerve, he tucked the gift in his bag with his sheet music, dressed in his concert attire, and walked to St. Margaret's, arriving a record thirty minutes early.

He and Sophia always went out for dessert together after the Children's Mass, after the singers and parishioners had departed, after they had cleaned up for the adult choir's performance at Midnight Mass. They usually went to a favorite café to celebrate with coffee and pie and to exchange gifts, usually CDs or concert tickets or books. Once Sophia had given him a huge bucket of LEGOs so he could construct a multitude of houses and cityscapes, take them apart, and rebuild anew. Anyone else would have considered it a gag gift, but not Sophia, and not Lucas. Whenever he grew frustrated with classes or work, he would pull out the little plastic bricks and build something impossible, something never before dreamt of, and afterward he would remember why he loved what he had chosen as his life's work.

Sophia's gift was one of the best he had ever received. That year, he hoped to give her one as meaningful.

His hopes ran so high on Christmas Eve that when Sophia took him aside before the concert and profusely apologized for the late notice, it took him a moment to understand that she could not go out for their customary post-concert dessert. She — she and Brandon — had to hurry off to her parents' home to share some very good news with them.

When she took a deep, shaky breath and clasped her hands together, interlacing her fingers, he knew what was coming before she spoke. The jewelry store — Brandon

77

had not really been shopping for a bracelet for his mother but analyzing Sophia's preferences in engagement rings. Earlier that day, Brandon had proposed, and Sophia had accepted.

Lucas went numb. He could only stare at her, nodding automatically and frowning thoughtfully as if he were in a lecture hall listening to a professor expound on a particularly inscrutable architectural concept.

"We can still do our gift exchange," Sophia was saying apologetically. "I just can't go out tonight. Or maybe we could do it another time?"

"Yeah, why don't we do that instead?" Lucas's voice sounded as if he were strangling. "Actually I — I couldn't believe it when I checked my bag just now but — well, I forgot to bring your gift."

"Oh, okay." Smiling, Sophia reached out and touched his arm. "You look so upset. It's no big deal."

He forced a smile and agreed.

They settled on December 27 and lunch at their favorite Indian buffet, and then it was time to warm up the choir for the concert. Lucas had never played more mechanically, but somehow he got through the hours, and afterward he remembered to congratulate Sophia. Her radiant smile when she thanked him struck him like a punch in the gut.

If he had known then that the engagement would come to an abrupt and inglorious end ten months later, he wouldn't have shown up at his parents' house that night in a daze of misery, wouldn't have had too much wine at dinner and more after dessert, wouldn't have ranted drunkenly to his brothers or cried to his sisters, wouldn't have woken up the next morning in the bottom bunk of his old bed in his old room with a throbbing head and a sour throat. His family treated him kindly, gently, when he staggered down the stairs, knowing most of the story and piecing together the rest. They knew him, and they knew how he felt, and no one tried to comfort him with falsely cheerful declarations about the millions of other women out there who would consider themselves lucky to have him. For that, he was thankful.

Two days after that bleak Christmas, he had unwrapped the jeweled combs, had found the receipt in his wallet, and had made it as far as the entrance to the store before deciding not to return them for a refund. Why he had not, and why he had kept them ever since, he could not say. The exchange period had long ago expired and he could not imagine giving them to anyone else. Nearly a year later, they were still in the box, still at the back of a drawer in his bedroom.

He should give them to one of his sisters, if only to make more room for socks.

Lucas dragged out the warm-up as long as he could, but he finally ran out of ideas. "Well done, kids," he said, rising from the piano bench. "As soon as Miss Sophia arrives —"

"She's over there," Alex interrupted, pointing. Startled, Lucas turned to look, evoking giggles from the sopranos.

"We're all here now, so let's continue," Sophia replied as she joined Lucas at the piano, her eyes bright, her cheeks flushed, and the faint scent of cinnamon in the air about her. "Let's begin with 'I Heard the Bells on Christmas Day.' " As the children opened their binders, Sophia inhaled deeply, sighed, and quietly added, for Lucas alone, "Some very lucky person nearby has coffee."

"Yes, you." He would have handed it to her except he would have dropped his sheet music, so instead he nodded to the mug and paper bag on the floor beside his bench. "I figured your concert would run late and you

wouldn't have time to stop. There's a cranberry scone in the bag if you're hungry."

"Lucas, you didn't," she exclaimed, picking them up. "You're a lifesaver, a saint, an
angel."

"Not really. Just a guy who walked past a
coffee shop on his way here." He spared a
glance for the children, who were becoming
cheerfully restless. "How was the concert?"

"The concert was great, but —" To his
astonishment, her face fell. "I lost my job.
Or I'm going to. In June."

"You're not going to teach us anymore?"
shrilled Alex. "Father Ryan fired you? He
can't do that! We like you too much."

"No, no, Father Ryan didn't fire me," said
Sophia quickly. "I meant my other job. I'm
not leaving St. Margaret's. Everything's
fine." As the anxious looks faded from the
children's faces, she murmured to Lucas,
"Curse his sharp young ears. I didn't mean
for him to hear that."

"It's okay," said Lucas, his brow furrowing. "Take a deep breath. Have some coffee.
We can talk about it afterward."

Cradling the mug in her hands, Sophia
nodded, closed her eyes, and took a long
drink of coffee. Lucas hoped it retained at
least some of its warmth.

The children were waiting.

"Trebles, let's hear from you first." Sophia straightened her shoulders, but her smile seemed forced. "Remember the eighth rest before you come in. Lucas, if you will?"

He nodded, wishing he could comfort her, waiting for her to raise her baton in the signal to begin. He could not help imagining how beautiful her long, dark hair would look held back from her lovely face by the jeweled combs. He ached to run his fingers through the silken locks, draw her to him, and kiss away her tears.

# CHAPTER FOUR:
## JANUARY–APRIL 1861

The people of the North were shaken by the news of South Carolina's secession, but Major Anderson's daring occupation of Fort Sumter heartened them. In Henry's study at Craigie House, Charley and Ernest spread maps of Charleston Harbor on the floor, studied them eagerly, pondered Major Anderson's defenses, and speculated about the likelihood of a rebel attack upon the fort, what South Carolina militia forces would be involved, and from which direction they would strike.

"I'd love to be with Major Anderson when the battle finally opens," Charley declared fervently, and not wishing to appear a coward, Ernest chimed in that he would too. Henry, a lifelong pacifist, recoiled at the thought of his sons marching off to war, and he said a silent prayer of thanksgiving that they were too young to enlist. Only after he murmured a final amen did he realize that he had not prayed for war to be averted. It troubled him that some element of his understanding, deep within his mind or heart, had assumed that war was the inevitable outcome of secession.

"It pains me to admit this," he confided to Fanny when they were alone in the parlor one snowy night early in the New Year, "for it contradicts some of my most ardent convictions, but war would be preferable to appeasement. If we simply let South Carolina quit the Union, our democracy will fail and the scourge of slavery will endure. It may even spread to the west."

"You're torn," Fanny said soothingly. "I am too. All peaceable abolitionists are. We want slavery to end, but is war too great a price to pay? We want to avoid bloodshed and destruction, but if war is the only way to end slavery, should we not be willing to make that sacrifice for the sake of the long-suffering people held in bondage? These are the great questions of our time."

"We may yet avoid war."

"Perhaps." Fanny stared into the fire, pensive and beautiful in profile. He reached out to stroke her hair, and she turned to smile wistfully at him. "Another question for our times: How long will Major Anderson and his men be able to hold out on that little island in the harbor?"

Henry had posed the same question to his friend Sumner, who by virtue of his position in the Senate knew more than he could share even with his closest friend. What Sumner could entrust to the mails was deeply troubling. Fort Sumter had been planned about forty years earlier as a bulwark to defend the shipping channels of Charleston Harbor. Its large, octagonal structure could accommodate 650 troops and 135 guns, but construction had never been completed, and scaffolding, stone, and piles of other building materials littered the interior. Only fifteen cannons had been installed, and the brick-and-mortar walls, though five feet thick and satisfactory to the standards of the 1820s when the fort had been designed, could not long withstand bombardment by modern artillery. Major Anderson's garrison was comprised of only eighty-seven officers and enlisted men, insufficient to fully staff the defenses, but too many for their limited supplies of food, beds, and blankets. Isolated by the same deep waters that protected his garrison from an infantry attack, the major was limited to only sporadic communications with military headquarters. In his reports, he emphasized that he and his men were determined to hold the fort, but they would eventually need reinforcements and supplies.

While Anderson's commander in chief, President Buchanan, dithered in Washington, Southern militiamen eager to wrest Fort Sumter from federal control poured into Charleston. Before long 3,000 armed men were organized under the command of General Pierre Gustave Toutant Beauregard, a vain, fastidious Louisianan who had resigned as the superintendent of West Point to join the rebellion. Henry found it both ironic and ominous when he learned that, years before, Beauregard had been one of Anderson's students at the military academy.

"Major Anderson will hold out longer than his enemies would ever expect," Henry told Fanny, recalling certain telling phrases from Sumner's letters. "He won't surrender unless he sincerely believes he has no other choice."

"Imminent starvation may compel him to," said Fanny, "unless President Buchanan summons the courage to act before it comes to that."

Henry could not disagree, and he worried that starvation was the likelier outcome, for the president seemed content to wait out the rest of his term twirling his thumbs in the White House rather than take measures to resolve the crisis.

Henry had lost all faith in the hesitant, immobile commander in chief, so he was astonished a few days later to read in the *Boston Daily Advertiser* that Buchanan had authorized a civilian steamer to carry provisions to Major Anderson and his men. The *Star of the West* had sailed from New York the previous Saturday afternoon with a cargo of beef, pork, and pilot bread, enough to sustain the beleaguered garrison for several weeks. "But yesterday the rumor gained ground in New York," the report continued, "and is doubtless true, that she stopped in the lower harbor and received 200 or 300 troops (marines, according to one account), after which she went to sea."

In subsequent reports, other newspapers confirmed the story, noting when and where the *Star of the West* had been spotted as it traveled south along the coast. Henry's astonishment that President Buchanan had finally taken action was tempered by grave concerns about the frequent accounts of the steamer's journey. Editors customarily studied one another's papers and reprinted stories of particular interest to their own readers, and if anything, secession had augmented the practice. Surely the citizens of Charleston knew that the *Star of the West* was on the way, and their military forces would be ready and waiting when she arrived.

A few days later, his concerns were proven justified by shocking headlines in the morning papers. The previous day, the *Star of the West* had sailed into Charleston Harbor and had been fired upon by militia and young military cadets positioned on the shores. Struck in the mast but not seriously damaged, the steamer nonetheless had been forced up the channel and back into the open sea.

Major Anderson and his men had not been harmed in the firefight, but the departing steamer had carried off any hope that they would be resupplied and reinforced anytime soon.

Even as the South Carolina militia and cadets were driving away the *Star of the West,* delegates in Mississippi were voting in favor of secession. "Our position is thoroughly identified with the institution of slavery," they declared in a statement explaining why they were obliged to leave the Union, which was published in papers throughout the North soon thereafter. "There was no choice left us but submission to the mandates of abolition, or a dissolution of the Union, whose principles had been subverted to work out our ruin."

The next day Florida seceded from the Union, and the next, Alabama.

One after another they broke off, like the edges of a sandy bluff that had withstood years of steady pounding of the surf only to crumble into the sea at the strike of a single, long-expected but overpowering tempest.

"Does no voice of reason and prudence remain in the South?" Fanny asked, pushing the papers and their dreadful reports aside. As if in response to her plea, former president John Tyler, writing from Richmond, Virginia, called for a peace convention in Washington where both sides could make one last attempt to resolve the crisis. Privately, Sumner told Henry that he had no hope for its success.

Two days after John Tyler published his call for a summit, Georgia seceded, as if in contempt of the former president's plan. Two days after that, five senators from Alabama, Florida, and Mississippi — some defiantly, others in sorrow — rose to offer farewell speeches before resigning from the Senate and departing Washington for their Southern homes. The papers somberly described how Senator Jefferson Davis, the last to speak, had declared that states did have the constitutional right to leave the Union, and that his home state of Mississippi had justifiable cause for doing so. Even so, he regretted the conflict that had divided them. "I am sure I feel no hostility toward you, senators from the North," he had said. "I am sure there is not one of you, whatever sharp discussion there may have been between us, to whom I cannot now say, in the presence of my God, I wish you well; and such, I feel, is the feeling of the people whom I represent toward those whom you represent." He expressed hope that their separate governments would eventually enjoy cordial diplomatic relations, and he apologized for any pain he might have inflicted upon any other senator in the heat of debate.

There was something very ludicrous, Henry thought, when seen from a distance, about the theatrical strut of the Southern senators as they quit the Union. "Our future Molière will have a fine field for comedy," he wrote to Sumner, who had witnessed the spectacle, "and the Southern Planter will figure as funnily as any of his farcical characters."

In truth — and Sumner knew him well enough to understand this — Henry was not at all amused, but outraged and apprehensive. He felt powerless to do anything but observe and record his impressions as the dissolution of the Union wore on, slowly and inexorably. Behind it all he imagined he heard the low murmur of the slaves, like the chorus in a Greek tragedy, prophesying woe.

Five days after Jefferson Davis and his compatriots made their farewell speeches in the Senate, Louisiana seceded. Nevertheless, and in what increasingly seemed to be a futile effort, delegates from both sides of the conflict scrambled to arrange the peace conference. Soon it was agreed that the summit would open at the Willard Hotel in Washington City on February 4, with former president John Tyler himself serving as chairman.

Three days before the conference opened, Texas seceded from the Union, as if to mock any lingering, vain hopes for peace. "Perhaps some good may yet come of the summit," said Fanny, but her expression betrayed her doubt, which Henry shared.

They were disappointed, but not surprised, when the papers declared the conference a failure from the outset. Only twenty-five of the thirty-four states had answered the opening roll call; none of the seven seceded states had sent delegates, nor had

91

Arkansas, nor five western states. Meanwhile, on the same day far to the south in Montgomery, Alabama, representatives from the seceded states met to organize a unified Confederate government. John Tyler's own granddaughter raised the Confederate flag at the opening ceremonies.

As February passed, gray and cold and bleak, the conference proceeded doggedly on. President-elect Abraham Lincoln departed his hometown of Springfield, Illinois, to embark on a long, winding journey to Washington City for his inauguration. Cheering crowds greeted him at cities and train stations along the way, and his eloquent speeches won praise for their brevity and moderate tone, but threats upon his life had been made as well. Throughout the North, tensions soared as his train drew ever closer to the capital.

Early one morning in the last week of February, the pealing of bells beckoned Henry, still in his dressing gown, to the window. The world outside seemed strangely still, the eastern sky glowing crimson with the sunrise. On the snow-dusted sidewalk a laundress bustled past, a heavy, covered basket on her hip; then a grocer's wagon rumbled over the cobblestones, its driver slouched wearily upon the seat, the reins clasped in one gloved hand. It seemed an ordinary morning. Nothing except the tolling of the bells — no distant rumble of cannon, no panicked citizens thronging the streets — indicated that anything was amiss.

He heard the rustle of Fanny's nightgown before he felt the touch of her gentle hand upon his back. "It's the twenty-second," she murmured. "They're ringing the bells in honor of George Washington's birthday."

"Of course." Henry put his arm around his wife's shoulders and drew her close, his gaze fixed on the street outside. To him, the bells ringing in celebration of the great national hero had a melancholy sound, reminding him of the wretched treason in the land. What would Washington, triumphant general and first president, think if he had lived to see the nation he had helped establish splintering into contentious fragments?

For several months, Washington had fought the war for independence from within the same walls that now sheltered Henry, Fanny, and their children. When the Revolution commenced, the house's original owner had remained loyal to King George, and when he had fled Boston in fear for his life, his property had been confiscated, his estate occupied by the colonial Marblehead

Regiment. In July of 1775, during the Siege of Boston, General Washington had made the residence his headquarters, and for nine months he had commanded the Cambridge Common of the Colonial Army from the gracious residence on Brattle Street. In December his wife, Martha, her son, and her daughter-in-law had joined him; the family had chosen the two eastern rooms on the second floor for their private quarters, while the southeast room on the lower level became the general's study and dining room, the adjacent room a parlor for his wife, and a chamber in back an office for his staff. Henry often wondered in which room Washington had received the news that General Henry Knox, a Boston bookseller, had succeeded in bringing the cannon from Fort Ticonderoga over the mountains and through the snow to the heights of Dorchester south of the city, where they forced the astonished British to evacuate in haste or risk the destruction of their fleet.

George Washington had once looked out upon the view Henry now regarded, had surely contemplated the future of his fledgling nation as Henry was doing. Henry could only hope that the Illinois lawyer and onetime congressman who would soon succeed him would prove to be as capable a leader. The nation's very survival depended upon it.

Less than a fortnight later, and only a few days after the Washington peace conference sputtered to an ignominious end after resolving nothing, Abraham Lincoln took the oath of office on the East Portico of the Capitol and became the sixteenth president of the United States. His inaugural address appeared in the evening papers, and Henry was pleased by the simple eloquence of his words, the clarity and compassion of his thought. His foremost duty was to preserve the Union, the new president had told a crowd of 30,000 massed on the muddy Capitol grounds on a raw, blustery day that had miraculously given way to sunshine just as he began to speak. Yet Mr. Lincoln had also addressed the fears of the Southern people, emphatically stating that he had no intention of interfering with slavery where it existed, and that even though the Fugitive Slave Law was offensive to many, he felt bound by the Constitution to enforce it.

That position, Henry and Fanny agreed, would not play well in progressive Boston, but her citizens would cheer his assertion that despite the claims of certain factions, according to the Constitution and the law, the Union was not and could not be broken.

" 'We are not enemies, but friends,' " Henry read aloud to Fanny in their chairs by the fireside while Charley and Alice paused in a game of checkers to listen. " 'We must not be enemies. Though passion may have strained, it must not break our bonds of affection. The mystic chords of memory, stretching from every battle-field, and patriot grave, to every living heart and hearth-stone, all over this broad land, will yet swell the chorus of the Union when again touched, as surely they will be, by the better angels of our nature.' "

"Our new president has something of the poet in him," remarked Fanny, smiling.

"That can only be to the benefit of us all," Henry replied, "just as any poet who writes for the world beyond his own threshold should have something in his nature of the statesman."

As spring came to Massachusetts, newly elected governor John Andrew, who had taken office in January, began preparing the state militia for whatever conflict might come. Men who were no longer fit for active service were replaced by stronger, more vigorous men capable of responding swiftly to an emergency call, like their Minutemen forefathers. The state legislature procured

$100,000 to outfit the troops with new overcoats, blankets, and knapsacks, and the men's training was redoubled.

Though no enemy ventured near the borders of the Commonwealth, Governor Andrew's preparations seemed warranted when word came to Washington, and from thence spread throughout the North, that Major Anderson had informed his superiors that his garrison must be supplied with provisions by April 15, or they must be withdrawn.

Henry did not envy Mr. Lincoln his high office, for even King Solomon would have been stymied by the choice the new president then faced. If he withdrew the federal garrison from Fort Sumter, he would tacitly acknowledge that Major Anderson's men occupied foreign soil, and that the Confederacy had become a separate, sovereign nation. If Mr. Lincoln defied South Carolina's demands and dispatched supplies to the starving soldiers, the South would view it as an act of aggression tantamount to a declaration of war.

While people throughout the divided land waited for Mr. Lincoln to decide, a hint that secret diplomatic efforts were going on at a frantic pace came to the Longfellows from a most unexpected source. One evening, after they dined with Fanny's parents at their elegant home in Beacon Hill, her father waited until the youngsters had been excused from the table before informing their parents that he had received a letter from his first cousin, William Appleton, still serving proudly in Congress at age seventy-five. "My cousin departed from New York on the afternoon of the ninth aboard the steamer *Nashville*," Nathan said. "He is, at this moment, en route to Charleston."

"Charleston," exclaimed Fanny, exchanging an astonished glance with Henry. "Whatever for?"

"His exact words as he wrote them," her father said, raising his eyebrows and casting a significant glance around the table, "were, 'I give the purpose for my excursion as reasons of health.'"

"An intriguing turn of phrase," said Henry. "How likely is it that the purpose he gives is not his true purpose, or at least not his only one?"

"If he has any other impetus for undertaking this journey," said Nathan, "he didn't wish to entrust it to a letter."

"And yet, we can but wonder," said Fanny's stepmother. "William has been dreadfully unhappy since his wife passed last year, and lately he's been afflicted by a painful, persistent cough. It may very well be that he does travel for the sake of *his* constitution, not *the* Constitution."

"If that's so, why go to Charleston, of all places?" asked Fanny. "Isn't it terribly dangerous to sail there now?"

"If he is indeed on some clandestine mission to secure peace," said Henry, "it may be far more dangerous if he does not go."

The following day, Nathan sent word to Craigie House that he had received a telegram from his cousin noting that the *Nashville* had arrived off the Charleston Bar and was awaiting high tide so the ship could enter the harbor. Though apprehensive of what dire news it might contain, Henry looked forward to William Appleton's next telegram, and the lengthier accounts he would be able to provide upon his return to Boston. Henry trusted the eyewitness impressions of a man he knew more than anonymous accounts in the press, which too often were frustratingly inaccurate and overwrought.

But before Nathan heard from his cousin again, the Boston papers blazed with terrible news: At half past four o'clock on the morning of Friday, April 12, Confederate batteries had opened fire on Fort Sumter. "The War Begun!" the headlines in the *Bos-*

ton *Daily Advertiser* raged. "The South Strikes the First Blow! The Southern Confederacy Authorizes Hostilities!" Major Anderson had returned fire, but the federal fleet had not responded, though three war steamers had arrived off the Bar.

"One of those ships is surely Cousin William's," Fanny said as she and Henry read the papers together. "Henry, what do you suppose has become of him?"

Henry quickly scanned the rest of the article. "There's no mention of the *Nashville,* and nothing to suggest that any federal ship came under fire. I'm sure he's safe and sound."

He would not venture to say the same for Major Anderson and his men.

None of them slept well that night, and the next day, as reports from correspondents in the South began to appear in the Boston papers, the Longfellow and Appleton families urgently sought out every scrap of news and pieced together what had happened as best they could. They learned that thirty-four hours after the first bombshell exploded in the air above Fort Sumter, the soldiers' quarters had been burned to the ground, the main gates destroyed, the gorge wall seriously damaged, and the magazine surrounded by an impassible wall of flame, its door so warped from the heat that it could not be opened. The fort's flagstaff had been shot away, but the flag itself had been rescued and attached to a short spar, where it had become a target of rebel marksmen. The Union garrison had only three cartridges of powder remaining, and no food but a small ration of salt pork. The fort had sustained so much damage that it would have been indefensible even if, somehow, it could have been provisioned and reinforced. Only when Major Anderson concluded that his position was utterly untenable had he felt obliged to accept the terms of evacuation offered by General Beauregard: Major Anderson would be permitted to evacuate his command without surrendering his arms, and he and his men would be granted safe, unimpeded transport to the North.

The federal garrison evacuated the fort with great dignity, taking their tattered Stars and Stripes with them as they were escorted aboard a steamer and delivered to the Union ships waiting beyond the bar. Fort Sumter, so long bravely defended, was under Confederate control, and Charleston Harbor with it.

There was no news of the *Nashville,* but to their enormous relief, on Sunday morning William Appleton telegraphed Nathan and other members of the family to assure them although the twelve-hour firefight had delayed his steamer from entering the harbor, he was now safely ashore in Charleston. They should not worry if he did not return to Boston immediately, for he intended to visit acquaintances, inspect plantations, and, if he could secure permission from General Beauregard, tour the battered Fort Sumter. He said nothing of the failure of his secret peace mission, if one had ever existed, but it was futile to wonder what might have been if his ship had arrived only a day earlier. The course had been set, and civil war had begun.

On April 15, three days after the surrender of Fort Sumter, President Lincoln issued a call for 75,000 militia to suppress the uprising, with a certain quota required from each state. Later that same day, Secretary of War Simon Cameron contacted Governor Andrew to formally request that he immediately send 1,500 troops to defend Washington City. In swift reply, the governor ordered four Massachusetts regiments, more than 3,000 men, to muster on Boston Common forthwith, uniformed, fully outfitted, and prepared to depart at once for the capital.

Henry marveled as a new patriotic fervor swept through Boston and Cambridge. Old political divisions were set aside and dissent fell silent as outrage replaced sympathy for the South. Demands for a swift, forceful military response filled the streets and newspapers. Impromptu rallies and marches sprang up in parks and squares; the Stars and Stripes flew from nearly every mast and flagpole and balcony. Even the Democrats and the Irish, well known for their affinity for the South and their hostility toward the abolitionist cause, declared their support for the Union.

Late the next day, Henry read in the evening papers that earlier that morning, three companies of the Massachusetts Eighth Regiment had arrived in Boston. Despite strong winds and torrential rainfall, they had marched from the depot to Faneuil Hall — banners waving, drums pounding, and fifes shrilling "Yankee Doodle" — where some of the men exchanged their old, smoothbore muskets for new rifles, and all were issued new overcoats.

Charley was so disappointed to have missed the spectacle that the following morning, as word spread that the Sixth Massachusetts had joined the Eighth in the city, Henry reluctantly agreed to take him and Ernest to observe their departure for Washington. At noon, Henry and his sons joined the throngs of eager onlookers lining Beacon Street and watched as the two regiments marched past and halted before the State House, proud and smartly attired in new uniforms, gleaming new rifles on their shoulders. His gaze riveted upon the soldiers standing at attention, Charley fairly quivered with excitement as Governor Anderson descended the broad staircase and presented the regimental colors to their colonel.

After the brief ceremony, the command rang out, and the regiments marched off past cheering crowds to the train station to board the cars that would carry them south to Washington City. Grinning, eyes shining with pride and admiration, Charley and Ernest applauded, shouted, and waved their caps in the air in a salute to the departing men.

"I'd do anything to be going with them right now," Charley said fervently, nudging his younger brother. Ernest nodded vigorously in reply.

Henry felt a chill so intense he was obliged to suppress a shudder. Silently, as he had many times since hostilities erupted, he thanked God that his sons were too young to join the fight. The authorities expected the rebellion to be quelled within ninety days, time enough for tremendous loss of life and destruction of property, but short enough to spare his sons.

He could only hope and pray that the actuality would prove to be no worse than the predictions.

# CHAPTER FIVE:
# THE CHOIRBOY'S TALE

Alex never meant to upset his mother, but sometimes things just happened. Sometimes, but not always, Charlotte was involved.

He never thought she would ever see his stupid vocabulary homework. Every week Mr. Donaldson gave the class ten new words, and they had to learn what they meant and how to spell them, and to prove it they had to use each in a complete sentence. Charlotte had really annoyed him at choir practice that day, and to make things worse, she was sitting across the kitchen table from him working on her homework as if there wasn't anything she'd rather be doing, when all he wanted was to get it over with so he could spend some of his screen time playing Minecraft. So when he saw that the first word was "hardship," he wrote, "Having an older sister is a *hardship.*" After underlining the vocabulary word with a flourish, he pondered the next on the list before coming up with, "My sister thinks she is the best singer in the *entire* choir." Inspiration struck, and one sentence after another came to him with astonishing swiftness: "She was *furious* when Miss Sophia gave me the solo for the concert. She did not *congratulate* me because she was jealous. I *conclude* that I am a better singer than my sister. If she wants to sing better, she should *practice* like I do. She thinks it is *tragic* when she isn't the best at something. My sister should be more *humble*. She has lots of *envy* because I sing better than she does." He struggled with the last word before finally settling upon "An *orchard* would be a weird place for a choir concert."

He'd turned in the page of sentences, pleased with a job well done. The next day, Mr. Donaldson told him to stay behind while the rest of the class put on their coats and boots and went out to morning recess. "What did I do?" Alex asked dejectedly after the other, luckier, kids had left. He wasn't pretending. Most of the time he didn't realize he had done something wrong until he was being punished for it.

Mr. Donaldson studied him through rectangular glasses that made him look like he was constantly squinting. "Your vocabulary homework was . . . interesting."

He didn't sound angry, which made Alex curious. "Yeah?"

"It was very creative of you to use the words in sentences that formed a complete paragraph." When the teacher glanced at a paper on his desk, Alex stole a quick peek and recognized his homework, marked with the usual spattering of red ink. "Is it fiction or nonfiction?"

"Nonfiction, I guess." They had learned the terms earlier in the semester, but from the way Mr. Donaldson was smiling, Alex suspected it was a trick question.

"I see." Mr. Donaldson beckoned him forward and held out the paper. "I noted a few places where your grammar wasn't quite right or you didn't clearly define the word within the context of the sentence. Nothing major. However —" He winced slightly and shook his head. "I had your sister in class two years ago, and I wonder if you're being a little tough on her. What do you think?"

"I don't know." Alex shrugged. "I guess. Maybe?"

"As I recall, Charlotte is a talented singer, and a very talented writer." Mr. Donaldson smiled and handed Alex his homework.

"Apparently it runs in the family. May I suggest that you not let your sister see this?"

"Okay." Quickly Alex tucked the paper into his take-home folder. "Can I go to recess now, please?"

Mr. Donaldson gave him permission, so Alex threw on his coat and raced outside, where he found his friends sliding down a huge pile of snow the plow had left behind after clearing the parking lot. It was only later, after lunch, when his mind was wandering during math workshop, that he realized with a jolt that Mr. Donaldson had called him a good writer.

Charlotte would be so mad. He would wait for the perfect time to tell her.

Before he could, Charlotte found his homework, and totally freaked out, and then their mom got that sad, weary look on her face that never failed to make him feel ashamed of himself. He tried to explain that he really hadn't meant to hurt his sister's feelings when he had written all that stuff. He should have stopped there, but instead something compelled him to point out that everything he had written was his true opinion, and wasn't that better than lying?

"What you wrote isn't *true*," Charlotte countered, her face red with rage. "It's just *mean*."

"It can be both," he insisted.

That was when their mom announced that there would be no television, no computers, no video games for the rest of the week. Charlotte didn't care about the loss of screen time — she had tons of books to read and homework to do and music to pound out on the piano — because to her the disgrace was an even worse punishment. But Alex cared. He felt the loss of Minecraft keenly, and after slogging through his homework, with nothing better to do he went to his room to practice his choir solo. He left the door open, and he had barely finished the first measures when Charlotte stomped by, paused in the hall, and, careful not to break the off-limits barrier of his doorway, hissed, "You're doing that on purpose, you obnoxious little show-off."

"Doing what?" he protested, but she had already disappeared into her own room and slammed the door. Oh, the solo. Right. Well, what was he supposed to do? Disobey Miss Sophia and not practice because it reminded his sister that he had been given the solo instead of her? That was just stupid. And *irresponsible,* which happened to be on that week's vocabulary list, although he'd have to think of a different sentence for it.

He knew Charlotte hated that he was a

good singer. Of the two of them, she had always been the best at everything — better than Alex in school, at piano lessons, in keeping their rooms clean, in being co-operative, in helping around the house, in staying tidy, in remembering to wash hands before supper, in remembering to use soap, in everything.

When their mother drove them to choir practice the next afternoon, Charlotte closed her book and said, "You can just pull up in front and let us out, Mom."

"Thanks, honey," she replied, passing the church and pulling into the narrow parking lot in the alley, "but I'd rather walk in with you."

Charlotte glanced over her shoulder at Alex. "You mean, to make sure we get there."

"It was only that one time," he retorted. A few weeks before, their mother had been in a rush, so she had dropped them off at the curb with strict instructions to go straight inside. Charlotte had wanted to obey, but as soon as their mother had driven off, Alex had heard dogs barking down the alley, and it sounded like they were fighting so he had to go see.

Charlotte had yelled at him to stop, to

come back, but he ignored her. By the time he found the source of the excitement a block away — two dog walkers tangled in the leashes of three dogs, their angry insults drowned out by barking and snarling — she had caught up with him. "You can't go running off like that," she had scolded. "Now we're going to be late."

"You didn't have to follow me," he had said, his gaze fixed on the spectacle across the street.

"Of course I did. You're just a little boy."

He resented being called a little boy, considering that he had just started the fourth grade, so although he had seen all that he wanted of the battle of the dog walkers, he stayed right where he was to prove that Charlotte wasn't the boss of him. Even then, they were only fifteen minutes late by the time Lucas came searching for them, and although Miss Sophia looked worried she didn't yell. Their mother never would have known except Charlotte tattled.

As he climbed out of the car, Alex spotted Father Ryan sweeping the sidewalk from the parking lot to the side door. "Hi, Father Ryan," he called, waving as they approached. "Nice hat. The Bruins are gonna crush the Penguins tomorrow."

"You'd better believe it," the priest said,

grinning. His smile changed a little as he turned to their mother. "Hey, Laurie. How's everything going?"

She gave him a big smile. "Oh, everything's fine. The usual."

"Have you heard from Jason?"

"Oh, sure. We hear from him all the time, don't we, kids?" She looked at Alex and Charlotte, nodding. Charlotte stared deliberately at her boots and shrugged, but Alex nodded happily back. "But you know how it is. The Internet over there is always breaking down, and it takes forever to get online again, but as soon as it's fixed, we're going to get to chat with him again —"

"I get to talk with him first," Alex broke in. "Mom promised. I want to make a rocket for the science fair and I have to ask Dad some stuff."

Father Ryan nodded, his forehead wrinkled and serious. "That's wise. I've heard about you and rockets. It's best to consult with an expert first." To Alex's mom, he added, "Please let me know if there's anything I can do."

"Thank you, Ryan. I will." Alex's mom and dad could call the priest Ryan instead of Father Ryan because he and their father were real friends and had been roommates in college. Alex's dad had showed him old pictures of Father Ryan from when he played hockey for Notre Dame and from when they had sung together in a men's choir there. Once his dad had said that after you've seen someone chug a yard it was a little difficult to call him "Father." Alex had laughed, even though he didn't really get the joke — chugging a yard sounded more like football than hockey — but his mom had looked shocked and declared that his joke wasn't funny. But then she had smiled, so maybe it was funny after all.

"And tell Jason Merry Christmas from me when you speak with him," Father Ryan said.

"Of course." His mom gave Father Ryan another small smile, placed her hands on Alex's and Charlotte's backs, and steered them toward the door.

As they entered the church, the adults' last words sank in. "Wait a minute," said Alex. "Why can't Father Ryan tell Dad Merry Christmas himself? Isn't Dad coming to church with us?"

"Of course not, honey," said his mother, a little breathless, probably from the cold and from climbing the stairs. "Your dad is in Afghanistan."

"I know that, but isn't he coming home for Christmas?"

"Dad won't be back until next summer," said Charlotte, throwing a look at him over her shoulder. It was a familiar look, the one that said she couldn't believe she was related to such a dummy.

Alex stopped short on the landing. "But he'll miss the concert."

His mother held open the door at the top of the stairs. "He's missed a lot of things. Come on, honey. We can't be late."

Alex trudged up the stairs, heart dragging somewhere near the bottom of his chest. "But who will make gingerbread pancakes? Dad always makes us gingerbread pancakes on Christmas morning."

To his shock, tears sprang into his mother's eyes. "I know you're disappointed, honey, and I am too. Maybe we can get something special from the bakery instead, okay? Would you like that?"

"Sure," said Alex, because he knew there was no other acceptable answer and he didn't want to make his mother cry.

Inside the church, Alex and Charlotte shrugged out of their coats and scarves and left them on the pew next to their mother while they went to join the other singers in the choir. "Nice going," Charlotte muttered as she flounced off to join the sopranos. Feeling slightly ill, Alex took his place between Finn and Logan. Lucas was sitting at the piano, but Miss Sophia wasn't around. Other kids were still arriving, Michael and Bruno and a bunch of girls.

"Michael, check it out," Alex said, swinging his black music binder like a katana in slow motion and making a low howl just like he'd seen in a samurai movie. Michael grinned and blocked the thrust with his own binder-sword, and then Bruno and Finn joined the battle.

"I'll be right back," said Lucas loudly all of a sudden, and he got up from the piano and ran off. Nobody answered him as far as Alex could tell, but that was all right because he returned a few minutes later and announced that they were going to warm up even though Miss Sophia wasn't there.

As Lucas sat down at the piano and began to play, Alex glanced at his mom, who sat in a pew with her hat and coat on as if she wasn't planning to stay. He smiled at her as he sang, but even though she seemed to be staring straight at the choir, she didn't smile back. Her eyes looked like she was watching something a million miles away, something that made her sad and lonely.

She looked exactly the way Alex felt whenever he thought about his dad.

He wished eighteen months wasn't so

long. He wished his dad was in the church right that minute, sitting next to his mom and holding her hand and making her smile. If Alex couldn't have that, at least not right away, he wished he could at least talk to his dad on the computer again. He really wanted to make a rocket for the science fair, but he knew his mom would never let him do so much as light a single match without adult supervision. She wouldn't let him do that even before that stupid fire, and the stupid fire had made everything worse.

Alex and his dad used to drive out to the open fields by the school and launch model rockets almost every weekend as long as the weather was nice. His dad had saved all of his rockets from when he was Alex's age, and he knew everything there was to know about how to make a rocket go higher or to spin, how to know where the parachute would bring the fuselage safely down to Earth. He had taught Alex about how the weight of the rocket and the thrust of the engine affected the acceleration, and how the diameter of the fuselage and the shape of the fins and nose cone affected drag. Alex knew so much about rockets that his third-grade teacher had let him do a special report to the whole class for extra credit in science. It was the first time he had earned an A-plus in anything, and his mom had been so happy that she had made his favorite dinner that night — spaghetti with meatballs, crusty garlic bread, and a chocolate cake for dessert.

On the last Saturday before his dad shipped out, he bought a ton of engines and they fired off rockets all afternoon. Afterward they had gone out for pizza, just the two of them, and his dad had told him seriously that Alex would be the man of the house while his dad was gone, and he trusted that Alex would take care of his mom and sister.

Alex had felt a surge of panic. "But I can't even drive."

His dad had laughed. "Okay, fair enough. But when I say take care of them, I mean to help your mother however she needs you. And don't wait to be asked. If you see the trash can in the kitchen is full, take the bag out to the garage. That kind of thing. You understand?"

Alex nodded.

"As for taking care of Charlotte," his dad continued, leaning forward on the table and regarding him seriously, "that means don't pick fights, don't call her names —"

"What if she picks a fight or calls me

names?"

"Just let it go. Just walk away."

"What if we're in the car and I can't walk away?"

His dad had smiled. "You're very smart, Alex. I bet you can figure out what you should do."

When they said goodbye to him, it wasn't as hard as Alex had expected. All the other families were there at the airport with signs and flags like the ones he and Charlotte and their mom carried, people from the VFW served big pieces of cake, and a marching band played, so it was almost like a party. His dad and the other soldiers looked really cool in their uniforms, and a senator's wife made a speech since the senator was sick, and it was a short speech so that was good. Charlotte cried quietly the whole time, and when it was time for their dad to go, their mom got tears in her eyes, but there was no way Alex was going to cry in front of all those brave soldiers.

Then their dad gave each of them one last hug, and he kissed their mom so long that Alex had to look away from sheer embarrassment, and then he was gone.

The ride home was quiet. Charlotte didn't complain when he kicked the back of her seat, so he soon lost interest, and when he asked their mom if they could get burgers and fries for supper, she replied, "Sure, honey," almost as if she wasn't really listening, as if she had totally forgotten that they had brought home burritos the day before and she would be breaking her own rule about no takeout more than once a week.

But their house seemed strangely hollow and echoey when they carried their paper bags and cups with plastic straws into the kitchen, and Alex couldn't help staring at his dad's empty chair as he forced himself to chew and swallow, and the bacon cheeseburger that had made his mouth water when he had seen the picture on the board sat in his stomach like a rock. When he told his mother that the house felt weird, and he felt weird too, she stroked his hair and told him she knew exactly what he meant. "We'll just have to get used to it," she told him, kissing him on the forehead.

As the weeks went by, Alex did get a little more used to the empty place at the dinner table, and the quiet, and his mother's red eyes and determined jaw, but things never felt right, not completely. He never felt bad when he was singing, though, and when he mentioned that in a video chat, his dad said, "That's great, Alex. You should keep doing the things that make you happy. It'll make the time go faster, and before you know it, we'll be doing fun stuff together again."

Alex wanted to take his dad's advice, but most of the things he liked to do best, he couldn't do without his dad. He could sing with the choir, of course, but he couldn't play hockey in the driveway with their sticks and a tennis ball, he couldn't go to Bruins games, and he couldn't launch model rockets. He could still play hockey on the ice with his team, of course, and he could watch the Bruins on television, but all he could do with his model rockets was count the engines left over from their last launch — one B6-4 and two C6-5s, the tally never changed — repaint them, or fix a few bent tail fins.

"Mom," he finally asked one Saturday as she was helping Charlotte make a poster about Abigail Adams for history class, "can Jeff and I launch model rockets today?"

"I'm sorry, honey," she said, glancing up from the paper and glue sticks and poster board scattered across the kitchen table. "I don't have time to take you today."

He had anticipated that response and had already planned for it. "We can ride our bikes to the field behind the baseball diamonds. Everything we need fits into my backpack."

"Maybe so, but I would still have to take

121

you. You can't launch model rockets without adult supervision."

"Dad said so," added Charlotte, unhelpful as always. "I heard him."

Alex scowled at her and she smiled brightly back.

"If Jeff's dad or mom can take you, that would be fine with me," his mother said, and with a whoop of delight, Alex ran off to call Jeff, only to learn that his dad was at a football game and wouldn't be home until late.

Discouraged, Alex glumly emptied his backpack of rockets, engines, parachutes, and tools and returned them to their shelves over his father's workbench in the garage. The next time he talked to his dad on the phone, even though he had been told over and over that they were supposed to act happy and optimistic, he complained that he was never going to be able to launch rockets again. "We'll launch them in four-teen months, I promise," his dad assured him, smiling.

"That's forever."

"That's not forever. It's just a little more than a year." When Alex groaned, his dad added, "The first Saturday after I get home, we'll launch rockets. Just the two of us, or you can bring Jeff if you want."

"Jeff can come the next time after that," Alex said quickly. "The first time, it'll be just us."

"Good plan," his dad said, nodding seriously. "In the meantime, why don't you find something else cool to fly? Paper airplanes or kites, maybe. Remember the kind we made last summer? Do you still have those books?"

"Yeah," said Alex, warming to the idea. "Yeah, I know exactly where they are."

His dad looked really happy, and asked him to mail him the best paper airplane he made so he could show it to the other soldiers. In the days that followed, Alex dug the books out of the pile of outgrown clothes at the back of his closet and tested dozens of designs until he found one that, when launched from the roof of their house, flew all the way across the street, did a huge loop, and landed in Mrs. Beswick's rosebushes. Unfortunately he celebrated with a loud cheer that brought his mother to the window, and when she saw the ladder propped up against the garage, she figured out where he was and yelled at him to come down from there immediately. He did so cheerfully, since he had already tested all the airplanes he had folded and had picked the winner.

He sent it to his dad, and his dad loved it. He showed it to all his buddies and they all thought it was awesome and said that Alex would probably be an aerospace engineer when he grew up. Alex just about burst from pride when his dad told him, and he tried again to persuade his mom to let him launch rockets because it would help him practice for his future career, but she still said no.

Before long Alex had made every single paper airplane model described in the book, some of them twice, and he had made a few original designs of his own. He found the kite book too, and made traditional kites, triangular kites, flying wing kites, box kites, and even a kite shaped like an umbrella before he lost interest.

Then one day, in social studies class, they watched a video about a lantern festival in China. Alex watched, impressed and awe-struck, as thousands of small, illuminated hot-air balloons rose into the night sky above a calm sea reflecting their pinpricks of light. They were made of oiled rice paper on a bamboo frame, the narrator explained, with a stiffened collar around the opening at the bottom from which a candle or other flame source was suspended. The flame heated the air within the lantern, causing it to rise.

Alex thought about those lanterns all day, and later, as soon as his mom got home from work, he ran to meet her at the door and asked if he could make a Chinese lantern.

She hung up her coat, her eyebrows drawing together in puzzlement. "You want to make a what?"

"A Chinese lantern," he said quickly, eager to get permission so he could get started. He had already found instructions on the Internet. "We watched a video about them in school and I think it'll take me a few days but I could finish it on Saturday. Please, Mom?"

"That must've been some video," she murmured, not really talking to him, but then she shrugged and said, "Sure. I remember making them in art class when I was around your age."

"You did?"

"Yes, a thousand years ago." She smiled, finger-combed his hair, and kissed him on the forehead. "Let me know if you need any help."

When he replied that he thought he would ask Jeff to help him, at least with the last part of the project, she looked surprised again but told him that was fine. He got started right after supper, collecting supplies — a plastic dry cleaner bag he found in his parents' closet, tape, three pieces of thin wire each a foot long cut from the spool on his dad's workbench, and a bunch of cotton balls from his mom's bathroom. He would also need lighter fluid and matches, but he knew exactly where to find those in the garage, so he decided to wait to get those until right before the launch.

Working alone in his room every night between homework, supper, and bedtime, Alex labored over his Chinese lantern with mounting excitement. He made the stiff collar by running strips of tape around the opening of the bag, then poked one end of each of the three wires through the tape, evenly spaced around the collar and twisted upon itself so it would stay in place. Then he twisted the free ends of the three wires together, then gave the wires another couple of twists about an inch above that one to make a little wire cage.

On Friday night, just as he finished putting away his project for the night so he could play some Minecraft before bed, his mom surprised him by knocking on the door and then opening it right away. "Hi," she said, peering around the room, her hand lingering on the knob. "What have you been doing in here, so quiet for so long?"

"Just working on my Chinese lantern."

"Where is it? Can I see it?"

"Can you wait until it's done? It really doesn't look like much now, and I want to test it first."

"Test it?" she said, smiling, though she looked a little confused. "To make sure it works?"

"Well, yeah." Was it a trick question? Parents and teachers loved trick questions.

"Do you need any string?"

Alex stared at her. This *had* to be a trick question. "No. Why would I?"

"To hang your lantern, of course." His mother folded her arms and leaned against the doorframe. "When my parents had outdoor parties in the summer, they would hang lots of Chinese lanterns around the patio. They always looked so pretty, illuminated by the tiki torches and the moonlight." Suddenly her eyebrows rose. "You aren't planning to use tiki torches, are you?"

"No way," said Alex emphatically. He didn't even know what those were. "Or moonlight."

On Saturday morning before breakfast Alex stuffed the little wire cage full of cotton balls, but then he had to set the lantern aside and wait impatiently for three o'clock, when Jeff was due home from his soccer game and would be able to help him launch it.

"I thought we were going to do this at the baseball diamond," Jeff whispered, glancing over his shoulder as he followed Alex, carefully holding the lantern, from his bedroom through the garage and outside to the driveway. Jeff was the biggest kid in class, but also the most nervous, at least when he was around Alex.

"I didn't want to carry matches and lighter fluid on my bike in my backpack," Alex replied. "Hold the lantern up."

Jeff looked doubtful, but he held the lantern away from his chest a few feet above the driveway while Alex uncapped the lighter fluid and doused the cotton balls.

"T minus one minute and counting," Alex intoned. He licked his finger and held it in the air, where it quickly became cooler on one side. A slight breeze stirred the plastic bag in Jeff's hands, or maybe Jeff's trembling shook it. It was hard to say.

Counting down from ten, Alex lit a match and held it to the soaked cotton balls, which quickly caught fire. Throwing the spent match aside, he held open the bottom of the bag to allow it to fill with hot air.

"No way," Jeff marveled as the bag expanded. "This might actually work."

"Get ready to let go," Alex said, interrupting his countdown. Jeff gulped and nodded. "Three, two, one. All systems go. Launch!"

Together they released the lantern, and it steadily rose into the air.

"It flies," Jeff exclaimed, watching it climb and move down the driveway with the breeze.

"Of course it flies," said Alex proudly, his gaze fixed on the lantern. "I wish we could've done this at night. It would look so awesome in the dark."

"It looks pretty awesome now," Jeff breathed as they watched it float off, moving up and away, following the street as if a tiny navigator was aboard. They exchanged quick high-fives, then instinctively began to follow in the lantern's wake, quickening their pace as it picked up speed. "Dude, I thought it was supposed to go up."

"It *is* going up."

"Not *straight* up. It's also going down the street." A note of panic came into Jeff's voice. "It's going toward my house."

"It'll start going straight up again when the wind dies down." But the wind wasn't dying down, and soon they had to break into a jog just to keep up with the lantern.

Alex tried to jump up and grab it, but it soared along at least six feet over his head.

"It's going to land on my roof," Jeff shrieked, but he was wrong, because the plastic bag got tangled in the branches of the willow tree in the front yard before it could reach the house. Alex slowly backed away, watching in horrified fascination as the plastic bag folded over upon itself and came to rest on the burning cotton balls. Soon flames began to lick the branches and travel lazily from one to another.

He was aware of Jeff yelling and sprinting for the house, and soon he came running back dragging the garden hose. As the flames multiplied, Alex shook off his shock and ran to help him, and fortunately they both had very good hand-eye coordination, proving that all those video games weren't a waste of time after all. Eventually the lantern, the willow tree, and they themselves were thoroughly soaked. The fire was out, and as Alex sank to his knees on the wet grass, he realized that neighbors had come outside to their porches and driveways and were watching and pointing. Jeff's mother had seized him by the shoulders and was scolding him, and Alex's mother was striding across the street, her hands balled into fists, her expression grim.

Jeff wasn't allowed to play with Alex anymore after that, even though they had been best friends since first grade. "That boy needs professional help," Jeff's mother told his mom crisply the next day when she brought Alex over to apologize. He had to pay with his own money for the arborist, who was sort of like a doctor for trees, but the willow would survive, which was a relief because Alex had never intended to hurt the tree. He hadn't intended any of the stuff that had gone wrong.

The worst part wasn't upsetting his mom, although that was definitely very, very bad. The worst part was telling his father the next time they video chatted. His dad looked so disappointed and worried, all Alex could do was lower his head and blink back tears and nod as his dad urged him to be good, to think things through, to make better choices, to remember that he was supposed to be helping his mother, not giving her more things to worry about.

"I'm sorry," Alex said, and he really, really meant it. He said it over and over again but it didn't make anything any better.

He had to do better, Alex told himself as Lucas led the choir through what felt like the longest warm-up in choir history. He hated the heavy, sick feeling that filled his stomach whenever he had done something bad and he knew everyone was mad at him. He wished he could talk to his dad and tell him that he would definitely do better. He wouldn't make his mom worry anymore. He would do something for her, something special for Christmas, something to make her smile again, a good surprise to make up for all the upsetting ones he had sprung on her ever since he was little, but more often since his dad had gone away, which was exactly the opposite of what he should have been doing.

He felt so awful that he had to look away and blink furiously so he didn't cry. He spotted his mom, motionless and pale, sitting in exactly the same position as when she had sat down. Then he saw Miss Sophia, smiling as she took off her coat. Instinctively he waved, and just as he remembered that he shouldn't, she gave him a tiny wave back, followed by an amused look of warning and a quick shake of the head. Alex quickly turned to face front again, just in time, because at that moment Lucas stood up. "Well done, kids," he said. "As soon as Miss Sophia arrives —"

"She's over there," Alex interrupted, pointing. Lucas jumped, and the sopranos

132

giggled, and soon Miss Sophia joined Lucas at the piano. She made a bad joke about being fired, which wasn't funny at all, but then rehearsal really began, and Alex was singing with his friends and a bunch of other kids he didn't know as well and also his sister, who really did have a beautiful singing voice and probably wasn't as jealous of him as his vocabulary homework had made it sound. And she was pretty smart too, so if he asked her to help him come up with a perfect Christmas surprise for their mother, she probably would.

The more he sang, the happier he felt, until gloomy thoughts of burning willow trees and disappointed parents and the stupid broken Internet in Afghanistan faded to the back of his mind. He felt himself filling up with music and with the promise of Christmas only a few short days away, and even though his dad wouldn't be there, Alex would make the holiday better for his mom and Charlotte. He didn't know exactly how, not yet, but he would.

# CHAPTER SIX:
## APRIL–JULY 1861

While Massachusetts and other Northern states promptly organized volunteer troops in response to the president's call to arms, the governors of Kentucky, Missouri, North Carolina, and Virginia declared that they would furnish no regiments to make war upon their Southern brethren. Then, on April 17, the same day Henry took his sons to watch the Eighth and the Sixth Massachusetts Militia depart Boston for Washington City, delegates in Richmond voted in favor of secession. The loss of Virginia was a terrible blow to the Union, and the other rebellious states surely rejoiced, for it was only a matter of time before the new independent commonwealth of Virginia added its military and economic might to the Confederacy.

Charley avidly followed reports of the Sixth and the Eighth Massachusetts Militia as they traveled by rail to Washington, and he seemed to know their movements before anyone else in the household. From Boston they had gone south to New York, where they had spent the night, and where the next morning vast crowds of cheering citizens had lined Broadway waving flags, banners, and handkerchiefs to send the volunteers off with great fanfare as they marched to the Hudson Ferry. Later that evening they arrived in Philadelphia, where they were welcomed with the pealing of bells, a grand display of fireworks, bonfires, bands, artillery salutes, and the glad applause of thousands of loyal citizens.

By all accounts, the troops' commanders did not expect such a warm reception in the next city on their route — Baltimore, about forty miles northeast of the capital. Although Maryland had remained in the Union, it was a slave state, and the city's loyalties were sharply divided. Even before the attack on Fort Sumter, Henry had read stories in the Boston papers of boisterous demonstrations in the streets. One day Union men would march through the city singing "Hail Columbia" and waving the Stars and Stripes; the next, Southern sympathizers would parade, singing "Dixie" and waving home-sewn flags bearing the South Carolina palmetto or the three stripes and seven stars of the Confederacy.

"Why didn't the militia travel by steamer?" Fanny asked when ominous rumors warned that thousands of Marylanders, clamoring for their state to follow Virginia out of the Union, were plotting to block the passage of Northern troops through Baltimore. The city had a history of mob violence, so the rumors could not be lightly dismissed; moreover, due to laws prohibiting the operation of steam engines within the city limits, upon arrival at the President Street Station, Washington-bound trains would be towed by teams of horses several blocks west through the city streets to Camden Station, where they would resume their journey by locomotive. The system, merely inconvenient in peacetime, was potentially disastrous in war.

"I suppose the generals decided that the railroad would be swifter," Henry replied, "and time is of the essence while Washington City lies unprotected."

"I trust that's the right decision," Fanny said pensively, and although she said no more of the matter that evening, Henry knew she was anxious and full of doubt.

All too soon, Fanny's worries proved to be prescient.

"Father," Charley shouted two days later

as he burst into the house carrying the evening papers. "The Sixth Massachusetts was attacked in Baltimore!"

"No, no, no," Henry murmured as he bolted from his chair and strode from his study to the foyer, where he met Charley, wide-eyed and quivering with excitement as he scanned the headlines.

"The soldiers that we saw off at the State House were attacked by a mob," Charley exclaimed as Fanny, Ernest, and Alice rushed to join them. Henry took a paper from the pile in his eldest son's arms, Fanny took another, and the children craned their necks, reading over their shoulders.

Ashen-faced, her gaze fixed on the page, Fanny pressed a hand to her throat. "Was anyone hurt?"

"They say two soldiers were killed, maybe more," said Charley, "and a few civilians too."

"What about the Eighth?" asked Ernest.

Charley shook his head. "The papers don't say. I think they were still in Philadelphia."

"Let's pray they escaped the melee," Henry said grimly. If there was any lingering doubt that their nation was at war, the deaths of the Massachusetts soldiers had abruptly dispelled it.

Over the next few days, as rumors spread and were quashed and fact could not always be distinguished from wild speculation, the truth of what had unfolded eventually came out. On the morning of April 19, the Sixth Massachusetts had left Philadelphia on a train bound for Washington by way of Baltimore. The commanders had been informed that their passage would be impeded, and they had warned their men that as they made their way through the city, they would almost certainly receive insults and abuse, and might even face assault — all of which they must ignore. Even if they were fired upon, they were not to fire back unless their officers gave the command.

The train carrying the Sixth Massachusetts had arrived in Baltimore unannounced, and several train cars carrying a few companies had made their way through the city without incident. But word of the soldiers' presence had spread quickly, and soon a hostile crowd had converged upon them, shouting insults and threats as their horse-drawn cars had pressed onward. Then the mob had torn up the train tracks, forcing the last four companies of the Sixth to abandon their railcars and attempt the crossing on foot. Immediately, several thousand enraged men and boys had swarmed them, hurling bricks and paving stones; from upstairs windows, other angry citizens flung dishes and bottles down upon them as they passed. The soldiers had marched onward at quick time, but when the furious mob had blocked their path and one rioter had shot a pistol into their ranks, they had opened fire upon their assailants. As the frenzy escalated, a man waving the flag of the Confederacy had become a rallying point for the mob, more shots had been fired, and the wounded had fallen bleeding to the ground amid screams and chaos. Eventually the soldiers had fought their way to the Camden Street Station, and after other sabotaged railway lines had been repaired, the train and its battered and bloodied passengers had sped off to Washington.

At least three soldiers and nine civilians had been killed and scores more injured on the streets of Baltimore. After the federal troops had escaped, the frenzied mob had turned its rage upon government property, destroying railroad tracks leading to the North, burning bridges, and severing telegraph lines. When the Sixth Massachusetts had finally reached Washington City, they had discovered that they were the only troops to have arrived, and that the destruction in Baltimore had completely isolated the nation's capital from the rest of the Union.

For six days Washington City stood alone, stranded, imperiled, and surrounded by enemies, with the Sixth Massachusetts its sole defenders against an attack by Confederate forces. But the attack, feared imminent, inexplicably did not come, and on April 25, the Sixth Massachusetts was joined by the New York Seventh Regiment, the First Rhode Island, and at last, the Massachusetts Eighth.

Washington City was safe, for the moment, and no longer cut off from the North, but concerns about its vulnerabilities shocked the people of the North into more urgent action. While young men rushed to join regiments and engineers raced to repair the damaged bridges and railroad tracks, governors ordered their newly mustered regiments to the capital and military officers contrived other ways to transport them there, since Baltimore remained impassable.

In Boston, Henry observed a new, energetic, and unified spirit among the populace. News that sons of Massachusetts had been killed and wounded in an unprovoked attack by hostile rebel sympathizers — and on the eighty-sixth anniversary of the revolutionary battles of Lexington and Concord — compelled them to abandon old political distinctions and animosities and to proclaim their allegiance to Governor Andrew, President Lincoln, and the Union. It seemed to Henry that the people's pride had soared to unprecedented heights, for the Commonwealth had endured a harrowing test and had kept faith with their country.

And yet Henry found the talk of war and the martial display woeful and wearying. Faces in the streets were stern and serious. The drums pounded an ominous rhythm. Even the coming of May with its sunshine and flowers and birdsong seemed to him bleak and cheerless. May had always seemed a perfumed word, breathing life, youth, love, song, but in such troubled times, the air had a bitter gunpowder taste and he could take no pleasure in it. Once, while strolling past the State House, his heart sank when he observed two youths of no more than twenty standing sentry at the gateway. Charley envied young men like them, but he envied even more their counterparts bivouacked in Washington or at Fortress Monroe. He understood nothing of the sadder aspects of war and saw only the glory and adventure.

As May unfurled her beauties day by day,

buttercups burst from the grass, the purple buds of lilacs tipped the hedges, and birdsong mingled discordantly with martial drums. Near the end of the month, Henry received a note from a friend, the writer and orator George W. Curtis, urging him to write a national song or hymn to rally the people of the Union behind their great cause.

"Will you attempt it?" inquired Fanny, smiling up at him as they walked along Brattle Street. They had set out hoping that the fine weather and perfumed air of spring would distract them from the war and from concerns over her father's declining health, but after they had chatted of the children and the garden and of their plans to move to their summer home at Nahant on Massachusetts Bay later that summer, the conversation turned back to work and to war.

"I think I'll decline," said Henry reluctantly.

"But why?" she asked. "It seems to me these dark times call for another great work like 'The Building of the Ship.'"

Henry patted her arm and smiled his thanks for the implicit praise. He had written the poem in 1849 in response to the growing animosity between slave states and free, when secession was still only a distant threat, a shoal few truly believed the nation would break upon. Its heartfelt call for the Union to endure — "sail on, O Ship of State! Sail on, O UNION, strong and great! Humanity with all its fears, With all the hopes of future years, Is hanging breathless on thy fate!" — was said to have moved Mr. Lincoln to tears when he had first heard it recited.

"It isn't that I wouldn't like to honor Curtis's request, but the command, 'Go to, let us make a national song,' doesn't inspire me. In fact, it has quite the opposite effect." Henry shook his head, wishing it were otherwise. "A national song will likely arise in some other way, if not from my pen, then from some other poet's."

"Oh, I hope it shall be from yours. Who else can move the people's hearts as you do?" She smiled up at him. "The children would be so proud."

"Ernest and Alice, perhaps," he replied. "Edith and Annie are too young to understand what their papa does."

"Charley is not too young. Why do you not mention him? Wouldn't he be as proud of you as Ernest and Alice?"

"Ah, Charley." Henry sighed, wistful. "You and I both know that our eldest boy is not overfond of literature. He's impressed by men of deeds, not men of letters."

"Charley admires you as much as the other children do," Fanny protested. "Perhaps more."

"He loves and respects me, but he does not admire me." Henry felt a pang of loss as he spoke the words, for giving voice to his great regret somehow anchored it in truth. "He admires men who fight, who risk their lives for noble purposes, who embody manly courage and daring. And I —" He shrugged and tried to smile, though he knew himself incapable of disguising his true feelings from his wife. "What do I risk in defense of my country? Ink-stained fingers? Injured pride from a scathing review?"

"Courage takes many forms," Fanny replied, squeezing his arm for emphasis, "and there are many honorable ways to contribute to the Union cause other than fighting on the battlefield. Charley knows this."

Henry raised her hand to his lips to thank her for her loving reassurances. He wished he could believe her.

Spring blossomed into summer, and the arduous work to build armies and navies continued apace, even as dismaying accounts of skirmishes in Virginia and Missouri, and the inevitable loss of life, appeared more frequently in the papers.

On the night of July 3, Henry invited Fanny outside to the garden to observe the night sky, where a splendid comet blazed in the north, near the constellation of the Great Bear. "If we were less scientific and more superstitious than we are," he remarked, his arm around her shoulders, "we might believe this to be an omen of a great Union victory yet to come."

She shuddered. "Or a terrible defeat. Weren't strange, celestial phenomena also considered portents of doom?"

"Oh, surely this one cannot presage anything so dire," he assured her with mock solemnity, kissing her forehead. "It shines in the northern sky, upon the North. It can mean only great things for the Union."

"I hope you're right." She gave a small, shaky laugh. "Of course, if I am to be brutally honest, I confess I believe this comet portends nothing, but serves only as a reminder of the endless wonder of God's creation."

"It's good for us to pause and remember that."

"Henry," she said with sudden urgency, "I

don't want our sons to go to war."

"Neither do I, darling."

"I have missed our precious Frances every day for almost thirteen years. I cannot lose another child. I couldn't bear it."

Henry's throat constricted. They almost never spoke of their precious, lost daughter, who had succumbed to illness at only seventeen months of age. "You needn't fear," he said. "Charley and Ernest are too young to enlist, and the war cannot last long."

"Charley is seventeen, and what war ever ended sooner than expected?"

"If the worst happens, and the rebellion is not put down for months, or even years, we will forbid Charley to enlist." Henry could not believe the conflict would last long enough for Ernest to be eligible to serve.

"Do you promise me?"

He took her hands. "I'll do everything in my power to prevent it."

"Thank you." She took a deep, tremulous breath and squeezed his hands, eyes downcast. "I'm ashamed of myself for demanding this of you, when other mothers' sons are risking their lives for the Union even as we speak. It seems almost treasonous — and yet I cannot take the words back."

"I'd be more astonished if you *didn't* want

146

to keep our boys out of the fight," Henry told her soothingly. "Darling, I truly believe, and I fervently pray, that they'll never have the opportunity."

He put his arm around her shoulders again and drew her close, and she sighed as she rested her head upon his shoulder. For a while longer they watched the comet in silence, but gradually, and without changing a single spark of its appearance, to Henry the celestial marvel had assumed a sinister aspect.

In Cambridge and Boston, Independence Day was celebrated with impressive patriotic fervor even for cities renowned for patriotism. Parades wound through the streets led by brass bands playing rousing martial tunes, and orators and politicians declaimed from many a park and street corner. Red, white, and blue bunting graced nearly every window and storefront, and the sidewalks were filled with citizens, young and old, waving flags and chanting patriotic slogans. Churches invited passersby to join them in solemn worship, prayer services to appeal to the Almighty for the restoration of the Union, while at the State House thousands gathered to hear the governor's annual address. Beneath a high banner declaring,

"Massachusetts for the Union Forever," Governor Andrew proclaimed the importance of preserving the Union, and of heeding the call to arms to fight for liberty and freedom, and of the noble courage of the Commonwealth's brave youth, who would gladly offer up their lives for their country. It was a stirring speech, but Henry and Fanny exchanged wary, knowing glances every time Charley and Ernest nudged each other, whispered together, and nodded eagerly.

After calling on Fanny's parents, Henry and Fanny took the children to the Music Hall for a special concert of patriotic music, with a program designed to appeal to the young. Afterward they enjoyed popped corn and ice cream sold by street vendors, and then went to the Common to view a hippopotamus, a magnificent creature that had come to America directly from touring the Continent and meeting the crowned heads of Europe. Henry and the children agreed that it was surely one of the most astonishing curiosities ever seen in Boston.

The weather on Independence Day was hot but tolerably so thanks to freshening winds that swept in from the sea, but soon thereafter the weather took a turn for the unbearable. Temperatures soared, the humidity steadily rose, until Henry could not wear a shirt for five minutes before it was soaked through with perspiration, and Fanny fanned herself and complained that she felt as if she were trying to breathe underwater.

"Perhaps we should retreat to Nahant sooner rather than later," Henry suggested wearily to Fanny less than a week after Independence Day. They were sitting listlessly in his study where the open windows gave them something of a cross-breeze, Henry in his favorite armchair by the fireplace, dark and swept clean, Fanny on the sofa between seven-year-old Edith and Annie, all of five years. They had intended to retire to their summer home in early August so that Henry could devote July to his work, but the sultry air so enervated him that he could hardly focus his thoughts enough to compose the salutation of a letter, much less a few lines of poetry.

"I'd like that very much," said Fanny, stroking Edith's limp curls. The back of the poor child's neck was damp with perspiration. "I daresay the children would too. But would that not interrupt your writing?"

"There's nothing to interrupt," he complained mildly. It was too hot to complain more vigorously. "If Nahant can afford us some relief, I may be able to tap into a wellspring of poetical inspiration."

"Say the word and I'll begin packing."

"We'll go as soon as I can make arrangements." Henry folded his hands across his waist and sank deeper into his chair. "I feel cooler already."

"I wish I could say the same." With a sigh, Fanny rose and reached for Edith's hand. "In the meantime, I can give this little one some relief. Come, darling. Let's go trim those overgrown curls."

Edith nodded obediently and slid down from the sofa. Little Annie promptly did too, taking Fanny's other hand.

"Save a lock or two, won't you, dear?" Henry called after them as Fanny led the girls from his study.

"I'll seal a curl in paper, just for you."

"For us," he mumbled drowsily. "For all posterity."

He smiled at the trill of her laugh, fading as she moved off down the hall.

Alone, he dozed in the quiet of his darkened office, his thoughts drifting from Nahant to his unfinished poem to a few letters he ought to answer before the week was out. His friend George Curtis had written to lament that the Committee on the National Hymn had received more than twelve hundred manuscripts, yet not one was considered suitable. Henry suspected that he would be obliged either to submit a piece or contrive a better excuse for not doing so. Either way, he did not relish the effort —

"Henry!"

The anguished cry jolted him from his doze. Horrorstruck, he beheld in the hallway his beloved wife, her light muslin dress engulfed in flame.

"Fanny!" He bolted to his feet, snatched up the hearth rug, and threw it around her in an attempt to smother the flames. The rug was too small; he could cover only a part of her.

"Henry," she gasped, her eyes rolling back into her head. Her skirt was but ash and charred steel hoops; the bodice burning yet as the flames crept upward to her face, her beloved face. The rug was too small. He flung his arms around her, crushing the flames with his chest, his arms.

"Papa!" Annie shrieked.

He glanced up to discover his daughter unharmed but watching in terror from the library doorway. "Get help," he shouted.

She darted off. As he fought to extinguish the flames, Fanny struggled in his embrace, pulling him with her as she staggered down the vestibule and into the front hall. At the foot of the stairs, she fainted; he eased her to the floor, flung the rug over her, ran to the dining room, snatched up a pitcher of water, and raced back to poured it over her. The smell of burning flesh stung his eyes and seared his nostrils.

"Mr. Longfellow!"

The servants were running down the stairs toward him; he was on his knees beside Fanny, dousing the last of the flames with the pitcher and the rug. "Fetch the doctor," he ordered hoarsely. She was unconscious — oh, merciful God, Fanny, his beloved — and he bent over her to kiss her smooth, untouched face. "Fanny, darling, stay with me, it will be all right." To the servants, he added, "Help me get her upstairs and into bed. Carefully, for the love of God, carefully!"

As his servants lifted her, he tried to stand, but his legs collapsed beneath him. Suddenly he felt someone seize him from behind and help him to his feet — it was Miss Davies, the governess. "Thank you," he murmured automatically, then hurried up the stairs after Fanny as quickly as he could. By the time he entered the room they had her lying atop their coverlet. The sight of her pale face and charred legs and torso nearly made his heart stop. "The doctor.

Where is the doctor?"

"He's been sent for, sir," said the butler, his voice breaking.

With a sob, Henry knelt beside the bed and stroked Fanny's brow, desperately listening for the sound of her soft breaths, to be sure she yet lived. It seemed an eternity until the doctor hurried in, his face a careful, impassive mask, his dismay betrayed only by the grim set of his mouth. Obediently Henry moved aside when asked to make way, but he paced at the foot of the bed, tormented, clenching his jaw so he did not scream.

"Mr. Longfellow —"

"Miss Davies." Distraught, he turned about and seized her by the shoulders. "The girls. Are they all right? Were they also burned?"

"The girls are safe, Mr. Longfellow. All the children are safe."

"You must take them away. They mustn't see their mother like this." His thoughts darted wildly. "Take them at once to the Dana home on Berkeley Street. Do you know it?"

"Certainly, but Mr. Longfellow —"

"What is it?" he barked.

"You must let the doctor tend to you as well."

Henry stared at her, bewildered, and then glanced down at his hands. They were red and charred, as were his arms, as was his chest. Suddenly searing pain crashed down upon him, an agony of fire from his neck to his waist. He felt himself growing faint, but strong hands seized him and kept him on his feet. Distantly he was aware of stumbling along between two servants down the hallway to the guest bedroom, where he was eased onto the bed, and the blackened tatters of his shirt and waistcoat were peeled away. He cried out in pain, in misery, and then the doctor was at his bedside and he breathed in sickly sweet ether and darkness engulfed him.

When he emerged from the stupor of ether and laudanum several days later, he wished the silent blackness would engulf him again.

His beloved wife was dead, taken cruelly from him after suffering beyond human endurance.

She had been buried, he learned, at Mount Auburn cemetery on July 13, their eighteenth wedding anniversary. The funeral had been held at noon in the library of Craigie House, the scene of so much domestic happiness, and of one horrific tragedy. Her coffin, covered in a fragrant blanket of flowers, had rested on a table in the center of the room; white roses had adorned her bosom and she had worn a wreath of orange blossoms upon her head.

As he grappled to comprehend the unimaginable, Henry learned that the family had suffered a second loss. After Fanny's funeral, Nathan Appleton, of fragile constitution at eighty years of age, had sat for the rest of the day clutching a lily saved for him from her coffin. "She has gone but a little while before me," he murmured whenever anyone offered him condolences. He died the next day, and soon thereafter he was buried beside his daughter.

As for Henry, when the doctor informed him that he was severely burned, but that he would live, and that his physical wounds would heal in time, he felt both relieved and utterly devastated.

At first, he was dosed too heavily with laudanum to see anyone, but when he overheard that Fanny's brother Tom was in the library, he asked for his brother-in-law to be shown to his sickroom.

Tom looked pale and haggard as he sat down at Henry's bedside, and his voice broke as he struggled to express his sorrow.

Henry could not bear it. He raised a hand to silence him. "How?" he croaked.

It was a single, despondent word, but Tom understood. It was a candle, he replied haltingly. Fanny had trimmed Edith's curls and had saved a pretty lock for Henry. As was the custom, she had placed it within a piece of folded paper, intending to seal it with a stick of wax, melted over a candle. Somehow she had brushed the sleeve of her light muslin dress against the candle, or a sudden breeze from the open window had spread the candle's flame, or the candle had fallen over — no one knew precisely — and her dress had caught fire.

Henry nodded and thanked Tom for the story, knowing that it pained his brother-in-law to tell it almost as much as it grieved him to hear it.

A candle. All his happiness lost forever because of a candle.

A week after Fanny's death, Cornelius Felton, professor of Greek literature and president of Harvard University, called at Craigie House. Since the accident, Henry almost never consented to see anyone other than family, but as Felton was one of Henry's oldest and closest friends, he asked him to be shown upstairs.

Felton expressed his condolences as gracefully as any man could, but each word was a stab in the heart. When Felton asked about his health, Henry gestured absently to his bandages. "I am still suffering from the burns, especially to my hands, but the doctor says I will recover."

"I'm very relieved to hear it." Felton scrutinized him, his worry unmistakable. "Does the pain disturb your rest?"

"On the contrary, I sleep best when the pain is greatest." Just then Henry glimpsed Annie lingering in the hallway just beyond the doorway, her face contorted in misery, and he decided to say no more of his suffering. "I'm sorry I haven't responded to your letter, but I have not felt up to it."

Felton hastened to assure him that no reply was necessary, that he had written in hopes of providing some small measure of comfort and would never dream of adding to Henry's burdens. Henry thanked him, and they chatted for a while longer, but then Felton, ever a kind friend, rose and bade him farewell rather than tire him.

Soon after Felton departed, Henry was sinking into a doze when he realized that Annie had reappeared in the doorway. Her face was streaked with tears.

"Dear little one," he said, holding out his bandaged arms to her. "Come. Come to Papa." Obediently she entered the room. He patted the bed, and she drew closer, but would not sit. "I'm getting better day by day. Does my appearance distress you?"

She nodded, and then she looked at the floor and shook her head.

"What is it, then, my dear little chick?"

"I killed Mama."

Henry felt as if he had been struck a blow to the heart with a blacksmith's hammer. "Oh, my precious girl, you did no such thing."

"I did," she sobbed. "I did."

"Annie, darling, it was an accident. A terrible accident. The candle —"

"It wasn't the candle. It was me."

He stared at her, wanting to draw her to him but powerless to move. "What do you mean?"

"Mama was cutting Edie's hair." Annie gulped air, trembling. "She folded the paper and put the curl inside. She got out the candle. I was playing with the box of parlor matches — opening the box, closing it. One fell out onto the floor. I went to pick it up, but it rolled under Mama's skirts and I don't know if she stepped on it or if I struck it on the floor but it lit, and then Mama's dress caught fire and she burned up and she's dead and I killed her."

Unable to speak, Henry held out his arms to his weeping child. She came to him, and he ignored the sharp, stabbing pains to his chest and arms as he enfolded her in his embrace. "It was an accident," he said in a voice that would allow no argument. "You are not responsible. You did not kill your mother. It was an accident."

Annie flung her arms around him and sobbed as if her heart had shattered from grief and guilt and would never be restored.

Later that day, he woke up from a fitful sleep just as Miss Davies passed quietly by his door, which had been left ajar. He called to her, and when she entered, he asked, "Is it true that a candle ignited my wife's dress?"

"Why, yes, Mr. Longfellow," she replied, puzzled, clasping her hands together at her waist.

"You're certain?"

"I myself heard the police captain tell Mr. Appleton so."

Henry inhaled deeply and sank back against his pillow. "Thank you, Miss Davies."

She nodded and departed, leaving the door ajar exactly as it had been before.

A few days after Annie's strange, disordered confession, Henry was able to rise from bed and take a few hesitant steps around his bedchamber. Soon thereafter, he attempted the stairs, and was able to sit up in the parlor. It was decided that he and the children would go to Nahant as soon as he was able, to convalesce and to find, if they could, some comfort for their broken hearts.

The day before they were to depart, Henry went to his library to search for a particular volume of Italian poetry he wanted to take on the journey. Suddenly, a few scattered objects on a table caught his eye — a candle, a slender bar of wax, a box of parlor matches, a piece of paper folded upon a golden curl.

Henry froze in place, scarcely able to breathe. Then he forced himself to cross the room, to examine the artifacts of his beloved wife's last day.

The folded paper had not been sealed. The slender bar of wax was whole, untouched. The candle had never been lit, its wick pure white without the slightest char.

Clenching his jaw to hold back a howl of anguish, Henry struck a match, lit the candle, melted the wax, and sealed his daughter's golden curl within the paper Fanny's gentle hands had folded.

# CHAPTER SEVEN:
# THE CHOIRGIRL'S TALE

Charlotte first heard of the terrible tragedy that had struck the poet Henry Wadsworth Longfellow's family when she was on a third-grade class field trip to the museum at Longfellow House. More than 150 years before, Mrs. Longfellow had died after her dress had caught fire in the library, and Mr. Longfellow had burned himself very badly trying to put out the flames.

"I don't see any burn marks," her friend Emily had whispered, frowning skeptically at the library floor as the tour guide described the artifacts on display.

"Mr. Longfellow probably cleaned them up," Charlotte had whispered back. "Would *you* want to see, every single day, burn marks on your floor from the fire that killed your wife?"

Emily had recoiled, shaking her head, and she might have replied except at that moment they had noticed Mrs. Hayes raising her eyebrows at them. Immediately Emily's expression had gone blandly innocent and she had gazed at the tour guide with rapt interest, but Charlotte had felt herself flush with shame. She had not spoken another word for the rest of the tour, and afterward, as they were boarding the bus to return to school, Charlotte had hung back so she could speak to Mrs. Hayes alone.

"Charlotte, it's all right," her teacher had replied, taken aback by her profuse apologies. "You and Emily weren't talking that loudly, and I trust you were discussing something about Longfellow."

"We were, really."

"As I thought." Mrs. Hayes had smiled and patted Charlotte on the shoulder. "You're a good girl and an excellent student. Please don't make more of this than I intended. We all need a little reminder about the rules now and then."

Miserable, Charlotte had nodded rather than blurt out that she didn't need to be reminded, not usually, not ever. No one knew the rules better or followed them more earnestly than she did. Her parents knew it, her friends understood it, the bullies teased her about it, and her teachers relied upon it. Everyone who knew Charlotte knew that she was trustworthy, honest, and responsible.

At least everyone had known that, until recently, until Charlotte had wound up in Mrs. Collins's sixth-grade English class and the reputation she had carefully protected since kindergarten had been shattered with one accusation.

Charlotte knew, deep down, that the trouble with the stern, mistrustful Mrs. Collins was not, as her mother would say if she knew about it, the end of the world. It was not a disaster. Alex almost burning down the neighborhood — *that* was a disaster. If her dad got wounded in Afghanistan, that would be one too. Mrs. Longfellow's suffering and death, and the terrible grief that had descended upon her husband and children — disastrous, every bit of it. Charlotte's failure and shame were nothing in comparison.

And yet her heart ached anyway.

The loss of his wife had broken Longfellow's heart and aged him almost overnight. Charlotte and Emily and thousands of tourists could not miss the difference between his image in photos and portraits from before Fanny Longfellow's death — handsome, dark-haired, elegant — and those that followed less than a year after, in which he appeared white-haired, stoop-shouldered, thickly bearded, deeply wrinkled, and utterly weary.

Sometimes Charlotte wondered if her mom would grow old overnight if something terrible happened to her dad in Afghanistan, but the thought was too upsetting to contemplate, so she quickly shoved it aside whenever it arose, unpleasant and sinister, from the darkest recesses of her imagination where nightmares lurked.

Charlotte remembered precisely the last time they had been able to speak with him because Mrs. Collins had announced the Christmas story contest the day before their scheduled chat, and Charlotte was eager to tell him about it. But the next day, her mom couldn't get him online at the proper time, and after testing the connections and emailing back and forth with some tech-services guy somewhere between Boston and Kabul, she had told Charlotte and Alex that they wouldn't be able to chat with their father after all. She shook her head slightly as she gave them the bad news, her brow furrowing, which told Charlotte that their mom was puzzled but not worried.

"That's not fair," protested Alex. "Dad said we could, and we waited patiently."

Charlotte agreed, but she knew that whining to their mother wouldn't help. "Can we try again tomorrow?"

"I'll see," their mother replied. "It can't hurt to ask."

The next day, their mother informed them that she had been in touch with the people in charge, and they had told her that their Internet was down and they did not know when the problem would be resolved. This time her face was pale and her mouth was strangely pinched as she delivered the bad news, but while Charlotte paused to wonder about that, Alex blurted, "It wasn't our fault we missed our turn, so they should let us go to the front of the line as soon as they're back online."

"That's right," said Charlotte. "Did you tell them that?"

"I did," said their mother carefully, "but other families before us had the same problem, so we have to go after them. We may not be able to talk to your father for quite some time."

"Wait a minute," said Alex slowly. "Does this mean we won't get to talk to Dad on Thanksgiving?"

Charlotte could not believe Alex had figured that out before she did. "Well?" she demanded shrilly, turning an accusing look upon their mother. "Does it?"

"I'm so very, very sorry." Her gaze dropped to her hands in her lap, and as she turned her wedding ring around her finger, Charlotte realized that she was fighting back tears, and she felt horrible for causing them. Quickly she apologized, and Alex surprisingly did the same, and their mother nodded wordlessly and held out her arms to them and they all clung to each other tightly.

At that moment, Charlotte resolved that she would try even harder not to upset their mother. Her mom missed her dad too. She wanted to chat with him as much as they did. Complaining wouldn't make the Internet expert work any faster. Charlotte would have to be patient, and she would have to remind Alex to be patient too.

"It's so hard to be patient," she confessed to Emily over lunch on the last day of school before Christmas. "I was really counting on talking to my dad at Thanksgiving, and when I couldn't I just wanted to cry, but I didn't want to make my mom sad, so I had to pretend that I was fine. 'Oh, this turkey is so good! Yum! Pumpkin pie! Sure, I haven't talked to my dad in forever, but who cares when I have all this food to distract me?' "

Emily shook her head, sympathetic. Charlotte trusted Emily with all her secrets. Of

166

all her friends, only Emily knew how long it had been since Charlotte had heard from her father. Only Emily had seen the nasty note Mrs. Collins had scrawled at the bottom of her Christmas story. And only Emily had heard Charlotte say that the only good thing — and it wasn't even that good — about the broken Internet in Afghanistan was that she could delay telling her father about her disgrace.

"Charlotte?"

"What?"

Emily drew in a breath and carefully asked, "Are you sure the Internet's broken in Afghanistan?"

"It's not broken in the entire country. Just where my dad is."

"I know that's what you mean, but . . . are you sure that's true?"

Charlotte studied her, uncomprehending. "What do you mean? My mom says it's broken."

"I know but . . ." Emily looked pained. "Do you think it is, really?"

"You mean you think she might be making it up?"

"I don't know. Maybe?"

"That's impossible. My mom hates lying. She never lies. Why would she lie?"

"Don't get upset," Emily begged. "I just

— it was just — I don't know. I'm just saying, it's really, really weird that no one over there has been able to fix it yet. I've seen the commercials for the Army. Don't they give the soldiers lots of training in electronics and computers and stuff like that?"

"They know how to fix it. My mom says they're probably just waiting for a part to be delivered or something." As Charlotte heard herself say the words, she realized how ridiculous they sounded. "Oh, my gosh. I'm so stupid."

"I shouldn't have said anything —"

"I am *so* incredibly stupid. I'm the stupidest person in the sixth grade. No, in our entire school. Our entire school *district.*"

"No, you're not." Emily touched her arm. "Charlotte, I'm so sorry —"

"You don't need to apologize. *You're* not the liar." The bell clanged. Charlotte bolted to her feet and seized her lunch tray. "I can't believe my mother thought I wouldn't figure it out."

She might not have, if not for Emily. Would her mother have told her eventually? It was so insulting to be treated like a little kid —

Then her heart plummeted. She gasped and stopped in the middle of the cafeteria so abruptly that a seventh-grade boy bumped into her and knocked over her carton of milk. As it dribbled onto the floor, onto her cute, retro navy-blue Mary Janes, as Emily scrambled for napkins, Charlotte was struck by the only question that mattered.

Why had her mother lied?

Had her father been injured? Before he left, he had assured her and Alex that he would be in a safe place fixing broken trucks and equipment far from any actual fighting, but later, when they were alone and Charlotte had pressed him, he had admitted that accidents happened and the base wasn't invulnerable. Was he, even at that moment, lying in a hospital bed somewhere? Was he — Could he be —

The thought was so horrible she could not let her mind hold it.

At last the school day ended. When her mother pulled up to the curb in their blue minivan, Charlotte scrutinized her through the window, hard, but nothing in her mother's expression suggested terrible grief, just the usual worry and strain. Maybe a bit more than usual. Charlotte opened the door and slid into the front seat, dropping her heavy, overstuffed backpack onto the floor between her legs.

"Hi, sweetie." Her mother leaned over to

give her a swift kiss on the cheek, which Charlotte tolerated in silence. Her mother threw her a quizzical glance as she merged into traffic. "Rough day?"

The car was overheated; Charlotte loosened her scarf. "Same as usual."

"How was English class?"

Charlotte felt her stomach lurch. "Fine. Why do you ask?"

"I don't know. It's always been your favorite subject, but you haven't mentioned anything lately about books you've read or papers you've written."

"It's not my favorite anymore." Feigning boredom, Charlotte slouched down in her seat, heart pounding. Her secret was apparently still safe.

Before long they pulled into the elementary school parking lot and spotted Alex on the snow-covered lawn, goofing around in the center of a circle of friends. When her mother beeped the horn, Alex high-fived his friends and bounded over, backpack mostly unzipped and bouncing wildly from the strap on his shoulder. "Hi, guys," he exclaimed as he climbed into the backseat. "Mr. Donaldson said it's supposed to snow tonight."

"I heard that too," their mother said, reaching back to ruffle his hair as he buckled his seat belt.

Charlotte dug a book out of her backpack and read as they drove to St. Margaret's, listening to Christmas carols on the radio and trying not to cry. "You can just pull up in front and let us out, Mom," Charlotte said when they arrived, closing her book and wedging it into her backpack.

"Thanks, honey, but I'd rather walk in with you."

Charlotte glanced over her shoulder at Alex. "You mean, to make sure we get there."

He scowled. "It was only that one time."

Charlotte sighed inwardly. Of course it had been only that one time, because their mother had never again trusted them enough to drop them off at the curb. It seemed unlikely that she ever would again. Suddenly her anger flared. Her mother didn't trust *her,* but Charlotte wasn't the one who had lied. In that way her mom was like Mrs. Collins, who punished the entire class when one student talked, who made everyone take a pop quiz when the first few students she called on didn't know the answers. Legend had it that once upon a time, a student had stolen a test from her electric typewriter and had made copies for the entire class so everyone earned an A the next day. Ever since, Mrs. Collins had expected the worst of every student she met, especially the high achievers, and she caught genuine cheaters so often that the principal accepted her judgment without question.

It wasn't fair, to use Alex's favorite phrase.

Father Ryan was sweeping the sidewalk by the side door as they approached the church. "Hi, Father Ryan," Alex shouted, waving. "Nice hat. The Bruins are gonna crush the Penguins tomorrow."

"You'd better believe it," the priest said with a grin, though Charlotte noticed it faded a little as he turned to their mother. "Hey, Laurie. How's everything going?"

"Oh, everything's fine," their mother said, giving him a huge, bright, obviously fake smile. "The usual."

The concern in his eyes told Charlotte that he was in on the secret. "Have you heard from Jason?"

"Oh, sure. We hear from him all the time, don't we, kids?" Their mother looked to Alex and Charlotte for confirmation, nodding, but although blissfully ignorant Alex nodded happily back, Charlotte stared at her boots and shrugged. "But you know how it is. The Internet over there is always breaking down, and it takes forever to get online again, but as soon as it's fixed, we're going to get to chat with him again —"

"I get to talk with him first," Alex interrupted. "Mom promised. I want to make a rocket for the science fair and I have to ask Dad some stuff."

Father Ryan nodded, obviously concerned. How could their mother think Charlotte wouldn't notice these things? "That's wise. I've heard about you and rockets. It's best to consult with an expert first." Gently, to their mother, he added, "Please let me know if there's anything I can do."

"Thank you, Ryan. I will."

"And tell Jason Merry Christmas from me when you speak with him," Father Ryan said.

"Of course." Looking close to tears, their mother gave him a small, forced smile, placed her hands on Alex's and Charlotte's backs, and steered them toward the door.

"Wait a minute," said Alex as they entered the stairwell and started up the steps. "Why can't Father Ryan tell Dad Merry Christmas himself? Isn't Dad coming to church with us?"

"Of course not, honey," their mom replied. "Your dad is in Afghanistan."

"I know that, but isn't he coming home for Christmas?"

Charlotte couldn't bear to have it all out in the stairwell, so she threw Alex a warning look. "Dad won't be back until next summer."

Bewildered, Alex halted abruptly. "But he'll miss the concert."

His mother held open the door at the top of the stairs. "He's missed a lot of things. Come on, honey. We can't be late."

Alex obeyed, for once. "But who will make gingerbread pancakes? Dad always makes us gingerbread pancakes on Christmas morning."

"I know you're disappointed, honey, and I am too." Her eyes were filling with tears. "Maybe we can get something special from the bakery instead, okay? Would you like that?"

Alex reluctantly agreed that bakery treats would be all right, and they took off their coats and left them on the pew with their mother. "Nice going," Charlotte scolded him in a murmur as they went to join the choir. Alex's face fell, and with a pang of guilt, Charlotte quickly put as many singers between them as Miss Sophia's seating arrangement allowed. She wished she hadn't scolded him. He was just a little boy, and he had no idea that their mother had much bigger problems on her mind than gingerbread pancakes for Christmas morning.

Eventually Lucas announced that they were going to begin rehearsal even though Miss Sophia hadn't arrived. Charlotte and her friends exchanged significant glances, acknowledging the strangeness of it. They all agreed that Lucas was handsome for someone so old, and they all knew that he was totally in love with Miss Sophia, and they thought it was funny that he thought no one knew. To be fair, most people didn't, including Miss Sophia.

With Miss Sophia absent, Charlotte had no conductor to watch as they warmed up their voices, so she let her gaze travel over the pews, coming to rest on her mother, sitting pale and motionless in the third row, still in her coat and hat. She was probably concentrating on making up new lies to cover up the old ones.

When Charlotte's voice began to quaver with anger and worry, she tore her gaze from her mother. Sister Winifred was tidying up the pews, smiling to herself; Charlotte always thought the little nun looked as if she were whistling merrily inside her head. Some other kids thought Sister Winifred was crazy and were a little afraid of her, but Charlotte thought she was nice. Once, long ago, she had overheard her parents agreeing that the elderly nun was eccentric, perhaps, but harmless. If she occasionally seemed to be chatting with someone no one else could see or hear, at least they were cheerful conversations punctuated with occasional merry laughter.

One day in late November, as Charlotte and Alex waited for their mother to pick them up after rehearsal, Charlotte had mentioned her Christmas story, which she had turned in earlier that day. "I should like to read it," Sister Winifred had remarked. "Would you email it to me?" Charlotte, astounded to discover that nuns used the Internet, had sent it to her that very day. Soon thereafter Sister Winifred had said that she had enjoyed the tale very much and declared that Charlotte was "a natural storyteller."

Charlotte had glowed from the praise, but it brought her no comfort now. What if the kindly nun asked what grade she had received on the assignment and how she had fared in the contest? Charlotte could imagine the sparkle fading from her eyes, sorrow and disappointment driving away all merriment from her expression. What would she think of Charlotte then? Grown-ups always believed one another before trusting a kid. If anyone found out, Sister Winifred or her mother or —

At that moment Miss Sophia hurried in and quickly shrugged out of her coat and scarf. She had just draped them over the back of a pew when a door closed at the back of the church and in walked the rich lady, the senator's wife. When Charlotte had first joined the choir, the senator and his wife used to show up at rehearsals together and sit near the back, listening and watching, always leaving before the end. For a long time, though — Charlotte couldn't remember exactly how long — the wife had come alone. Whenever Charlotte saw her, she was reminded painfully of the day her father had left for Afghanistan. The senator had been scheduled to speak, but he had been sick so his wife had filled in for him. She had done pretty well too. She had been funny when she could be and serious when she had to be, and she never said "Um" or lost her train of thought.

Maybe the lady could ask her husband the senator to look into the stupid Internet problems at her father's base, Charlotte thought fleetingly, before remembering with a sickening jolt that their Internet was probably working just fine.

Charlotte was so upset that her voice cracked on a high note. The other sopranos were kind enough to pretend not to notice, but she was so mortified that she clamped her mouth shut and stared stonily at the back of the head of the girl in front of her. She didn't utter another note until Miss Sophia picked up her baton and announced "I Heard the Bells on Christmas Day," and she only sang then because Miss Sophia would notice if she didn't, even if she mouthed the words. And yet, as much as Charlotte had once loved that simple, beautiful carol, at that moment she would rather sing anything else.

It was that carol — or, rather, the poem that had inspired it — that had gotten her into so much trouble.

For as long as Charlotte could remember, she had loved to write stories. Her mother said that she had begun writing as soon as she could hold a crayon, but since she hadn't known the alphabet, she'd had to read her stories aloud since only she could interpret the colorful marks on the paper. She always received the highest grades on her school compositions, and at the fifth-grade graduation ceremony the previous year, she had won a special award for the best historical essay in the entire class. Her name had been printed in a special place in the program and everything. So, in early

October when Mrs. Collins had announced the student Christmas story contest, Charlotte was elated. If she won first place in her school, her story would go on to the district competition. If it won there, it would be sent to the newspaper to be judged by a team of experts. The top three stories would be published in the Christmas Day edition of the *Boston Globe,* and the week before, the winners and their parents would be invited to a special lunch with the editors and judges, where they would read their stories aloud and receive an engraved plaque.

What a wonderful Christmas gift this would be for her mother, Charlotte thought. Mom always said that the best gifts were homemade because they were unique and came from the heart. Charlotte could give her mother her plaque and tell her that she owed her success to her, because her mother had read aloud to Charlotte from the time she was a baby and had never refused to drive her to the library no matter how busy she was. Her mother would be so proud. She would smile again like she hadn't smiled since her dad left. She might even forget, if only for a moment, how lonely she was without him.

The contest was officially called the Alice

Longfellow Christmas Creative Writing Competition, because it was sponsored by a foundation the poet's daughter had created in the early 1900s. Though Alice Longfellow had been only ten years old when her mother died, in time she had become the mistress of the household, taking care of her younger sisters and looking after their father. She had never married, and after Henry Wadsworth Longfellow died, she had become the curator of her father's legacy and a respected philanthropist, supporting many worthy causes that promoted historic preservation and education for women.

When Charlotte made the connection between Alice Longfellow, her father the famous poet, the historic residence she had visited in third grade, and the new carol Miss Sophia had chosen for the choir's Christmas Eve concert, it was as if a cartoon lightbulb had lit up above her head. Charlotte would write a story about a girl whose father had recently died (because to have her mother die would be too much like Alice's real life) and who was searching for her brother, a Union soldier who had been wounded on the battlefield and had gone missing after being taken to a military hospital in Washington, DC. Her only clue would be a scrap of a letter that had been left behind, but she was determined to find him, nurse him back to health, and bring him home in time for Christmas.

Inspired, Charlotte had thrown herself into the work, writing at a furious pace. She was fairly satisfied with her first draft and almost happy with the second, but she knew something was missing. It wasn't until Alex was given the solo in "I Heard the Bells on Christmas Day" that she realized what her story lacked: a Christmas poem. A Christmas story inspired by a Christmas carol inspired by a poet's Christmas poem really ought to include some poetry of its own.

Charlotte had already decided that the brother in the story was missing because he had been taken to recover in a makeshift hospital set up in a church rather than a regular one, so of course her story included a choir. She decided it would be smart to use Henry Wadsworth Longfellow's own "Christmas Bells" as a model, so she began her poem with the line, "I heard the choir on Christmas Day / Their new and favorite carols play / Nice and sweet the stanzas beat / Of peace on earth, every day."

"No," she had said aloud, disgusted, scribbling out the entire stanza. That was too much like Longfellow's original, except stupider. Choirs didn't play carols; they sang them. Stanzas didn't beat, and "nice and sweet" sounded like a commercial for Christmas cookies.

She had started over, and suddenly, again like a flash of light, a first line came to her, whole and clear: "The choir sang on Christmas night." Simple and clear, with a perfect rhythm. More ideas flowed, and soon she had an entire stanza:

The choir sang on Christmas night
Of a heavenly star that shone great light
Upon the manger where Jesus slept
While tender watch his mother kept.

Happily, she wrote the rest that evening, and over the next few days, she perfected the poem and nestled it snugly within her story. She typed it all up on her mother's computer, printed out the story on good paper, and put it in a clear plastic binder for safekeeping.

Then she submitted it to Mrs. Collins with fingers crossed, hoping she would receive not only an A-plus for the class assignment, but also the happy news that her story had qualified for the district competition.

She had read her story to her mother, who had loved it, and to Alex, who had told her it wasn't too bad but should have had more soldiers and fighting, and to Emily, who thought it was wonderful and declared that it would definitely be published in the *Boston Globe* on Christmas morning. Charlotte hoped she was right.

A few days later Mrs. Collins returned the stories to their authors, placing them facedown on the students' desks as she walked through the aisles, making general comments about what the class had done well as a group and where they clearly needed to improve. Eagerly, Charlotte turned over her story — only to discover a large red C at the top of the title page.

Horrified, she quickly turned the story facedown again.

"Did you win?" Emily whispered from the desk behind her.

Charlotte swallowed hard, stole a look at Mrs. Collins, still distributing papers and droning on about margins, and quickly shook her head.

"No?" came Emily's incredulous whisper.

Again Charlotte shook her head.

"That's impossible. What did you get?"

Carefully, so no one else would see, Charlotte shielded the front page with her cupped hand and raised it just above her shoulder so Emily could learn the shocking truth.

Emily gasped. "She must have given you the wrong paper."

For a moment Charlotte's hopes flickered back to life, but then, holding the story on her lap and paging through it to read the comments, all hope died. Mrs. Collins had made hardly any corrections to her story, but she had circled the poem several times with broad red strokes. In the margin beside it, she had written, "Is this yours?" At the end of the paper, she had added a lengthier comment: "Please refer to the student handbook for the school policy regarding plagiarism. The entire project must be a student's own original work."

Charlotte felt as if a giant fist was squeezing all the air out of her lungs. Of course the entire project was hers — the story, the poem, every word. She had written it in her bedroom, at the public library, and at the kitchen table with her favorite gel ink pen. Her name was on it. No one had ever accused her of cheating before, not even at Four Square or Monopoly, and she had no idea what to do.

Right before lunch, the winner was announced — a boy from one of the other sixth-grade classes who had written a story about a young tollbooth operator who overcame a lifelong stutter in order to wish a Merry Christmas to the drivers traveling on the holiday, the last of whom was Santa Claus in disguise. Charlotte knew everyone had expected her to win, but she ignored their curious glances and pretended she didn't care. If anyone asked, she would tell them that she had written her story the morning it was due and hadn't really expected to win. Fortunately, she was spared from telling that lie because no one asked.

Of course she shared the devastating accusation with Emily, who became outraged on her behalf and insisted that she go to Mrs. Collins immediately and explain that she had not cheated, that the poem was her own creation. "I did base it upon Longfellow's poem," Charlotte reminded her as they stood side by side at their lockers, packing up at the end of the day. "Maybe that's cheating."

"Maybe 'Christmas Bells' inspired you, but your poem is nothing like his. His verses have five lines and yours have four. He repeats that line about peace and goodwill and you don't. Your poems have the same meter and they're both about Christmas, but that's it."

"Maybe that's enough."

"Inspiration is not plagiarism. Explain to her. I'll come with you."

"Right now?" Charlotte said, dismayed, as Emily slammed both of their lockers shut and seized her hand.

"Yes, right now."

"We'll miss the bus."

"My mom's driving me home today. She'll give you a ride."

Emily was determined, and Charlotte was heartened by her support, so she allowed herself to be towed along to Mrs. Collins's room. Their teacher was erasing the blackboard when Emily knocked firmly on the open door, and her eyebrows rose at the sight of them.

"I'm glad you came by, Charlotte." She gestured to a desk in the front row. "Please sit. Emily, you may wait outside."

"Charlotte didn't cheat," Emily declared.

"Emily," Mrs. Collins said distinctly, "you may wait outside. Please close the door."

As Charlotte took her seat, Emily reluctantly obeyed, throwing her one last encouraging look through the window as the door closed.

Mrs. Collins sat down behind her desk, the ancient electric typewriter of school legend at her right hand. "Well, Charlotte?

186

Did you have something you wanted to tell me?"

Charlotte took a deep breath. "You wanted to know if the poem is mine. Well, it is. Every word. The rest of the story too."

Mrs. Collins regarded her with disappointment but not the least bit of surprise. "It would be better if you told the truth."

"I am telling you the truth." Her voice sounded very small and meek and not at all convincing.

"Charlotte, that C was generous, an acknowledgment that most of the story is clearly your own writing. I could have given you an F and reported you to the principal." Mrs. Collins sighed, frowning. "Perhaps I should invite your parents in and we can all discuss this together."

"No," Charlotte blurted. The knowing look Mrs. Collins gave her in reply told her the teacher completely misunderstood her urgency. "Please don't tell her. My mom is really stressed out and this will make everything worse."

Mrs. Collins folded her arms. "Then I understand why it would feel especially important to you to receive a good grade, and maybe even to win the contest, but plagiarism is never an acceptable means to that end."

"I didn't steal someone else's poem." Suddenly inspired, she dug into her backpack, took out her English binder, and took out a handful of loose-leaf papers covered in cursive and cross-outs. "See? These are my rough drafts. You can see how I started and how I changed it and how it became better."

Mrs. Collins barely glanced at the pages. "Charlotte, we both know you could have written all that after your assignment was returned to you."

"How could I have done that?" Charlotte protested, forgetting herself. "When would I have had time? I was in class all day."

"At lunch. In the passing periods."

"That's not what happened." Charlotte felt tears gathering. "It's my poem and my story, every word. I didn't cheat. I swear I didn't."

Mrs. Collins sighed and rose. "You should go now. If you want to discuss this matter further, we'll invite your parents to join us."

Charlotte rose, her vision blurry with tears, and zipped her backpack shut with force. "My dad can't come here all the way from Afghanistan to tell you I'm not a liar," she snapped icily.

"Charlotte —"

But she had heard enough. Wiping her

eyes with the back of her hand, she stumbled from the classroom, nearly crashing into Emily, who put her arm around her shoulders. "You should tell your mom," she said as they made their way outside to the curb.

"I can't. My mom has enough to worry about with my dad being gone and Alex — being Alex."

"Then tell another teacher. Every other teacher at this school who's had you in class knows you're smart and honest. They'll stick up for you to Mrs. Collins. They'll —"

"We can't tell any other teachers," insisted Charlotte. "The first thing they'll want to do is call my mom. You know that."

Emily clearly wanted to argue the point, but their arrival at the car brought their debate to an abrupt end. Emily's mother took one look at Charlotte's tear-streaked face and her daughter's indignant scowl and agreed to drive Charlotte home, no questions asked.

Charlotte had been so proud of her story, especially the poem, but Mrs. Collins had ruined everything. There would be no wonderful honor to brighten her mother's bleak season, no prize-winning story to read to her proud father over the Internet, no beautifully engraved plaque to present to her mother on Christmas morning. She was in disgrace, and there was no coming back from it.

Charlotte had considered that the worst day of her life. She never thought she would ever feel as horrible as she had at that moment, trying to convince her teacher of her innocence and hearing only bland rejections in reply.

Her mother's lie — and the unknown cause of it — had proven that she could feel worse, so very much worse.

She took a deep breath in the middle of the verse and tried her best to sing, but her heart wasn't in it. She couldn't bear to give voice to the sweet, poignant melody when she knew that eventually the secrets would come out, and as bad as she felt now, she would feel worse, infinitely worse, when her mother finally confessed the real reason why they had not heard from her dad in so long.

# CHAPTER EIGHT:
## AUGUST–DECEMBER 1861

Nahant. Aug 18. 1861.
Mrs. Robert Mackintosh
2 Hyde Park Terrace
London

Dearest Mary,

I will try to write you a line to-day, if only to thank you for your affectionate letter, which touched and consoled me much.

How I am alive after what my eyes have seen, I know not. I am at least patient, if not resigned; and thank God hourly — as I have from the beginning — for the beautiful life your beloved sister and I led together, and that I loved her more and more to the end.

I feel that only you and I knew her thoroughly. You can understand what an inexpressible delight she was to me, always and in all things. I never looked at her without a thrill of pleasure; — she never came into a room where I was without my heart beating quicker, nor went out without my feeling that something of the light went with her. I loved her so entirely, and I know she was very happy.

Truly do you say there was no one like her. And now that she is gone, I can only utter a cry "from the depth of a divine despair." If I could be with you for a while, I should be greatly comforted; only to you can I speak out all that is in my heart about her.

It is a sad thing for Robert to have been here through all this. But his fortitude and his quiet sympathy have given us all strength and support. How much you must have needed him! He goes back to you with our blessing, leaving regrets behind. We all love him very much.

I am afraid I am very selfish in my sorrow; but not an hour passes without my thinking of you, and of how you will bear the double woe, of a father's and a sister's death at once. Dear, affectionate old man! The last day of his life, all day long, he sat holding a lily in his hand, a flower from Fanny's funeral. I trust that the admirable fortitude and patience which thus far have supported you, will not fail. Nor must you think, that having preached resignation to others I am myself a cast-away. Infinite, tender memories of our darling fill me and surround me. Nothing but sweetness comes from her. That noble, loyal, spiritual nature always uplifted and illuminated mine, and always will, to the end.

For the future I have no plans. I can not yet lift my eyes in that direction. I only look backward, not forward. The only question is, what will be best for the children? I shall think of that when I get back to Cambridge.

Meanwhile think of me here, by this haunted sea-shore. So strong is the sense of her presence upon me, that I should hardly be surprised to meet her in our favorite walk, or, if I looked up now to see her in the room.

My heart aches and bleeds sorely for the poor children. To lose such a mother, and all the divine influences of her character and care. They do not know how great their loss is, but I do. God will provide. His will be done!

Full of affection, ever most truly,

H. W. L.

As mournful and bleak as it had been to spend the late summer at the cottage at Nahant, with its constant reminders of countless blissful, happy days lost forever to the past, Henry knew that returning home to Craigie House would be infinitely more painful.

In the aftermath of his beloved Fanny's death, Henry had plunged into a grief so deep and so complete that he had had no strength or presence of mind to demur when Charles Sumner and Tom Appleton and other friends had urged him to retire to the seashore. There, they had said, he could convalesce from his injuries and escape the distressing scenes of so much former happiness and present horror.

He had acquiesced, believing desperate flight preferable to paralysis, hoping that a change of scenery would ease the children's suffering, knowing that nothing could mitigate his own. For a time he had become so wildly melancholic that he had believed he was going insane, and he had feared that his friends would be obliged to commit him to an asylum. Only by sheer force of will had he stumbled back from the precipice of madness. He was greatly bereaved — entirely, wholly bereft — yet so were the children, and they needed him. They were

Fanny's greatest legacy. He could not forsake her by leaving them orphaned and alone in a world that had changed utterly in the matter of a few terrible hours.

At Nahant the fog of shock and laudanum faded, his burned skin itched and ached and yet healed. The relentless stream of letters of condolences followed them to the cottage, but there were few callers. Charley and Ernest sailed and fished and fervently discussed the war. The girls brought Henry shells they had collected upon the shore, begged him for stories, and went on various excursions with Miss Davies. The cottage was too quiet with the children gone, and though he sat at his desk with paper and pen, and tried to write poetry or respond to letters, he found himself counting the silent minutes until they returned. Miss Davies and his friends thought peace and quiet would ease his recovery, but what he desperately craved was his children's noise and activity, their liveliness and youth, the glimpses of their mother he perceived in a daughter's smile, in a son's clever witticism. He clung to such ephemera as if they would tether him to the Earth, restraining him from drifting away to join his beloved wife too soon, before his duty to his children was fulfilled.

At last that bleak, empty August ground to a halt, and with a rising sense of sickening dread, Henry made arrangements for their return to Cambridge. Charley would resume his studies at Harvard when the new term commenced, albeit reluctantly, and the younger children too would return to school. And since Henry must provide for them, he would have to take up his pen, though it seemed impossible that he would ever again find it within himself to write. It seemed that all poetry had drained from the world, that life had lost its flavor and color and fragrance. What was there to write about but misery and loss?

He brooded in silence as he and the children traveled homeward. He was grateful that Charley and Ernest were as ever boon companions, and that dear, good, wise little Alice distracted her younger sisters by pointing out interesting sights she glimpsed through the windows and reading aloud to them when they tired of watching the passing scenery. Henry smiled when the children spoke to him, and caressed their heads whenever they came near, but he was distracted by the conundrum of how, upon their arrival at Craigie House, he would make it across the threshold without collapsing in paroxysms of grief.

Upon their arrival in Boston they boarded a carriage for the last stage of their journey, and as they drove to Cambridge, the children peered through the windows and called out familiar landmarks they passed, as if they had been gone a year and everything they beheld was both new and familiar. Henry's heart pounded as the carriage turned onto Brattle Street. Their home would be barren, so bleak and desolate, without the loving presence that had once graced it. He was not sure he could set foot within the once cherished walls.

Too soon the carriage halted in front of Craigie House.

Henry found himself unable to move. The children did not seem to notice; Charley opened the door and bounded out, Ernest on his heels, and as the boys helped with the luggage, Miss Davies assisted the girls. They were halfway up the front walk, and then they were climbing the stairs, and still Henry had not yet descended from the carriage.

Then the front door opened and a woman emerged from the house. For a moment Henry felt as if his heart had stopped, and then recognition struck, and he inhaled deeply, both shaken and profoundly relieved. His sister Anne stood on the front porch, holding out her arms to her nieces and nephews, welcoming them home. She glanced past them, and her eyes met Henry's, and she managed a tremulous smile.

Anne. He descended from the carriage, steadying himself on his carved walking stick. What a compassionate sister, what a truly good woman she was! She had been widowed young, after only three years of marriage, and she had been the legal guardian of their nephew, Henry, ever since their brother Stephen's wife had divorced him on grounds of alcoholism and adultery. The poet's namesake was twenty-one now, and Anne had assumed the role of caretaker of the old family home in Portland, Maine. Now, it seemed, she had come to take care of her grief-stricken brother and his children. Her kindness knew no bounds.

As the children embraced their aunt and went into the house, she held out her hands to her brother. "Henry," she said, her eyes glistening with tears.

"My dear sister." He set aside his walking stick, took her hands, and kissed her cheek. "I cannot say how very happy and relieved I am to find you here."

"You're growing a beard," she said, studying him. "It ages you twenty years at least."

"It's not the beard that has aged me."

The house had been closed so long that the air tasted stale, but after the windows were opened to the fresh, autumnal breezes, the lingering scent of neglect dissipated. Henry marked changes that had occurred in his absence: The hearth rug had been discarded, the floor of the library and at the foot of the stairs scoured bare and refinished so that no trace of the fire remained. His wife's clothing had been removed from her wardrobe — by whom and where taken, he did not know. Her jewelry remained, packed carefully into two velvet-lined cases, one she had brought with her as a bride, another he had given her for Christmas five years before. When his daughters came of age, he would pass the jewels on to them.

Later Anne gently told him that she had packed away Fanny's wedding gown in her trunk, along with a few other precious mementos. "They're in her trunk in the attic," she said. "It may pain you to look upon them now, but someday they'll evoke fond memories, and they may bring you some comfort."

Henry could not imagine such a day, but he thanked her. "The girls will cherish the gown," he said. "Perhaps they'll wish to wear it in her honor when they marry — in twenty or thirty years, when I've reconciled myself to the idea of them marrying at all."

Anne smiled, her relief so evident that his breath caught in his throat. Truly he must appear most desperately bereft of all hope for such a simple, ordinary jest to bring her such relief.

The days passed, and grew somewhat easier in the passing, though no less lonely. The children returned to school. The servants bustled about industriously, ever solicitous of the family's grief, the master's strange bewilderment. Henry tried to resume his familiar routines and found that he could not, for Fanny had been involved in every aspect of his life, even those solitary pursuits of reading and writing. Fanny had been the perfect companion of his daily existence, his partner in every endeavor, the sharer of all his successes.

He did not know how to pick up and carry on without her. He was not sure he could.

He knew that he must.

He began with the simplest of tasks — responding to letters on matters of business. The burns to his hands had not yet completely healed, but he could hold a pen. There were accounts to settle, requests for charitable donations to honor, stationery to order, invitations to decline.

He resumed his customary morning walks before breakfast, feeling unsteady without Fanny on his arm. Sometimes Anne accompanied him, but often he went alone. The scenery became increasingly beautiful as autumn colored the countryside, but to him its splendor was inexpressibly sad. He took his daughters out for drives to enjoy the noonday warmth and sunshine, and together they strolled the gardens of Craigie House, admiring the glimmer of golden leaves in the sunlight, the lilac hedges shot with crimson creeper, the river sketching silver curves in the meadow. Everything he beheld was full of loveliness and sublimity, but within him was naught but hunger, the famine of the heart.

He knew he did not suffer alone. Charley hid his grief best, believing stoic strength to be the proper demeanor for a young man of seventeen contending with loss. In this Ernest tried to emulate him, but his mask of bravery often slipped, especially when he thought no one was watching. Tender-hearted Edith often wept, and was comforted by Alice, but of all the children, little Annie suffered the most. Sometimes, when Henry and his youngest child were alone and quiet, she would repeat her unhappy confession that she had killed her mother. He gently pleaded with her not to say such a terrible, untrue thing. He told her emphatically that whatever had happened, it had been an accident. She would nod obediently in response to his attempts to comfort and reassure her, but although she stopped professing her guilt aloud, he knew she still blamed herself, and the sense of her culpability oppressed her. "I used to call you Allegra," he told his melancholy child ruefully, drawing her onto his lap, kissing her brow when she rested her head on his shoulder. "I shall now have to call you Penserosa."

A few friends visited, Charles Sumner and Richard Dana one evening, James Fields the next day. All were kind and solicitous, and he found some solace in their company. He apologized for neglecting to respond to their letters and begged them to understand that his silence did not signify indifference. To a man, they hastened to assure him that there was no need for apologies, or even replies. Their only wish was to offer him whatever comfort and help they could.

To other friends, equally cherished but too far distant to visit, he did feel obliged to write, though the act of stringing words together had become painfully arduous.

Cambridge. September 28, 1861.
Mr. George William Curtis
New York City

My Dear Curtis,
   Have patience with me if I have not answered your affectionate and touching letter. Even now I cannot answer it; I can only thank you for it. I am too utterly wretched and overwhelmed, — to the eyes of others, outwardly, calm; but inwardly bleeding to death.
   I can say no more. God bless you, and protect your household!

H. W. L.


He owed his dear friend better than that, but he could do no more.

His sister Anne remained with the family throughout September, easing their homecoming with her tender, affectionate ways, her quiet conversation, her deft management of the household. But Henry had always known that other responsibilities beckoned her home, and when the time came for her to depart, he managed to restrain himself from begging her to stay. "You've done me tremendous good," he said as he saw her off at the train station. "I don't know how I shall ever thank you sufficiently."

"I know how," she promptly replied. "Write to me, and frequently, to let me know how you're getting on. Even if it's only a few lines about the weather and Charley's latest mischief and how tall the children are growing — or how long your dreadful beard has gotten — do write." She kissed him on the cheek, making a playful show of avoiding his whiskers. "Or better yet, shave it off and consider all debts fully paid."

"I will write," he promised, but said nothing of the beard.

Henry had not followed politics since the day of the fire, but soon after Anne's departure, on October 1, the state Republican convention opened in Worcester, about forty miles west of Cambridge. He could not help feeling a rekindled spark of interest, for his dear and loyal friend Charles Sumner had been invited to address the delegates, and Henry knew he intended to speak on the controversial subject of emancipation. The following day, his dormant curiosity creakily reawakening, Henry delved into the papers and was soon engrossed in reports of his friend's success — or shameful demonstration of his utter loss of reason, as the

Southern sympathizers in the press would have it. Delegates and spectators had filled the great hall, every one of them devoted to the Union, but divided in their opinion regarding a radical anti-slavery platform, some in favor, others firmly opposed. As he read Sumner's speech, Henry found himself shaking his head in admiration for his friend's audacity, his unwillingness to pander to the opposing factions in the audience. Declaring slavery to be the sole cause of the war and the fundamental strength of the rebellion, Sumner had insisted that slavery should be struck down with every power at the government's disposal — including martial law.

Many of Sumner's remarks had met with vigorous applause, often so sustained and thunderous that he had been obliged to pause and wait for it to subside. Even so, afterward, as the convention proceedings continued, it became apparent that many of the delegates disagreed that the slaves should be declared free. Others, though they agreed that slavery must end, argued that the time was not right for emancipation. Unfortunately for the abolitionist cause — and for the countless thousands of souls languishing in bondage — the opposition to Sumner's proposal was enough to compel the state Republican Party not to add a call for emancipation to the party platform.

Henry knew his friend was sorely disappointed, but not undaunted. In the aftermath of the convention, Sumner's speech was so well regarded — except in the most conservative circles — that he was invited to address other, more sympathetic audiences elsewhere.

Less than a fortnight later, he delivered a more elaborate and extended version of the speech, newly titled "The Rebellion: Its Origin and Mainspring," at the Tremont Temple in Boston, and Henry relinquished his mournful solitude for the evening in order to attend. He was escorted to place of honor in a box seat apart from the throng, for which he was thankful, and he listened, thoroughly absorbed and admiring, as Sumner boldly identified the institution of slavery as the source of the conflict between North and South, and the sole support of the rebellion. "It is slavery that marshals these hosts and breathes into their embattled ranks its own barbarous fire," he declared. "It is slavery that stamps its character alike upon officers and men. It is slavery that inspires all, from general to trumpeter. It is slavery that speaks in the word of command, and sounds in the morning drumbeat. It is slavery that digs trenches and builds hostile forts. It is slavery that pitches its wicked tents and stations its sentries over against the national capital. It is slavery that sharpens the bayonet and runs the bullet; that points the cannon and scatters the shell — blazing, bursting unto death. Wherever this rebellion shows itself, whatever form it takes, whatever thing it does, whatever it meditates, it is moved by slavery; nay, the rebellion is slavery itself — incarnate, living, acting, raging, robbing, murdering, according to the essential law of its being."

With the advance of the Union armies, Sumner insisted, emancipation had become a military necessity, not only because the Confederates benefited from slave labor but also because the Union must align itself with the forces of moral good. Emancipation would do more to weaken the rebellion than any other weapon in its vast arsenal. "To the enemy such a blow will be a terror," he said, his voice ringing with certainty. "To good men it will be an encouragement, and to foreign nations watching this contest it will be an earnest of something beyond a mere carnival of battle."

Henry was greatly pleased by the enthusiastic, vigorous applause that followed Sumner's speech, and afterward, as they dined together, he congratulated his friend. "I intend to renew the discussion of emancipation in the Senate," Sumner told him, every line of his face marked with determination. "If the president will not act, we will force his hand."

"You make a convincing case," Henry replied. "I don't see how Mr. Lincoln could fail to be persuaded."

"I'm certain the president abhors slavery, but I'll make no excuses for his inaction, which only prolongs the war and will lead to greater loss of life." Then Sumner's expression softened. "But never think, my dear Longfellow, that in my preoccupation with our great national struggle, I forget for a moment your own deeply personal one."

"Nor have I," said Henry, his throat constricting, "in the midst of my own tragedy, forgotten our nation's."

October trudged on, full of autumnal beauty and aching loneliness and dreadful news about the war. Whenever Henry walked into town, he invariably encountered a friend with a son or nephew in the army, and even as they voiced pride in their young men's service, every word and grimace betrayed their apprehension. Once Henry listened sympathetically as a physician of his acquaintance spoke at length about his son, a lieutenant with the Massachusetts Twentieth, from whom the family had not heard since before his battalion engaged the rebels in a battle on the Potomac. Suddenly the doctor, much embarrassed for his protracted narrative, said, "My good Mr. Longfellow, I fear I have detained you overlong."

"Not at all," Henry assured him, quite truthfully, for in listening to the anxious father's troubles he had almost, for a moment, forgotten his own. Three days later he learned that the physician's son had been wounded in the battle but was expected to recover, so some good news tempered the bad.

He tried, time and again, to compose poetry, but his thoughts were too full of his beloved Fanny to attempt to write about anyone or anything else, yet he dared not attempt to write of his lost beloved out of fear that his poor words would fail to do her justice. How could they but fail? She had been everything to him, his world, his all, and the thoughts that haunted his heart and brain he could not record.

In early November, James Fields wrote to request a poem for the January edition of the *Atlantic Monthly.* Henry resolved to discipline himself, to wrest control of his poetic gifts from the iron grasp of despair, and to produce something worthy, not only to gratify his friend but to prove to himself that he could. But his determination weakened by the hour, and within days of receiving the letter he wrote back to decline. "I am sorry to say No, instead of Yes; but so it must be," he wrote in haste, the sooner to finish the unhappy task. "I can neither write nor think; and have nothing fit to send you, but my love — which you cannot put into the Magazine."

Sometimes he feared that he would never write again, except apologetic letters to friends.

Massachusetts celebrated Thanksgiving on November 21, but the Longfellows made no feast of it that year. Tom Appleton joined the family for a quiet supper, and afterward, Henry took a long, solitary walk in the twilight.

December came, mild enough at first to allow him more solitary walks, sometimes through a grove of pines, gray clouds overhead, a carpet of russet pine needles underfoot. On rare occasion a friend would accompany him, uplifting and sustaining him with generous sympathy. More often he walked alone, the thin morning sunshine and light flurries heralding winter.

As Christmas approached, Henry realized he must mark the occasion with more care than he had given Thanksgiving or he would never endure the day. Fanny had always loved the Christmas season — the contrast of green holly and red berries, the hint of snow in the air, the crackling warmth of the Yule log on the hearth, the music, the games, the revelry, the gathering of friends and family, the sacred joy of the Nativity, the wonder and awe in the children's eyes. Whenever the merriment of the season reminded him — starkly, painfully — of his grief and longing and loneliness, he reminded himself that even a family as bereft as their own ought to mark Christmas with joy and thanksgiving. Was it not because of his Savior, whose birth they celebrated that holy day, that he was redeemed, and would be reunited with his dearest Fanny in the world to come?

And so he kept Christmas determinedly, in honor of his beloved wife. He purchased gifts for the children, marking the cards from their mother as well as himself. He instructed the cook to prepare a special feast for the family, he made contributions to benefit the less fortunate, and he remembered the servants generously. With his daughters' help, he packed a box full of presents to send to Portland for the aunts and cousins in his old hometown. On Christmas Eve, he had a beautifully decorated tree in the parlor for the children, and it met with such success that the following day, Edith and Annie made a tree of their own to present to their dolls in the nursery, using the top of the family tree and the candle ends. "It is, on the whole, rather prettier than the original," Henry mused aloud when they invited him to come and see.

The children delighted in their numerous presents, especially the sugarplums their aunt Anne sent from Portland with her love. Later, after a quieter but no less delicious feast than in years past, Henry called the children to join him by the fireside for their traditional story. Even Charley, restless as he was, listened, rapt, as Henry read aloud Charles Dickens's *A Christmas Carol,* a longtime family favorite. It brought Henry bittersweet comfort to think that benevolent spirits could visit the Earth at Christmastime.

"How inexpressibly sad are all holidays!" he wrote in his journal later that night. The children had gone to bed hours before, but memories of Christmases past had kept him long awake. "But the dear little girls had their Christmas-tree last night; and an unseen presence blessed the scene."

As he waited for the ink to dry upon the page, in his imagination he lived again his last Christmas with Fanny, saw vividly her loving smile, felt her touch upon his arm, heard her gentle, merry laugh close to his ear, felt her soft, tender lips brush his cheek.

A log crashed on the hearth, startling him from his reverie. He watched, grief seizing him anew, as it blazed before falling back into embers.

"Happy Christmas, darling," he murmured. He closed his journal and retired to his bed, relieved to have made it through the day, not daring to wonder what the lonely New Year would bring.

# CHAPTER NINE:
## THE MOTHER'S TALE

Her heart aching, Laurie sat motionless in the pew, transfixed by the choir's impossibly lovely song, staring straight ahead so she would not weep.

I heard the bells on Christmas Day
Their old, familiar carols play,
And wild and sweet
The words repeat
Of peace on earth, good-will to men!

The children's voices, sweet and pure, filled the church with enthralling, angelic harmony. The children weren't angels, of course, but very much human — willful, mischievous, friendly, often kind, occasionally cruel, serious or cheerful, thoughtful or careless — with all the endearing and exasperating habits that made them unique, that made their parents marvel and wonder and adore. Laurie's own children were certainly not angels — Charlotte with her moods and perfectionism, Alex who lived utterly in the present and gave no thought to consequences — and yet they were perfect, absolutely perfect, exactly as they were.

Laurie was grateful that the children had inherited Jason's perfect pitch and wonderful voice. She too had an excellent ear, enough to admire and appreciate their gifts, enough to lament her own mediocre instrument. Christmas, more than any other time of year, gave her abundant opportunity to enjoy their gifts, for she truly believed that the most profoundly glorious music ever composed had been created to celebrate that holy season. And at Christmas, children were encouraged as at no other time of year to raise their voices in harmonious song, to proclaim the good news of the savior's birth, to reflect upon the wondrous mystery, to encourage their listeners to rejoice with family and friends near and far.

She could not ruin Christmas for them. She could not let it become a season they would dread for the rest of their lives, a time of grief and mourning in a world that already provided too much of both.

"Oh, my," a merry voice chirped. "Are you preparing to do battle?"

Startled, Laurie glanced away from the choir and discovered Sister Winifred standing in the aisle nearby, studying her over the rims of her glasses with her head tilted to one side, giving her the air of a plump, inquisitive little bird. "I'm sorry, Sister. Preparing to do what?"

"To do battle — with the forces of darkness, perhaps." The elderly nun's arms were filled with hymnals, so she indicated Laurie's lap with a nod.

Laurie glanced down and discovered that her hands were balled into fists, tangled in her scarf as if she meant to wring the life out of it. Flustered, she immediately released the scarf and attempted to smooth out the evidence of her distress.

"Are you all right, my dear?" Sister Winifred inquired.

"Yes, Sister, I just . . . have a lot on my mind. It's a crazy time of year."

"It's a season of miracles," the nun replied, nodding agreement.

That wasn't quite what Laurie had meant. "Yes, that too."

Sister Winifred beamed as if Laurie had recited the Apostles' Creed in perfect Latin, and resumed tidying up the pews, humming along with the choir, occasionally making brief, quiet remarks to no one in particular,

216

in a tone that was both friendly and respectful. She was just thinking aloud, Laurie told herself uncertainly. Surely Sister Winifred wasn't really carrying on a conversation with an invisible friend. Laurie did not want to believe that the warm, cheerful nun was declining, just as she wanted to deny the evidence that Charlotte was transforming into a sullen, withdrawn teenager ahead of schedule, or that Alex was a budding pyromaniac, or that Jason —

Jason. For a moment she had to hold her breath so she did not cry out in anguish. It was torment, not knowing. She could almost wish to be told the worst, just to know, just to get this nightmare of waiting and not knowing over with — but no, she didn't. She didn't want to hasten terrible news even to relieve her worry. As long as she didn't know for certain that her husband was dead, she could hope that he lived.

She took a deep breath, clasped her hands together, and listened as the children sang.

And in despair I bowed my head;
"There is no peace on earth," I said;
"For hate is strong,
And mocks the song
Of peace on earth, good-will to men!"

"There is no peace on Earth," Laurie whispered, her lips barely moving. That was why Jason had gone overseas, far from his family, from his home. And until she knew all hope was lost, until an officer showed up at her door with his terse, irrevocable announcement that she was a widow, she would protect the children from worry. They would not know he was missing — lost, captured, or killed. They would not spend that sacred holiday crushed by grief. She would let them enjoy one last, happy Christmas as innocent children before she revealed that their father was gone, their family forever shattered.

To lose him at all would be devastating, but it would be especially heartbreaking to lose him at Christmas — not only because it was a season of peace, love, joy, and wonder but because Laurie and Jason had always considered Christmas their holiday, as essential to the story of their lives together as their wedding day.

It was in Advent that they had first met years before, as freshmen at the University of Notre Dame. Laurie's family had moved often while she was young, as her father was transferred from one naval base to another, but for the previous eight years he had been stationed in San Diego. There Laurie had become thoroughly, happily Californian, but when it came time to apply to college, she had refused to limit herself to schools in temperate regions.

When the first winter storm of her freshman year struck the Notre Dame campus, Laurie happily threw on her new blue-and-gold winter gear and raced outside for a snowball fight with her roommates, and soon she and the other residents of Breen-Phillips Hall paired up with the women from the dorm next door in a spirited battle against the residents of the two men's dorms on the opposite side of North Quad.

But by mid-December, winter had lost its allure, and so had letters from home. Her younger sister wrote cheerily of dressing in sandals and short skirts for bike rides along the beach, and from San Diego State University, her boyfriend described seminars held outside in the shade of palm trees and weekend surf parties.

Late December brought a weeklong ordeal of final exams, fueled by stress, determination, and far too much caffeine and junk food. Up until her Spanish final on the very last slot on the schedule late Friday afternoon, Laurie practically lived in the library, abandoning sleep, exercise, and leisurely meals at North Dining Hall with her friends for fast food gobbled down at the LaFortune Student Center.

When she submitted her Spanish final, she felt proud of herself, confident that she had done well, and relieved, exhausted, and happy. Only when she was nearly finished packing her suit-case for her flight home the next morning did she realize that she had completely neglected her Christmas shopping. She had no desire to spend her first days in the sunshine and warmth of San Diego battling the crowds at the mall, so she threw on her coat and boots and hurried to the campus bookstore to search for gifts before it closed for winter break.

She found a few perfect things for her family and was heading for the checkout line when a guy approached her carrying a hanger in each hand. "Excuse me," he said. His black pea coat was unbuttoned, offering a glimpse of a burgundy sweater. "Can I ask you a quick question?"

He was tall, at least six feet, with dark green eyes, curly reddish-brown hair, and a build that suggested he ought to be in the Irish Guard. "Sure," she replied, thinking that she wouldn't mind a lengthy question if he were the one asking.

"I'm trying to pick out a gift for my little

sister, and she's about your size. I don't want to insult her by getting something too big, but I want to make sure it's not too small and won't fit."

Laurie smiled. "Because that would insult her too."

"Exactly."

Lowering her voice confidentially, Laurie said, "I wear a size medium."

"That's what I was going to get. Do you have time for a second question?"

"Absolutely."

"Which would be a better Christmas present, this" — he presented one hanger, which held a sweatshirt with an embroidered university seal — "or this?" He held out the other, bearing a green cable-knit turtleneck sweater with the interlocking ND logo on the collar.

"It depends. If she's a student at USC, she'll hate them both."

He grinned. "She's a senior in high school, and she wants to go here next year."

"Then either one should be fine. Does she usually dress casual or more preppy?"

"Sometimes one, sometimes the other."

Laurie studied the two garments. "I'd prefer the turtleneck, but that's just me." She paused, considering. "Do you want me to try them on so you can get a better idea of how they look?"

"Would you really do that? Do you have time?"

"Sure. I'm done with finals and my flight home doesn't leave until tomorrow."

"Same with me. My roommate finished this morning and he's long gone, but I just took my last exam an hour ago."

"My roommates finished yesterday."

"I wish I'd been that lucky." He raised his eyebrows, hopeful. "You really don't mind?"

"Not at all." Laurie took the hangers, disappeared into the dressing room, and emerged wearing first the sweatshirt, and then the turtleneck.

"I prefer the sweater on you," he said, appreciatively, "but I think I'd want my little sister to wear the sweatshirt."

Laurie laughed. "Of course you would. But the gift is supposed to be about her, not you."

"Yeah, I guess you're right." He held up first one, and then the other. "I think I should go with the sweater."

"I think you've made the right choice."

"Me too. Thanks for your help." He replaced the sweatshirt on its proper display rack and turned back to her, smiling. "Hey, after you're finished shopping, do you want to go get a cup of coffee or something?"

She almost said yes, but then she thought of her boyfriend back home. "I can't."

"That's fine," he said, poorly concealing his disappointment. "You probably have to pack."

"Yes, that's it," she said quickly. "I'm sorry. Really."

"It's okay." Turning to go, he added, "Thanks again for your help. Have a great winter break."

"You too," she said. "Merry Christmas."

He smiled at her over his shoulder. "Merry Christmas."

As soon as she joined the line at the cashier, Laurie began to regret turning him down. So she had a boyfriend. So what? They still could have gone for coffee, just two fellow students relaxing after finals and killing time until they left for home. She craned her neck and searched the nearby aisles, but although his height should have made him easy to find, she saw no sign of him.

Upon her return to campus after winter break, newly single — she and her boyfriend had parted amicably over the holidays — Laurie hoped to run into "the cute book-store guy," as she called him when describing the encounter to her roommates, but January passed, and then February, and their paths never crossed. By March she had stopped hoping to catch a glimpse of him while walking across campus or studying at the Hesburgh Library or jogging around the lakes. Soon after spring break she began dating Matthew, a sophomore pre-med student who lived in Keenan Hall, and her encounter with the cute bookstore guy faded into myth.

One evening after supper in mid-December of her sophomore year, she was in her dorm loading her backpack for a long night of studying at the library when she heard men's voices — hushed questions, muffled laughter — in the hall outside her room. A moment later, a pure, rich tenor sang the opening measures of "The Holly and the Ivy." As two other tenors, a baritone, and a bass joined in, Laurie and her room-mate Mary exchanged quizzical glances, then darted to the door, threw it open, and peered out into the hall. At the far end of the hallway, five young men in formal evening dress — the apparel of the Notre Dame Glee Club, the renowned men's choir — were serenading a young woman, who stood framed in her doorway, enjoying the attention as much as the music. Up and down the hallway other doors opened and curious women looked out, and when the

224

song finished, they all broke into applause.

One of the baritones handed the young woman a flower, and as the singers bowed first to her and then to all their other admirers, Laurie gasped in astonishment. One of the singers, barely recognizable in white tie and severely close-cropped hair, was the cute bookstore guy.

Laurie clutched Mary's arm. "That's him."

Mary studied the singers as they approached on their way to the stairwell. "Who?"

"Him. The guy from the bookstore."

"Impossible. You invented him."

Laurie gave her a little shove. "I did *not.*"

The singers passed just as Mary burst out laughing. The cute bookstore guy halted, his eyes widening as he recognized Laurie. "It's you," he said. "I thought you were a hallucination brought on by sleep deprivation."

"I'm real," said Laurie, smiling.

"So I see." The other four singers continued on without him, but the bookstore guy seemed not to notice. "Now I know why I've never run into you in the dining hall. I live in Dillon."

"Of course. South Quad, South Dining Hall."

"Exactly. And I figured out you're not in the College of Engineering."

"No, Arts and Letters. Sociology. Which is why I've never seen you in class." Laurie bit the inside of her lower lip, realizing too late that she had admitted looking for him.

"I'm Mary," her roommate broke in. "And you are?"

"Jason." He turned to Laurie. "And you're?"

"Laurie."

"Nice to meet you, Laurie. And Mary."

"You sing beautifully," said Mary warmly, offering him her most disarming smile, the one that reduced cynical teaching assistants to tongue-tied boys willing to grant her extensions for late papers, penalty-free.

"Thanks," Jason replied. "We're doing a fund-raiser for the South Bend Center for the Homeless. For a donation, four or five of us will sing the carol of your choice to anyone on campus. It usually ends up guys sending us to their girlfriends, although we have sent three different quintets to a particular chemistry professor with requests for 'You're a Mean One, Mr. Grinch.' "

As Mary laughed, Laurie said, "Oh, that's right. I read about that in the *Observer*. Not the Grinch part, the fund-raiser."

"Laurie writes for the *Observer*," said

Mary. "She's a great writer."

Laurie felt her cheeks growing warm. "I wouldn't say *great.*"

"That's why I say it *for* you."

"Jason, dude, come on," called one of the baritones from down the hall. "Elevator's here."

"Be right there." Jason gave Laurie an apologetic shrug. "I've got to go. We have six more carols to perform before parietals."

"You'd better go a-wassailing, then." Mary withdrew from the doorway, but with one lingering glance over her shoulder, she added, "Very nice to meet you, Jason from Dillon."

"Nice to meet you too." Jason's gaze quickly returned to Laurie. "My friends think you're fictional, and they've been teasing me for almost a year. Will you help me prove to them that you exist?"

"Jaaaaason," one of the singers bellowed. "Elevator's gone. Now we have to take the stairs."

"Sorry, Ryan," Jason called back. In an undertone to Laurie, he confessed, "Not that sorry."

"It's terrible you had to endure a year of teasing because of me," Laurie said, with exaggerated regret, smiling. "I feel horribly guilty."

"You can make it up to me. There's a party on our floor tomorrow night. Want to come?" When she hesitated, he added, "You can bring Mary."

"I'm sure she'd love to go, but —"

"But what?" Then understanding dawned in his eyes. "You have a boyfriend."

Laurie nodded.

"Same boyfriend as last year?"

"No," she replied, taken aback. How had he known? She was sure she hadn't mentioned a boyfriend.

Grimacing, Jason glanced down the hallway, where his companions' voices had faded to echoes in the stairwell. "I have terrible timing."

"I imagine that's a liability in singing."

He laughed, rich and full, and Laurie felt a pang of regret. "Yeah, it is. Anyway, I should go. Good luck with finals."

"You too. Merry Christmas."

With one last nod, Jason hurried off after the rest of his quintet, and Laurie closed the door and resumed packing up her books.

Mary had put on her glasses and was sprawled on her bed reading a Penguin Classic paperback edition of Emily Dickinson. "Not. Bad."

"I agree."

"He has a real Mr. Darcy thing going on

in that tux, despite the ROTC haircut."

"Do you really think he's in ROTC?"

"No one gets that haircut unless they're in ROTC." Mary peered up at her. "Is that a problem? I thought your dad was in the marines."

"The navy. Which is how I learned I don't ever want to be a military wife." She raised a palm and shook her head vigorously. "Forget I said that. Do not analyze a single word of that sentence."

Mary smiled knowingly. "Consider it forgotten."

"I have a boyfriend."

"Yes, I know. I've met him."

Soon thereafter, in the midst of final exams, Laurie and Matthew exchanged Christmas gifts. She gave him a fascinating book by a Notre Dame professor about the history of medicine in the Middle Ages, while Matthew gave her a Notre Dame sweatshirt, size large. She didn't take offense, and she thanked him for it sincerely, but after supper she stopped by the bookstore to exchange it for a pretty cable-knit cardigan.

Snow was softly falling as she crossed the quiet campus on her way back to the dorm, and although the snow-covered scene was beautiful, serene, even reverent, she felt strangely lonelier for not seeing Jason, someone she hardly knew.

It escaped Matthew's notice that she never wore the sweatshirt he had given her. He never had the opportunity to impress her with a more thoughtful Christmas gift, though, for he broke up with her on the Wednesday before Thanksgiving the following year. "I'm a senior," he pointed out unnecessarily. "I'm graduating in May and I want to enjoy my last few months on campus."

"I never liked him," Mary remarked afterward, waving a hand dismissively.

"You can do so much better," said Jessica, their other roommate.

Laurie decided to believe them.

Term projects and final exams distracted her from her broken heart. Laurie threw herself into her work, determined to earn excellent grades and keep her grade point average high. Her internship at the San Diego Department of Public Health the previous summer had convinced her to pursue her master's of social work degree after graduation, and she knew she needed impressive qualifications if she hoped to be accepted by a top program.

On Tuesday of finals week Jessica and

Mary found her in the dorm's basement study lounge. "Put down that book," Jessica teased, lowering her voice to a whisper rather than disturb the four other students bent over books or staring at laptops nearby. "You're coming with us."

"I can't," Laurie whispered back. "I have to finish this paper by nine or I won't have time to study for my Contemporary Sociological Theory exam."

"You can spare an hour for a study break." Mary snatched the book from her hands, marked her place with a piece of loose-leaf paper, and slapped the book shut, startling the other students. "They're decorating gingerbread cookies at North Dining Hall."

When Laurie and her roommates arrived, they found a few dozen students mingling around long tables laden with gingerbread men — and gingerbread leprechauns and the ubiquitous interlocking ND logo — as well as frosting, raisins, and all manner of small candies for decorating. Feeling like kids at recess, the three friends each took a cookie on a small plate, gathered supplies, and claimed adjacent seats at a table. Laurie, in her love of gingerbread, was tempted to take a bite of her logo cookie unadorned, but instead she applied a layer of frosting and began outlining the letters in chocolate chips.

"Well, deck the halls." Mary nudged Laurie with her elbow and nodded toward the other end of the table. "Look what Santa brought."

Laurie glanced down the table and discovered Jason frowning thoughtfully at a gingerbread leprechaun. Beside him stood a slightly taller, good-looking blond guy whom Laurie quickly recognized as one of the baritone carolers. As Laurie watched, Jason's friend gestured toward an assemblage of small bowls filled with candy before them, shook his head in mock disgust, and said something that made Jason throw back his head and laugh. And then, as if he had felt Laurie's gaze upon him, he caught her eye, and a slow, disbelieving smile came upon his face.

"If you don't go talk to him, I will," said Jessica.

"What'll I say?" Laurie whispered frantically as she rose.

"Don't overthink it." Mary gave her a little push in his direction. "Ask to borrow some frosting or something."

Carrying her cookie in one hand and a plastic knife in the other, Laurie felt her smile growing as she approached Jason and his friend. "Hi."

"Hi, Laurie," Jason replied emphatically. "Laurie, I'd like you to meet my friend Ryan. Ryan, this is Laurie."

Ryan looked from Jason to Laurie and back. "Bookstore Laurie?"

"Bookstore Laurie."

"I don't believe it." Ryan brushed his right hand against the side of his jeans as if wiping off cookie crumbs and extended it to her. "Bookstore Laurie. I thought Jason invented you."

"As I've been telling you for almost two years," said Jason pointedly, "I didn't."

"We used to say he must've met you in the fiction section."

Laurie laughed and shook Ryan's hand. "We've met before, sort of. You serenaded a girl on my floor last year."

Ryan studied her. "Oh, that's right. You're the one who made us miss the elevator."

"No, that was my fault," said Jason.

"I went to your autumn concert," Laurie confessed, "so I saw you there too."

"And you didn't say hello afterward?" Jason protested.

"I couldn't fight my way through the crowds of admirers."

"They are legion," Ryan acknowledged.

"I was thinking," Laurie heard herself say, "when you're finished decorating your cookies, do you — both of you — want to join me and my roommates for coffee or something?"

"Gingerbread goes great with coffee," Ryan mused. "Or hot chocolate."

"I'm sure we could manage hot chocolate too." Laurie turned back to Jason, and saw his look of chagrined dismay, and felt her smile fading. "But if you have to get back to studying, that's fine."

"It's not that," Jason said, embarrassed, "it's just —"

"I found them," a pretty brunette cried triumphantly, bursting between Jason and Ryan, throwing her arms around their shoulders. "Cinnamon hearts!" She kissed Jason on the cheek and held up a plastic bag of candy. "I knew they couldn't have run out."

"Mission accomplished," said Jason, and when he shot a guarded look Laurie's way, she understood immediately.

Jason's girlfriend — because of course that's who she had to be — tore open the plastic bag and set it on the table. "Finally. Now I can start." She looked around. "Where's my cookie?"

Ryan winced. "Are you referring to the gingerbread man someone abandoned on that plate over there?"

Jason's girlfriend planted a fist on her hip. "It was not abandoned. It was awaiting cinnamon hearts."

"I might have eaten it."

"Ryan," she protested, punching him playfully on the shoulder. "Go get me another one."

"You'd better come with me to make sure I don't eat it on the way back."

She laughed, rolled her eyes, and led him off. Laurie watched them go, impressed with Ryan's maneuvering. "He should be a diplomat."

"Yeah, but he'll probably be a priest instead." When Laurie did a double-take, Jason added, "I'm serious. He moved into Old College this semester, and he's seriously considering entering the seminary."

"So your other friend," said Laurie, trying to sound casual and failing utterly. "She must be your girlfriend, not Ryan's."

Jason nodded.

"She seems very nice."

"She is."

"That's good." Forgetting that she still held her gingerbread cookie, she gestured toward her roommates. "I'd better get back."

"Sure. Of course." Jason managed a half-hearted grin. "It was good seeing you."

"Did your sister like the sweater?"

"What? Oh, yeah, she did. She loved it." Jason's smile deepened. "She's a sophomore here now."

"Really? That's great." Suddenly Laurie felt utterly weary and miserable. "My timing is terrible."

"I guess we have that in common."

Laurie nodded and turned to go.

Jessica and Mary had watched the entire debacle, but based on their expressions, Laurie guessed that they had not overheard the conversation. "Girlfriend," she said abruptly, stabbing her plastic knife into a bowl of frosting and dropping into her chair, disconsolate.

"Oh, Laurie, honey." Mary got out of her chair to embrace her, and for a moment Laurie closed her eyes and rested her head on her friend's shoulder. Then Mary placed her hands on Laurie's shoulders, held her gaze, and implored, "Don't let this ruin gingerbread for you."

Laurie couldn't help it. She burst out laughing.

In her senior year, the first snowfall of the season came in late October, and by early December, the entire campus was covered by a thick blanket of white that would endure until April. The weather during finals week was especially treacherous, with several inches of heavy, wet flakes falling every other day, and Laurie yet again had an exam scheduled for the last testing period on Friday afternoon. She had booked a flight home Saturday noon, but as thick flakes began swiftly falling as she made her way back to the dorm after supper, she realized with increasing dismay that her travel plans could — and probably would — be disrupted.

The next morning she rose before her alarm, awakened by strong gusts of wind scouring the windows with snow. She reached the South Bend Airport safely an hour before her flight, but once inside the terminal, the long line of exasperated would-be passengers told her that her ordeal had just begun. Travelers her own age milled about or slumped wearily in hard plastic seats clutching cups of coffee, their coats opened to reveal a variety of Notre Dame, Saint Mary's, and Holy Cross College sweatshirts.

As she approached her gate, the strap of her carry-on bag pressing uncomfortably against her shoulder, the passenger at the counter finished speaking with the agent and turned, boarding pass in hand. When his eyes met hers, Laurie felt a surge of unexpected delight.

"Hey, Laurie," said Jason. "Late Friday final?"

"Of course. Every semester." She glanced past him to the board behind the agents' counter. "Oh, no. An hour delay? Really? The monitor in ticketing said it was only fifteen minutes."

"I think even an hour is optimistic." Jason sighed. "I've already been here three hours. My flight to O'Hare was supposed to leave at nine, but it was canceled, so everyone's been scrambling for seats on the next flight." He held up his boarding pass, and Laurie glimpsed the same flight number as her own. "I'm one of the lucky ones."

At that moment he spotted a pair of empty seats and suggested they claim them. As they awaited the boarding announcement and braced themselves for more delays, their complaints about the weather and travel soon turned to more interesting topics. Laurie learned that Jason was the second eldest of four children, and that his hometown was Hartford, Connecticut, and that he had applied to graduate school in mechanical engineering but would probably have to defer admission until he served out his ROTC commitment. He had no plans for a lifelong career in the military, he confided. Although he was proud to serve his country, he had only joined ROTC to pay for college.

When Laurie told him about her hopes to attend graduate school, his brow furrowed in surprise. "I thought you were going into journalism."

"No," she replied. "Social work. You know, for the wealth and glamour."

He smiled, but he also shook his head. "But you're such a good writer. I've read your work in the *Observer*. I just assumed, since you've worked on the paper for four years, that you wanted to make it your career."

"Oh, no. That's just for fun." She couldn't help feeling flattered. "You've read my work? And . . . you like it?"

He assured her he did, and she was impressed when he mentioned a few particular articles to prove it. Another delay was announced, and then another, but they scarcely noticed, so engrossed were they in their conversation. And then came the news they had been expecting and dreading all along — their flight had been canceled.

A chorus of groans and a smattering of expletives nearly drowned out a second announcement: Since conditions were not expected to improve, the airline had arranged for a bus to carry them all to Chicago O'Hare in hopes that they would either make their original connections or they could be transferred to later flights.

"If it's too dangerous to fly, how is it any safer to drive?" Laurie asked worriedly as they hurried off to collect their checked luggage and board the coach. As they stowed their luggage and found seats together, Jason described, as only a mechanical engineer could, why they would be perfectly safe. They talked, and shared snacks, and confessed to each other that as satisfied as they were with their post-college plans, they were not looking forward to leaving Notre Dame.

More than two hours later, the coach reached the airport, and it had barely halted before everyone bolted from their seats, grabbed their carry-on bags, and scrambled to claim their luggage stowed below, recheck it, endure a security screening, and race off to departure gates or customer service.

Laurie lost sight of Jason in the chaos, though she searched the crowds for him. After she passed through security, she checked the overhead monitors and discovered that their flights departed from entirely different concourses, and that Jason's was already boarding.

Her heart sank as she hurried off to her gate. She had wanted to say goodbye, to wish him a merry Christmas, to ask him if he was seeing anyone, because in all their time together that day he had not mentioned his girlfriend even once. January would be soon enough to ask, she consoled herself as she stepped onto the escalator leading to the underground walkway. She knew his name and how to find him.

"Laurie!"

She glanced over her shoulder and spotted Jason above her on the landing.

He cupped his hands around his mouth. "Do you want to go to the ROTC ball with me next month?"

"Yes," she called back as the escalator carried her away.

"You don't even know when it is!"

"It doesn't matter! I'll be there!"

The escalator had descended too low for her to see him any longer, but she knew he understood.

It was a truth universally acknowledged that it was a mistake to begin a relationship in the last semester of senior year, but Laurie and Jason ignored conventional wisdom. And so Laurie's last months of college were happier than any that had come before, and in May, even her reluctant departure from the campus and friends she dearly loved was more sweet than bitter.

Laurie and Jason kept in touch while she began her graduate studies in the Luskin School of Public Affairs at UCLA and he fulfilled his obligation to the army in Afghanistan. She was tremendously relieved when he was safely stateside again, and when he enlisted with the Massachusetts National Guard to help pay for graduate school at MIT, she was less than thrilled, but she understood. As soon as she earned her degree, she found a job in the Boston public school system and moved there to be near him.

When they returned to Notre Dame for their fifth-year reunion — Notre Dame alumni loved their alma mater too much to celebrate reunions only once a decade — Jason proposed at the bookstore, where they had first met. They married a year later at the Basilica of the Sacred Heart, too soon for Jason's friend Ryan, a seminarian at that point, to officiate, although he did serve as best man.

The years passed happily and with dizzying swiftness, full of newlywed joys and work and, before long, children. When Charlotte was born Laurie resigned her job to stay home with her, and with Alex too when he came along two years later. When Alex entered first grade, Laurie found herself restless at home, and yet she was reluctant to resume her career in social work. She wanted nothing to distract her from her first priority, her family, and she had discovered that social work was more than a full-time vocation, and she could never learn to leave her work at the workplace.

"Why don't you get a job with the *Boston Globe*?" Jason suggested. "You always loved to write, and you were brilliant at the *Observer.*"

Many of her fondest memories of college involved the newspaper, but she had no professional experience, and her student experience was years out of date. Newspapers everywhere were cutting staff, not taking chances on long-dormant reporters. Then, miraculously, Ryan — who by then had taken holy orders and had been appointed to St. Margaret's — gave her a lead on a job with a local progressive weekly. It paid poorly, but Laurie liked her coworkers and found it enormously fulfilling to be writing again.

Jason had kept up his commitment with the Massachusetts National Guard, assuming it would mean a couple of weekends a month training and the rare local deployment in case of a natural disaster. He enjoyed the camaraderie and was proud of his service, but when word came that his unit was going to be deployed to Afghanistan, he was thunderstruck.

Laurie was staggered and angry — and terrified that Jason's position supervising a behind-the-lines machine shop would prove far more dangerous than he said. She had scarcely come to terms with that when he was assigned — only temporarily, he was assured — to a forward operating base, still relatively safe behind barbed wire and concrete barriers, but less so than the other.

When Jason missed his first video chat, she blamed technical difficulties. Then came the phone call from his superior officer, and the foreboding news that a transport had broken down while returning from an intelligence mission, and that Jason had volunteered to go with the team to fix it, knowing that he could do it better and more swiftly than anyone. On their return to base, one of the trucks in the convoy had hit a roadside bomb, and insurgents had attacked. Most of the soldiers escaped with only minor cuts and bruises, but some were killed, and Jason had gone missing.

That was what in her terror and anger Laurie could not understand. How could they lose track of a soldier? Laurie's imagination ran wild with terrifying possibilities — all manner of terrible fates that she absolutely must not allow the children to contemplate.

Tears filled her eyes as she listened to the choir, as she listened to her children sing so beautifully, so innocently, untouched by the grief and terror that clutched her and squeezed with an icy grip. She would protect them from worry as long as she could. If she held out long enough, perhaps good news would come. Perhaps she would learn that it had all been a terrible misunderstanding, that Jason had been found, safe and well, and that she had spared the children needless worry. And if the news was not good, then at least she had delayed the inevitable blow —

"God is not dead, nor does He sleep."

Startled from her reverie, Laurie turned in the direction of Sister Winifred's voice. "What? What did you say?"

"From the carol." Sister Winifred indicated the choir with a nod. "It's not scripture, of course, but poetry, and nonetheless true. God is listening, my dear. He knows your troubles and he hears your prayers."

Laurie fought back tears. "Sometimes I wonder."

"I suppose we all do, sometimes." The elderly nun's wrinkled features curved in a compassionate smile. "Everything's going to be all right, my dear. Have faith."

Laurie pressed her lips together to hold back a sob. Ryan must have told her about Jason, or the nun had overheard them speaking. Laurie had sobbed out her worries to the sympathetic priest on more than one occasion, for the burden of her secret had proven too much to carry alone. She had told Ryan what she could not bear to tell the children, her friends, her family. "Thank you," she managed to say. "You're very kind."

"Oh, that's not mere kindness." Sister Winifred paused and tilted her head as if listening intently, and then she nodded. "And I know for a fact that Charlotte wrote every word of her Christmas story. I don't think you ever would have doubted that, but it's nice to know for certain, isn't it?"

Bewildered, Laurie nodded. "Yes," she murmured, fighting back tears. "It's best to know."

Except when the truth would break her heart, her children's hearts. She would put herself between her children and the devastating truth until the last possible moment. Only when all hope was proven futile would she capitulate — then, and not one hour before.

# Chapter Ten:
## January 1862–March 1863

The days passed in dull monotony. The effort of accepting calls from Cambridge neighbors and acquaintances passing through Boston exhausted Henry, and it was more difficult still to focus his thoughts enough to write to friends afar like Sumner. And yet it pained him not to write, to shut himself away in Craigie House with the children and pretend the outside world had passed away with his beloved wife. Fanny would not have wanted him to become a recluse, and he knew he would inevitably fail as a father if he isolated himself. So he forced himself to write letters, to see friends, to attend to household business with what fortitude and patience he could muster, heavy in heart and head.

He felt himself adrift upon bitter waters, and as the winter passed, he struggled to drop an anchor, to chart a course. Poetry eluded him, his spirits too overwhelmed and crushed to sustain any spark of inspiration. Each day upon waking he found himself daunted by the task of building up again his shattered life, the remnants of which crumbled like sand between his fingers whenever he tried to grasp it.

Since words would not flow from his pen except by force, he sought escape in other poets' verse. The beautiful musicality of the great Italian works drew him, freeing him from his anguish for brief, blessed interludes of complete absorption. In late February, stirred by a memory of how he and Fanny, when first they met in Switzerland, had found solace from their separate griefs by translating poems of the German romantics, Henry translated the beautiful Canto XXV of Dante's *Paradiso.*

Unexpectedly pleased with the result, and struck by how unfamiliar the sensation of pleasure had become, Henry invited a few friends for dinner one evening, and afterward, he read aloud his translation. To his relief, his friends did not shower him with fulsome praise out of sheer thankfulness that he was taking an interest in literature again, but rather expressed sincere approval for his efforts and offered suggestions for alternative interpretations of the Italian here and there.

"I've contemplated translating all of Dante's *The Divine Comedy* into English," Henry confided. "I've long admired Dante, as you know. I included his work in many of the classes I taught at Harvard, and although I'm no longer a professor, introducing Americans to great works of European literature is still a sort of mission for me."

"*The Divine Comedy* is essential to the literary canon," mused his friend James Russell Howell. "A fresh translation is long overdue."

The others agreed that Henry was just the man to undertake the task. More gratifyingly still, no one pressed him to admit that he did not feel equal to the creation of any original work, and that he desperately needed some engrossing distraction from his heart's desolation. No words he could frame could adequately describe the ceaseless agony of his life. How his heart continued to beat he knew not, and sometimes he did indeed feel as if he were dying. The earth seemed to sink beneath him, and if it were not that the children held him fast, he should lose his grasp on life altogether, it had all become so shadowy and insubstantial.

The steady labor of translation gave shape to his days, offered him purpose, distraction. As his work progressed, once a week, several learned friends would meet at Craigie House to hear Henry read aloud from whatever canto he had recently completed, following along with the original Italian text and offering critiques and suggestions. Afterward, they would adjourn to the dining room for supper — oysters, carved cold turkey, venison, or duck, accompanied by excellent wine from Henry's esteemed cellars. The gatherings often lasted into the early hours of the morning, but eventually his companions departed for their own homes, and although Henry knew the children slept soundly upstairs, in those quiet moonlight hours, his solitude oppressed him.

As Henry immersed himself in Dante's *Divine Comedy,* the war that most authorities had predicted would be over in nine months entered its second year.

"I'll be eighteen in June," Charley reminded his father one afternoon as spring approached. "The Union needs good, steady men in the ranks."

"The Union may search elsewhere for them."

Charley frowned. "Massachusetts needs to fill her quota of recruits. When I come of age, I want to enlist, and I'd like to have your blessing."

"I cannot give it to you." Unable to bear the stark disappointment in his eldest son's eyes, Henry turned away and busied himself sorting papers on his desk. "Think of your brother and your sisters." *Think of me,* he added silently. "This house has seen enough grief and mourning. You're too young to know what it means to risk your life."

"I'd have to be a fool not to understand what serving my country means, what sacrifice may be required of me," said Charley. "I read the names of the killed and missing in the papers. I've seen the wounded soldiers suffering in hospitals, and I've seen the veterans too maimed to fight again. At this very moment, men younger than myself are marching on battlefields —"

"Young men who don't have your prospects," Henry interrupted. "You haven't yet completed your studies at Harvard."

Charley shook his head, impatient. "I'm not interested in my studies at Harvard, or in any position you might have the Appletons arrange for me. It is because I have such prospects, that I've enjoyed such privilege, that I should fight for my country. Everything I have I owe to you, to your accomplishments, to your genius. I want to earn my own position of honor and respect, not inherit it."

For a moment, Henry was struck speechless. Always before Charley had spoken of enlisting because he sought adventure, because he was eager to prove himself daring and heroic. He had never spoken of duty.

"You could not join the army even if I gave you my blessing," Henry said when he found his voice, gesturing to his son's maimed left hand. When he was but eleven years old, Charley had shot off his left thumb when his hunting rifle misfired. Henry never would have imagined he would one day be thankful for that accident.

"I can hold a gun. You know that."

"Well enough to hunt quail, perhaps, but not well enough to join the infantry on the battlefield, where enemies would be firing upon you and your fumbling would endanger not only yourself but your fellow soldiers."

Charley set his jaw, stubborn. "There must be some honorable way I can serve. I'm an excellent sailor. I could join the navy."

"You're a fine yachtsman. That does not make you fit to confront Confederate frigates or privateers." Henry rose and shook his head, signifying that the discussion was over. "No, son. We've known too much tragedy in this household for you to expose yourself to mortal danger unnecessarily."

"How can you call my service unnecessary?" Charley countered. "The Union needs every able man. You support the Union and President Lincoln. How can you ask me to sit idly at home when my friends are marching off to fight a war you've said the Union absolutely must win?"

"You shall not enlist," Henry insisted, wishing he had a better answer, one that would persuade his son to be content to sit out the war at home, one that did not ring with hypocrisy and fear.

Henry's admonitions did nothing to quell Charley's restlessness. With each passing day Henry became more anxious, knowing that he had only until Charley's eighteenth birthday, when Henry would no longer have the power to forbid it, to convince his son that he should not enlist.

Quietly, he made inquiries with reliable acquaintances, and in early March, his efforts bore fruit when Charley was presented with opportunity to see something of the war without being drawn into it. Charley's friend William Fay invited him along on an excursion aboard a supply vessel bound for

Ship Island in the Gulf of Mexico twelve miles off the coast of Mississippi, the staging ground for the anticipated Union assault upon New Orleans. Upon their arrival at the barrier island, Charley and the rest of the crew would live in the soldiers' camp while their ship was unloaded. Henry hoped the journey would allow his son to experience the adventure of war without the danger, and perhaps a taste of the hardships and deprivations soldiers endured, far from the glamour of parades and parties, would be enough to dissuade him from joining their ranks.

On March 6, Henry saw Charley off in Boston. His heart constricted as he shook his eldest child's hand, heartily wished him Godspeed, and watched from the pier as his son boarded the *Parliament,* his bag slung upon his back, his smile broad and proud, his eyes bright with excitement. "I'll write to you as often as I can," he called to his father, waving.

Henry was too overcome with misgivings to reply, but he managed to smile and wave his hat as the ship set off, carrying his boy far from home.

True to his word, Charley wrote often. His vivid, amusing descriptions of the ocean journey, the lively crew, the chronic inefficiencies of the military, and a few rare glimpses of "Johnny Reb" entertained and enthralled his siblings but did little to relieve Henry's worries. From Ship Island, which turned out to be little more than a wind-battered, sand fly–infested, disease-ridden sandbar, Charley wrote of meeting the wife of their commanding general, Massachusetts's own Benjamin Butler, "in her little ten foot house which is furnished with rebel furniture captured on its way to New Orleans." The floor was covered with sand, Charley wrote, the air thick with flies, "and there Mrs. B. sits in her glory and black silk dress languidly fanning herself and making rather flat remarks."

Perhaps it was because Charley saw so few ladies on his adventure that he was especially observant of those he did meet. In a letter written April 10, the staccato lines of his pen revealed his delight when he and some of his shipmates "were introduced to a real live woman and it was very pleasant to see one after a month's voyage. I feel half in love with her although she is married, as she is very pretty and only nineteen. Her history is this: She enlisted as a private in the 15 Maine with her husband and she was not discovered until she had nearly got here. When they did find her out they made her put on her own clothes and took her to the cabin where she is now staying."

"A lady soldier," Alice exclaimed as Henry read the letter aloud. "I never knew there could be such a creature."

"There wasn't for long," Ernest pointed out. "She's already in a dress again."

"What will become of her, I wonder?" piped up Edith. "Will they send her home to Maine or keep her on the island as a punishment?"

"If the Fifteenth Maine is encamped on Ship Island," mused Alice, "I suppose she would rather stay there to be near her husband, despite the dirt and disease and sand flies."

Quickly Henry cleared his throat and resumed reading Charley's letter rather than let his daughters dwell too long on the romantic notion of a devoted wife turned lady soldier. He had enough to worry about keeping Charley and Ernest out of the army than to fear for his daughters too. To his dismay, it was evident that rather than giving Charley his fill of the military life, the adventure had only whetted his appetite, and Ernest's too.

At the end of May, Charley returned home, more determined than ever to enlist in the army as soon as he wore down his father's resistance or turned eighteen, whichever came first. Determined to leave him no opportunity, Henry decided to take him and Ernest to see Niagara Falls, leaving the little girls at Craigie House in the care of his sister Anne. The journey was pleasant, the scenery sublime, and it offered Henry great relief that Charley spent his birthday sketching the falls with his brother and several charming young ladies rather than signing away three years of his life — and possibly his life itself — to the army. And yet Henry suffered pangs of grief, for the inspiring panorama reminded him constantly of his European travels with Fanny, and he found himself often thinking how she would have enjoyed the magnificent rush and crash of the falls. He missed his sweet daughters so intensely that the sight of another little girl holding her father's hand as they strolled along a forest path moved him to tears. He was all too glad to return home with his sons, and soon thereafter, determined to forestall Charley's enlistment, he quickly arranged for Charley and his friend William Fay to embark upon a European tour, which Henry fervently hoped would outlast the war.

He was thankful an ocean separated Charley from the war when tales of fresh horrors from the battlefield filled the newspapers. He could not deny — as his eldest son knew he could not — that the war must be fought and won, not only to preserve the Union but to destroy slavery once and for all throughout the land. The Civil War was not a revolution, as the rebels boasted, but a Catilinarian conspiracy, a plot devised by disaffected aristocrats to overthrow the legitimate government. It pit slavery against freedom, the strong, freshening north wind against the southern pestilence. One day while walking in Boston, Henry observed on display in a jeweler's window a slave collar of iron, with an iron tongue as large as a spoon to cram into the slave's mouth. Every drop of blood in his veins quivered at the sight. The world forgot, or never knew, what slavery truly was, if it could turn away from such cruelty, indifferent to the plight of millions of suffering men, women, and children throughout the benighted South.

But Charley was far removed from the struggle, and all of Henry's children were safe, well, and enduring the unspeakable loss of their beloved mother bravely, and that comforted him, gave him courage. On one beautiful day not long after he had shuddered in horror at the sight of the slave collar, he sat in his study attending to his correspondence while his daughters flitted about like blithe little birds, preparing to celebrate the birthday of one of their dolls. When Edith presented him with the program, neatly written and illustrated in her own hand, Henry marveled at how beautiful their childhood world was, so instinctively alive, so illuminated with imagination. Although his heart remained desolate, aching and bleeding from its fatal wound, he could yet find tender consolation in his children's happiness and pleasure.

But he could not resign himself to the one request Charley insisted would gratify him most.

Charley returned from his European tour with the war seeming no nearer its conclusion and his determination to serve stronger than ever. Stalling for time, Henry took the children to the family summer retreat in Nahant, and when swimming, boating, and lazier indulgences did not distract Charley, Henry tried to appease him with vague suggestions of other ways he might serve his country nobly. At the end of August, he wrote to his brother Alexander that despite his best efforts, Charley was still eager for the war. "I wish you would make him assistant on the Coast Survey, to keep him quiet," Henry wrote, adding the last phrase in confidence, for although Charley had endorsed the request, he could not know Henry's foremost impetus or all would be undone. "I will pay his salary."

The letter was safely delivered, the matter investigated, but nothing could be found for Charley, so he reluctantly resumed his studies at Harvard when the autumn term began. Henry was greatly relieved to have his son safely back at his books and lectures, but no small measure of apprehension lingered, for he knew Charley's hunger for the war remained unsatisfied — and he was not the sort of young man who could stoically ignore his appetites.

On September 17, less than a fortnight after Charley resumed his studies, the Boston press announced that Union general George McClellan had managed to repulse General Lee's advance into the North in an enormously costly battle along Antietam Creek in Maryland. Henry was horrified to behold the interminable lists of the dead and wounded, and even as he prayed for the deceased and their families, he also thanked God that thus far his sons had been spared. Soon thereafter, Sumner wrote from Washington that although President Lincoln had been greatly displeased that General McClellan had not pressed his advantage but had allowed the battered Confederate army to withdraw to Virginia, he had declared the stalemate a victory — to serve some other purpose, or so Sumner suspected.

Only a few days after Henry received Sumner's letter, the president's greater purpose was revealed when newspapers across the North published a proclamation in which President Lincoln declared that "on the first day of January in the year of our Lord, one thousand eight hundred and sixty-three, all persons held as slaves within any State, or designated part of a State, the people whereof shall then be in rebellion against the United States shall be then, thenceforward, and forever free."

In progressive Boston, people of color and abolitionists of all races rejoiced, for Mr. Lincoln's proclamation had brought the country significantly closer to that glorious, inevitable day when slavery would cease forever, for everyone. Governor Andrew expressed regret that the president would delay bestowing freedom upon the slaves until January, but still he declared the proclamation "grand and sublime after all." At the Boston Music Hall on Winter Street, famed orator and abolitionist Wendell Phillips announced that at long last, he could finally rejoice beneath the Stars and Stripes, while in Washington, Sumner delivered a speech in the Senate praising the president's long-awaited decree.

That was not to say that the preliminary proclamation escaped criticism, even among those who celebrated it, for many believed that it did not do enough to ensure liberty for all. The proclamation called for the abolition of slavery only in states that were in rebellion as of January 1, 1863, so if a state agreed to return to the Union before then, slavery could continue there. The proclamation did nothing to free the enslaved people living within the loyal Union border states of Delaware, Kentucky, Maryland, and Missouri, as well as Confederate territory that had come under Union control in Tennessee and parts of Louisiana. Upon reflection, Henry found it difficult to disagree with Horace Greeley, editor of the *New York Tribune* and frequent critic of the Lincoln administration, when he complained that the president had emancipated slaves where the Union could not free them and had kept them enslaved in places where the Union did enjoy the power to give them liberty.

Henry could not deny that the proclamation was far from perfect — and yet, despite its limitations, he rejoiced in it, for it proved that the nation was finally moving toward freedom and liberty for all. The old Union was gone forever. When the war was won and the country restored and whole, it would be a new United States, truly a more perfect union.

Perhaps the proclamation and its promise of freedom had inspired him, or perhaps the work of translating Dante's *Inferno* had rekindled his dormant creative spark, or perhaps observing Charley safely ensconced at Harvard had eased his troubled mind, but somehow Henry found himself writing poetry again.

He had no title for his work as yet, but he envisioned a long narrative poem in the manner of Chaucer or Boccaccio, a series of stories told by an eclectic gathering of men from various walks of life, all uniquely American, telling tales as their travels brought them together fortuitously at an inn. The Red Horse Tavern in Sudbury, a stagecoach stop twenty miles from Cambridge, inspired the setting for his poem, just as several of his acquaintances provided models for the storytelling characters. Henry worked on the poem between translating cantos of Dante, and as the autumn passed, he enjoyed visiting the quaint country inn in his imagination, and he found comfort in composing poetry again, even when it required great effort.

By the end of October he had completed "The Legend of Rabbi Ben Levi" and had begun "King Robert of Sicily." On the last day of the month, he visited the Red Horse Tavern with his friend and editor James Fields to refresh his memory and invigorate his imagination. Beautiful summery weather blessed their journey as they passed through a lovely valley on a winding road shaded by grand, ancient oaks. The rambling, dilapidated building had been constructed more than two hundred years before and looked every decade of it, but in its heyday it had been an essential wayside for all travelers heading west from Boston. Even in its hoary old age it possessed a certain ineffable charm that delighted Henry, and that he was determined to capture in his poem.

He was especially pleased to discover a verse some long-ago traveler had engraved upon a window in the parlor. " 'What do you think! / Here is good drink,' " he read aloud to Fields. " 'Perhaps you may not know it, / If not in haste, do stop and taste, / You merry folks will shew it.' I wonder who the author could have been, and when he left these lines to mark his visit."

"I rather wonder if he obtained the inn-keeper's permission before scratching medi-ocre poetry into the glass," Fields replied.

"I hope he didn't. It makes for a better story that way." Henry turned away from the window and regarded his friend thoughtfully. "Perhaps I should have one of my characters do the same."

"The college student might," Fields mused, "although I do hope you'll have him scratch a more elegant verse."

"A playful, simple poem might suit the character better."

"Then choose a more eloquent character to vandalize the window. You do have quite an unlikely assortment to select from."

"Unlikely? How so?"

Fields waved a hand and shrugged, con-veying that he thought it obvious and had meant no offense. "A college student, a Yankee innkeeper, a musician, a poet, a theologian, a Sicilian, and a Spanish Jew. One would not expect to encounter such men gathered around the same table at any inn I've ever entered."

"Ah, perhaps not, but their very differ-ences affirm the nature of our immigrant land," Henry said. "*E Pluribus Unum.* In my view that does not refer only to states, but also to our varied people. Whatever brought these strangers together in this place — chance, fate, or divine intervention — their lives will be forever transformed, forever bound together even if only by the slenderest of threads, because they shared stories."

Fields tugged at his ear, considering. "I suppose they must have something in common, or they would not have been at the inn at that particular day and hour."

"Yes, precisely," said Henry, pleased that his friend had discovered the implicit truth within his poem, one he suspected would elude many a reader. All people — white and colored, slave and free, Union and Confederate — shared a common humanity belied by their outward differences. In a time of discord, in a land torn by war, no truth was more important to remember than that.

Autumn faded into winter, and before long the Christmas season was upon them again, but as the citizens of Boston and Cambridge prepared for their restrained wartime celebrations, the Longfellow family received frightening news from the battlefields of Virginia: Henry's nephew Stephen, a private in the Twentieth Massachusetts Volunteers, Company H, had been wounded in the bloody, calamitous Battle of Fredericksburg, and no one knew what had become of him.

Henry's eldest brother, dissipated and unreliable, was of no use to Stephen's desperate, frightened mother, so Henry immediately wrote to Sumner to ask his friend to use his connections to learn where his nephew was, and how he was. After several harrowing days, Sumner discovered the young soldier's whereabouts, and reported that his wound appeared slight and he seemed to be recovering well.

Much relieved, Henry and his sister Anne swiftly wrote letters and made arrangements for Stephen's care. All the while, Charley passed in and out of Henry's study, his hands thrust in his pockets, his expression dark and full of consternation. Henry assumed that worry for his injured cousin had evoked Charley's bleak, smoldering mood and tried to reassure him that his cousin would survive.

"They call the Massachusetts Twentieth the Harvard Regiment," Charley responded. "All the officers are Harvard graduates, and nearly all the privates had attended Harvard."

"Yes, I've heard that."

"I should have been there in the thick of it, with my classmates, by my cousin's side."

"I'm heartily glad you were not," said Henry sharply. "The Union suffered more than twelve thousand casualties in that terrible battle. The Confederates suffered more than five thousand. It's the height of hubris to wish yourself among them, where so many were slain, wounded, or captured by the enemy."

Charley glowered. "Better to die nobly than to cower within a fortress of books and lecture halls."

As Charley stormed from the room, Henry rested his elbows on the desk and buried his head in his hands. "Better to live," he murmured, though he knew his son was beyond hearing. "Better you should live."

Later, when Charley's temper had cooled, he returned to his father seeking permission to go to his cousin and tend him in his infirmary. Henry refused, but diplomatically, pointing out that Charley knew nothing of nursing, and that his aunt Anne had Stephen's care well in hand. He did not admit that his predominant reason for forbidding Charley to go was that he feared his son would not come home again. While some young fellows would be repulsed by the horrific sights and smells and sounds of a military hospital, the ever contrary Charley would probably discover in the harrowing scenes more inspiration to enlist, more evidence that his country needed him.

Henry sent a parcel of food and other necessities to Stephen rather than send his eldest son, and a few days before Christmas, he received a letter in reply, a simple note of thanks and wishes for a merry Christmas, brief but reassuring. And then Christmas was upon them, Henry's second without his beloved wife. His brother Alexander sent presents for the girls' Christmas tree, and Henry sent gifts and letters to all the family in Portland, but for him Christmas was but another melancholy day, and at the end of it, he felt exhausted and drained from the effort of making the holiday merry for his children.

On New Year's Day, however, all the joy and exultation that had eluded Henry at Christmastime descended with dizzying intensity, for on that day President Lincoln would enact the Emancipation Proclamation, declaring all slaves within rebellious states "then, thenceforward, and forever free."

It seemed to Henry that all of Boston and Cambridge held its breath anxiously as they awaited the announcement from Washington by telegraph that the president had signed the document. Henry marked the day in

quiet reflection at home, but restless, irrepressible Charley went out to witness the
momentous event in the company of like-
minded friends, those few who had not
marched off to war. When he returned home
later that night, he told Henry that he had
attended an enormous gathering at Tremont
Temple, nearly three thousand determined,
impatient abolitionists including Frederick
Douglass and William Lloyd Garrison.
When evening descended and still no word
from the capital had come, apprehensions
soared, and voices rose in uneasy murmurs
and angry grumbles that President Lincoln
had been persuaded not to enact the Proclamation after all.

"When the people could bear it no longer," Charley reported, flush with lingering
excitement, "Judge Thomas Russell went to
the *Boston Journal* offices to see whether
the Proclamation had been signed. He
discovered that the news had just arrived
over the telegraph, and so he asked if he
could take the dispatches to Tremont Temple and read them to the waiting crowd.
Although he vowed to return them promptly
afterward, he was refused — so he seized
the dispatches and fled back to Tremont
Temple with the night editor in hot pursuit."

Henry had to smile at the scene so comically and vividly depicted. "And did the judge succeed?"

"Oh, yes. He had a bit of a head start and proved the faster runner. The night editor didn't stand a chance of overtaking him." Grinning, Charley dropped into an armchair and leaned forward to rest his elbows on his knees. "When the great news was announced and the Proclamation read aloud, a thrill shot through the crowd. I've never seen such intense enthusiasm. The people seemed almost wild with jubilation, and the celebration spilled out into the streets — parades, speeches, bands playing, men cheering, ladies waving their handkerchiefs."

"It is the dawning of a new day, and well worth celebrating."

"You should've been there. Emerson was."

"Then the fellowship of Massachusetts poets was well represented despite my absence." Henry regarded his eldest son fondly. "I think I enjoyed your retelling of the events more than I would have had I experienced them myself."

"But I forgot to tell you the most astonishing news of all." Charley straightened in his chair, his eyes alight with eager anticipation. "President Lincoln made a few changes to the preliminary document that appeared in the papers last September. Among them, he announced that men of suitable condition among the newly freed slaves would be received into military service to garrison forts and other places, and to man vessels of all kinds."

Henry stared, dumbfounded. "President Lincoln means to create regiments of colored soldiers?"

"And sailors too, from the sound of it."

"Sumner has been calling upon the president to put rifles into the hands of colored men from the outset of the war," Henry said in wonder. "Time and again Mr. Lincoln has rejected his proposals out of hand. I can only imagine what Sumner is thinking and feeling at this moment. I wish he were here now, so I might see the expression on his face and shake his hand."

"It is a glorious thing that colored soldiers will at last be permitted to take up arms in defense of the Union."

"And to fight for the freedom of their race."

"How will it look to the world if I, who have enjoyed every privilege of wealth and success, every benefit of education and good family, sit comfortably at home while these brave men who have already endured so much will fight for the country whose blessings they have been denied, but which I have enjoyed as my birthright?"

Again Henry found himself without words, so taken aback was he by the sudden turn the conversation had taken. Never would he have expected Charley to turn the Emancipation Proclamation into an argument for his own enlistment. "I care nothing for the opinion of a judgmental world," he managed to say.

"I don't think that's true, and even if it were, *I* care. I care very much. Every day I safely stroll the paths of Harvard, or idle away hours with my nose in a book, I feel my honor being weighed and found wanting."

"The president's own eldest son has not enlisted."

"That's Todd Lincoln's business and none of mine." Charley regarded his father with steady determination. "Perhaps his father won't bestow his blessing and he can't bring himself to ignore the wishes of a beloved parent. Perhaps a time will come when duty to honor and country outweighs his duty to his father."

Henry's gaze was equally determined. "I hope he is wise enough to forgo any rash decision that would break his father's heart at a time when Mr. Lincoln must remain strong and steadfast for the sake of all those who depend upon him."

Charley inclined his head, but whether in acquiescence or simple acknowledgment Henry could not say for certain.

Their disagreement was the only unpleasantness to mar what had been a beautiful day full of sunshine, culminating in a tranquil, moonlit night. As he wrote in his journal before retiring, Henry fervently hoped that the moonlit serenity would prove a proper metaphor for the working of the Emancipation Proclamation — and of the quietude he prayed would fill his restless son's heart and mind.

Winter passed, and although Charley rarely spoke of enlisting after their confrontation on New Year's Day, Henry knew the subject was ever in his thoughts. Charley plugged away at his studies with none of the enjoyment Henry had known as a young scholar, but he often escaped the confines of lecture hall and library to travel to New York with friends or to visit family in Portland. He always remembered to keep Henry apprised of his whereabouts, so when he went missing one March afternoon with no warning, without even a note left behind to explain where he had gone so suddenly and when they could expect him to return, Henry was filled with apprehension.

Four days passed in dread and frustration with no word from Charley — and then a letter arrived at Craigie House bearing a Portland postmark.

Dear Papa,

You know for how long a time I have been wanting to go to war. I have tried hard to resist the temptation of going without your leave but I cannot any longer. I feel it to be my first duty to do what I can for my country and I would willingly lay down my life for it if it would be of any good. God bless you all.

Yours affectionately,
Charley

Henry's cry of anguish brought Alice running, but it was several moments before he could bring himself to tell her what dreadful revelation had rendered him tearful and trembling.

Charley had gone to war.

# CHAPTER ELEVEN: THE WIDOW'S TALE

The holiday party at Paul's Boston offices on the last Friday before Christmas had always been one of his favorite traditions, one Camille was determined to honor in his memory. She had chosen the staffers' gifts in late October, when Paul had still been aware enough to approve her choices, an ability he had lost by the time she wrapped them and added a personal note of thanks to each card.

His loyal staffers would understand that the message was Paul's, though the handwriting was Camille's. She had been writing on his behalf for years, as his penmanship inexorably declined into an indecipherable scrawl. What his staff would not know was that she had not taken his dictation for months, and that she alone had composed the heartfelt messages in their cards, writing what she thought Paul would have, if the gift of speech had not forsaken him.

She and Paul had hoped for one last Christmas together at their Back Bay home with Grace and Ella, his two daughters from his first marriage, and their husbands and children. But the day after Thanksgiving, Paul had taken a sudden turn for the worse, and although he rallied at the hospital, his legendary indomitable strength was unmistakably faltering. Heart aching, Camille had phoned the girls to come at once to say their farewells, which they did, and an agonizing forty-eight hours after they reached his bedside, Paul breathed his last. He left the world peacefully, easily, with less resistance than anyone would have expected from a man even his political opponents grudgingly admired as a tireless fighter for every person, cause, and bill he believed in.

No one would have complained if Camille had canceled the holiday staff party, but she summoned up her resolve and quietly insisted it must go forward. That was what Paul would have wanted, and she had fought by his side for too many years through too many crises to collapse in grief and leave a task unfinished. She had always been her father's daughter, as persistent and stubborn and driven as the revered and feared Graham McAllister had ever been, and yet this decision owed perhaps more to the influence of her mother, who had instilled in her from childhood that one's personal disappointments did not release one from one's obligations to others, and that loyalty must always be rewarded. And so while Camille made funeral arrangements and consulted with lawyers about her husband's estate, she continued to take calls from caterers and florists and DJs. As she forged ahead, checking the tasks off her list one by one, she gradually realized that she was actually planning another memorial service, one more intimate than his enormous public funeral attended by thousands of mourners, including the president and his wife, at least half of Congress, dozens of foreign dignitaries, and so many grief-stricken constituents that the line outside the door of St. Margaret's Church had wound around the block.

Paul's funeral in Boston had been for the world. The holiday party would be for Camille and his loyal staff, many of whom had worked with him and for him for decades, others fresh from college, bright-eyed, idealistic, and impossibly young. She would thank them on her late husband's behalf for another year of hard work and dedication; they would celebrate the year's accomplishments as they always did. But unlike every other year, Paul would not be present to accept their applause and ardent admiration with sincere thanks and self-deprecating humor, and he would offer no inspiring words about all the good and great things they would accomplish together in the New Year. This time when they parted for the holidays they would truly say goodbye, to Paul and to one another.

The party officially began at one o'clock with the opening of the sumptuous buffet and, perhaps more important, the bar, but when Camille and her assistant, Kendra, arrived early to supervise the last-minute details, they discovered that office work had already sputtered to a halt. Clerks and assistants and interns were dazedly packing up for the winter recess or wandering aimlessly from office to break room, hands thrust in pockets, tears glinting in eyes. Camille had received assurances from the governor and the state party leadership that Paul's staff would remain employed well into the New Year to assist with the transition, and most would keep their jobs well after that, although the interim senator, whomever was eventually appointed, would probably replace a few with trusted aides of his or her own. Camille was deeply moved to realize that in their genuine mourning,

Paul's staffers had forgotten to worry about their own futures, and she was grateful that she had secured their jobs at least for the time being. Letters of recommendation and a few well-placed called-in favors would help those whom Paul's replacement might choose to let go.

"I've never seen them so grim," Kendra said in a practiced undertone as Camille made the rounds, greeting everyone and urging them to help themselves at the buffet. "This may go down as the most dismal holiday party in recorded history."

"It's our responsibility to make sure it doesn't," Camille murmured back as she subtly gestured for the DJ to turn down the volume to a more tolerable level to allow for easier conversation.

"Even so, if you need me to extract you, give the signal."

"Kendra, dear, you know I can't do that, not tonight, not under these circumstances." On a more pragmatic note, Camille added, "Besides, everyone here knows our signals."

Camille had been prepared to spend the first hour of the party accepting condolences, but she had not expected to find herself comforting tearful interns, assistants, and advisors as often as she was comforted. Everyone had a story to share about how

Paul had inspired them, how he had helped them, how he had transformed their political cynicism into hope.

"I've always thought all politicians were the same," Paul's director of social media admitted, shaking his head, swallowing hard, his eyes red-rimmed. "Slimy, opportunistic, power-hungry narcissists more interested in padding their offshore bank accounts than making a real difference in people's lives."

"Oh, Jim, no," she protested. "You're too young to be so jaded."

"That was what I thought *before* I came to work for the senator." Jim cleared his throat. "I've never known anyone with as much integrity, compassion, and genuine love of country as your husband. He inspires me to be a better man, to give more than I take, like he always did."

Camille needed a moment to compose herself. "You're very kind," she said, with scarcely a tremor in her voice. "Thank you."

Soon thereafter, a dark-haired, strikingly pretty intern named Marisol approached, carrying a glass half-full of white wine in one hand and a plate of delicacies from the buffet in the other. Unlike the glass, the plate appeared untouched, as was Camille's. Lately nothing could tempt her appetite.

"Mrs. Barrett?" Marisol began tentatively. She was a political science major at the University of Massachusetts, and easily both the shyest and one of the most insightful of Paul's interns.

"Yes, Marisol?" Camille felt a stab of alarm as she spotted tears welling up in the younger woman's eyes. "Deep breath," she murmured, as much for herself as for Marisol. Camille was barely holding herself together, and if anyone else broke down, she would surely follow.

Marisol nodded and inhaled deeply. "I have some news — good news. I wanted to share it with the senator, but it came too late —" She took another deep, shaky breath. "You must know what an inspiration your husband was to me, to all of us."

"Yes, I do know."

"He encouraged me to apply to law school. He advised me about where to apply, he wrote letters of recommendation, and —" Marisol's pride shone through her grief. "And it paid off. Yesterday I received my acceptance to Harvard Law School."

"That's wonderful! Congratulations, Marisol. I'm delighted for you."

"Thank you, Mrs. Barrett. I owe it all to the senator."

"Not all, surely. You've been a diligent

student on top of all the hours you've put in here, and you alone earned those excellent grades."

Marisol nodded modestly, acknowledging her part in her success. "Still, I know Senator Barrett's recommendations made the difference, and without his encouragement, I probably wouldn't have set my sights so high."

"Let this be a lesson to you never again to underestimate yourself," said Camille emphatically. "I know the senator would be very proud of you."

Marisol smiled, though her eyes glistened with tears. "Thank you, Mrs. Barrett. That means more to me than you could possibly imagine."

Camille smiled rather than contradict her, for she thought she knew very well.

And so the party unfolded, in anecdotes that gratified and pained Camille in equal measure. Paul had profoundly affected the lives of everyone in that room, and by their own testimony, they were resolved to carry on his progressive vision of politics as public service, of improving the lives of ordinary people through sensible legislation and commonsense reform, strengthening the nation from the ground up.

What greater legacy could any man hope

for than to inspire younger generations to make the world a better place? As she studied his staffers' faces and heard their stories, Camille felt herself overcome with longing and gratitude, and she wished with all her heart that she could tell Paul how much he was loved, admired, and respected. He had always been too self-effacing to endure such talk, even from his devoted wife. She hoped that somehow he had known what he had been too modest to hear.

Paul had often told her that humanity's most precious commodity was time — "Not love," he had emphasized, "not because it's less important, but because you can run out of time, while love can be endlessly replenished" — and so by tradition, the holiday party always ended by late afternoon, granting the staff the gift of a few precious extra hours to spend as they wished — picking up their kids early from day care, shopping for Christmas gifts, catching an earlier flight home for the holidays. And so at half past three, Camille distributed gifts and offered a few words of gratitude and hope, adding a liberal dose of humor to keep things from becoming too maudlin. She found comfort in their laughter, in their shining optimism, in their enduring love for the best man she had ever known, the man she had been blessed to call her husband and most cherished friend for more than thirty years.

Camille wished everyone a Happy New Year and safe journeys; they thanked her with a crash of applause. On that note the party ended, but nearly everyone paused to wish her a Merry Christmas on their way out the door. Several asked her to keep in touch, and a few young women flung their arms around her and wept. Camille embraced them as long as they needed, murmuring words of comfort, suddenly reluctant for the gathering to end, dreading the task that awaited her when the staff departed.

Too soon, only Camille, Kendra, and Paul's executive assistant, Alicia, remained. The cleaning crew arrived, and for a moment Camille stood near the reception desk, taking in the cheerful decorations and the depleted buffet, hugging her arms to her chest, utterly at a loss as to how to proceed. Then she became aware of Kendra and Alicia studying her, exchanging worried glances, and so she nodded briskly and said, "I suppose we should get to it."

They nodded wordlessly and followed her into Paul's private office.

It was tidier than he had kept it in the old

days, for he had not entered it for many weeks and Camille preferred an orderly workspace when she held court there. "Let's begin with his papers," she said, more decisively than she felt. "Keep everything in chronological order, but separate his personal correspondence into other boxes." She would have everything delivered to her home, where she would sort the wheat from the chaff at some unimaginable later date when she felt up to the task.

She glanced around at his prized books autographed by their esteemed authors, the framed photographs on the desk and the credenza — Paul beaming as he walked hand in hand with his pigtailed daughters on Cape Cod, Paul surrounded by his grandchildren in front of a glorious Christmas tree, Paul shaking hands with an impressive array of presidents, prime ministers, and Nobel Peace Prize winners, childhood heroes and colleagues, rivals and friends. Ella would cherish the photo of her father with Dr. Martin Luther King in Montgomery in 1966, Camille decided, while Grace would gratefully accept the two photos of her father with Mother Teresa, one taken at her first Home for the Dying in Calcutta, the other in Washington at the White House ceremony at which she received the Presidential Medal of Freedom. One of his favorite perks of his high office, Paul had often remarked, was the opportunity to meet the people he most admired.

Once Camille had entered his office to find him studying the photographs and shaking his head in bewilderment. "See that guy with the goofy grin?" he had asked, gesturing toward the framed photos, arranged in pride of place on a sturdy oak bookcase. "That kid from Watertown, the son of a plumber and a kindergarten teacher?"

"Of course," she had said, coming around behind his chair to rest her hands on his shoulders and kiss the top of his head. "But I would argue that his grin is utterly adorable, with nothing goofy about it."

"Tell me something." He had placed a hand on hers and had gazed up at her quizzically. "How'd he end up in these pictures with those people?"

She had laughed and had kissed him again, and had teased that all those renowned world figures undoubtedly kept the same photos in their offices, to impress visitors with evidence that they had shaken hands with the distinguished Senator Paul Barrett. She remembered the moment well, for it had occurred during those heady, anxious days when the party leadership was urging him to run for president, an honor that after much contemplation he had declined. He had not yet completed all he had set out to accomplish for the people of Massachusetts, he confided to Camille, and he was unwilling to abandon the work unfinished. Neither of them would have imagined that years later, illness would force him to leave so much undone, or that his untimely death would leave the way open for his political opponents to tear down all he had built. Already newspaper editors and television talking heads were heatedly debating who might fill Paul's place until the next election, perennial rivals from the other party were loudly promising to repeal measures he had so wisely and thoughtfully crafted —

The sound of sobbing tore her from her reverie. With a start, Camille turned to discover Alicia sitting on the floor transferring manila folders from a filing cabinet into a carton, her shoulders shaking, tears streaming down her face.

"Oh, no," Camille murmured, heart cinching as she hurried to Alicia's side. Paul's loyal assistant was forty-six, a mother of three, a model of steadfast composure at the heart of any political storm, and yet she clung to Camille and wept as if her heart had broken. "It's going to be all right," Camille murmured, holding her and patting her on the back gently, soothingly, as if she were Ella or Grace. "Everything will be all right."

Eventually Alicia composed herself and accepted the handkerchief Kendra offered, her face contorting as if she too might at any moment burst into anguished tears. This would never do. Camille rose and helped Alicia to her feet. "Why don't we close up these boxes, water the plants, and call it a day?" she said. "I think this task can wait until after Christmas."

Alicia sniffled into the borrowed handkerchief and nodded, but Kendra looked uncertain. "We still have to clear out his Washington offices," she reminded Camille. "You said you wanted to take care of this office first, by the end of December, to divide up the work."

"We have plenty of time. The interim senator hasn't even been appointed yet." Briskly, Camille put her arms around the other women's shoulders and turned them toward the door. "It's the last Friday before Christmas, and I'm sure we all have other, more urgent, matters to attend to."

"I was just going to go home and decorate my tree and order takeout," Kendra replied, an uncharacteristic tremor in her voice, "but you're introducing the keynote speaker at the benefit dinner for Boston Children's Hospital."

"Oh, yes, that's tonight." After Paul died, the organizer had kindly offered to let her off the hook, but Paul's younger brother had been treated for cancer at Boston Children's Hospital and Paul had always given the institution his staunchest support. "Clearly we don't have time to finish now even if we wanted to. Let's adjourn until the first Monday of the New Year, nine o'clock sharp. Agreed?"

Kendra and Alicia could hardly disagree, so they nodded, looking somewhat dazed. Camille helped them into their coats, distracting them with chat about the snowy forecast and holiday travel as she shooed them out the door. The caterers and the cleaning crew were still finishing up, so she wished them happy holidays, put on her coat, collected her purse and a file of documents she had to look over for the lawyers, and hurried from the office without looking back, down the stairs and outside to where Robert waited with the car.

"Where to, Mrs. Barrett?" Robert asked

as he opened the back door for her.

"The Fairmont Copley Plaza, please."

"Right away, ma'am."

He shut the door, and as he came around to take the driver's seat, she settled gratefully into the warmth and comfort of the car, closing her eyes and letting her head fall against the headrest, her thoughts drifting on the melodious strains of classical music playing on the radio. She shut out the clamoring stresses of the day so effectively that she had traveled more than a mile before she remembered that she had allotted several hours to the sorting of Paul's office. If she continued on to the Fairmont Copley Plaza, she would arrive ridiculously early for the dinner. She would interrupt the preparations, her hosts would feel obliged to entertain her, and she would end up making more work for everyone — and subjecting herself to attention and condolences she really could not bear at the moment.

"Robert," she said, "could we stop by Saint Margaret's on the way?"

"Certainly, Mrs. Barrett." He put on his turn signal and changed lanes, too professional to point out that the church was not at all on the way.

Snow was falling as the car pulled up to

the curb in front of the church, icy crystals whisked smoothly aside by the windshield wipers. "I won't be long," she told Robert as he helped her from the backseat. He nodded, shut the door, and offered to escort her up the stairs, but a glance told her they had been recently swept and salted, so she declined.

The children's choir rehearsal was under way when she entered the church, and the sweet loveliness of their voices and the rich, achingly familiar tones of the piano struck her with such force that she forgot to ease the tall, heavy door gently shut. It closed behind her with a muffled boom, drawing the attention of Sister Winifred, who had been quietly walking the aisles, raising kneelers and replacing hymnals and missals, and the young choir director, who was inexplicably standing near the front pew rather than with the choir. Camille offered the choir director an apologetic smile as she unbuttoned her coat and settled into the back pew, and the younger woman smiled back.

The choir director joined the accompanist at the piano, and the choir began to sing "I Heard the Bells on Christmas Day," a lovely carol that Camille knew better as the Longfellow poem "Christmas Bells." A few years before, Camille and Paul had discovered an original manuscript of the poem — or rather, one of Camille's most reliable contacts in the auction world had — which they had donated to the Longfellow House on Brattle Street in Cambridge. "Do you remember . . ." she murmured, before shock and remembrance choked off her words. For a moment she had forgotten that Paul was not sitting beside her listening to the choir, to the piano, as he had so often before. For a moment she had forgotten he never would again.

Overcome, she closed her eyes against tears. She knew it comforted everyone else to see her bearing up so well, so bravely, but in the sacred peace of St. Margaret's, she could set the mask aside. She missed Paul desperately, with every thought, with every breath. She kept busy — everyone advised her to keep busy — but what would she do when she ran out of distractions? How would she bear the long, bleak, empty years without him? Thoughts of the future chilled her heart as if nothing lay ahead of her but cold, grim, endless winter, wind-swept and barren.

Intellectually, she knew this was not so. In her darkest hours, she reminded herself that all around her, life was flourishing, that she had important work yet to accomplish, that she would not always feel so rawly despondent as she did at that moment. But her heart — her heart declared that solace and resignation would forever elude her.

She had loved Paul too long to imagine any happiness without him — life, surely, but no joy.

She had never thought to marry, much less to know truly great love. She had known marriage was expected of her; from childhood, her mother and a series of nurses, governesses, and headmistresses had taught her that young ladies of her class had no greater duty and ought to have no other ambition but to marry suitable young gentlemen and carry on as their mothers and grandmothers had done since time immemorial — acting as her husband's hostess, furthering his ambitions and discouraging his vices, bearing children to carry on the family line, managing the household staff, supporting charitable endeavors, displaying perfect manners and elegant dress, shrewdly managing her fortune.

Camille loved her mother and grandmothers but found their lives astoundingly dull. Instead, from the time she could read a newspaper well enough to understand her family's role in the industry, she longed to emulate her father — Graham McAllister, Pulitzer Prize winner, scion of the McAllister media empire that had begun in 1861 when his grandfather founded a Republican newspaper in Hartford to champion Abraham Lincoln's policies throughout Connecticut. By the time Graham assumed the role of CEO upon his father's retirement, the McAllister News Group consisted of hundreds of newspapers in cities large and small from coast to coast, dozens of radio stations, and several television networks. In recent decades, Camille's brother, Asher, had survived the decline of print media by diversifying into the Internet and new media well ahead of his competitors.

From the cradle Asher had been groomed to take over the corporation from their father one distant day; from an equally early age, Camille had been expected to play no part whatsoever. When she became the editor of her preparatory academy's newspaper, her parents had been charmed but not impressed. When she decided to major in journalism at Radcliffe, her mother had been taken aback — she had been somewhat skeptical of the need for Camille to attend college at all — but her father had approved her choice, evidently perceiving it as a sign of filial admiration. Both parents expressed the appropriate amount of sincere pride when Camille won a national student journalism award for her insightful, elegant feature biography of one of Radcliffe College's founders, Alice Mary Longfellow. And yet somehow they were utterly astonished when, upon receiving her degree, she announced her desire to come to work for the McAllister News Group, as Asher had done two years before.

"Hear, hear, sis," said Asher, raising his glass to her from the opposite side of the dining table. "Welcome to the sweatshop."

"Congratulations are a bit premature," said their mother, maintaining her composure admirably well. "Camille, darling, what could you possibly be thinking?"

"I want to be a journalist," Camille declared. "I want to cover the big stories — Watergate, Vietnam, nuclear testing in Nevada. The IRA. The Soviet Union breaking our trade agreement."

Martha — Muffy to family and friends — shook her head. "I can't imagine there are any positions suitable for young ladies on the staff of our papers. Isn't that so, Graham?"

"There aren't many," he acknowledged, but Camille was aware of his appraising gaze. "So, Camille, writing for the school papers all these years hasn't been just a diverting hobby?"

"No more than studying for my degree has been."

"Graham, don't encourage this folly," Muffy admonished. "Camille doesn't need a job — goodness, the very idea! If she finds she has too much time on her hands now that she's finished school, I can find any number of worthwhile charities that would be glad to have a McAllister on the board."

"I want to be a journalist," Camille repeated firmly. "Not out of boredom but because the work is important and I happen to excel at it."

"We have a few girl reporters," Asher remarked. "We could always use a few more. Camille could write circles around most of them."

Camille threw him a grateful look, which he answered with a grin and a wink. "All I want is the same opportunity you offered Asher," she said, turning to her father. "If I were a man, we wouldn't be having this discussion. You would've already told me where to report on my first day."

Graham shrugged, but he seemed to be suppressing a grin. "I suppose that's true."

"With good reason," her mother said, incredulous. "A man has to support a family. Some less fortunate girls have to earn their keep. Camille shouldn't take a job that ought to go to someone who truly needs it. She'll only have to resign when she marries."

Camille thought it wiser to refrain from admitting that she was not certain she would ever marry. "All I want is a chance," she said, keeping her gaze fixed determinedly on her father. "If I can't hack it, fire me, but at least give me an opportunity to sink or swim instead of demanding I stay on the shore."

"Asher started at the bottom, in the mailroom," her father reminded her. "I would expect no less of you. How fast can you type?"

"Graham," Muffy protested.

"Eighty words a minute," Camille replied

"You can do better." Her father sat back in his chair and folded his arms. "Very well. I'll give you a job. You won't like it, but if you want something better you'll have to work for it. I won't show you any special favors. No one will know you're my daughter."

"Trust me," Asher broke in. "He'll be harder on you than anyone."

"I want to go on the record as opposing this ridiculous scheme in no uncertain terms," Muffy declared.

"Noted, my dear," said Graham, smiling. "Remember, Camille, your mother did try to warn you, as did I."

As it happened, her parents' warnings were not without merit. The entry-level job was in Bridgeport, a twenty-five-minute train ride away, and it paid barely enough to cover her fares and lunch. Camille loathed fetching coffee and dry cleaning for harried editors, and she gritted her teeth every time some leering cub reporter addressed her as "doll" or "girlie," but she loved the energy of the newsroom, the frantic pace, the insistence upon confirming sources, the relentless pursuit of the truth. Some days she typed other writers' copy until her fingers ached, longing to put her own words down on paper, fighting the urge to revise clumsy phrases or correct dangling modifiers. Usually she succeeded, but on one particularly frustrating day — first she had been sent out in a torrential downpour to bring back lunch for the editorial board and had spent the rest of the day with bedraggled hair and damp clothes, and later a copyeditor had communicated the need for haste not by telling her a particular errand was urgent but by smacking her on the bottom with a rolled-up newspaper —

her pride got the better of her. In part because she feared her writing skills would atrophy if she did not put them to good use, in part because she was angry that her bosses could find no better use for a summa cum laude graduate of Radcliffe than Girl Friday, she rewrote an article for the financial page rather than merely transcribing it, cutting three hundred words, polishing the dull prose that remained, and bringing the point into much better focus.

She filed the story, barely making deadline, and stayed two hours late to clean up other people's messes before finally storming home, nearly the last to leave the office. "Rough day?" her father inquired when she dragged herself across the threshold.

She refused to complain. "No worse than most," she replied lightly, climbing the stairs with a spring in her step, keeping her chin up until she was safely out of sight in her own bedroom. There she sank blissfully into a hot bath, silently cursing the copyeditor, taking great satisfaction in imagining him going home to a dim, one-room flat half the size of her bedroom and munching a cold bacon and cheese sandwich on stale bread for supper, while an excellent four-course meal with her family awaited her downstairs in her parents' elegantly appointed dining room as soon as she dressed and descended. If those arrogant men only knew who she was — but no, she didn't want that. She wanted to earn their respect through her own merits, not because of her surname.

The next day she arrived at work with the usual double box of doughnuts only to discover the bullpen in disorder, puzzlement intermingled with consternation and amusement in her coworkers' expressions. "Mr. Myers is on a rampage," the senior typist warned her, and only then did Camille remember the article.

"Who rewrote my piece?" Myers thundered, waving the early edition over his head as he stormed through the newsroom. "It cleared editorial. Who changed it afterward?"

Camille's heart plummeted as she envisioned her short-lived newspaper career fluttering out the window on wings of ink-stained newsprint. "I did," she announced clearly. Why not own up to it? They would find out sooner or later, and she was no coward.

"You?" Myers gaped at her. "The coffee girl?"

"I also pick up doughnuts and dry cleaning."

Someone guffawed, but Myers strode over

to her, cheeks florid, cigarette clenched in his teeth so tightly she expected it to snap in half. He halted only inches away, but she was taller and he had to tilt his head to glare up at her. "Who do you think you are, Brenda Starr? Lois Lane?"

"Your article was too long and too imprecise," she replied coolly. "I did you a favor by cleaning it up before it went out into the world with your name attached to it."

She heard a hoot of laughter and a low whistle. Myers spluttered an angry rebuttal, but Camille did not flinch. She scarcely listened. She was too busy silently berating herself for losing the first, and probably only, job she would ever have in the newspaper business.

"The girl's right."

Everyone turned at the sound of the low, gravelly voice of the editor in chief. Just outside the doorway to his office, he stood puffing on his cigar as he compared Myers's handwritten draft to the printed article above the fold on the front page of the finance section.

Camille held her breath. The room was silent. Everyone watched as the editor finished reading. "You should thank her, Myers. Buy her lunch or send her flowers. You've never sounded better." He shot a pointed look around the room. "Now, get back to work. We've got another issue coming out tomorrow."

Everyone leapt to obey, except for Camille, who stood frozen in place as it dawned on her that she had not been fired. Myers shook a finger in her face before storming off to his desk.

"I admire your nerve," the senior typist murmured as she hurried past with an armful of mimeographs. Camille managed a weak smile in reply, sensing, or hoping she sensed, a seismic shift in the newsroom.

She was wrong. She spent the rest of that day typing advertising copy and fetching sandwiches, and the next few weeks brought more of the same drudgery. Then, just as she had convinced herself she had let her best opportunity for advancement slip through her fingers, the features editor asked for a volunteer to cover a local flower show. She shot her hand in the air and told him he would have three hundred words by deadline. "Make it two hundred," he replied, and ducked back into his office without asking her name. She gave the editor two hundred fifty words, swallowed her protests when he cut it down to an even hundred, and glowed with triumph the next day when it appeared at the bottom of the last page of the features section, sans byline.

That evening, over a pre-dinner cocktail, Asher presented her with a clip of the piece, beautifully matted and framed. Their father smiled, but their mother cast her gaze to the heavens and sighed. Camille flung her arms around her brother and kissed him on the cheek, and as soon as supper was over she hurried upstairs and gave the memento pride of place on her bedside table.

As trivial as it was, the article marked a breakthrough. Other assignments to cover similarly banal events followed, but Camille imagined her mother and her mother's friends as her audience, and infused the stories with the detached humor and inner-circle asides they would appreciate. Readers actually wrote in to praise the work of the anonymous new reporter, and before long Camille found herself a regular reporter for the society page, deserving of a byline.

"McAllister, huh?" the copyeditor mused when he finally noticed her last name. "The guy who owns this paper is named McAllister."

"No kidding," Camille remarked, typing away at one hundred words a minute. "People might think we're related."

The copyeditor barked out a laugh. "You wouldn't be working here if you were."

"It would make a great story, though, wouldn't it? Rebellious debutante toiling away anonymously at her father's paper, determined to prove herself and earn her own accolades."

"No one would ever believe it," he said, shaking a cigarette from a pack, shaking his head too. "The problem with fiction is that it has to be plausible."

"Then I'll stick with reporting the facts," said Camille, nodding to the story emerging from her typewriter.

By the time the team of crack reporters who were her coworkers figured out her identity, two years had passed and she had accumulated enough clips to land a staff reporter job at the larger, more prestigious newspaper in Hartford. At first there too she was relegated to the social and sentiment stories she and her few female colleagues disparaged as the "pink ghetto," but eventually she wised up. She could wait forever for an editor to discover her talent and assign her a plum story, or she could pursue her own leads, discovering the most important stories of the day before her editors could assign them to someone else.

Year by year she worked at her craft, honing her skills, establishing contacts, garnering acclaim and the occasional promotion.

Her mother attended her friends' children's weddings and bemoaned Camille's unmarried state, while her father critiqued her clips and offered her more prestigious, lucrative positions he insisted she had earned. Camille refused to lament her lack of a husband and declined her father's well-intended offers to propel her career forward more rapidly than he would have any other reporter not named McAllister. She had become fiercely protective of her independence, all the while ruefully aware that her sizable trust fund emboldened her to take risks that her less affluent colleagues could ill afford.

Ten years out of college, she was happily single, increasingly well regarded in her chosen profession, and firmly ensconced in the political and national news sections of Connecticut's most respected newspaper, with her articles frequently picked up by papers all across the country. Her days of describing society teas and flower shows were well behind her.

Her work kept her on the move, from New York to London, Paris, Lisbon, Berlin, and, more often than not, Washington. When colleagues and the occasional envious rival declared she would run the McAllister News Group someday, Camille laughingly dismissed the idea. "I'll leave running the corporation to my businessman brother," she would say. "I just want to write."

Nevertheless, she faithfully kept her filial commitments to the McAllister Foundation. One snowy mid-December evening in Washington, she was attending a charity gala at the Smithsonian when her attention was drawn by the sound of a piano prelude by Claude Debussy, flawlessly and beautifully executed, though the six-piece band had taken a break. Curious, champagne flute in hand, Camille traced the sound to the piano, where she found a dashing, dark-haired man playing for a small group of admirers. She needed only a moment to recognize the three-term congressman from Boston, Paul Barrett. They had never met, but he was known for his idealism and uncanny ability to walk away from negotiations with everything he wanted and yet leaving his opponents with the satisfied sense that they had triumphed.

More than a year before, it had been almost impossible to open a newspaper or turn on the television without glimpsing Paul Barrett striding from office to car to apartment in a fruitless attempt to avoid the media circus — haggard, angry and miserable, not relaxed and happy as he was when she saw him, his fingers dancing with ef-fortless grace upon the piano keys. His recent ex-wife had been caught in a tawdry affair with a governor whose presidential ambitions had been quashed, along with both of their marriages when the sordid details came out. At the time, Camille had found the whole matter pathetic and had refused to write about it.

"You play wonderfully," she told the congressman when the band returned and he relinquished the piano with a grin and a joke about keeping his day job.

"Thanks." Congressman Barrett eyed her warily, and for a fleeting moment she felt chagrined, as if she should apologize on behalf of journalists everywhere for all he had endured at their hands. "You're putting on a great party tonight."

Camille waved a hand dismissively, not surprised that he knew who she was. "I agree it's a lovely event, but I didn't have any part in the planning. All the credit goes to my brother and his wife."

"I see. Are you covering the event, then?"

"I'm not working tonight, so you needn't censor yourself." Camille sipped the last of her champagne and placed the empty glass on the tray of a passing waiter. "I'm here to support the family's charitable endeavors, and to enjoy myself."

Before the congressman could reply, the band began to play. Couples returned to the dance floor, and after a moment's hesitation, and probably more out of politeness rather than anything else, he asked her to dance.

She had not expected to like him. She despised the cloying sense of neediness and excessive, false bonhomie that enveloped most politicians, but she quickly learned that Paul was not of that sort. He was funny and smart, with a self-deprecating sense of humor that could have been annoying but was refreshing and charming instead. To her pleasant surprise, they spent most of the evening together, dancing and talking and wryly commenting on the not-entirely-accidental meetings and barely clandestine deal making going on all around them, until an aide appeared and apologetically whisked Paul off to meet some important potential donor or another.

The next day, a lovely bouquet of flowers was delivered to her office, along with Paul's card and an invitation to call if she would like to continue the conversation his aide had interrupted. After a day of weighing the possible consequences, both personal and professional, Camille called.

When they began appearing in public together, Camille found herself uncomfortably thrust into the role of subject rather than reporter. When they announced their engagement two years later, concerns over the appearance of a conflict of interest compelled her to resign from the paper, wistfully, and not without regret. Some society observers looked askance at their twelve-year age difference and murmured that the marriage would never last. Several of Camille's professional acquaintances accused her of crossing inviolable professional boundaries, while others seemed to regard her engagement as a betrayal, as if she had defected to the enemy. Political opponents and even a few cynical members of his own party publicly speculated that the congressman was only interested in the young heiress for her money and her father's influence. Muffy, despite her relief that Camille was finally marrying, was sorely disappointed in her choice of husband — a politician of no particular family or fortune, and a mere congressman at that — and Graham took to proclaiming, adamantly and often, that his future son-in-law should expect no special dispensations from the rigorous scrutiny of the McAllister News Group. There were many awkward, uncomfortable, and chilly encounters with Ella and Grace, her stepdaughters-to-be, until they got to know one another better.

But Camille loved Paul deeply, and despite everything, she was eager to face the challenges of her new role as political wife. She was inspired by Paul's noble ambitions and lofty goals, and she resolved to do all she could to help him achieve them.

To Muffy's satisfaction, Paul did not remain "merely a congressman" for long. They were still newlyweds when he narrowly won election to the Senate; every six years after that, he was reelected by ever wider margins. There were days Camille missed journalism, the thrill of discovering a cover-up, the satisfaction of putting words on paper and sharing ideas with thousands of readers, but she found great fulfillment in being Paul's partner, in love and in politics, and she was pleasantly surprised to discover that all of her education and experience up to that point — even the lessons she had unwillingly absorbed at the Muffy McAllister School of Deportment — had prepared her well for her second career.

Music played an important role in their marriage, as it had in their meeting and their courtship. Camille first realized she was in love with Paul late one winter night in his Washington apartment, while she sat on the sofa wrapped in blankets and sipping mulled wine while he serenaded her with Gershwin tunes on an electric keyboard. As a boy Paul had sung in the church choir, and when he had begun lingering after rehearsals to pick out melodies on the ancient upright piano, a nun had taken notice and had offered to give him weekly lessons. When he had learned all Sister Winifred could teach him, she had arranged for a parishioner, a pianist and professor at the Berklee College of Music, to take him on as a pupil, pro bono. Although Paul played for sheer enjoyment and had never intended to become a professional musician, he had attended Boston College on a music scholarship, and had paid his way through law school with loans and regular gigs at piano bars.

Muffy and Graham had bought them a beautiful residence in the Back Bay as a wedding gift, far more spacious and luxurious than their town house in the capital. Since they finally had enough room, as a gift for their first anniversary, Camille presented Paul with a magnificent Shigeru Kawai grand piano. "I heard somewhere that the first anniversary is the musical instrument year," she teased as Paul stood staring in wonderment at the beautiful, gleaming piano, struck speechless with amazement and delight.

"Paper," he said, stepping forward to test the Middle-C key, shaking his head at the pure, rich, perfect tone. "I'm pretty sure the first anniversary is paper."

"I have that covered." She lifted the top of the bench to reveal a storage space, which she had filled with sheet music.

He often told her that he had never received a more wonderful gift, and she always replied that the piano had really been a gift to herself, for she loved to hear him play. Whenever they were at home rather than traveling throughout the state to meet with constituents or around the globe to meet world leaders, he played for her every day, bright American standards to start the morning, elegant classical music to unwind after supper.

Paul played with such skill and passion and obvious joy it was perhaps inevitable that clumsy notes in the lower register were the first signs of his illness.

At first he blamed infrequent practice, as the demands of the Senate kept him from playing as often as he liked. When the problem persisted, they both attributed it to fatigue or too much caffeine or the natural process of aging, which they ruefully bemoaned and resolved to resist tooth and claw. Then Camille noticed the faint tremor in his left hand; she asked how long it had afflicted him, and shocked by the answer, she insisted that he see his doctor at once.

It was Parkinson's disease, his doctor told them, suggesting they seek a second opinion with a specialist just to be sure. The specialist confirmed the original diagnosis, as they had dreaded, as they had expected he would.

For years they were able to keep the knowledge of Paul's illness within the family and their innermost circle of friends, but as his condition deteriorated, his most trusted aides were informed, and the party leadership. Camille assisted Paul in every way she could, compensating for his exhaustion and distraction, and disguising his physical symptoms to the extent she was able.

Despite the doctor's recommendation that Paul avoid stress and fatigue, his work took on a new urgency. He redoubled his efforts to push important measures through the Senate, and he called in favors he had been saving for a prolonged political career that had suddenly become unlikely. They had good days when they thrived on their work and accomplished so much that they almost forgot his disease. They had bad days when friends warned them that sharp-eyed observers had noticed Paul's tremor and rumors were circling that he was suffering from alcoholic withdrawal. The worst day came when Paul sat down at the piano, attempted a simple étude, and discovered he could no longer play.

That was the only time Camille saw him weep for all he had lost, for all the inevitable losses yet to come.

The beautiful piano sat in their living room for months, untouched except for regular dusting by the housekeeper. Camille wished she had learned to play, but as a young girl she had endured three years of piano lessons until her constant complaining wore down her exasperated parents and they had allowed her to quit. The piano had brought them so much joy, but to see it silent and neglected day after day brought them immeasurable pain.

Paul had confided this to his priest, but it was Sister Winifred who suggested they donate the piano to St. Margaret's. The music ministry still used the tinny upright Paul had picked out tunes upon as a choirboy, and it was an ongoing struggle to keep it in tune. "You can come and visit it whenever you like," the white-haired nun promised cheerfully when they lingered at the church one Sunday after Mass. "I have it on the highest authority that it belongs here and will do untold good."

"Highest authority — does she mean God?" Camille asked Paul in an incredulous whisper afterward as she helped him down the front stairs to the car. "Does she mean that God speaks to her directly, and that he put in a special request for your piano?"

"It *is* a magnificent piano," Paul reminded her, and Camille had to agree he made a fair point.

They were longtime anonymous benefactors of St. Margaret's, the church where Paul had been baptized, where his family had worshipped, where his parents had married. They had paid for a new roof when insurance fell short, they had funded the complete revamping of the aging HVAC system, and they always contributed generously to annual appeals. Donating the piano was simply another way to honor the church that had played such an important role in Paul's upbringing, and that continued to sustain them through their most recent, most arduous trial.

It was heart-wrenching, and yet a relief too, when the movers came to transport the piano to its new home. And what an unexpected joy it was to hear it played again whenever they returned to Boston. The young accompanist for the children's choir lacked Paul's extraordinary talent, yet he was a fine pianist, playing with skill and heart, and when the children sang along, the music they created was as close to divine as Camille ever expected to hear on Earth.

Paul had intended to break the news of his illness in his own time, after he had prepared himself for the onslaught of sympathy and premature eulogies that would surely follow, but someone leaked his medical records to the press, and suddenly he found himself in a maelstrom of lamentations from his supporters and accusations of deception from his opponents. Camille stood by his side at the hastily arranged press conference on the steps of the Capitol in which he acknowledged the truth and vowed to keep fighting in the Senate for as long as he was able.

Camille had never been prouder of him, never more inspired by his boundless determination, his deep humility.

Near the end, Camille had for all practical purposes taken over all of his duties that could be performed from his office. Then came the day he asked to go home, and she knew he meant their Boston residence. He declined most visitors and went out rarely, but once a week, and sometimes twice, he asked to be taken to St. Margaret's to listen to the children's choir and the beautiful piano Camille had given him for their first anniversary nearly thirty years before.

And then Paul was gone, and forevermore Camille would sit alone in the pew where they had once listened together.

She felt his presence strongly there, and it comforted her even as it made her miss him all the more. When she closed her eyes, she could almost imagine that her beloved husband rather than the young accompanist sat at the piano, bringing forth rich, sonorous music, as marvelous and ephemeral as life itself.

"What now?" she heard herself murmur aloud. She had devoted the last few years and every ounce of her time, energy, and attention to caring for Paul, to doing all she could to help him fulfill his life's ambitions in the time remaining to him. She had focused so determinedly upon that vocation that she had given no thought to what might follow. She had plans for the immediate future, to be sure. Listening to the rest of choir practice. Attending the benefit dinner for Boston Children's Hospital. Hosting the best Christmas she could manage for Paul's grieving family. Clearing out his Boston offices, followed by those in Washington. But that would see her only through the end of January, at most. What then? How would she fill the empty days, the lonely years, after those last duties were completed?

The future, once so rich with possibilities with Paul by her side, now stretched out before her like an unfathomable void, impossible to fill.

# CHAPTER TWELVE:
## MARCH–JUNE 1863

Charley had run off to join the army without receiving his father's blessing, without informing him of his intentions. Heartsick, Henry folded the letter, fumbled it into his waistcoat pocket, and went in search of Ernest, calling his name as he strode through the house. The alarm in his voice brought his younger son running, but when Henry queried him, Ernest denied knowing anything of his elder brother's plans. His look of shocked abandonment convinced Henry that he spoke the truth.

The Portland postmark was almost certainly a ruse meant to mislead pursuers and give Charley a few days' head start, but it was a clue nonetheless. Charley's good friend and third cousin George Rand resided in Portland; in all likelihood he was the accomplice who had posted Charley's letter and might know his plans. After Henry had determined that no one at Craigie House had any idea where Charley had gone, he wrote to his headstrong, impulsive son, though he harbored little hope that he could persuade him to abandon his reckless scheme and come home.

Camb. March 14 1863.

My Dear Charley,

Your letter this morning did not surprise me very much, as I thought it probable you had gone on some such mad-cap expedition. Still you have done very wrong; and I hope you will so see it and come home again at once.

Your motive is a noble one; but you are too precipitate. I have always thought you, and still think you, too young to go into the army. It can be no reproach to you, and no disgrace, to wait a little longer; though I can very well understand your impatience.

As soon as you receive this, let me know where you are, and what you have done, and are doing.

All join in much love to you. I have not yet told anyone of your doings, but have said only that you are in Portland, that being the Postmark on your letter.

Ever affectionately<br>H. W. L.

Next Henry wrote to his sister Anne in Portland to inform her of the family's latest troubles, and to implore her to ask family and friends to search Portland for Charley in case he was indeed in the city. "He is under a strange delusion," Henry lamented, "and I hope he will think better of it and come back. He is altogether too young to go into the army." If Charley were found before he enlisted, he should be sent home immediately, preferably with an escort. If he were found too late, Henry asked that they arrange for Charley to be suitably outfitted before he departed for the front lines. "Please give the enclosed note of mine for Charley to George Rand," Henry concluded, writing swiftly, frantically, as if minutes would make all the difference. "He is evidently in the secret, and will know where to find him."

Henry continued his desperate search through letters and telegrams, and a few days later, he received a letter from Captain William Henry McCartney, a Boston lawyer serving with the First Battery Massachusetts Volunteer Light Artillery, which solved the mystery of Charley's disappearance but otherwise brought Henry little comfort.

Camp Batty "A" Massacts
Brooks Div 6 Army Corps
March 12th 1863.

To H W Longfellow Esq.
Sir:
Yesterday in coming from Philadelphia to this camp I was met by your Son: who desired to enlist in my Battery. I knew him by sight; and being as you may well suppose somewhat surprised; I began to question him — I ascertained that he was both clandestinely absent from his home, and very determined to enlist as a private Soldier. Indeed I learned that he had actually applied to be received in the Regular Infantry but had been rejected on account of the loss of a thumb. I did not consider him the proper person to enlist — as he was evidently intending — Then for the purpose of retaining him and in order to prevent his enlisting elsewhere I promised him to receive him as a recruit. I took him into my Hotel, and brought him down here this PM. He has made me promise to enlist him tomorrow, under pain if I don't that he

will go elsewhere; and where he is not known, and enlist. My object in writing you Sir — is to inform you; that I shall endeavor to make him suppose; that he is enlisted lawfully — and so to keep him here: until I shall be advised by you in the matter. He is very shrewd. So much so, that I was utterly unable to advise you last night, in Washington, of his whereabouts. So constantly did he look after me. I beg leave to add Sir that I have taken these steps both on account of the respect; which I entertain for his family, and for his own sake.

I am Sir
with much respect
W H McCartney
Capt Comdg —

P.S. I have to beg as a favor, that he may not know: that you receive this information from me.

Thunderstruck, Henry was nonetheless relieved to know where Charley was, that he was under Captain McCartney's protection, and that the illusion that he had been properly enlisted would prevent him from running off to another unit that would take him in readily, gladly. Though Charley was encamped on the Rappahannock, safely beyond the range of the Confederate guns, he was still too close to danger for Henry's peace of mind — and since General Hooker was a fighting general, McCartney's artillery battery would surely soon move upon the fields of war.

Resigned to Charley's decision, knowing that he was likely to do more harm than good if he tried to extricate him from the army by coercion, Henry resolved instead to secure Charley a commission. The idea of wielding whatever influence his fame and fortune offered to maneuver Charley into a place of privilege he had not earned pricked at Henry's egalitarian conscience, but he could not refrain from doing all that he could for his boy. He knew well that even junior officers received better food, housing, supplies, and medical care than the most experienced enlisted man — and the harrowing accounts of exchanged prisoners of war confirmed that captured officers received significantly better treatment in Confederate prisons, often making the difference between survival and death. Charley was Henry's firstborn son, and although he had enlisted without his consent, Henry could not bear to punish him by refusing to provide whatever relative comforts and protection he could.

On March 17, Henry wrote to Sumner, seeking his advice, asking him to call on Captain McCartney if possible, to intervene however necessary to make Charley an officer. As soon as the letter was posted, Henry set out to call on his friend and editor James Fields to ask him to speak with Governor Andrew on Charley's behalf, but along the way he encountered a military funeral, and the sight so upset him that he returned home and wrote Fields a letter instead. He next wrote to Dr. Edward B. Dalton, a longtime family friend and the medical inspector of the Sixth Army Corps, requesting that he pay a surprise visit on Charley in camp and to report back with all haste.

Before evening fell on that long, distressing day, Henry sent off two more letters, written with great reluctance and pain. The first was to Captain McCartney to inform him that he could proceed with Charley's enlistment ceremony, for Henry knew that withholding his permission, which the captain had sought out of respect and not legal obligation, would only delay the inevitable. The last letter was to Charley, expressing his love, and that of all the family, and assuring him that he would not insist that Charley return home.

Anxious and increasingly melancholic,

Henry awaited word from his eldest son, making do in the interim with secondhand reports from friends. Sumner was the first to reply to his frantic series of letters, informing Henry that he had written to Charley and had invited him to Washington, surmising that Charley would be more amenable to persuasion if he were separated from his would-be comrades in arms. Not surprisingly, Charley had easily detected the stratagem and had replied that he would be most happy to visit Senator Sumner in Washington — after the war was over or his three-year term of service fulfilled.

"I feel better about Charley now than I did at first," Sumner acknowledged, "partly from thinking of his case, and partly from what has been said to me by others." He had sought advice from Secretary of War Edwin Stanton, who understood Henry's circumstances as well as any father could, for he too had a son who had enlisted without permission. When his son first began agitating to join the army, Secretary Stanton had enrolled him in college in Ohio to remove him from temptation, but soon thereafter his son left school to join up with a Union regiment in Tennessee. Three hundred similar cases had been presented to him at the War Department by parents seeking advice or action, and Secretary Stanton had absolute confidence that the course he had taken with his own son was appropriate for Henry too. "He left his own son in the ranks," Sumner explained, "fully and fairly to try the life he had selected." Secretary Stanton also urged them not to secure Charley a commission "until he had really earned it," for rewarding his deception with a high rank and a staff would encourage "idleness and vulgar dissipations."

After kindly promising to do whatever he could for Charley, Sumner encouraged Henry to accept the young man's decision and let him make his own way. "I see clearly that this act is the natural cropping out of Charley's character," Sumner added. "It was *in* him to do so, and, I believe also, it will be *in* him to persevere. I doubt if you could change him. You could not win him back. He could not return without mortification, that would be worse than any experience before him."

Henry could imagine an infinite number of terrible experiences on the battlefield that would be far worse than any embarrassment Charley might suffer if he were persuaded to come home. Even so, Sumner's sympathetic, rational letter — and Secretary

Stanton's wisdom born of experience — helped Henry reconcile himself to the misadventure. So too did the report from Dr. Dalton following his surprise visit to Charley in camp. "He was glad to hear from you," the doctor wrote, "sent his love, & says he is as happy as a lark all day long — likes his captain, thinks himself very fortunate in getting into this Battery, & says he is 'the luckiest bird round,' & would not leave for anything." Dr. Dalton vowed to look after Charley and care for him personally should he fall ill, but he assured Henry that the battery was encamped on good ground, with no especial danger of disease.

Taking what comfort he could from his friends' reassurances and advice, Henry sought distraction and solace in Dante as he had so often before, translating a canto each day, staving off depression and paralyzing fear with the beauty of the Italian language and the magnificence of the poet's vision. His *Sudbury Tales* was going to press, still in want of a more elegant title, and he had a good deal of correspondence to attend to on its behalf. But distractions were not remedies.

At long last the post brought a letter from Charley himself, his pride and exuberance fairly leaping off the page. "You dont know how glad I am to hear that you wont make me come back," he wrote, entirely mistaking Henry's restraint for approval. "I would not back out now for anything in the world." He was in the best Massachusetts battery, he boasted, and their captain was "a tip top soldier," and with great enthusiasm he described guard duty, the "little huts" in which the soldiers slept, recent snows, drills undertaken, horses tended, comrades befriended. "If I had taken my pick of our whole army I don't think I could have joined anything more to my idea than this Battery," he declared, unwittingly paining Henry with every word. Charley concluded his letter with a request for certain essential belongings — his India-rubber coat, his largest pair of brogans, a few cents' worth of matches, whatever preserves the family could spare from the larder — and he warned Henry to fasten the box securely, for nearly every shipment received by the battery of late had been broken into during transit and half the contents removed.

Henry immediately set himself to the task of gathering the things Charley required, his efforts mechanical, a strange, fatalistic grief welling up within him. Somehow Charley's first letter from the encampment marked a milestone, a point beyond which he would not return home except as a veteran soldier — if he returned at all. Henry fought back tears as he bound up the parcel, the twine digging painfully into his hands as he pulled the strands fiercely tight.

"Would you like some help?"

It was Ernest, lingering tentatively in the study doorway. "Yes, please, my dear boy," said Henry, forcing heartiness into his voice. Ernest hurried over and helped him hold the twine, tie the knots, and cut the loose ends, and when all was done to Henry's satisfaction, Ernest offered to see the box sent on its way.

Ernest picked up the parcel, but he hesitated before carrying it off. "Papa?"

"Yes, Ernie?"

"I understand the trouble and worry Charley has caused, even if he doesn't." Ernest shifted the box in his arms, and suddenly Henry was struck by the realization that Charley's impetuous act had placed a very real burden of worry upon his younger siblings, one that in his fears for his eldest son Henry had neglected to assuage. "I want you to know that even though I'm almost eighteen, and I love my country no less than Charley does, I promise I'll never enlist without your permission."

Henry's throat constricted, but he forced himself to speak steadily. "Do you seek it?"

After a moment's hesitation, Ernest shook his head. "What I would really like, Papa, is to go to West Point and study mathematics and engineering."

Ernest was already diligently studying both subjects at the Scientific School in Cambridge, and Henry thought one soldier in the family was quite enough, but he said, "I'll inquire about how you might obtain an appointment."

As Ernest nodded and departed with his brother's parcel, Henry sank into a chair, rested his head in his hands, and prayed that the war would be brought to a swift and merciful end before Ernest could join his brother in the army, before Charley experienced more of soldiering than camping and drilling and tending horses.

For days, Henry had been mulling over the advice Stanton had given and Sumner had seconded, and Charley's letter finally convinced him to follow it. Just as he reconciled himself to the idea of Charley serving as a private, he received a telegram from Lieutenant Colonel Greely S. Curtis of the First Massachusetts Cavalry, sent from Potomac Creek, Virginia. "Col Sargent recommends Charles Longfellow for commission today," read the terse message, rendering Henry more mystified than hopeful. Colonel Curtis was engaged to Hatty Appleton, the daughter of Nathan Appleton and his second wife, which made her Charley's "half-aunt," though she was only three years his elder. Whatever Charley might want for himself, the Appletons would consider it unseemly for a member of their illustrious family to serve as a lowly enlisted man.

Soon thereafter, a letter from Charley elaborated upon the cryptic telegram. "The day before yesterday I had a call from Lieut. Col. Curtis," Charley wrote, "and he said he had come to offer me a commission in his cavalry. Yesterday I rode over to the camp of the 1st and was introduced to the Colonel, he said he would write to Boston for my commission that afternoon so now that Col Sargent has recommended me I suppose I shall get it."

Whether Charley had managed to impress his superior officers during his very brief tenure as a private, or whether someone from the wealthy and powerful Appleton side of the family had arranged for the commission, Henry could only wonder, although he suspected Hatty Appleton had taken a particular interest in her nephew's military career. However it had come about, Charley was appointed a second lieutenant with the First Massachusetts Cavalry under General Joseph Hooker.

While Charley awaited his commission and deployment, he continued to serve under Captain McCartney with Battery A, practicing the care and management of horses, learning cavalry exercises from one of the sergeants, enjoying the camaraderie of the campfire. In the meantime, back in Cambridge, Henry hastened to assemble the clothes and equipment required by a cavalry lieutenant, carefully following the list Curtis had provided. "A good young horse, not white, short backed, quick & meant for work not show," the list began, followed by "a servant who must be young & used to horses," and continuing with a lengthy inventory of saddles, tack, and other supplies for the horse; garments for Charley's uniform, including spurs and a long blue overcoat; a sword, revolver, pistol, and ammunition as well as the appropriate belts to carry them; items for grooming and cleanliness; a three-volume work on cavalry tactics; a rubber blanket; and a strong leather traveling bag that Henry could not imagine would accommodate it all. He was astounded by the expense, but he bore it willingly for Charley's sake.

On the first day of April, Charley received word that his commission had been granted. He promptly reported to the First Massachusetts Cavalry's camp at Potomac Creek, Virginia, where Henry arranged for his uniforms and equipment to be delivered. Soon afterward, Henry received a letter from Captain McCartney written the day Charley left the battery. "It affords me much pleasure to say of him: that he exhibits all the characteristics of a thorough soldier," the captain wrote. "I am also very much pleased to know; that I have contributed somewhat; to his success — present — and that which awaits him, in the future." Henry firmly believed that the solicitous captain had done even more for Charley than he modestly claimed; if he had not taken the impetuous young man under his protection, Charley surely would have run off to enlist elsewhere, and might never have received his commission, and might even at that moment be on the front lines, mere yards away from the enemy's bayonets. As a token of his gratitude, and after consulting with Sumner to make sure it did not violate any War Department regulations, Henry arranged for a basket of champagne to be delivered to Captain McCartney, with his most sincere compliments.

He found himself unexpectedly heartened by the captain's praise, and he could not help wondering if perhaps his impulsive son had at last found his true calling. It was not the profession Henry would have chosen for him, but as his kind and thoughtful friends had reminded him when Charley first ran off to enlist, and as William Godwin elucidated so well in his essays, a son is a being independent of his father, and will not necessarily follow him, and the sooner the father accepts this, the better.

But not even the first stirrings of pride in his son's burgeoning career could diminish the sharp pangs of guilt he felt when he recalled the promise he had made to his beloved wife one summer night in the garden as they had watched a comet blaze in the night sky, in the north near the constellation of the Great Bear.

For two weeks Charley encamped at Potomac Creek with the First Massachusetts Cavalry, drilling, foraging for provisions, drilling, spending idle hours in talk and card games, drilling, passing in review, and yet more drilling. The new second lieutenant wrote enthusiastically about the improved rations his higher rank had bestowed, and he described his comrades and their training, especially their mishaps, with characteristic good humor.

When the muddy roads dried enough to become passable, the Army of the Potomac broke winter camp and began to move, and on April 10, Charley embarked on his first campaign as the cavalry marched out to the Orange and Alexandria Railroad and took up positions along the Rappahannock to guard the river crossings. Back home at Craigie House, his family anxiously awaited his letters and studied the papers for news of the cavalry's movements. At the end of that first day's march, Charley later reported with casual pride, Colonel Curtis had appointed him regimental adjutant, which was "a mighty fine position," he wrote, "as you see so much of what is going on." His new role had other benefits, he noted in his next letter. "My tent has to be next to Col Curtises so as to be handy for orders which is very pleasant, we are now sitting out in front of our tents on logs toasting our boots before the fire."

Then followed several long days of silence.

When word reached Cambridge of the fierce and bloody Battle of Chancellorsville, Henry felt sick with fear, haunted by gruesome visions of battlefield carnage. So certain was he that Charley must have been wounded in the terrible defeat that he wrote to his brother Samuel in New York and asked him to hurry to Washington City to meet him at the trains carrying the injured from the battlefield to hospitals in the capital.

It was just as well that Samuel decided to wait for an official report from the regiment before setting out, for a few days later, Henry received a letter from Charley expressing his disgust and disappointment that the First Massachusetts Cavalry had missed the entire engagement. Their first day's march had brought them within range of the Confederate army's artillery, but heavy rains had swelled the Rappahannock, rendering the fords too hazardous to cross. Instead the regiment had watched in consternation while rebel troops on the opposite shore constructed earthworks from which they could easily control the fords. The cavalry was commanded to withdraw, then ordered to make another advance that brought them near White Sulphur Springs, a town on the northern fork of the Rappahannock near Warrington. There too heavy rains had prevented them from mounting an attack. "It seems as if Providence was against us really although it is wicked to say so," grumbled Charley, "for if we once got across and the rivers did not rise and cut off our supplies we should sweep the whole country west of the Rappahannock."

Even as Charley lamented that "these confounded rains spoil all the General's plans," Henry could not help blessing the storms that had prevented his son from joining in so costly a battle. It was a great relief to know that his son had spent most of the campaign guarding wagon trains, occasionally able to hear the distant roar of cannon and disturbed by the grim parade of wounded being carried to the rear in ambulances, but otherwise safe and sound. Henry knew it would not always be thus.

Henry's unquiet mind rested easier when he learned that the First Massachusetts Cavalry had returned to camp at Potomac Creek, exhausted from the twenty-four-day campaign if not truly battle-scarred and blooded. After the excitement of the battle-fields, even though Charley had not penetrated much beyond the fringes, the camp life he had once found so invigorating now seemed dull and tedious. "It is mighty stupid coming back to this old camp again," he wrote, disgusted. "It is ten times as pleasant to be in the field on the march. I enjoy that very much, one has such an appetite after a days march, and it seems so good to lie at full length on the ground and stretch yourself under the trees. You cant imagine our feelings at this bringing the troops back to this side of the river just as we had received orders to hold ourselves in readiness for an immediate and rapid pursuit of the enemy."

Compounding his dissatisfaction, Charley had not yet received the parcels of supplies Henry had sent weeks before, nor any of the boxes his loving father, siblings, and aunts had sent to him since. He was also still making do with a borrowed horse and a reluctant enlisted man in place of a servant, although army regulations required him to provide his own. Demand for both horses and servants exceeded supply in the vicinity of the army, so Henry purchased two mares in Boston, a bay and a black, and hired William Locklin, an Irish-born Cambridge laborer in his early fifties, to transport the horses to the cavalry's encampment and to stay on to serve Charley for twenty dollars a month. The horses were the very ideal, Charley noted when he wrote home to thank his father, but regrettably, Locklin had quickly proven poorly suited for the military life. He and the horses had arrived in a torrential downpour, which lasted several days and made it impossible for anyone to dry out. "This rather dampened Locklin's courage," Charley wrote, "and gave him the rheumatism so that nothing will do but he must go home. He is a very nice man but rather an old bird for the army. You see the young ones stand it the best. I lent him ten dollars to help him home as he had only twelve dollars at hand."

Henry hired another man to serve Charley in the field as quickly as the matter could be accomplished, frustrated that he could do no more for his son than to conduct such business, send parcels of food and necessities, and write encouraging letters. Charley's letters from the encampment were invariably sanguine and confident despite the dull routine of his duties — preparing official documents for the colonel, exercising his horses, drilling his men, and debating past battles, campaigns yet to come, and the arcane workings of the War Department around the campfire. He expressed great indignation when his general, Fighting Joe Hooker, came under sharp criticism in the press for his failures of command at the Battle of Chancellorsville. "It is wonderful how the papers lie," he wrote. "They praise up fellows whom we know to be miserable sneaks and others who have done very brave and splendid things are never so much as mentioned."

Yet neither the controversies encircling his commanding officers nor the failure of the Union Army to win a decisive battle diminished Charley's enthusiasm for the military life. His letters home revealed that despite his experience of the discomforts of camp and the grim aftermath of battle, somehow he still perceived war as romantic and exciting, and he still considered soldiering the greatest expression of heroism. He longed to ride with General George Stoneman, whose splendid attack on General Lee's rear before the Battle of Chancellorsville had won him great acclaim from Northerners desperate for a Union victory. He expressed great regret that the cavalry had not descended upon Richmond while General Lee was distracted by General Hooker on the Rappahannock, and he overflowed with praise and pride for the First Massachusetts Cavalry. "I hope for the honor of the Regiment that we shall have a good slap at the Rebs yet," he declared, "as I think our men can whip them all to pieces as we are much better drilled."

Henry was glad for Charley's good spirits — how much more anxious he would be if his son were demoralized and miserable —

but he winced at Charley's hubris and prayed it would not prove to be a fatal flaw.

Henry had long supported an idea that Sumner had championed on the floor of the Senate and elsewhere, that men of color ought to be permitted to take up arms in defense of their country and the liberation of their race. Like thousands of abolitionists throughout the North, he had rejoiced when President Lincoln's Emancipation Proclamation had declared slaves in lands under rebellion henceforth and forever free, and he had welcomed the provision that men of suitable condition among the newly freed slaves would be received into military service.

For months, Henry knew, Governor Andrew and prominent abolitionists from Boston and throughout Massachusetts had been working quietly, diligently, to organize an infantry regiment of worthy men of color. Henry had contributed to the appeals to raise funds for publicity and travel, and he followed with great interest reports of recruitment efforts, which extended beyond the borders of the Commonwealth into northern cities such as New York, Philadelphia, and Pittsburgh. The Massachusetts Fifty-Fourth, as it would be called, would be under the command of Colonel Robert Gould Shaw, the twenty-five-year-old son of one of Boston's most prominent, prosperous, and staunchly abolitionist families.

On the morning of May 28, vast throngs of Bostonians, white and colored alike, their expressions eager and earnest, lined the sidewalks as Henry made his way to the Appleton residence at 39 Beacon Street. There, from an upstairs window in the company of Appletons, Curtises, and other friends, he observed a spectacle that would have been inconceivable only a year before — colored soldiers marching through the streets of Boston to the Common, where they would be reviewed by Governor Andrew before embarking for duty in South Carolina.

Smartly dressed, splendidly equipped, and preceded by a full band of musicians, the men of the Fifty-Fourth Massachusetts marched proudly and well, their expressions stern and stoic, their backs straight and eyes bright. The city resounded with glad shouts and thunderous applause so that Henry and his companions anticipated the regiment's arrival well before they turned onto Beacon Street.

When Colonel Shaw appeared on horseback at the head of the column, Henry watched him pass, marveling that someone so young would be called upon to fulfill so great a duty. Then his gaze traveled across the street and down the block to 44 Beacon Street, where the young officer's family watched proudly from the second-story balcony of the Shaw residence as the newly appointed colonel led his troops to meet the governor. Henry had never witnessed a more imposing spectacle, and he found it somehow both wild and strange and invigorating, as if a hazy, distant dream had sprung to vivid life.

He watched, inexpressibly moved, as the regiment reached the bottom of the hill, turned left onto Charles Street, and marched toward the gate of Boston Common, where Governor Andrew and other dignitaries awaited them. In that glorious moment it seemed as if there might be no limit to what the colored race could accomplish in the years to come, unhindered by slavery, when peace reigned over a united nation.

Henry knew that when the ceremonies concluded at noon, the Fifty-Fourth Massachusetts would march down State Street to Battery Wharf, board the steamer *De Molay,* and set out for South Carolina and for war. There was no doubt that their actions would be closely, even skeptically, observed and reported, and many people, North and South alike, would expect them to fail. Henry knew he was not alone in his glad satisfaction that men of color were at long last allowed to take part in the great conflict that would free their people from bondage. With their success and sacrifice, in victory and defeat, they would prove to a judgmental world the true strength, courage, and intelligence of their race, and not only freedom but true equality would surely follow.

A few days later, on a lovely spring morning ripe with the warm breezes and abundant flowers of early June, Henry and the girls sent off a box full of gifts to Charley, who would mark his nineteenth birthday one week hence. As the day approached, Henry felt his son's absence, and that of the beloved mother who had brought him into the world, ever more sharply. Henry could not explain why he found the summer even gloomier and more lonely than the winter, full of bittersweet memories and difficult to bear.

For some time Alice, Edith, and Anne had been imploring him to take them to Portland to visit their dear aunt Anne, and

Henry was inclined to oblige them. He delighted in pleasing his sweet little daughters — their smiles and kisses broke like sunbeams through his skies overcast with sorrow — and he believed a change of scene might do him some good.

Two days after Charley's birthday, Henry took the girls north to Portland, where family and friends welcomed them with affectionate joy. In the company of his sympathetic, compassionate sister, he felt something too long tightly bound up in his heart and head gently loosening, enabling him to sit quietly, peacefully, to breathe more deeply.

He scarcely had time to marvel at the unfamiliar sensation of contentment when it was brutally shattered by word from Dr. Dalton that Charley had been stricken with camp fever, and was so desperately ill that he was being evacuated to a military hospital in Washington.

Fighting off overwhelming dread, Henry entrusted his daughters to his sister's care and departed immediately for the capital. His train arrived at ten o'clock in the morning on June 13, but even in his haste to make inquiries and locate his ailing son, Henry was startled to discover that the city was so packed full of soldiers' tents and overcrowded hospitals that it seemed to be one vast military encampment.

At last Henry found his eldest son, not in one of the makeshift military hospitals as he had feared and expected, malodorous and full of stomach-turning horrors and disease, but in the private F Street residence of the Reverend James Richardson, Massachusetts-born Unitarian minister, prominent official with the United States Sanitary Commission, and good friend of Henry's brother Samuel.

Charley struggled to sit up in bed when Henry hurried into the sickroom. "No, my dear boy. Lie back," Henry urged, easing him down upon the pillow.

"I'm not as ill as I might seem," said Charley hoarsely.

"I'm sure you're not," said Henry. His son's cheeks were flushed, his skin seeming taut and strangely translucent, his fever no doubt exacerbated by the stifling heat and humidity of the city. "But rest benefits even the healthiest of men, so you have no reason not to make good use of this comfortable bed."

"It is far better than a cot in a tent," Charley acknowledged, his voice no more than a rough whisper.

As dreadful as it was to see his firstborn

ill, finding Charley able to speak, and even to joke, relieved Henry greatly, for he had expected to find him barely clinging to consciousness, tossing and turning, soaked through with fever sweat, delirious. As soon as Charley dozed off, Henry sought out the doctor, who assured him that although the fever was nothing to dismiss lightly, Charley presented no alarming symptoms that suggested his life was in danger. "He was doing far better this morning, until he decided to disobey orders and leave his bed," Dr. Clymer said wryly. "Reverend Richardson managed to talk him out of taking a turn in the garden, but even descending the staircase was enough to bring about a relapse. He needs rest, Mr. Longfellow, rest and quiet."

"He shall have them," Henry replied firmly, "whether he wants them or not."

For the next few weeks, Henry remained with Charley in Washington in the home of their generous host, rarely leaving his son's bedside. He arranged for a tent of blue gauze to be draped over his bed to keep off the harassing flies, and fed him a steady, nutritious diet of beef tea, blancmange, and ice cream, an especially welcome dish, sweet and soothingly cool upon the patient's sore throat. As a staunch homeopath, Henry was astounded by the vast quantity of mixtures, powders, and mysterious draughts Dr. Clymer insisted upon pouring into Charley. It staggered belief, but Henry held his tongue and followed instructions, for the doctor had an excellent reputation for curing such cases and Henry dared not put Charley's recovery at risk. Even so, he preferred the prescriptions of Miss Dorothea Dix, the Superintendent of Women Nurses and occasional visitor to Charley's sickroom, who provided pure Bermuda arrowroot and homeopathic cocoa and recommended that they remove Charley from the oppressive climate of Washington as soon as he was able to travel.

Day by day Charley improved, and they began to hope that Dr. Clymer would soon release him so they might travel to Nahant. Miss Dix agreed that the fresh sea breezes and sunshine would quicken Charley's convalescence, but Dr. Clymer was reluctant to discharge him, warning that any disturbance could bring about another relapse.

To no one's surprise, as the fever abated and his strength returned, Charley became increasingly restless and bored confined to his sickbed. He chafed at the doctor's orders so vigorously that Henry quietly rejoiced, thankful to see his son's familiar restless energy restored. Henry distracted him with letters, which they exchanged in great numbers with family and friends, and by reading aloud Miss Mary Elizabeth Braddon's novel *Lady Audley's Secret,* an immensely popular murder story that was just scandalous enough to make for rather entertaining reading.

Eventually Charley was allowed out of bed, and soon thereafter he was permitted to sit up in the parlor. Occasionally a friend or acquaintance or even strangers would call, having heard that the son of the illustrious poet was ill and wishing to express their hopes for his swift recovery. Other well-wishers sent flowers and letters, and several charming young ladies of the neighborhood brought him enticing delicacies from their kitchens, but nothing could sweeten Charley's temper when he learned that the First Massachusetts had engaged the five regiments of the Virginia Cavalry in a fierce battle at Aldie in Loudoun County, Virginia, without him. "I am the most unlucky fellow to have missed it all," he grumbled, kicking his bedsheets and punching his pillow in frustration. "The war will be over before Dr. Clymer lets me leave this house, much less return to the field."

"You have perfectly articulated my most ardent wish," Henry replied lightly, but

Charley merely heaved a sigh and asked for paper and pencil so he could write to his brother.

The war seemed no closer to its end when Henry finally convinced Dr. Clymer to let him take Charley to Nahant. After thanking Reverend Richardson profusely for his generosity and kindness, Henry and Charley departed Washington by sea and arrived at Nahant on the last day of June. The fresh, cool sea breezes seemed to invigorate Charley, though he was already in good spirits, so delighted was he to be released from his sickroom, but the next morning his fever returned, brought on, no doubt, by the rigors of travel. Henry ordered him back to bed, and Charley, grumbling, obeyed, although by evening Henry relented enough to allow him to move to a reclining chair on the front porch.

The rest of the family soon joined them at the cottage, and in the cheerful company of his adoring sisters and doting aunt, Charley steadily regained his vitality. By the middle of July, he was enjoying walks on the warm, sandy beaches and refreshing swims in the ocean. He had missed another fierce battle in which the First Massachusetts Cavalry had acquitted themselves with distinction, having engaged Confederate general J.E.B.

Stuart's cavalry in Maryland and Pennsylvania, preventing them from joining up with the main body of General Robert E. Lee's forces at Gettysburg. Charley again lamented his misfortune, and vowed that as soon as he was given leave to rejoin his regiment, he would set out with all haste.

The day came too soon to suit Henry. On August 14, Charley bade farewell to his family and left Nahant in the company of a newly hired servant, a man called Chamberlain. First they stopped in New Market, Maryland, where Charley's horses had been stabled during his convalescence, then onward to Washington, where, until the First Massachusetts Cavalry returned to its rear base and he could rejoin them, he was assigned to command the rear guard of a squadron protecting a train of sutlers' wagons en route to the front. "It was pretty good fun being head of the rearguard," Charley wrote to Henry on August 22, "as whenever a wagon would break down or get mired the sutlers would treat us to grub to keep us around as they were dreadfully frightened of being left alone to be captured by the rebels." The rearguard would not have abandoned the wagon train, Charley was quick to point out, but they were too glad for the extra food to emphasize that point to the sutlers.

By the time Henry received the letter at Nahant, Charley had already reunited with his regiment near Warrington and had joined in the hunt for Confederate colonel John Singleton Mosby — the Gray Ghost — and his band of raiders, the notoriously swift and elusive First Virginia Cavalry.

Charley was thrilled to be in the thick of it again, but Henry could not share his cheerful enthusiasm. His son had missed violent battles that had cut down thousands of young men like wheat before the scythe. He had recovered from a serious illness that had claimed the lives of countless thousands more. How many narrow escapes could one young soldier survive before his luck finally ran out?

# CHAPTER THIRTEEN:
# THE PRIEST'S TALE

The smell of coffee brewing woke Ryan well before dawn, but even before he glanced at the clock he knew Sister Winifred had yet again tiptoed into his room after he had fallen asleep and had shut off his alarm. Sister Winifred called him "Father," but she often seemed to think of him as a grandson.

Yawning enormously, he rose, knelt on the small braided rug beside the window to pray, and then quickly showered and dressed, only a half hour behind schedule. When he went downstairs to the kitchen, he found the elderly nun standing at the counter humming "Angels We Have Heard on High" as she plucked two slices from the toaster and set them on a plate.

"Sister Winifred," he admonished mildly, reaching into the cupboard beside the sink for a coffee mug. "This was your day to sleep in. We're supposed to take turns getting up early to make coffee, remember?"

"Oh, I was awake anyway, Father." She smiled brightly and she carried her plate to the small table where the newspaper, a small glass of orange juice, and a steaming cup of milky coffee already awaited her. "A growing boy like you needs his rest."

He had to laugh. "Sister, I'm more than a decade beyond fitting that description."

"Really?" Frowning, she removed her glasses, polished the lenses with her napkin, replaced them on the bridge of her upturned nose, and peered up at him. "Well, I suppose maybe you are, but you still needed the rest. You have a very busy day in store."

"As do you." He poured himself a cup of coffee, added sugar, and pulled out a chair at the other end of the table. "I know you mean well, but you really need to stop turning off my alarm."

"If I hadn't, it would have woken you up."

"Well, yes. That *is* the point of an alarm clock." He took a deep drink of coffee and settled back into his chair, amused. "We've talked about this. What if I'd had an important appointment first thing this morning, and I slept through it?"

"I wouldn't have turned off your alarm if you really needed to be up so early."

"How would you have known?"

"I would have known," she said, with such

conviction that Ryan knew it was futile to try to persuade her otherwise. Besides, she probably *would* have known, and not because she checked his calendar. Sister Winifred had uncanny intuition, and she observed much more than anyone gave her credit for. Most people assumed she was distracted because she often talked to herself aloud, which wasn't uncommon in people her age. The habit troubled Ryan only because members of the parish often approached him privately to express their concerns for her health. He always assured them that the elderly nun saw her doctor regularly and never failed to receive a clean bill of health, except for the usual minor, inevitable physical issues associated with aging. The well-meaning parishioners would nod, express their relief, and walk away, as dubious as before.

As for himself, Ryan was certain he had never met a saner, happier, or more optimistic person than Sister Winifred. His only worry about her admittedly disconcerting chattiness was that word of it would filter upward to higher offices within the diocese, and some authority with good intentions would insist that she retire. Ryan knew that Sister Winifred would be heartbroken if that came to pass. She had entered religious life long before he was born, and she had been with St. Margaret's as long as anyone could remember. Ryan depended upon her, and he knew she needed the parish as much as it needed her.

"You have a grief-counseling appointment at ten o'clock," she reminded him, "and a pre-Cana session at eleven."

"Thanks, Sister."

"Also, Jerome Duffy will be stopping by after lunch to discuss an important question of theology, so you might want to prepare yourself."

"Jerry?" said Ryan, bemused. Jerry attended Sunday Mass regularly and could be counted upon for most Holy Days of Obligation, but he had never engaged Ryan in a serious theological discussion before. "When you spoke with him, did he give you any hint what this important question of theology might be?"

"Oh, I didn't speak with him."

"Did he explain in his message?"

She shook her head. "There was no message. He didn't call."

Sister Winifred often made such predictions, and was more than often right. Ryan figured she probably drew upon intuition, common sense, longtime familiarity with their parishioners, and overheard conversations, but he could not explain her astonishing accuracy rate, which would put most professional prognosticators to shame. "I guess he'll tell me when he arrives."

"I'm sure you'll be on the edge of your seat with suspense until then. Oh, before I forget, your mother would like you to call, and we're going to get a few inches of snow this afternoon. Perhaps you'd like to plan to clear the steps and sidewalks before choir rehearsal, so the children don't take a tumble."

It was a safe bet that his mother wanted him to call, because she always did, but for Sister Winifred to claim she could predict measurable snowfall was too much. "How could you possibly know that it's going to snow this afternoon?"

Bemused, the elderly nun tapped the newspaper lying folded on the table between them. "I read the forecast in the *Globe*. How else would I know?" She smiled indulgently and rose. "I'm not going to finish my toast. Do you want the last piece?"

"No, thank you." Ryan usually fasted before morning Mass, not only to properly receive the Sacrament of Eucharist but to make him more mindful of his many neighbors who also would not have anything to eat that morning, and not by choice. "I'll get something after."

"I'll turn the lights on in the church," she said, and left him alone to finish his coffee and prepare.

He sipped his coffee and contemplated the day's Gospel reading. At one time he had wondered if he should avoid coffee before Mass too, if indulging in a cup was undermining his purpose at best and cheating at worst. He had confessed his uncertainties to his friend Jason, who had known him since college and therefore was not intimidated into deference by his collar and title. Jason, who knew him better than almost anyone, had told him frankly that it was not self-indulgence but a courtesy to his parishioners to have a cup of coffee before he faced the day.

Jason. A sudden stab of worry compelled Ryan to set down his cup, bow his head, and murmur a fervent prayer for his friend's safety and deliverance. Laurie had not heard from her husband in two months, and Ryan could well imagine her anxiety and fear. Her son, Alex, seemed unaware that anything was amiss except that his father was away from home, but Charlotte was precocious and observant, and Ryan knew it was only a matter of time until she realized that something was very wrong, that her mother was not telling them the whole truth.

Ryan crossed himself, rose, washed the dishes, and went to prepare for morning Mass.

About twenty-five worshippers attended the eight o'clock service, including the parish's two secular employees, Gene, the custodian, and Lisa, the part-time office manager. The rest of the congregation, which skewed older, included the usual fifteen or so regulars and a few unfamiliar faces — guests of the regulars, he learned when they introduced themselves afterward, as well as a few curious tourists drawn by the church's history and architecture.

After worship, he passed the morning in office work and counseling sessions, writing his customary letter for the parish bulletin, and brief calls on housebound parishioners. He returned to the parish house at half past noon, in time for a quick sandwich before the doorbell rang.

When Ryan answered, he was not surprised to find Jerome Duffy standing on the doorstep. "Sorry to drop by unexpected, Father," he said. "Something's been bothering me, and I thought maybe I could talk it over with you on my lunch break, but if this is a bad time —"

"Not at all." Ryan opened the door wider

and beckoned him inside, tempted to remark that Jerry had been expected. "Come on in."

Ryan showed Jerry into the living room, which was elegantly and comfortably appointed with gently used furniture donated almost thirty years before by the church's most generous benefactor, a boy from the neighborhood who had become a senator. Ryan had met with him often in his final months as his health declined, offering him spiritual guidance and comfort, and sometimes just a sympathetic ear. His widow still visited St. Margaret's regularly. She seemed to particularly enjoy hearing the children's choir sing to the accompaniment of the wonderful piano the couple had given to the church, anonymously, as they did all their generous gifts, in the spirit of Matthew 6:1–2.

"What can I do for you, Jerry?" Ryan asked as they seated themselves in opposite chairs by the fireplace, swept clean and long unused.

Jerry removed his knit cap. "I had a religious question for you, Father, and I really hope it doesn't seem disrespectful."

Ryan prepared himself. "I'm sure it won't. What's on your mind?"

"I've been wondering . . . does God care

about sports?"

Ryan blinked at him. "Say again?"

"Does God care about sports?" Jerry leaned forward, rested his elbows on his knees, and regarded him earnestly. "I mean, you always hear players giving Jesus the credit when they make a goal or score a touchdown or win the playoffs, but doesn't that mean Jesus wanted the other team to fail?"

"Well, I don't know if I'd say —"

"That just doesn't seem fair, Father. It's not like the other team's full of Satan worshippers, right? They probably go to church as much as the guys who won. They probably prayed for victory too, and they're probably not any more sinful. So why would Jesus listen to the prayers of one team and ignore the other?"

"You must be a Red Sox fan."

"Of course," Jerry replied stoutly. "From the cradle."

"It's appropriate to give thanks to God for blessings received, and for the good health and the physical and mental gifts that help a player achieve victory." Ryan paused to consider his next words. "Whether the Lord actually prefers one sports team over another is quite another matter — and I say that as a Notre Dame fan."

"It's just hard for me to imagine that with so much war and poverty and suffering in the world, Jesus is sitting up in the clouds wearing a sweatshirt and cap with one team's logo, shouting their cheers and booing the other guys, you know?"

Smiling, Ryan shook his head to clear it of the irreverent image. "Look at it this way. What if Patrick and Daniel were playing on opposing soccer teams in the most important match of the season? Soccer's their game, right?"

"Yeah, but they'd never play each other. My boys are three years apart in age."

"Let's say for the sake of argument that they *are* playing against each other. You wouldn't cheer for one son and ignore the other, or pray for one to win and the other to lose, right?"

"Of course not."

"You might instead hope that both boys both would perform to the best of their abilities, that they would play fairly, that they'd avoid injury, and that they'd show good sportsmanship, win or lose."

Jerry nodded. "Sure."

"If that's how you feel as a father, putting these more noble values ahead of simply winning a game, how do you think our divine Father, in His perfect love for all His earthly children, would regard it?"

"I get what you're saying, Father."

"We all like to win, but sometimes we learn more from losing. Sometimes, although we might not like it, God's plan is for us to endure a defeat."

"So tell me, Father." Jerry lowered his voice confidentially. "With all that in mind, is it okay to pray for the Bruins to beat the Penguins tomorrow night?"

"I don't think it's wrong," said Ryan. "Let's just hope a victory is part of God's plan, and that if it isn't, that we'll accept it with good grace."

"Thanks, Father." Satisfied, Jerry pushed himself to his feet. "I feel much better."

"Anytime." Ryan rose and shook his hand. "My door's always open."

He saw Jerry out, unexpectedly cheered by the conversation, and by Sister Winifred's idea of what constituted an important question of theology. It was not unusual for parishioners to approach him with concerns like Jerry's, and he always strove to give them thoughtful, prayerful answers. He drew upon experience and knowledge of scripture rather than doctrine when presented with topics that had never been addressed specifically in the seminary, or in any of the undergraduate philosophy and theology classes he had taken when he was first seriously discerning his vocation.

Ryan had not come from a particularly religious family, as his bewildered mother had often reminded him after he announced his intention to enter the seminary. His parents had taken him and his younger brother to church on Sundays, and saw to it that they received the sacraments, and refrained from serving meat on Fridays during Lent. They said grace before supper and made weekly contributions to the parish, but otherwise religion was something restricted to Sunday mornings, Christmas, and Easter.

Only in hindsight did his parents detect a pattern in his childhood play: He had always liked to build churches instead of spaceships and castles with his LEGOs, he had often played Mass with his Star Wars action figures, and twice he had dressed as Saint Francis of Assisi for Halloween. He had sung with the church choir from a very early age, but they had attributed that to his love of music, and a few years later when he asked to become an altar boy, they assumed he was dutifully responding to the priest's request for volunteers. He was a good, loving boy, certainly, but a future priest? The thought had never occurred to them, and if anyone had suggested it, they probably would have laughed. Surely future priests were more obedient, less likely to squabble with their brothers, and disinclined to gleefully check their opponents on the rink or to boast the highest shooting percentage in the high school league. Ryan was far more likely to join the NHL than the priesthood.

But Ryan had always found an inexpressible joy and beauty in the Mass, qualities he quickly realized went unnoticed by his brother and his friends, who groaned about going to church and waited impatiently for the torturous hour to pass. Uncomfortable, he kept his feelings to himself, except in the confessional. His parents had no idea he went to confession every Thursday on his way home from school; they assumed he stayed late to get help with his homework, and Ryan did not correct their mistake out of embarrassment and a vague sense that they would think he was strange. Every week his confessor gently suggested that deceiving his parents even with the best of intentions was a kind of sin, and that honesty could lead to greater understanding and acceptance. "They'll just think I'm weird and tell me to stop," Ryan would reply gloomily, and the kindly priest would drop the subject until Ryan brought it up again the following week.

In his junior year, Ryan and his classmates were inundated with standardized tests, personality inventories, and career aptitude assessments. The results of the first type of test told him that he was a good student; the second that he was outgoing, optimistic, and happy, which he had already figured out. It was the last kind that made him inexplicably anxious, because they consistently reported the same results: He should pursue a career as an athlete, coach, trainer, or teacher; or he should consider work in counseling, nursing, teaching, or religious life.

"I guess it's teaching for me," Ryan had muttered after receiving the results from a test taken in his psychology class.

A friend overheard and turned around in his chair. "What'd you get? I got finance or business. That totally blows. I want to play electric guitar."

Ryan had pretended to study his results. "According to this, I'm supposed to be the starting forward for the Bruins. Can't argue with that."

His friend had guffawed, prompting the teacher to call on him, abruptly ending the conversation.

Ryan brooded over the test results and his

inexplicable yearning as he accompanied his parents on campus visits and diligently filled out applications and fielded inquiries from college recruiters. In his senior year, after receiving several acceptance letters, he discussed his options with his parents and school advisor — and then had a very different conversation with his priest.

"I think maybe I'm supposed to become a priest," he said hesitantly. Saying the words aloud and hearing them echo in the quiet church made the idea somehow more real, frighteningly so. "The problem is, I'm not sure. I like hockey too, and I really like girls." Embarrassed, he studied the floor. "I'd really hate to give up either one."

Father David nodded, seeming not at all surprised by any part of the admission. "What do your parents think about this?"

"They don't know."

"This isn't something you'd feel comfortable sharing with them?"

"I don't think they'd exactly celebrate."

"They might surprise you."

Ryan shrugged.

The priest sighed, thoughtful. "What are your other choices?"

"I got into a few universities, but I've kind of narrowed it down to applying to St. John's Seminary or attending Notre Dame.

They gave me a hockey scholarship."

The priest's eyebrows rose. "Full ride?"

"Yeah, all four years, maybe even a fifth."

"Well done." Father David smiled kindly. "Have you spoken to anyone at St. John's?"

"No." Ryan shifted uncomfortably in the pew. "Not yet. I wanted to talk to you first."

"Did you know that they only accept applicants who have already earned a bachelor's degree?"

Ryan's heart sank a little. "No, I didn't."

"There are other seminaries that accept young men with a high school diploma, of course, and I could certainly recommend some for you to consider." Father David studied him for a moment. "It's very good that you want to discover God's will for you, very good indeed. Do you want my advice?"

"Absolutely, Father. That's why I'm here."

"I think you should take the scholarship. Play hockey and earn your degree. Study philosophy and theology, and find a religious advisor to help you prayerfully and thoughtfully discern your vocation." Father David smiled. "I've heard that Notre Dame is a fine place to do that."

A sudden rush of happiness convinced Ryan that he should follow the priest's advice.

The following August, he enrolled at the

University of Notre Dame, moved into Dillon Hall on South Quad, and quickly befriended his roommate, Jason, an aspiring engineer. He played hockey, joined the Glee Club, participated in campus ministry events, and even dated now and then, although his acknowledgment that he was considering the priesthood tended to deter any long-term romantic relationships. At the end of his first year, he declared his major in philosophy, which from the moment he returned home for summer break inspired many pointed questions from his parents about what he intended to do with a philosophy degree after graduation. All he could bring himself to say was that he was still figuring it out, which satisfied his parents not at all.

To his surprise, as the summer passed, his younger brother, a straight-A high school senior-to-be, became his staunchest supporter. "An education in the humanities teaches critical thinking and essential analytical skills," Liam declared. "It develops oral and written communications skills, the ability to synthesize information, and the ability to ask the right questions. Skills like those appeal to employers, and they never become obsolete. Studying the humanities opens the mind."

Liam was likely to become his class valedictorian, and his stratospheric standardized test scores had already earned him the avid attention of Harvard, Yale, and Columbia, so their parents found it impossible to dismiss his argument out of hand. To Ryan's relief, as he prepared to return to campus for the fall semester, they did not insist that he choose a more practical major, and he knew he had his brother to thank for it.

"No problem, bro," Liam replied, slapping him on the back and grinning. "I did it for myself as much as for you. I plan to major in history."

Over the next few years, Ryan studied and prayed. He met weekly with his rector, who had become his spiritual advisor during his time of discernment, and he volunteered with Campus Ministry and the Center for Social Concerns out of an intense desire to serve his community. For release he had hockey, for fun the Glee Club, and for friendship his roommate Jason, the other guys in the dorm, and a small circle of friends he had met in clubs and classes, fellow students drawn together by their contemplation of religious life. Some, like Ryan, were reluctant to tell their parents and had confided in only a few close friends. Others had been urged so often since childhood to consider the priesthood or had been told so many times that they would make an excellent priest that they were uncertain whether they heard God's call or merely an internalized echo of their parents and parish priests. But for Ryan, every year brought greater certainty that God wanted him to become a diocesan priest, and greater happiness with that choice.

As much as Ryan enjoyed his undergraduate social life, in the second semester of his junior year, he moved from Dillon Hall into Old College, an undergraduate seminary for the Congregation of the Holy Cross that offered residence, community, and support to undergraduate men discerning a call to religious life. It was there that Ryan became more certain of his calling and more determined to heed it.

With that knowledge came acceptance that he could no longer hide from his parents the truth of what he was and what he wanted to become.

A few weeks before graduation, while home on spring break, he broke the news to his family one evening after dinner. His parents were stunned, and as the week passed they asked him again and again if he was absolutely certain. His mother lamented that he would never marry or have children, and in the tearful discussions that erupted and subsided in the days that followed, she confessed that she feared he would be lonely and unhappy for the rest of his life. His father took it remarkably well, and after much throat clearing told Ryan that he was an adult and capable of making his own decisions, but he should be sure, absolutely sure, before he took any irrevocable vows.

To his sorrow, his younger brother took the news very badly.

"How could you willingly enlist in a sexist, moribund, archaic, patriarchal, scandal-ridden institution like the Catholic Church?" Liam demanded. "You're an intelligent, rational, educated person. What possible appeal could that life have for you?"

Ryan tried to explain, but Liam refused to listen. A chasm opened between them that day, one that Ryan tried in vain to bridge. He wrote to Liam often from the seminary, but Liam rarely replied, and only in anger. When they gathered at their family home for holidays, their conversations were strained and formal. Ryan missed their old closeness terribly, but Liam, who as the years went by earned his PhD from Princeton, accepted an endowed chair in the Department of History at Harvard, married, and welcomed two children into the world, rarely spoke to him except to debate Church doctrine or to challenge him to defend the Church from scandals that Ryan himself deplored as indefensible.

Over the years his parents came to accept his vocation, even to respect it, but Liam rejected organized religion, and he would have considered himself a hypocrite if he had not rejected Ryan too. Ryan had always known that the path he had chosen could lead him away from people he loved, but he felt the loss of his brother's friendship keenly, and he felt responsible for the sorrowful burden their estrangement conferred upon their parents.

Ryan's vocation had cost him his brother's friendship. That was his only regret about his choice, but even if he had known, he could not have chosen otherwise.

"Your mother called," Sister Winifred told him brightly when their paths crossed in the hallway outside the parish office, where Ryan had just finished meeting with the office manager about year-end accounts. "She wants to know when you're available to celebrate Christmas with the family."

Ryan nodded, remembering her earlier prediction. "Thanks, Sister. I'll call her back later."

"She said she understands if it can't be on

Christmas Day itself, or even Christmas Eve. She realizes that you're quite busy this time of year, and that you can't easily reschedule commitments. She wants you to know that they'll arrange the family celebration around you. The important thing is that you be there."

"Of course," said Ryan, taken aback. Why wouldn't he show up? Even at that busy, holy time of year he had days off between Christmas and New Year's Day, and he had never missed a family Christmas celebration. "Well, that's . . . very considerate of her."

Sister Winifred put her head to one side and studied him. "Your mother would also like you to reconcile with your brother as soon as possible. She and your father are still quite distressed about your last argument at Thanksgiving. They're worried that one of you will refuse to come for Christmas in order to avoid the other."

Ryan inhaled deeply and ran a hand over his jaw. "My mother told you all that?"

"Why, no," said Sister Winifred, indignant, "but I would hardly expect her to. These are private family matters." She smiled and continued on her way, then paused to say over her shoulder, "Oh, my. The snow has arrived ahead of schedule."

Ryan stared after her until she disappeared around the corner, then he shook his head, his glance taking in all sides of the windowless hallway. He knew that if he stepped out onto the front porch, he would discover snow falling quietly upon the churchyard, and the streets and city beyond.

He found himself equally certain that however the elderly nun had come by her information about his parents' unspoken worries — intuition or eavesdropping or otherwise — she was probably right.

Lost in thought, Ryan made his way to the sacristy, where he sat down heavily in a chair, his errand forgotten. It was true he and Liam had exchanged heated words over the pumpkin pie and coffee while their parents and Liam's wife had sat in silence, glancing unhappily at one another across the dining-room table. To Ryan, however, nothing had distinguished that argument from its many predecessors.

Liam had brought up the usual criticisms of the Catholic Church in general and the Boston archdiocese in particular, and Ryan had responded as honestly as he could, but even when he agreed that certain actions were utterly indefensible and described ongoing reforms, Liam disparaged him. "How can you acknowledge these glaring faults in the Church and remain a part of it?"

"You mean aside from having taken sacred vows? How would my leaving the Church help solve any of the problems you've mentioned? Don't you want people who acknowledge past mistakes and care about justice to stick around to resolve these issues?"

"Leaving would make a stronger statement," Liam retorted. "By staying you align yourself with an authoritarian institution that treats women as second-class citizens and puts maintaining its own power and authority above everything that Jesus professed."

"My vocation isn't about power and authority," said Ryan, taken aback by his brother's vehemence. "It's about a life of service."

Liam barked an ironic laugh. "You forget that I've known you all my life. You're the guy who wouldn't think twice before checking an opponent into the boards if the ref was looking the other way. You used to cheat at Monopoly. I know you, and I know you aren't any holier than anyone else."

"I wasn't called to the priesthood because I was holy. I was called to *become* holier. We all are, whether our vocation is the priesthood or married life or something else."

"I just don't get it." Liam sat back in his chair and studied him, his expression bewildered — and to Ryan's astonishment, deeply pained. "How can you, of all people, shut yourself away in your church? How can you turn your back upon the world instead of engaging in real life, where you could make a difference?"

For a moment Ryan could only stare at him, speechless. "Liam, believe me, I've never been more engaged in real life."

"Maybe that's what you think, sheltered as you are."

"Sheltered?" Ryan shook his head, incredulous. "Listen, Liam. You couldn't be more wrong."

In reply, Liam pushed back his chair and stood, frowning.

"Liam, come visit me at St. Margaret's."

"Are you kidding? I know where I'm not wanted."

"Don't say that. Let me show you around, give you a better idea of what I do. Maybe then you'll understand —"

"I'll never understand you," said Liam angrily, looking suddenly as if he might weep. "I'll never understand the choices you've made."

He stormed from the room, and a few moments later, Ryan heard him telling his children in a falsely cheerful voice that they should kiss their grandparents goodbye, because it was time to go.

It had been a heated, ugly argument to be sure, but had it been their worst? Alone in the sacristy, Ryan played the scene over again in his mind, wishing he had handled it differently. Upon reflection, he realized that he and Liam had not spoken or exchanged a single email since Thanksgiving, but they had not been in daily contact since high school, and Ryan had thought nothing of it.

Evidently he should have. He prayed that he had not become aware too late.

By midafternoon, snow was falling in thick, downy flakes upon St. Margaret's, just as Sister Winifred and the *Boston Globe* had predicted. Gene was busy tinkering with the furnace, so Ryan pulled on his black peacoat and favorite Bruins cap and headed outside to clear the stairs and sidewalks before the children arrived for choir practice.

He was sweeping snow from the front landing when Lucas, the accompanist, walked past on his way to the side entrance.

He carried two cups of coffee, his bag was slung over his chest, and he was muttering angrily to himself. "Get over it," Ryan heard him say. It was practically a shout.

"Get over what?" he called.

Lucas glanced around wildly for a moment before spotting him at the top of the stairs. He hesitated before saying, chagrined, "You know."

"Oh, that." Ryan nodded and continued sweeping. He knew he probably should stay out of it unless Lucas asked for advice, but he could not resist adding, "You should ask her out."

"Are you kidding? Less than two months ago she broke up with her fiancé."

"Which means she's single."

"It's too soon."

"I think I would've heard if there was an official mourning period."

"Sophia doesn't think of me as anything more than a friend."

"Only because you've never given her reason to think of you as anything else."

Lucas's expression revealed that the remark had hit home. "Father," he replied, not unkindly, "no offense, but I'm a little skeptical about taking romantic advice from a priest."

Ryan acknowledged that he made a fair

point, and since he couldn't do anything else to ease the younger man's heartache, he invited him in through the front entrance to save him a bit of a walk in the cold.

Lucas was always the first to arrive, and Sophia, the choir director and unwitting object of his affection, usually followed soon after, but Ryan had finished clearing snow from the front of the church and had moved on to the side without seeing her. A few singers arrived and greeted him cheerfully as they passed on their way indoors, and still there was no sign of her.

Not long before rehearsal was scheduled to begin, a familiar car pulled into the narrow parking lot and a mother and two children he knew well climbed out. "Hi, Father Ryan," Alex called, waving as they crossed the lot. "Nice hat. The Bruins are gonna crush the Penguins tomorrow."

"You'd better believe it," Ryan said, grinning, but when he caught sight of Laurie he felt his heart clench with apprehension. "Hey, Laurie," he said carefully, mindful of Charlotte's watchful gaze. "How's everything going?"

"Oh, everything's fine." Her smile was too bright, falsely cheerful for the children's sake. "The usual."

He thought he knew what that meant, but

he had to ask. "Have you heard from Jason?"

"Oh, sure. We hear from him all the time, don't we, kids?" Laurie turned to Alex and Charlotte, nodding to prompt the response she sought. Charlotte stared deliberately at her boots and shrugged, but Alex nodded happily back. "But you know how it is. The Internet over there is always breaking down, and it takes forever to get online again, but as soon as it's fixed, we're going to get to chat with him again."

"I get to talk with him first," said Alex. "Mom promised. I want to make a rocket for the science fair and I have to ask Dad some stuff."

"That's wise," Ryan said, nodding seriously. "I've heard about you and rockets. It's best to consult with an expert first." To Laurie, he added, "Please let me know if there's anything I can do."

"Thank you, Ryan. I will."

"And tell Jason Merry Christmas from me when you speak with him," Ryan said.

"Of course." Laurie offered a wan smile, looking as if she wished she could say more — and maybe she would later, when the children could not overhear. She placed her hands on her children's backs and guided them toward the door.

Ryan finished clearing the walk, greeting children and parents and babysitters as they arrived for choir rehearsal, chatting briefly with one mother about her daughter's upcoming first communion, conferring quietly with another about her father's longtime battle with cancer. He took prayer requests, referred one young father to the parish food pantry, and offered a kind word to everyone, because it never hurt, and for all he knew, it might be just the thing to help someone get through a difficult day.

The arrivals tapered off, and by the time Ryan finished the sidewalk, he had been alone with his thoughts for quite a while. He returned inside, but just as he took off his coat and hat, Lucas appeared at the top of the stairs. "Have you seen Sophia?"

Ryan tried to hide his amusement. "You're worried she might have gotten stuck in a snowdrift somewhere between here and school?"

Lucas shrugged. "You never know."

"You stay here and start rehearsal," said Ryan, pulling on his coat. "I'll keep watch for Sophia."

"Thanks, Father."

Ryan tugged on his hat and waved Lucas back into the church. Turning, he opened the door and stepped outside — and narrowly avoided colliding with the missing choir director. "There you are," he said, catching the door as it swung shut. "Lucas was getting worried, so he sent me out to search for you."

Shivering, Sophia quickly stepped into the warmth of the stairwell. "I'm not late, am I? I should've taken the bus."

"No, you're right on time, but you're usually early, and that was cause enough for worry." A tightness in her expression told him that something weighed heavily on her mind. Thinking that she might benefit from confiding in a friend, he added, "Lucas cares about you, you know."

Sophia laughed and shrugged out of her coat. "He just doesn't want to be left alone with that pack of wild hooligans."

"That's not fair," said Ryan, smiling. "Not to the kids and not to Lucas. He's great with them and you know it. He's leading them in warm-ups as we speak."

Sophia's quick intake of breath revealed that she was even later than she thought. "Thanks, Father." She stamped her boots on the mat, draped her coat over her arm, and hurried up the staircase and through the doorway into the nave.

Ryan wiped his feet, removed his coat and hat, and followed after, wondering what he could do to encourage Sophia and Lucas to have a long-overdue conversation about their feelings for each other. He couldn't do much, he concluded ruefully, not without being overbearing and intrusive. There were some matters of the heart people had to figure out on their own.

When he entered the church, the children were singing "I Heard the Bells on Christmas Day," a beautiful, poignant arrangement of the familiar carol he had never heard until Sophia and Lucas began teaching it to the children. Smiling to hear Alex hit every note of his solo with sweet perfection, he did not realize Sister Winifred had joined him until she spoke almost at his elbow. "It's painful to be the one not chosen," she murmured sympathetically, her gaze on the choir director and the accompanist who watched her, surely believing himself unobserved, his yearning and resignation plainly visible in his face, evident in every note he played. "Even when you acknowledge, deep down, that the choice was the right one, it hurts to think that the one you love prefers someone else." She smiled and patted his arm. "Call your mother tomorrow. Tell her everything will be all right. And then call your brother and see that you make it so."

"I will," said Ryan slowly, staring at her, wondering. "I will."

# CHAPTER FOURTEEN:
## SEPTEMBER–DECEMBER 1863

Mosby's Raiders proved maddeningly elusive, and in his letters home Charley's mood oscillated between proud resolve and fuming exasperation. The hottest summer in memory seared and exhausted the First Massachusetts Cavalry as they chased phantoms through the woods and fields of Virginia, their horses' hooves churning up clouds of choking dust as they rode. Once verdant meadows turned brown and brittle beneath the unrelenting sun, and with grazing limited the horses grew thin and tired. At night, bands of rebels stealthily crossed the Union picket lines to capture a sutler's wagon or to cut down an unsuspecting sentry before vanishing without a trace, keeping the federal soldiers constantly on edge.

From late August to the middle of September, the regiment bivouacked at Waterloo and Orleans, to the rear of Plum Run, setting up pickets along the creek and sending frequent patrols into Flint Hill. Though the heat lingered, Charley reported, the weather was otherwise delightful, the scenery beautiful, and food plentiful, although foraging soldiers tempted by farmhouses too far from the road often found themselves betrayed by resentful Confederate sympathizers and captured or killed by partisan rangers.

Autumn brought relief from the enervating heat and humidity but not from danger. On September 13, General George Meade sent the army across the Rappahannock, the cavalry taking the advance. While the Second Massachusetts crossed the Rixeyville Ford, Charley and the First engaged General Lee's cavalry near Culpepper, eventually forcing them down to the Rapidan River, but not before the rebel troops dug in and made a stand. "Here our regiment was ordered up to support a battery," Charley wrote a few days later. "The shot and shell were flying over our heads, by this time pretty lively, and the first thing I knew I saw a 12 lb shot coming bounding along it made two jumps in front of us and then went zip close by my leg and hit Sergeant Reed, my quartermaster sergeant below the knee taking his leg off, he was the next man to me."

Shaking, heart pounding, Henry put the letter aside and went out to the garden, but his awareness of his son's narrow escape followed him. He sat on a bench, planted his hands on his knees, and took deep breaths to steady his nerves, forcing the horrifying, all-too-vivid images from his mind's eye. The unfortunate sergeant had been the next man to Charley. The difference between survival and life-shattering injury had been a matter of only a few inches, a minuscule alteration to the angle of the cannon.

Before long, curiosity and concern for his son overcame his dread, and he returned to his study and the letter. For weeks the family had wondered anxiously where Charley was and what he was doing. The papers reported that the entire army was in motion, which seemed unlikely, but they offered little specific news of the First Massachusetts Cavalry. Charley's letters, as alarming or vague as they could sometimes be, were a far better source of information — and they assured Henry that, at least on the day his son had written them, he had been safe and unharmed.

As the rebel shot had flown thick and fast over their heads, Charley's letter continued, the men had not shown much courage at first, ducking and flinching whenever any shells burst near them. Even so, they did not falter but stuck to the task, driving the rebels back all afternoon and into the evening. The next day the First Massachusetts Cavalry was in the advance, and Charley had charge of his company. "We met the rebs at Cedar Mt. but they retired to the Rapidan," he wrote, his haphazard grammar and spelling revealing the lingering thrill of danger survived. "There we got into it as thick as I ever want to. They had seen pieces of artillery playing into us (the 1st Mass 1st R. I. and 6th Ohio) we had to manoeuvre under this fire it was not over jolly. Our squadron dashed across a field where we were peppered finely but we got behind a hill where they could not hit us. Our men were sent out to skirmish and one regiment of rebs charged them but were driven back by our men they try to frighten our boys by yelling and howling but it is no go."

Charley and his men dug in behind a fence, where they stayed up all night under arms. The next morning they were at last relieved, having had nothing to eat for more than twenty-four hours. As they had been in the saddle nearly all of that time, their horses were dreadfully spent as well.

"I had several narrow escapes being covered with dirt from shells several times," Charley reflected somberly, "one bursting so close to my face as to make me feel the blast of hot air but thank God none of our officers are hurt. I don't know yet how many men are killed. They may talk about the gaiety of a soldiers life but it strikes me as pretty earnest work when shells are ripping and tearing your men to pieces."

The First was resting that day while the remainder of the brigade engaged the enemy, hoping to provoke them into revealing their strength. "I shall write again and more fully as soon as I get a chance," Charley promised. "Don't be anxious. God bless you all at home."

Henry choked out a laugh. " 'Don't be anxious'?" he echoed, a second laugh escaping his throat as a sob. "What a cold and stoic father I would be if I were not anxious!"

When he had composed himself, he read aloud selected excerpts to Alice, Edith, and Anne, but let Ernest read the letter in its entirety. Ernest should know what horrors awaited him should he decide to enroll at West Point and follow his brother into war.

"My Dear Charley," Henry wrote in reply

a few days later. "Your letter of the 16th relieved our minds; and we are very thankful that you are safe, and have escaped thus far, without harm, from so many dangers, and so much exposure. I cannot help wishing, that you were still acting as Adjutant, but perhaps you know best. You do not tell me how your health and strength hold out; nor whether you have coats and blankets enough. You must guard against chills in the cold nights." Then, since he knew his eldest son would tolerate only so much fatherly advice, he shared the news from home, hoping that fond reminders of family and friends would hearten his young soldier.

The weeks passed in an exchange of letters between Craigie House and the regiment's encampment, in work and in the sweeter distraction of playful moments with his daughters, in prayer and in anxious reflection. Henry frequently sent parcels of supplies to the front — beaver gloves and silk handkerchiefs, cigars and brandy for medicinal purposes, seed cakes and gingersnaps, tinned bologna and syrup — but more than one shipment mysteriously vanished along the way until Henry, thoroughly exasperated, learned to circumvent would-be thieves by sending Charley's packages directly to the regimental sutler in

Washington, an honest and reliable fellow who could be trusted to carry them safely to their intended recipient.

Letters, at least, traveled fairly reliably through the mails, and helped raise the morale of the young cavalryman in the field and his anxious family back home. Charley told of early-morning skirmishes, of foraging patrols, of nuisance raids intended to provoke a more significant confrontation between the two armies, which seemed almost permanently fixed along the Rappahannock and the Rapidan. He seemed eager to move, to exchange tedium and discomfort for action, but beneath his son's yearning for battle and glory, Henry discerned an emerging maturity forged in the kiln of hardship and danger. After weeks of sleeping through the night in the saddle, awaiting the alarm of a rebel raid; of days when water, hardtack, and a bit of salt pork were his only sustenance; of exposure to the deafening roar of artillery and rifle fire, the chilling wail of the rebel yell, and the gruesome sight of dead and wounded men, Charley had become a reliable patrol leader, an adept skirmisher. Experience had spoiled his boyhood fancies of the glamour and glory of war, all flashing sabers and wind-tossed banners and gallant cavalry charges, but it had not lessened his enthusiasm for military life or his commitment to the Union.

For all his worry, for all his longtime pacifism, for all his regret that Charley had enlisted without permission, Henry found himself increasingly proud of him.

In the first week of October, President Lincoln had issued a Proclamation of Thanksgiving, noting that despite the destruction of war, the year 1863 had been bountiful, with fruitful fields, steady industry, widening national borders, increasing population, and plenteous mines. Even in the midst of a civil war of unprecedented magnitude and severity, peace had been preserved with foreign nations, order had been maintained everywhere except the theater of war, and laws had been made, respected, and obeyed. It seemed fit and proper, the president declared, that these blessings "should be solemnly, reverently and gratefully acknowledged as with one heart and one voice by the whole American People. I do therefore invite my fellow citizens in every part of the United States, and also those who are at sea and those who are sojourning in foreign lands, to set apart and observe the last Thursday of November next, as a day of

Thanksgiving and Praise to our beneficent Father who dwelleth in the Heavens."

Massachusetts had long celebrated Thanksgiving as a state holiday, and Henry approved of the president's wish to unite the country in a national day of gratitude and prayer on one particular, common date. He decided to mark the occasion with a feast at Craigie House, and he invited his brother-in-law Tom Appleton, and Harriott Appleton, Fanny's widowed stepmother, to celebrate with him and the children.

Thanksgiving Day dawned with heartening news from Tennessee, where General Ulysses S. Grant had broken the Confederate siege of Chattanooga with decisive victories at Lookout Mountain and Missionary Ridge.

"It will not be long now until the war is over and Charley will come home," Mrs. Appleton said as the family lingered at the table, warmed by the company and the fire and renewed hope for victory, peace, and reunion.

Henry wanted to agree, but the war had already dragged on more than two and a half years, and despite General Grant's victories in the west, he could not foresee an end to it anytime soon. "Let us drink to the health of all the lieutenants in the Army of the Potomac," he proposed, raising his glass.

The others lifted their glasses and joined him in the toast, their voices solemn and prayerful, ever mindful of the absent loved ones whose presence would have made their holiday complete, of the empty places at other families' tables, North and South alike, the empty arms of grieving wives and mothers, the empty hopes of bereft fathers and children.

The next day, Henry wrote a short letter to Charley, to wish him well as always, to describe their Thanksgiving feast and to say how much they had longed to have him among them. He sent off the letter and turned his thoughts again to his work; he had begun to have his translation of Dante put in type, in order to have a clear copy to work upon while making his notes. On Saturday he hoped for a letter from Charley, but the only news from the front he received that day came via the papers, which announced that the Army of the Potomac was advancing on General Lee's position at Mine Run.

Three days later, on the first of December, Henry had just sat down to supper with his children when he was summoned to the door to receive a telegram. A sudden hush fell over the dining room. The last time he had received a telegram, a thunderous knock upon the front door had awakened the household at midnight and Henry had learned of the death of the good and generous Reverend Richardson, who had so kindly taken Charley into his home the previous summer while he was stricken with camp fever.

But this was not the middle of the night, and Henry would not have his children learn to jump in fear at every knock upon the door. "You may begin without me, children," he said calmly as he pushed back his chair and rose. Edith and Annie happily complied, but Ernest and Alice exchanged guarded looks across the table.

Henry hurried to the front door. "Who sent it?" he asked as he took the folded paper from the messenger.

"I don't know, sir," the lad replied. "I only carry them. Another fellow takes them off the wire."

Henry knew that, just as he knew he was delaying the inevitable. It could be news from Washington, he thought, Sumner announcing some bold new measure passed by the Senate, or better yet, arrangements for a long-overdue visit. It could be word from his publishers, news about the recently published *Tales of a Wayside Inn* or an editorial note about the forthcoming Dante. Nevertheless, he steeled himself and opened the telegram.

The first glance told him that it had indeed come from Washington; the second, that it was not from his friend Sumner but from the Department of War: "Our dispatches state that Lieut Longfellow of First Mass Cavalry was severly wounded in the Face at Mount Hope Church on Friday Nov 27th. No chance of any wounded being sent in at present."

A strange, distant roaring filled his ears, and as he stood staring at the slip of paper, he felt his vision going gray around the edges, his hands and feet going tingling and numb as if from too lengthy exposure to cold.

"Sir?" an urgent voice prompted him. "Mr. Longfellow, sir?"

With a start, Henry glanced up to find the messenger regarding him curiously. "Yes?"

"Do you wish to send a reply, sir?"

"No — no, thank you." Henry fumbled for the doorknob. "Not at present. Good evening."

"That'll be three dollars and fifty-three cents, sir," the messenger blurted before he could close the door.

Henry kept his anguish in check as he paid the lad and sent him on his way, his thoughts racing with plans and with the inescapable imagery the telegram evoked in his mind's eye. Then he returned to the dining room, where Ernest and Alice were finishing their soup and conversing in murmurs while the little girls happily discussed a Christmas tea party they were planning for their dolls.

"I'm afraid I must depart for Washington City immediately," he interrupted, his voice miraculously steady. "Charley has — I'm quite sorry to say that he has been rather badly injured. I must get to the capital at once, so that I may be there to receive him when he is brought to the hospital."

Anne let out a muffled shriek and seized Edith's arm, while Alice nodded gravely, her stricken gaze fixed on his. Ernest bolted to his feet and blurted, "I'll come with you."

Henry was about to refuse, but then he realized how useful his steady, sensible son would be to him in such a time. "Of course. We'll leave at once."

The girls would be well looked after by their governess in his absence, Henry knew, but he hastily sent off notes to trusted neighbors to inform them of his unexpected journey and where they could reach him in

Washington. He and Ernest quickly packed their bags, and after the girls saw them off in a flurry of tearful embraces, promises to pray for Charley, and earnest pleas for them to write as soon as they had word of their dear brother, they raced to the wharf, where they caught the five o'clock Fall River steamer for New York.

There were no staterooms to be had, so Henry and Ernest retired to the saloon, where they settled into uncomfortable armchairs, which would serve as their beds for the night. "We must not imagine the worst," Henry said, as much to inspirit himself as to comfort his son. "The telegram said it was a severe wound, not mortal."

"Of course, Papa," Ernest murmured, pale and quiet.

The night was stormy and a severe gale rocked the ship in the Sound, so although Henry and Ernest tried to sleep, they managed no better than a fitful doze. The storm delayed their arrival in New York City, and moments after they raced down the gangplank to the pier, they realized they had just missed the first train to Washington. They waited impatiently for the next, endured what felt like an interminable journey by rail, and at long last arrived in the capital at ten o'clock in the evening of December 2.

They took rooms at the Willard Hotel, checked with the clerk for telegrams from home or the War Department — there were none — and dispatched a messenger to Sumner's residence to inform him of their arrival in Washington and the dreadful circumstances that had brought them there.

After a restless night, Henry and Ernest awoke to the dismaying realization that they had received no news of Charley overnight, nothing regarding his condition or his whereabouts. Nevertheless, in expectation of his arrival, they quit the Willard and took a more spacious suite at Ebbitt House, three doors down the street from Sumner's home. Then they began their urgent search for Charley, not knowing in which of the many official and makeshift hospitals scattered throughout the city he could be, desperate to see for themselves that he lived, that he was being given every attention. To their dismay, an officer of the Sanitary Commission informed them that Charley had not yet arrived from the front, and worse yet, that no one could tell them where he was or when he might arrive.

After signing an oath of allegiance, Henry managed to secure a military pass that allowed them to cross military lines. He and Ernest immediately boarded a steamer that carried them across the Potomac, past several ships of the Russian fleet, and on to Alexandria, Virginia, where they sought out Colonel John H. Devereux, the superintendent of military railroads.

"I'm searching for my son," Henry explained, breathless from exhaustion, haste, and worry. "Two days ago I received word that he was severely injured, but I've heard nothing of him since, and of course —" Ernest rested a hand upon his shoulder, lending him his strength. "As his father, I will imagine the worst. You understand."

"Certainly I do," the colonel replied kindly, and he offered to telegraph stations along the railroad line to ask for news. Gratified, Henry thanked him, and after the message was sent down the wire, he and Ernest settled down to wait in the seats the colonel offered them in his office.

All afternoon, Henry and Ernest waited for a reply, starting at every first click of an incoming message, sinking back into their chairs again when the operator glanced their way and shook his head in regret. With each passing hour they grew more dispirited, until eventually, reluctantly, they departed on the last steamer of the day back to Washington.

"What could this bewildering silence

mean?" Ernest asked as they made their weary way back to Ebbitt House.

"I hope it signifies nothing but the usual inefficiencies of the military," Henry replied, reluctant to confess what more dire occurrence it could portend.

Back in their suite, Ernest wrote to Alice to let her know they had arrived but had not yet seen Charley. Exhausted, they then retired for the night, determined to resume the search at daybreak.

At midnight, a brisk rapping upon the door woke Henry from unsettling dreams. Groggy, he drew on his dressing gown and opened the door to a messenger carrying a telegram from Colonel Devereux. "Lt Longfellow is in Hospital at Brandy Station and doing well," the colonel had wired. "He will be sent to Washn tomorrow so says Capt Beckwith A.D.C. to Gen Patrick you can meet him at Alexa without difficulty as it will probably be late in the day before your son arrives."

Greatly relieved, Henry was tempted to wake Ernest and share the encouraging news, but good sense and parental concern won out, and he let his steadfast boy sleep. Instead he sat on the edge of the bed, buried his head in his hands, and silently wept. Charley was doing well, the colonel had

405

said. He might be disfigured and enduring great pain, but it seemed that he would live. Surely Colonel Devereux would not have encouraged Henry's hopes if it were not so.

Henry returned to bed and claimed a few more hours of troubled sleep, his dreams haunted by scenes of Charley, his face swathed in bloody bandages, crying out in pain with every jolt of the railcar as it rumbled through Virginia.

In the morning, Ernest agreed that the news from Brandy Station was promising, and they were just going down to breakfast when another telegram from Colonel Devereux arrived: "Lt Longfellow shot in chest not in face. If the wounded are embarked at the time proposed they will arrive at Washington about six o'clock this p.m."

Henry and Ernest exchanged startled looks. "Not shot in the face, but in the chest?" said Ernest. "This sounds like good news, don't you think, Papa?"

"Many a soldier has perished from a chest wound," said Henry, uncertain, "but yes, it does seem somehow less dire, as wounds go."

"I wish we could see him and judge for ourselves." Frustration sharpened Ernest's voice. "I half expect to receive another telegram before we sit down at the breakfast table, informing us that Charley has been wounded not in the chest but in the back-side, and he'll arrive in Washington a week from Tuesday."

Henry almost laughed. "Patience is a virtue, son."

"Even the most virtuous of saints would agree that after our haste to get here, this interminable waiting is unbearable."

"All the more so because somewhere Charley is waiting too," said Henry, "aboard a train or detained at a station, surely in great discomfort, and with his wounds unat-tended."

He had very little patience left for the military's inconsistencies and inefficiencies, but he was powerless to speed Charley's journey. He and Ernest had no choice but to wait, but they found some consolation in knowing the specific hour Charley was expected to reach the capital — and that perhaps he had not been as badly hurt as they had feared.

With a long stretch of empty hours to fill, after breakfast Henry wrote cheery, optimis-tic letters home to Edith and Annie, as Ernest had written to Alice the night before. Then Henry sent a brief note down the block to Sumner. His steadfast friend promptly replied by offering to escort

Henry and Ernest to the Capitol to view *Westward the Course of Empire Takes Its Way,* a magnificent fresco the German artist Emanuel Leutze had painted on the wall of the landing in the west stairway the year before.

Sumner's company provided a welcome distraction, but Henry was ever mindful of the time, and by six o'clock he and Ernest had parted company with the senator and were anxiously waiting at the railway station. For hours they sat or paced on the platform, rushing to meet every train, frantically scanning the disembarking passengers for Charley — and soon, for any wounded soldier at all, for although numerous men in uniform were riding the trains, it was evident from their dress and manner that they had not come from the front.

"They will put all the wounded on one train," Henry speculated, dismayed and increasingly restless. "Surely it will come soon."

Ernest made no reply, but strode to the edge of the platform and gazed off down the tracks to the south, as if he could draw his brother's train to them by sheer force of longing.

They waited at the station until the last train arrived at ten o'clock, but Charley was not on it. Discouraged and disbelieving, they returned to Ebbitt House, where they contemplated all the possible reasons for the delay over a late supper. Then, after reassuring each other that someone would have telegraphed them if Charley had taken a turn for the worse, they retired for the night.

Again a brisk rapping upon the door woke Henry shortly after midnight. "Charley," he murmured, swiftly rising and snatching up his dressing gown. When he tore open the door, his heart plummeted to discover not his missing son, but the now familiar messenger, bearing yet another telegram.

"Have just seen your son," Colonel Devereux had written not twenty minutes before. "He is bright & feeling well. Has a slight wound in shoulder ball glancing upward and no bones broken. He remains here tonight & will leave on train for Washington at 12.50 PM tomorrow I have informed him of your Hotel in case anything should cause you to pass each other accidentally in trying to meet."

"The colonel writes as if Charley is up and walking around," said Ernest, who had woken at the knock and had read the telegram over his father's shoulder.

"That may simply be an imprecise turn of

phrase," Henry cautioned him, "and yet I feel immeasurable relief knowing where he is, and that Colonel Devereux has seen him, and has spoken to him."

Ernest concurred, and with an enormous yawn, he hugged Henry and returned to bed. Henry, his head buzzing with questions and plans, lay awake in bed long after a church bell struck one o'clock, but eventually fatigue overcame him and he drifted off to sleep.

In the morning, Henry and Ernest made sure the suite was ready to receive their injured soldier, and Henry wrote to Alice to share the good news of Charley's condition and imminent arrival, concluding with what he hoped was a note of reassuring levity. "Think of the mischief done by leaving out the little word 'not' in the first telegram!" he wrote. " '*Not* severely injured,' it should have been."

At breakfast Henry and Ernest resolved that if Charley were not aboard the anticipated train, they would travel to Alexandria and transport him to Washington themselves. At noon they returned to the station, where they joined dozens of other anxious civilians waiting on the platform, gazing worriedly down the tracks, straining their ears for the rumble of iron wheels and the shriek of the whistle.

At long last they heard it — the chugging of the engine, the squealing of brakes. Henry took Ernest by the arm and steered his son alongside the train, weaving their way through the crowd, craning their necks to peer in through the windows.

"Papa, look there," said Ernest, gesturing to a baggage car near the end of the train. The doors had been flung wide, and haggard, bloodied, limping soldiers were disembarking, their soiled uniforms littered with pieces of the yellow straw strewn about to absorb bodily fluids and perhaps offer a modicum of comfort. As Henry and Ernst hurried toward it, they observed other soldiers carried off on stretchers, their bandages soiled and soaked through with blood.

Ernst glimpsed him first. "Charley," he shouted, waving his hand in the air. Henry spotted him then, and felt a chill when the huddled figure on the stretcher beneath the blue wool blanket did not stir at his brother's cry. Seized by a sudden panic that Charley would be swallowed up by the throng and lost within the vast system of military hospitals and converted public buildings, Henry pushed his way through the crowd, all politeness and dignity forgotten, until he reached his stricken boy's side.

"Charley," he gasped, taking hold of one pale hand folded across Charley's chest. "Charley, it's Papa. We're here, Ernest and I. We're here."

Charley's blue eyes fluttered open, bleary and bloodshot. "Hello, Papa," he said faintly, managing a wan smile before his eyes drifted shut again. He looked utterly bedraggled, his face gaunt and whiskered, his hair disheveled and flecked with straw.

"Come with me," Henry commanded the two soldiers carrying the stretcher, fixing them with a look that precluded dissent. With Ernest following behind, Henry led them to the ambulance Sumner had arranged, but just as they were loading Charley on board, he roused himself enough to explain that his friend Captain Henry Pickering Bowditch was among the wounded, and to ask if they could see to him as well. At Henry's nod, Ernest raced back to the luggage car, found the injured captain, and arranged for him to be carried onto the ambulance beside Charley.

They sped off to Ebbitt House, and before long the two wounded officers were resting in comfortable beds in a large, airy suite, where cheerful sunlight streamed in through three tall windows. Bowditch had been shot in the right arm just below the elbow, but he said it was only a slight injury, and he seemed otherwise well and in good spirits. Charley's bandages had not been changed in three days, and when Henry unwrapped the soiled cloths, it was immediately evident that his injury was far more serious than his companion's. As Henry washed and dressed the wounds, Charley explained that he had been shot in the back while on patrol near New Hope Church. The bullet had struck him beneath one shoulder blade and had plunged through his torso, nicking his spine and exiting on the other side. Another officer had dragged him back through the Union lines, where he was briefly examined and given up for dead. But inexplicably, the ball had missed his lungs and heart and arteries and had not severed his spinal cord, so although he had endured great pain as he had languished in a church converted into a battlefield dressing station, he had not perished.

Charley's long, halting, agonizing journey to Washington was an ordeal best forgotten.

Henry ordered beef tea and custard brought up to the room, and was gratified to observe his two patients digging in with hearty appetites. Afterward, Bowditch immediately sank into a deep sleep, but Charley had only just begun to doze when they heard the tramping of boots in the hallway and the bang of a fist upon the door — the army surgeon come to check on his patients. Charley sat up obligingly as the physician examined him, but sank back against his pillow gratefully as soon as it was over and closed his eyes. "Keep him quiet," the army surgeon instructed Henry, who nodded. Next the physician approached Bowditch's bed, peered intently at his bandaged right arm, and then turned, nodded, and departed, all without a word.

"I suppose we should keep the other fellow quiet too," remarked Ernest, and Henry was so overcome with sudden relief and thankfulness that he was obliged to smother a laugh, lest he dissolve into tears.

Charley and Bowditch slept well that night, and in the morning, Dr. Hoskins, who had accompanied the wounded soldiers on the train, came by to examine them. Bowditch he declared quite well indeed, but after announcing that Charley was much improved, he took Henry aside. "Mr. Longfellow," he said, lowering his voice so no one else would overhear, "my duty to myself and to you requires me to say that your son's wound is very serious."

"Yes," Henry replied. "So I have seen."

"You should know that although he seems to be on the mend, the injury to his vertebrae may yet result in paralysis."

Henry's heart plummeted, but he steeled himself and asked, "When might he be stricken? At what point in his convalescence will we know he has escaped that fate?"

"As to your first question, paralysis might ensue next week, next year, or never. As to your second —" Dr. Hoskins frowned and shook his head. "I regret that because of the damage to the bone, the chance of paralysis will persist for the rest of his life."

"I see," said Henry faintly, sickened by the picture of his vibrant, active, athletic boy confined for the rest of his life to bed, to inaction, to misery.

"I will, of course, leave to your discretion what you tell him of this, and when."

"Thank you, doctor." Henry took a deep, shaky breath. "I'll say nothing at present. We must say nothing to alarm him, nothing to bring on melancholy. What good would it do to warn him of a tragedy that may never come to pass?" He shook his head vigorously. "No. No. We must encourage optimism, keep his spirits up. That will speed his healing."

The doctor bowed assent.

With Ernest's help, Henry kept the young officers comfortable, well fed, and rested throughout the day, tempting them with rich custards and nourishing broths, taking dictation when they wished to write letters home, reading aloud from novels and newspapers. Two physicians and a medical inspector came by in the evening, and when the latter, a Dr. George M. McGill, gave Charley a more optimistic appraisal than Dr. Hoskins had done, Henry waited until the doctors left the suite, then hurried after Dr. McGill and asked to speak to him alone. "You believe Charley will continue to improve?" he asked.

"As long as he rests properly and does not overexert himself too soon, I do indeed," the doctor replied. "However, the wound will be long in healing. Your son will not be fit for service for more than six months."

This too was good news, of a sort, for Henry was in no hurry to have Charley rejoin his regiment. "Then you don't expect that he will suffer any latent effects — sudden paralysis, for example?"

Dr. McGill regarded him kindly. "There is a very small chance, so small that I didn't bother to mention it. I do hope you won't trouble your son — or yourself — with worries about such an unlikely occurrence."

Greatly relieved, Henry shook the doctor's hand and thanked him profusely, but he could not entirely dismiss Dr. Hoskins's warning. Nothing would do but to see Charley safely home to Craigie House, where he could convalesce properly.

On December 7, district surgeon Dr. Bates — a modest, deft little man, kind and obliging — took charge of Charley's case, and Henry soon persuaded him to issue a certificate for a leave of absence so Charley could recover from his wounds at home. While Charley rested at Ebbitt House, gaining strength for the journey, friends called to wish him well, and he was heartily grateful for the distraction, never having been the sort to enjoy lounging about in bed with a good book or his own thoughts. Bowditch's parents had arrived from Boston earlier that day, much alarmed despite Henry's telegrams attesting to his good condition. "We lost our eldest son earlier this year, in March," Bowditch's father quietly confided to Henry while his wife fussed with her son's blankets. "He was wounded in the abdomen in the first charge at Kelly's Ford."

"My dear Mr. Bowditch, I'm so sorry."

"He might have survived, except the two surgeons who discovered him lying on the ground beside his horse had no means to carry him from the battlefield, and the ambulance corps never approached him there." He gestured toward his younger son, who was lying in bed, smiling up at his doting mother. "So you understand, Mr. Longfellow, why neither of us could have a moment's peace until we saw our boy safe and sound."

Henry understood perfectly.

Once assured that Charley and Bowditch were in good hands and good company, Henry accompanied Sumner to the Capitol for the opening of the Thirty-Eighth Congress. Outside the Senate chamber, he chanced upon several old friends — Senators William Pitt Fessenden of Maine, James Dixon of Connecticut, and John P. Hale of New Hampshire — and while they were chatting, others recognized him and joined the growing circle of admiring onlookers. When Henry mentioned that he would be leaving Washington shortly, Congressman Caleb Lyon blurted, "Mr. Longfellow, you must sit for a photograph before you go." When Henry demurred, the congressman insisted, "Yes, sir, you and Senator Sumner together. What a fine memento of your visit such a portrait would be!"

Henry and Sumner exchanged a look;

Sumner shrugged, and Henry decided it would be easier to acquiesce than to explain that the only memento of that visit he wanted to take home was his two sons, both hale and hearty. Thus the following morning, Henry, his sons, and Sumner visited the studio of Alexander Gardner at Seventh and S Streets to have their portraits made. The renowned photographist took images of Charley and Ernest separately, but he sat Henry and Sumner together. "I shall call this portrait *The Politics and Poetry of New England,*" he declared in a proud Scottish brogue.

At eight thirty that evening, Henry, his sons, Bowditch, and his parents left Washington on the late train to Boston. Henry organized berths for the two wounded soldiers, but the rest of the party were obliged to make do with regular seats, ill suited for a comfortable night's rest. They arrived in New York at half past seven the next morning, stiff and weary, and with several hours before their connection to Boston, Henry took rooms for them at the Fifth Avenue Hotel. When they were comfortably settled, he sent word to Dr. William H. Van Buren, the distinguished surgeon and founder of the Sanitary Commission, asking him to send an associate to examine the young soldiers. Instead, Dr. Van Buren attended them himself, and after he dressed their wounds and proclaimed them none the worse for their railway journey, he refused to accept any fee. "I am not often sentimental," he said, "but I feel disposed to be so this morning."

Before they boarded the noon train to Boston, Henry telegraphed Alice to let her know that they expected to reach home at ten o'clock, and that he wanted Dr. Morrill Wyman to meet them there. Many hours and more than two hundred miles later, the Longfellows and Bowditches parted company at the station in Boston, and a hired carriage took Henry and his sons the last few miles of the journey home.

Alice, Edith, and Anne greeted them at the door, overflowing with sisterly devotion and concern for their wounded brother. A hot supper awaited them, and Charley's expression as he gazed around the table at the affectionate company, felt the warmth of the hearth, and tasted the nourishing food told Henry that his runaway soldier had never appreciated his home and family more than at that moment.

Shortly after the family finished supper, Dr. Wyman arrived to examine and dress Charley's wounds. It was nearly midnight by the time Charley was finally put to bed, exhausted and in some pain, but well fed, warm, and content.

The road ahead of Charley would be long and difficult, Henry knew. His convalescence would be painful and slow and surely frustrating. But at that late hour, all of Henry's children were safe and happy and together, and that was enough.

# CHAPTER FIFTEEN: THE NUN'S TALE

For as long as Winifred could remember, she had wanted to become a nun. As a girl she had daydreamed about entering the convent the way her friends had wistfully imagined heading out to Hollywood to become movie stars. Her parents were devout, and since she was the fifth eldest of eight and her father's earnings as a vacuum cleaner salesman could stretch only so far, when she was sixteen and asked her parents' blessing to enter the convent, they cried a little but agreed.

Winifred had never regretted or even doubted her decision, but that did not mean she did not, from time to time, wonder and question. Fortunately, the mother superior of her order, Sister Mary Joan, kindly encouraged Winifred to come to her whenever she was puzzled or unsure. They would drink tea in her office and chat, or walk around the gardens in fair weather, and afterward Winifred always understood things at least a little better than before.

One winter afternoon, shortly after taking her vows as a novice, Winifred sought out Sister Mary Joan and asked how to know when she truly heard God speaking to her. "I've been reading about the subconscious," she said. "When I pray, how do I know that what I hear is the Lord's voice and not merely an echo of my own thoughts?"

Sister Mary Joan rested her chin on her hand and regarded her fondly. "How do you know that the Lord isn't speaking to you through your subconscious?"

Winifred stared at her, startled. "Well, I don't know. Can He do that?" When the mother superior smiled, Winifred quickly added, "Of course He can. I just . . . didn't realize that He did."

"Our heavenly father doesn't always speak to us through a burning bush," said Sister Mary Joan. "How much easier it would be for us if He did — but if we wanted the easy path, we wouldn't have chosen this life."

Winifred nodded agreement.

"When you think you're hearing God speak to you in a moment of quiet contemplation, ask yourself if what you hear reflects the truth of God's word," said Sister Mary Joan. "Is it something Jesus would affirm?

Does it draw you closer to Him?"

"What if I'm not sure?"

"You should always feel free to talk with me, or with another trusted spiritual advisor." Sister Mary Joan smiled. "Remember that sometimes God speaks to us through other people."

"Really?" Winifred brightened at a sudden thought. "Does that mean that God might sometimes use us to speak to other people? Maybe when we don't even realize it?"

"Logically that would follow — and so we should be ever mindful of what we say and do, and try always to be instruments of God's peace and love."

The mother superior's reflection so impressed Winifred that for a time thereafter she said very little, worried that she might mistranslate something God wanted her to say. After praying earnestly about it and talking it over with Sister Mary Joan, she realized that if God wanted to speak through her, she should trust that He would manage to get His message across properly. The best thing she could do would be to get out of the way and let it happen.

As the years went by and God's plan led her from the beloved convent to St. Margaret's Church, Winifred remembered Sister Mary Joan fondly and longed to discuss questions of theology and faith with her over a cup of tea. Often when she wrestled with the day's challenges or contemplated an ethical matter, she would imagine herself back in Sister Mary Joan's office at the convent, and without fail her thoughts would become clearer, solutions came to mind, worry fell away.

As she grew older, she developed the habit of unwittingly talking aloud instead of keeping the conversations all to herself. Maybe speaking helped her to think. Maybe — although she hoped not — she had become vain in her old age and simply liked to hear the sound of her own voice. She hadn't considered the habit a matter of much concern until she began to notice worried glances from parishioners who came upon her unexpectedly in the church or parish house and found her apparently engrossed in conversation with an imaginary friend. Once a darling little girl from the choir, Charlotte, had asked her soberly if she spoke to angels. Winifred had laughed, delighted, and reminded Charlotte that perhaps they all sometimes entertained angels unawares. Still, she tried to remember to practice the mental exercise in solitude rather than upset anyone, and she supposed she succeeded more often than not.

Yet it was far too easy to forget when she was distracted, as she was at that moment by the lovely music of the choir, and by the sight of the blond woman in the red beret sitting in a pew near the front, staring at the choir and looking utterly bereft. She was Alex and Charlotte's mother, Winifred recalled, and her husband had gone missing in Afghanistan. How frightened she must be, the poor dear, having no idea where her husband was, if he had been captured or injured or killed. She probably thought God had abandoned them.

As Winifred watched, Laurie twisted and knotted up her scarf as if she meant to strangle it or fashion it into a garrote to strangle someone else. "Oh, my," Winifred exclaimed. "Are you preparing to do battle?"

Startled, Laurie glanced away from the choir. "I'm sorry, Sister. Preparing to do what?"

"To do battle — with the forces of darkness, perhaps." Winifred's arms were filled with hymnals, so she indicated the poor, battered scarf with a nod.

Glancing down at her lap, Laurie gasped, released the scarf, and quickly tried to smooth out the wrinkles.

"Are you all right, my dear?" Winifred inquired.

"Yes, Sister, I just . . . have a lot on my mind. It's a crazy time of year."

"It's a season of miracles," Winifred agreed, nodding.

"Yes, that too."

Winifred smiled in reply, but Laurie looked so upset that Winifred observed her from the corner of her eye as she continued tidying up the pews. When the choir sang the carol's most profound lyric, she echoed, "God is not dead, nor does He sleep."

"What?" Laurie said, startled from her reverie. "What did you say?"

"From the carol." Sister Winifred indicated the choir with a nod. "It's not scripture, of course, but poetry, and nonetheless true. God is listening, my dear. He knows your troubles and he hears your prayers."

"Sometimes I wonder."

"I suppose we all do, sometimes." Winifred smiled, her heart overflowing with compassion and concern. "Everything's going to be all right, my dear. Have faith."

Laurie pressed her lips together, and for a long moment, she seemed to be fighting back sobs of anguish. "Thank you," she managed to say. "You're very kind."

"Oh, that's not mere kindness." Winifred paused and tilted her head, thinking. Should she leave it at that? But what about darling little Charlotte? A few weeks ago, Winifred had been straightening the pews when she happened to glance into the girl's open backpack. She had seen the Christmas story — which she had already read, in both draft and finished form — and it was delightful. She could not imagine what sort of teacher would write such thoughtlessly cruel comments on the work of a student as conscientious as Charlotte.

Winifred decided to speak up.

"And I know for a fact that Charlotte wrote every word of her Christmas story," she declared. "I don't think you ever would have doubted that, but it's nice to know for certain, isn't it?"

Laurie nodded, looking utterly bewildered. "Yes," she murmured, fighting back tears. "It's best to know."

Winifred put away a few of the hymnals, enough to free one of her hands so she could pat Laurie reassuringly on the shoulder. Laurie returned her gaze to the choir, her expression suddenly both wistful and resolved. Winifred decided to leave her to her prayers and private thoughts, and moved quietly down the pew.

As she put away the last of the hymnals, she heard the side door close softly, and she glanced up to see that Father Ryan had

428

entered, having finished clearing away the snow, greeting the children as they arrived for rehearsal, and going out in search for their tardy choir director. Winifred hoped he would mend fences with his brother soon, whatever the cause of their most recent disagreement. Father Ryan had not mentioned it, but his mother often phoned to chat with Winifred, to check in on her son without seeming to do so. "I don't know what gets into those boys," she had told Winifred tearfully just that morning. "They've always suffered through a bit of sibling rivalry, but their argument over Thanksgiving dinner was over the top."

"They'll reconcile before Christmas," Winifred had reassured her confidently. "What sort of example would Father Ryan set for the children of our congregation if he didn't?"

Father Ryan's mother had seemed to take comfort in that, and she declared that she was determined to persuade the brothers to talk over their differences before the holidays — because she absolutely insisted that they celebrate together as a family, as always.

Winifred couldn't appeal to Father Ryan's brother, but she could try to nudge Father Ryan in the right direction. He was so intent on the choir rehearsal that he did not notice her approach until she was at his side. When she followed his line of sight, it seemed that he was watching Sophia and Lucas. The pianist was gazing at the choir director with such obvious love and longing it seemed impossible that she could be unaware of it.

"It's painful to be the one not chosen," she murmured to Father Ryan, watching the younger pair. "Even when you acknowledge, deep down, that the choice was the right one, it hurts to think that the one you love prefers someone else."

Father Ryan was watching her, an inscrutable expression on his face. He had probably guessed that she had not really approached him to discuss the two young people, who from the look of things really ought to fall in love, get married, and live happily ever after.

She smiled, patted Father Ryan's arm, and got to the point. "Call your mother tomorrow," she urged. "Tell her everything will be all right. And then call your brother and see that you make it so."

"I will," Father Ryan replied slowly. "I will."

Winifred knew she could count on him to follow through. Smiling, she left him to contemplate how he would broker peace. She was glad to have promising news to share with his mother the next time she called.

Winifred continued her work at a leisurely pace, entertained by the choir. When they were nearly finished, she observed Mrs. Barrett, who had been quietly listening from a back pew, glance at her watch, sigh, and rise. Winifred hurried over as she was putting on her coat and caught up with her just as she exited to the vestibule. "Will you be joining us for the Christmas Eve concert, Mrs. Barrett?" she inquired.

"I think I might." The elegant widow smiled, but her eyes were sad. "The children are splendid singers, and you know how much I enjoy hearing Paul's piano making such beautiful music."

"I do know," Winifred replied kindly. "Our two young volunteers do such a wonderful job with the children."

"Oh, I agree. The boy who sang the solo in the first carol has such a beautiful voice."

"Yes, he does." Without thinking, Winifred added, "The poor dear. What a Christmas he and his sister will have this year."

"What do you mean?"

Winifred hesitated, reluctant to trespass on the family's privacy. "Well, you see, his father is serving in Afghanistan. About two months ago, a convoy was in a terrible accident — a truck struck some sort of bomb on the roadside. Lieutenant Moran is a genius with machinery, and he volunteered to go out and help get the convoy moving again."

"They were attacked while he was making the repairs?"

"Yes, I'm sorry to say that they were. Some soldiers were killed, others injured, and somehow in the midst of it, Lieutenant Moran went missing."

"How does a soldier just go missing?" It sounded to Winifred like a rhetorical question. "Surely with all their resources and contacts, the military ought to be able to find him, or —" Mrs. Barrett hesitated. "Or his remains."

"I don't know," said Winifred, spreading her hands. "I can't pretend to understand the military."

"I happen to know a few people who specialize in it." Briskly, Mrs. Barrett took a small steno notebook and slender black pen from her purse. "Would you spell his name for me, and tell me anything else you know about his disappearance? I can make a few calls. They might turn up nothing new, but it doesn't hurt to try."

Gratified, Winifred told the senator's widow all she knew, and as Mrs. Barrett put away her notebook and pen, they agreed not to mention it to Laurie until they knew more. When Winifred thanked her, Mrs. Barrett waved it off. "It's no trouble at all, really. It's the least I can do, considering how much pleasure his children and their friends have given me and Paul with their singing."

"Oh, yes, the choir has come such a long way since Sophia took on the role of choir director." Winifred turned her gaze back to the choir and sighed. "It's such a shame about her job."

"What do you mean? Is Sophia leaving St. Margaret's?"

"Oh, no, certainly not. It's her other job — her paying job. She teaches music at Peleg Wadsworth Elementary in Watertown."

"That's where Paul attended school."

"Yes, I remember," said Winifred, thinking of the boy she had known so many years before, the bright lad with an ear for music and no piano at home to play upon. His school music classes had made a great difference in his life. He had told her so. "Our Sophia found out earlier this afternoon that her position is being eliminated. It's terribly unfortunate, not only for her but for her students. The state budget for education was slashed, as I'm sure you know, and a local tax levy measure failed in last month's election. Since the federal funding almost certainly won't come through —"

"Why is that?" Mrs. Barrett interrupted. "Why almost certainly?"

"Well, with your late husband's passing," said Winifred delicately, "the vote in the Senate is guaranteed to go the other way, isn't it?"

"I most definitely disagree. Let's not concede defeat until the Senate reconvenes and we see where the votes lie."

"Of course you know much more about politics than I do, but isn't the fellow who's expected to replace your husband entirely set against it?"

"You must mean the governor's brother-in-law." Mrs. Barrett frowned. "The governor hasn't appointed an interim senator yet, but you're right, rumor has it that his brother-in-law is the front-runner."

Winifred refrained from admitting that she had a more reliable source than mere rumor. A certain member of the governor's staff served on St. Margaret's Altar Committee, and she liked to chat. "Perhaps the governor will have a change of heart," she said, although her source suggested otherwise.

Mrs. Barrett folded her arms and

shrugged, her black purse dangling from the crook of her arm. "The governor should want to avoid charges of nepotism. What he really ought to do is choose someone as qualified as his brother-in-law but more appealing to voters. Someone likable, perhaps someone other than a career politician."

"Someone who cares about education and the poor." Winifred smiled brightly. "Perhaps I should volunteer."

Mrs. Barrett smiled. "Why not? I could put in a good word for you if you like. I expect to see the governor tonight."

"No, no, dear me, no," Winifred exclaimed, until she realized Mrs. Barrett was teasing her. "Very well, then, if you insist. It's not a position I would seek out, but if I'm asked to serve, I couldn't possibly refuse."

After promising to be in touch with any news, Mrs. Barrett explained that she was expected at a benefit dinner and hurried off to her car. By then rehearsal had concluded, so Winifred went to the front of the church to bid the children farewell. When she found Alex putting on his coat, it was difficult not to confess that Mrs. Barrett was making inquiries on his father's behalf. "I hope you have a very Merry Christmas, Alex," she said instead.

"Thanks," he said, suddenly glum. "It won't be the same without my dad around."

"I'm sure that's true, dear."

"There's stuff he does to make it special, you know? It won't feel like Christmas without him, especially if the stupid Internet is still broken and we can't even talk to him."

"Well —" Winifred paused to think. "Is there anything you can do to fill in for your father?"

"Like what?"

"The stuff he does to make Christmas special, as you say. Can you do any of it in his place?" Quickly Winifred added, "Only safe things, of course. Nothing involving fire or rockets."

Alex grinned. "Christmas fire rockets. Cool."

"Only safe things," she repeated emphatically. At that moment, Charlotte approached to collect her brother. "Oh, Charlotte, dear, I have a favor to ask."

"Sure, Sister. Anything."

"Miss Sophia put me in charge of making the programs for the choir concert, and I thought it would be lovely to include the poem from your Christmas story."

A smile briefly lit up the girl's face before worry replaced it. "I'd like that, but . . ."

"But what, dear?"

She winced and tucked her hands into her coat pockets. "I was kind of hoping everyone would forget about it."

"But it's such a charming story," Winifred protested. "At the very least, I think you really ought to share it with your mother."

Charlotte's eyes widened in alarm. "You told her I got it back?"

"Didn't she know?" One look at the girl's stricken expression gave Winifred her answer. "Oh, dear. My apologies, Charlotte. I assumed you had told her."

"Told her what?" Alex queried.

Ignoring him, Charlotte gulped air. "It's okay. She knew about the assignment, and the contest. I read the story to her before I turned it in. She would've asked about it eventually, or my teacher would've told her."

"What story?" Alex persisted. "What contest?"

"Your sister wrote a wonderful Christmas tale," Winifred told him.

"Oh, that. I thought it was a poem." Alex frowned at his sister, confused. "I know it was. I saw you working on it — I mean, I *heard* you working on it, and working on it, and working on it. You kept repeating lines and changing one word and changing it back."

Winifred and Charlotte exchanged a look. "You remember that clearly?" Winifred asked him.

"Well, yeah. It was really annoying. And now that poem is stuck in my head. 'I heard the choir on Christmas Day, I'd rather go outside and play, than hear my sister's poem all day.' "

"That's not how it goes," Charlotte snapped.

"Maybe that's how it *should* go."

Charlotte took a deep breath, let it out, and regarded Alex with barely contained exasperation. "I'm not going to get mad at you, and you know why? Because we're in church, and because you're a witness."

Alex's face wrinkled up in bewilderment. "What did I witness?"

"My creative process."

"I don't get it."

"That's okay. Mom will." Charlotte smiled tentatively up at Winifred. "Thanks, Sister. You can use my poem for the concert program. See you Christmas Eve." She tugged her brother's coat sleeve, and the two children hurried off to meet their mother at the door.

Winifred watched them go, smiling.

The church had fallen quiet as the children departed, and when Winifred glanced around, she realized that Father Ryan had left as well — to phone his brother, she hoped. A laugh caught her attention, and she turned around to discover Sophia and Lucas putting away sheet music and tidying up the choir seats. "Should I meddle?" she mused aloud. "Oh, why not. I've already caused so much mischief today, what's a little more?"

It was not exactly the soundest ethical argument she had ever made, but when she considered how Sister Mary Joan might have responded if Winifred had asked her advice, she imagined her old friend and mentor smiling in amusement and raising no objections.

"Nothing ventured, nothing gained," she murmured, crossing the transept to join the young people at the piano. "Such a delightful rehearsal," she declared, and they broke off their work and conversation to smile back. "That first carol the children sang, the one based upon the poem by Longfellow — I'm not as familiar with it as the others but I'm quite taken with it."

"I'm glad you enjoyed it," said Sophia. "Every year I like to include a song or two with a connection to the community."

"Oh, yes, Longfellow was a local boy, wasn't he?" Winifred gave a little start. "Oh,

I shouldn't keep you two, tonight of all nights. Don't you have a traditional date after the last rehearsal before the Christmas Eve concert? You go out for a bite to eat and exchange Christmas gifts, isn't that right?"

"Well —" Sophia threw Lucas a quick glance. "I guess it *is* a tradition, but I don't think we would call it a —" She fell abruptly silent and glanced at Lucas again.

"We usually go out and celebrate after the concert," Lucas quickly explained. "Not that, I mean, not that we're going out in any sense other than, you know. Going. And out."

"So it's a tradition," said Winifred carefully, making sure she got it right, "but not a date, and you aren't going out tonight, but on the night after the concert, and you may be going *outside,* but you are not *going out.*"

Sophia and Lucas looked at each other, and then at her, and then in unison they nodded, Sophia embarrassed, Lucas pained.

Winifred shook her head and laughed. "Well, I might have gotten it word perfect but I don't understand half of what I just said. Goodness, young couples today certainly have a way of making simple things

440

unnecessarily complex! I blame social media."

"We're not a couple," Sophia blurted. When Lucas winced, Sophia's regret was clearly deep and immediate. "I said that about ten times more emphatically than I should have. I was only trying to clarify — I didn't mean —"

Lucas managed a smile. "It's really okay. I understand."

Winifred knew it was time to make her exit. "I'll leave you to it, then, whatever your plans for the evening are." She turned and began to walk away, but then she paused to smile back at them. "I must say, in this festive season, there's something so absolutely wonderful and life-affirming about seeing a young couple in love. It just warms my heart."

With one last nod for each of them, she continued on her way.

Just as she reached the door, she heard Sophia ask Lucas, "Do you think she meant us?"

Winifred waited for the door to close behind her before she burst into merry laughter.

# Chapter Sixteen: Christmas 1863

Although Charley chafed to be confined to the house and lamented his absence from the First Massachusetts Cavalry, Henry knew that his eldest son was happy to spend Christmas at home among his family. He grew stronger every day, and he whistled and sang as he went about the house, playing chess with Ernest, singing at the pianoforte with Alice, and delighting Edith and Annie by attending a series of dainty tea parties in the nursery. Once Henry even came upon Charley in the study, propped up with a lotus-leaf pillow in the largest chair, ordering supplies for his next campaign.

"One would think you were returning to the field tomorrow," Henry had exclaimed, able to regard his son's eagerness with good humor knowing that Dr. McGill had forbidden him to rejoin his regiment for six months. "That tomorrow is a good way off."

"I want to be prepared," Charley had said, grimacing slightly. He never uttered a single murmur of complaint, though he had a wound through his back a foot long. He pretended it did not hurt him, but Henry knew better. Every morning he had to help Charley wash and dress, and even those simple tasks caused him pain. Henry admired his son's newfound sense of responsibility, but Henry considered the six-month prescribed convalescence to be a great gift, and not a day passed but he was thankful for it.

Christmas Eve at Craigie House was a simple but joyous affair, with a tree for the children on Christmas Eve and the reading of Charles Dickens's thrilling *A Christmas Carol* by the fireside in the evening. The next morning there were gifts to open and carols to sing, and at midday the family enjoyed a delicious feast, with a menu that boasted many of Charley's favorite dishes.

In the late afternoon, after bidding farewell to a few last callers and seeing the children settled down to new books and toys, Henry decided to go for a stroll. He had brought home a bothersome cold from Washington, and he hoped a turn in the brisk, frosty air would clear his head.

As Henry passed through the gate and

stepped onto the sidewalk, a sudden gust of wind jostled his hat. He pulled it on more firmly, tightened his scarf, and set out with his back to the wind. In the distance he heard a church bell ringing out a poignant carol, like a voice calling out a joyful Christmas greeting to listeners far and near, a wish for peace on Earth and goodwill to all.

Henry smiled, remembering the great, sonorous pealing of bells that had heralded the dawn of Christmas that morning. Every belfry had proclaimed the good news of the birth of the Christ Child, in Boston and Cambridge and throughout Christendom, one unbroken song of peace and love as the sun rose and darkness gave way to light.

Then a shadow fell over his thoughts. Had the young men on the battlefield heard the distant bells welcoming Christmas morning, or had the sublime carol been drowned out by the thundering of cannon? How many sons, brothers, fathers, and husbands in camps, on battlefields, or in hospitals had perished in the time that the bells had tolled the promise of peace and goodwill? The nation had been rent asunder, and many a family with it. It seemed impossible that there could be a single household, North or South, that did not grieve on that Christmas Day, missing a beloved soldier shivering in a camp or hospital or prison hundreds of miles from home, mourning one who had fallen to artillery or illness, suffering all the deprivations and dangers of war, appealing to the Lord for deliverance that never came.

Did those forlorn households hear the joyful ringing of Christmas bells or the sorrowful tolling that marked a funeral? Did they hear merry pealing, or only an echo of the bleak misery of war?

Henry's throat constricted. It seemed absurd to celebrate Christmas in such dark days. Songs of peace on Earth and goodwill to men mocked the last cry of a soldier cut down by a bullet, the unfathomable grief of an enslaved mother whose child had been snatched from her arms and sold away from her forever, the endless mourning of countless wives, children, mothers, sisters, and sweethearts whose hearts had died with the men they loved, uncounted casualties of war. There was no peace on Earth, only war, war and death and abandonment and mourning. Where was God's peace? Where, for that matter, was God? When countless voices cried out His name in the hour of death, in the endless years of mourning, why did He do nothing?

"God is not dead," a gentle voice spoke behind him, "nor doth He sleep."

"Fanny —" Henry whirled about, but no one stood behind him. A horse pulled a sleigh a block away down Brattle Street, light spilled through the windows of dozens of houses, merry laughter and music momentarily broke the stillness as a front door opened to welcome guests and closed again — but Henry stood on the sidewalk alone.

A steady wind stirred his whiskers and scarf; a few lacy flakes of snow fell upon his eyelashes. He blinked them away, his breath trapped in his throat, aching and raw. He had heard Fanny's voice so clearly, so unmistakably, so warm and compassionate and familiar and close that he should have felt her breath on his cheek.

"Fanny," he murmured, tears filling his eyes.

He was alone, and yet he was not.

"God is not dead, nor doth He sleep," Henry repeated, committing the phrase to memory. Quickly he strode down Brattle Street toward home. He could not pretend to comprehend God's plan, but he had faith that there was one, and in the fullness of time, all would be revealed. Evil would fail and good would triumph. Surely someday there would indeed be peace on Earth and goodwill to all — Union and Confederate, slave and free, man and woman, believer and skeptic.

He would write about it, and perhaps, in his way, he could help bring about that better, peaceful, harmonious world the bells proclaimed when they filled the skies with their joyous carols on Christmas Day.

# CHAPTER SEVENTEEN:
## CHORUS

Lucas watched Sister Winifred bustle cheerfully away, reluctant to face Sophia, to ascertain how horrified, amused, or repulsed she was by the elderly nun's unwittingly devastating remarks.

"Do you think she meant us?" Sophia asked.

"I think she did," Lucas replied cautiously.

Sophia uttered a small, helpless laugh. "Well, that was embarrassing, wasn't it?"

Stung, Lucas managed to keep his voice light. "How so?"

"To be called out like that. For her to assume we're a couple — not only that, but a couple in love."

Lucas shrugged, put away the last of his sheet music, and zipped his bag shut. "Is it really such a bizarre assumption? We're friends, we spend a lot of time together —"

"I didn't say it was bizarre —"

"Merely insulting, then."

"Lucas —" Sophia studied him, confused and hurt. "Why are you acting like this?"

"No reason." Lucas pulled on his coat and slung the strap of his bag over his shoulder. "I'm sorry. Never mind. See you at the concert."

"Lucas, don't." Sophia caught him by the sleeve as he passed her on the way to the door. "Let's talk about this. I'm sorry if I gave you the impression that I was insulted. I'm not. I was just surprised. It was —" She paused, thinking. "It was an unexpected comment from an unexpected source."

"Fair point," Lucas admitted. "I expect unexpected comments from Sister Winifred, but maybe not the matchmaking kind."

Sophia winced from embarrassment, but even then she was beautiful. "Do you think that's what she was doing?"

Lucas sighed. "Not exactly, since she thinks the match has already been made."

"Right." Sophia nodded, and her features relaxed into a tentative version of her usual smile. "Are we still on for dessert and coffee after the Christmas Eve concert?"

"I'm up for it if you are. Crema Café?"

"Don't they close at nine?"

"Right." He tried to come up with another option, but suddenly he felt so overwhelmingly frustrated and weary that nothing else came to mind. "We'll think of something."

"Maybe Turkish coffee and baklava at Café Algiers?"

Lucas thrust his hands into his pockets and managed a smile. "Yeah, that sounds great."

"Lucas," said Sophia, pensive again, "you're not angry with me, are you? I'm sorry if I acted weird about what Sister Winifred said, but it was just so —"

"Unexpected. Yes, I know. You've said."

"Wasn't it unexpected for you?" she countered. "You've never been interested —"

"No, Sophia. *You've* never been interested. I've always been interested. Even when you were with someone else, when I was with someone else —" He took a deep breath and spoke as clearly as he could, because he had said too much already not to make absolutely sure she understood him. "I will always be interested, Sophia."

Sophia stared. "Lucas, I —"

"You don't have to say anything. Actually, I think it would be better if you didn't." He forced a smile, but it felt like a grimace. "I'm going to leave now, before I do any more damage."

She nodded, speechless.

"I'll see you Christmas Eve." Lucas turned and strode from the church, silently berating himself. It was impossible to be angry with Sister Winifred — she was kind and sweet and hadn't meant any harm — and as he thought about it as he trudged home through the snow, she had done him a favor. His secret was suffocating him, and if the truth ruined their friendship, he would have to live with that. He would rather endure rejection now than suffer in silent hope waiting for — what? For Sophia to read his mind and discover how he felt, for her to suddenly fall in love with him? As Father Ryan had said, Lucas had never given Sophia any reason to think of him as more than a friend. It was far more likely that she would have remained oblivious, and eventually, when she got over her broken engagement, she would start dating someone else, someone brave enough to tell her that he loved her.

Thanks to Sister Winifred, Sophia knew Lucas was interested — the understatement of the century. He couldn't leave it at that. He would tell her the whole truth and hope for the best.

"Thank you for taking my call, Richard," said Camille into her cell phone. "Please give my love to Julia and the boys. Merry Christmas."

"Sounds like that went well," Robert remarked from the driver's seat as she ended the call.

"Absolutely. He's going to make locating Lieutenant Moran a top military priority, and no one will want to disappoint him." Camille settled back into her seat, smiling. "Richard has so much on his plate that I hate to impose, but what's the point of having the personal cell phone number of the chairman of the joint chiefs of staff if you don't call him every once in a while?"

"I'd say it was for a good cause."

"The very best of causes — locating a lost soldier, reuniting a husband and father with his family." That was the outcome Camille hoped for, although she knew there were other, crueler possibilities. "The chairman promised that the search will be thorough and it'll continue until Lieutenant Moran is found. He says it may just be an unfortunate paperwork error, and that at this very moment the lieutenant might be recuperating in a hospital in Kabul or Germany with no idea that he's officially missing."

Robert nodded, but Camille had studied the back of his head and the set of his shoulders for too many years not to know when something troubled him. Sure enough, after they drove a block or two in silence, he said, "Mrs. Barrett, I hope the general's right, but if Lieutenant Moran's been at an army hospital all this time, wouldn't he have gotten in touch with his family by now?"

"If he were conscious and able," Camille acknowledged. "If he knows who he is. Remember he was involved in a deadly attack. He might have been seriously injured."

"I'll keep him in my prayers, ma'am."

"As will I." Camille tapped her cell phone against her palm, thinking. Richard wasn't her only friend with connections in the region. Three of her former colleagues from her reporting days had gone on to become foreign correspondents, with networks of contacts and informants not only in the military but in the villages and marketplaces. Civilians often quietly confided to the press when they would not speak to any military authority. Surely someone had witnessed the attack and knew what had become of the lone American soldier left behind. Someone knew and someone would talk.

Quickly Camille called her old friends, speaking with one and leaving urgent messages with the others. By the time the car pulled up to the Fairmont Copley Plaza, Camille was satisfied that some of the cleverest people she knew were on the case.

Robert assisted her from the car, and the doorman swiftly welcomed her in from the cold. She was a few minutes late, but not unfashionably so; by the time she checked her coat and entered the ballroom, they were still serving cocktails and passing the hors d'oeuvres. Before she had a glass of white wine in her hand, she had been greeted warmly by several friends and twice as many acquaintances. Other people she had never met, but who had known or admired Paul, came forward to offer their condolences, which Camille accepted graciously. Although it pained her to be forcibly reminded of his absence — as if she could forget, as if she were not constantly aware of it — she was nevertheless moved to see how much Paul had meant to so many of his constituents and colleagues, and how they wanted to comfort her and honor him.

Just as the master of ceremonies invited the guests to be seated for dinner, Camille spotted the governor in the crowd and gracefully maneuvered to his side. "Governor," she greeted him, smiling, feigning pleasant surprise at a chance encounter. "How very nice to see you."

"Camille, hello." He took her hand and

kissed her cheek, smelling faintly of cigar smoke and gin. "You're looking lovely, as always. It's good to see you back in Boston."

"It's good to be home," she said, emphasizing the last word ever so slightly. The governor had once famously accused Paul of being a Washington insider, which was absolutely ridiculous. "I had hoped we'd be seated at the same table so we could chat. But alas —" She gestured to a table just ahead. "I'm there, and you're much closer to the front."

His eyebrows rose, and there was a hint of wariness in his smile. "Something on your mind?"

"Yes, actually, there is." She slowed her pace to prolong the conversation, and he obligingly did the same. "I understand you haven't made up your mind about whom you'll appoint to finish out Paul's term."

"No, not yet, although I have a short list." He gave her a sidelong glance. "Do you intend to lobby for someone in particular?"

"Yes, Governor. Myself."

He stopped abruptly. "You?"

"Why not? I know the job; I've been doing it for many months now, some might argue for several years. I know Paul's constituents and I care deeply about the future of our state." She touched him on the arm and leaned forward confidentially. "And I think we can agree that nothing will show your commitment to bipartisanship and transparent governance more than if you were to appoint someone who is not in your back pocket. Appointing your brother-in-law sends quite the opposite message."

"He's not on the short list."

"That's not what I hear."

She could see the wheels turning in his mind as he studied her appraisingly. Paul had always been more popular than the governor among Massachusetts voters, and Paul's approval ratings with registered members of the governor's party were remarkably high. The governor surely was aware of the long and honorable tradition of widows finishing out their late husbands' terms; the practice had become less common in recent decades, as women had proven themselves able to campaign and be elected on their own merits, but for more than one hundred years, it had been the only way a woman could serve in Congress.

"That is an inspired idea," the governor told her. Almost everyone else had taken their seats, and their conversation was in danger of becoming conspicuous. He held out Camille's chair, and as she smiled and seated herself, he bent low and said, "Let's talk soon and work out the details. I'd like to make an announcement Monday morning."

"Certainly. Shall I call you tomorrow?"

"Why not have dinner with me and Julia instead?"

"I'd be delighted."

"I'll have my assistant call yours." He straightened and, ever the consummate politician, he addressed the others seated at her table, offering a few cordial remarks that left everyone feeling pleased and appreciated, as if he had come by especially to meet them. Then, with a last nod for Camille, he went off to find his own place.

Elated, she took the first opportunity to slip away between courses, and from a secluded corner of the lobby, she phoned her assistant and told her of her impromptu meeting with the governor.

Kendra was guardedly optimistic. "Are you sure you have the job?"

"I'm sure. From his perspective he has as much to gain by appointing me as I do."

"He wants to bask in your popularity," Kendra speculated, undoubtedly correct. "Are you *sure* you have the job?"

"I'm so sure that I want you to phone everyone on Paul's staff and tell them to report to work as usual on the first Monday morning after New Year's Day." With a gasp, she said, "Most of them have probably found new jobs already."

"I've kept track of those who haven't, in case we heard of any openings. If we consolidate your staff and what remains of the senator's, you'll have everything covered, and I don't think you could find a more qualified, more dedicated team anywhere."

"I like the sound of that. Thank you, Kendra."

"You're very welcome," she replied. "Well, Madame Senator, what will be your top priority once you take office?"

"Funding for education," Camille immediately replied. "It's absolutely essential that we provide the children of Massachusetts with the best possible chance for success in life."

She knew it was what Paul would have wanted.

Charlotte watched the passing scenery as her mother drove her and Alex home from rehearsal. "Mom," she eventually said, "I have some good news and some bad news. Which would you like first?"

"The bad news," said Alex eagerly.

"I asked Mom."

"Oh, I don't know, honey." Their mother

sighed and glanced down the street to her left before making a right turn on red. "I could use some good news. Let's start with that."

"Okay." Charlotte steeled herself with the memory of Sister Winifred's praise. "Remember that Christmas story I was working on?"

"The one for the Alice Longfellow Creative Writing Competition? Of course I remember. It was excellent, and I say that as a professional."

"The thing is . . ." Charlotte took a deep breath. "Remember the poem I put in it, about the choir? The good news is that Sister Winifred wants to print it in the programs for the Christmas Eve concert."

"Charlotte, that's wonderful! Congratulations."

"What's the bad news?" Alex demanded.

Charlotte prepared to speak — and discovered she couldn't.

"Honey?" Her mother threw her a wary glance before returning her gaze to the road. "There's something else?"

"The bad news is that Mrs. Collins thinks I plagiarized the poem."

"What? How could she think that?"

Charlotte shrugged and knotted her fingers together in her lap, her eyes filling with tears.

"That's crazy," said Alex. "You'd rather get run over by a car than cheat at school. You don't even need to cheat."

"No one *needs* to cheat," said their mother emphatically. "Charlotte, are you sure? Is it possible you misunderstood her?"

"No. Definitely not. You can read what she wrote on my paper. It's pretty clear."

"That's preposterous." Her mother gripped the steering wheel tightly and her voice carried an edge. "You've had straight A's since the first grade and she can't see fit to give you the benefit of the doubt?"

"I guess not." Disbelieving, Charlotte peeped at her mother from the corner of her eye. Wasn't she going to ask if the poem was really hers? Without any evidence or cross-her-heart testimony, was her mother really going to side with Charlotte against a teacher? Grown-ups always believed one another before trusting a kid, or so she had always thought.

"Her poem is so good that Mrs. Collins thinks a real poet wrote it," Alex speculated. "I mean, obviously."

Their mother shook her head, her mouth tight, her expression indignant and angry. "It's a sign of something very wrong in our schools that students are penalized for doing too well."

"Next time I'll throw in a few spelling mistakes," said Charlotte glumly, but before her mother could protest, she quickly added, "I was just kidding."

"Always do your very best work, both of you," their mother emphasized. "Oh, sweetie, I can't believe this. What grade did you get?"

In a small voice, Charlotte said, "She gave me a C."

"What?" cried Alex. "You got a C? You?"

"Alex," their mother admonished, but she was too distracted to put much force behind it. "Charlotte, I'd like to read your teacher's comments tonight. I'm curious to see her reasoning. Either way, as soon as we get home, I'm going to email her and schedule a conference. I might ask the principal to join us."

"You don't have to do that."

"Actually, I think I do." Their mother fell silent for a long moment. "Honey, I think it's wonderful that your poem will be printed in the concert program, but I'm sure you must be disappointed about the contest."

Charlotte nodded, thinking of how much she had wanted to see her mother's face shining with pride as Charlotte read aloud her story at the special lunch with the editors and judges, how she had wanted to give the plaque to her for Christmas and tell her she owed her everything, how she had looked forward to running out to the end of the driveway on Christmas morning to bring in the newspaper and show her mother and Alex her story, running in a neat, wide column beneath her name and her school photo.

"I know it's not the *Boston Globe*," her mother continued, "but my editor wants some Christmas features for the next issue, and he might be interested in your story. Would you like me to submit it?"

"Yes," cried Charlotte. "Yes, please! Except — can I change a few things first? I thought of a better introduction and I don't like the description of the choir director on the second page."

Her mother laughed. "Spoken like a true writer. Of course you can revise it first. I won't need to show it to my editor until Monday morning, but that deadline is absolute."

"I'll have it done," Charlotte promised. Her heart sang; her head felt light and merry. She should have told her mother ages ago.

462

"Mrs. Collins is so stupid," said Alex scornfully. "She should've known Charlotte didn't cheat."

"I think we can all agree on that," said their mother.

"All Mrs. Collins had to do was type part of the poem in Google and she would have known in five seconds that it hadn't been published anywhere before."

"Oh my gosh." Charlotte turned in her seat to stare at him, astounded. "You're not only a witness, you know how to find the evidence."

"Your word is evidence enough for me," their mother said.

Gratified, Charlotte smiled at her. "But not for everyone." Turning back to Alex, she shook her head in amazement. "You're a genius, Alex, and not just at setting things on fire."

Alex grinned, pleased and proud. "But *especially* at setting things on fire."

Ryan would have called his brother as soon as rehearsal ended, but he needed time to plan what to say. Sister Winifred's wise words were a revelation that had rendered him stunned and enlightened. All those years, all those cutting remarks about the Church and the priesthood — Ryan had always assumed that Liam scorned his calling. It had never occurred to him that perhaps his brother envied it.

Somehow that changed everything. Liam had always deserved his compassion and understanding, but it was a lot easier to be understanding when one actually understood.

He braced himself with a strong cup of coffee before dialing his brother's number. The conversation was stiff and awkward, so Ryan cut the small talk short and apologized for their argument over Thanksgiving dinner. Liam replied that it wasn't Ryan's fault and it wasn't an argument, more like a heated discussion. "Whatever it was, I regret it," said Ryan. "Especially since it upset Mom and Dad."

"Yeah," said Liam, his pained tone perfectly conveying a wince. "That was unfortunate."

"Let me make it up to you," said Ryan. "I know you love local historical architecture. Why don't you come by St. Margaret's and I'll give you the grand tour?"

"Isn't this your busy season?" Liam said archly, but then his tone softened. "Actually, I've read about St. Margaret's, and it's intriguing from both historical and aesthetic perspectives."

"Two words, bro: grand tour."

"Well —"

"Why don't you come on Christmas Eve, you and Eileen and the kids? You could bring Mom and Dad too. We have a great children's choir, and they're putting on a concert before Mass. I could show you around afterward."

"I don't know." Liam hesitated. "I don't know. I'll need to check with Eileen. She might already have something else planned for our Christmas Eve."

"Oh. Well, it is kind of last-minute."

"I'll let you know, okay?"

"Sure. Sure."

"Either way, thanks for asking."

Ryan assured him it was no problem, and if Christmas Eve didn't work out he'd be happy to give Liam a tour another time. Heart heavy, he hung up the phone, stared into space for a long moment, then sighed, washed his coffee cup, and returned to the chapel to find solace in his evening prayers.

As the weekend passed, Ryan hoped Liam would call to let him know his plans, but the busy days swiftly passed without a word from his brother. And then it was the morning of Christmas Eve, sunny and cold, crisp and blue-skied, although as she spread jam on her breakfast toast, Sister Winifred put her head to one side, listened intently, and declared that it would snow after nightfall. Somewhat unnerved, Ryan glanced at the table and was relieved to see the same prediction on the front page of the *Globe*.

Ryan did not know whether his brother intended to accept his invitation until an hour before the Christmas concert, when Liam texted, "On our way." Eagerly, nervously, Ryan waited in the vestibule, welcoming parishioners and stealing quick glances outside whenever someone opened the front doors. At last they arrived — Liam looking wary, his wife hopeful; their mother on Liam's arm, beaming; their father stoop-shouldered and keen-eyed; Liam's sons looking around with interest, nudging each other and whispering private jokes.

Overwhelmed with joy and relief, Ryan hurried forward to greet them, but as soon as the others in the vestibule realized the newcomers were their priest's family, so many came forward to be introduced that Ryan had no opportunity to speak with his brother before they were obliged to take their seats for the concert.

Ryan was very happy that his family had chosen that day to come to St. Margaret's. The children's choir performed beautifully, their sweet voices the perfect joyful noise to celebrate the sacred anticipation that was Christmas Eve. Young Alex performed his solo with exceptional grace and richness, astonishing in a boy his age. Afterward, Ryan saw him glance over at his sister, grinning, and she returned a proud smile — a Christmas miracle in miniature. He hoped Laurie had seen it too, and he decided that if Charlotte and Alex could set aside their sibling rivalry in honor of Christmas, surely he and Liam could.

After the concert, Ryan celebrated Mass with an abundance of reverence and joy. The children's choir sang for the Mass, their pure, clear, youthful voices a touching reminder of how Jesus had come into the world as a child, as a helpless infant, beloved of his parents, subjected to the persecutions and political turmoil of his day. As Christians professed to love the baby Jesus, so too should they love all children — their own, of course, but also their neighbor's, and the stranger's, and the children who would enter the world in generations to come, long after they themselves had moved on.

After the service, Ryan returned to the vestibule to wish his departing parishioners a merry Christmas, and then, while a beaming Sister Winifred led the rest of the family to the parish house for coffee, apple cider, and gingerbread cookies, Ryan took Liam on the grand tour of St. Margaret's. "I hope I didn't oversell this," he remarked as they put on their coats and headed outside.

"You raised my expectations when you called it the 'grand tour,' " Liam warned, smiling faintly as in unison the brothers tucked their hands into their pockets. "I feel like I already know quite a lot about St. Margaret's from your pianist."

"Lucas?"

Liam nodded. "He took my History and Theory of Historic Preservation class a few years ago. I assigned a paper on a local building of historical significance and its role in the community, and he wrote about St. Margaret's."

"I remember. Lucas told us he picked St. Margaret's from a list his professor made." Ryan stopped short and put his hand on his brother's shoulder. "This is amazing. You sent Lucas to us."

"Hardly. I gave the class a list. Lucas picked your church."

"You put St. Margaret's on the list." In spite of Liam's envy or sense of rejection or whatever other emotions complicated his feelings, he had included Ryan's parish on the list.

"It's architecturally and historically significant," said Liam, somewhat defensively.

"Yes, and we all know that places fitting that description are hard to come by in Boston and Cambridge."

Liam punched him lightly in the arm. "Shut up."

"Or what?" said Ryan, laughing. "You'll tell Mom?"

"Don't think I won't."

Ryan elbowed him. "Idle threats."

"We'll see who's laughing when you find coal in your stocking."

Ryan's laugh rang out, and Liam grinned, and the snow fell lightly upon them.

The sidewalk needed clearing again by the time the tour was finished, but instead of joining the rest of the family at the piano, where Sister Winifred was merrily leading them in Christmas carols, Liam offered to help shovel.

They tackled the front stairs first, the snow light and powdery enough that a broom would have served well enough. "Your nephews were very impressed with the children's choir," Liam remarked, planting his shovel in a snowbank. "Connor loves to sing. He asked me if he could join."

"That depends. Is he any good?" Ryan ducked when Liam flung snow at him.

"Seriously, he's welcome to join. Sophia and Lucas are fantastic teachers."

Liam shrugged, considering. "When do they practice?"

"Tuesdays and Fridays from four thirty until six. They sing at nine o'clock Mass every Sunday morning, and at the afternoon vigil Mass on the first Saturday of the month. They also have a few holiday concerts during the year, like today's."

"Nothing on Wednesday?"

"Not unless Christmas or Easter happen to fall on a Wednesday."

"That could work. Connor has this other thing on Wednesdays, a rocketry club."

"Really," said Ryan, intrigued. "That sounds like fun."

"Yeah, it is. I wish they'd let me join. A few Harvard students started it a few years ago, and it's really taken off." He winced. "Sorry, bad pun."

"I forgive you."

"From a priest, that really means something." Liam grinned. "Anyway, it's a great organization. The kids learn all about rocketry — the science to it, not just the awesome explosions. Force, aerodynamics, thrust, lift, and lots of other things Connor could explain much better than I."

"It sounds perfect for a kid I know, one of

the boys in the choir."

"I can email you the details. Or we can talk about it tomorrow at Mom and Dad's." Liam hesitated. "You are coming, right?"

"I won't be able to leave St. Margaret's until three, but I'll be there."

"So we'll talk then."

"Sounds good."

With a sigh, Liam pulled his shovel free from the snowbank and resumed clearing the stairs, and after watching him for a moment, Ryan did too.

They would talk tomorrow. Everything would be all right between them as long as they kept talking.

Sophia was immeasurably proud of her young singers, and she told them so after Mass, lighthearted and smiling, glowing in the aftermath of their musical triumph. Before they bundled into their coats and departed with their parents, she gave each child a candy cane and a Christmas ornament shaped like a quarter note and wished them a Merry Christmas. They all happily echoed the phrase, some flinging their arms around her waist in spontaneous hugs, and most offered her small gifts — homemade treats, hand-knit scarves, gift cards to local shops and restaurants, always welcome on a public schoolteacher's budget.

Her heart plummeted. At least for the next few months she could still claim that title. She should probably save the gift cards until then, when she would be forced to make severe budget cuts — unless somehow the funding came through for her school.

Deliberately, she shoved aside all worry and dread over her pending unemployment. It was Christmas Eve, and the choir had performed the best concert of her tenure as director, and she did not want to spoil the moment.

After the children were gone, Sophia and Lucas tidied up, joking and laughing as they recapped the concert. "Sister Winifred's programs were a big hit," Lucas remarked as he finished packing up his sheet music.

"I think Charlotte's poem deserves the credit." Sophia slipped into her coat, wrapped one of her new scarves around her neck, and then, suddenly shy, she asked, "Are we still on for dessert?"

"Of course. Why wouldn't we be?"

Sophia shrugged. "No reason." She had spent every day since their last rehearsal contemplating Sister Winifred's words, but if Lucas wanted to pretend the incident had never happened, so would she.

Gathering up their gifts — between them

they had received enough tasty baked goods to see them through all twelve days of Christmas — they left St. Margaret's and walked down the block to Café Algiers for Turkish coffee and baklava. They chatted for a while about their plans for Christmas Day and New Year's Eve — they both confessed that they planned to stay home on the last night of the year, Lucas to work on his thesis, Sophia to revise her résumé. After the server came by to refill their cups, Sophia smiled and reached for her bag. "Do you want to open your gift first?"

"Absolutely." He grinned and rubbed his hands together, feigning avarice.

She laughed. "I hope you like this. If you don't, feel free to regift it, because I can't return it." She took a thick, red envelope from her bag and set it on the table beside his coffee cup.

He picked up the envelope and shook it close to his ear. "Is it a bowling alley?"

"No, just the deed."

He grinned and carefully tore open the flap. "A card," he said, peering inside. "Yeah, I'm definitely going to regift this."

"The gift is *in* the card, silly."

Obligingly, he looked. "Tickets to . . . something." He studied them more carefully. "Oh, wow, this is great. Tickets to a lecture by Anders DeWitt."

"It's next month," Sophia explained, in case he hadn't seen the fine print. "In New York. I know that's inconvenient, but he isn't speaking anywhere closer."

"Not a problem." He regarded her, happy and amazed. "Are you a fan of Anders De-Witt?"

"I thought you might be, and that's what matters. I know only what I've read on the Internet."

"He's one of the most prominent urban planners and designers of our time. I couldn't even tell you how many awards he's won. I have all of his books." Then he paused. "Two tickets."

"Right. I thought we could go together, take the train and spend the day in New York and then go to the lecture." Quickly she added, "But the tickets are yours. If you'd rather take one of your friends from school, that would be perfectly fine."

"No, let's go together."

"One of your fellow students might get more out of the lecture than I would."

"Sophia." He caught her eye and smiled. "I'd rather go with you. Really."

"Okay." Relieved, she smiled and sat back in her chair. "Good."

He carefully tucked the tickets and the

card back into the envelope and set it aside. "I have something for you too."

"You'd better."

He smiled as he took a small box from his bag, but something in his eyes suggested nervousness. "You know, I actually bought this for you last year."

"Really?" Intrigued, she studied the box as he placed it before her. "Why didn't you give it to me then?"

He shrugged. "Bad timing."

Her curiosity rising, Sophia unwrapped the box, lifted the lid — and discovered, resting on a soft bed of white cotton, a pair of exquisite combs with jeweled rims.

With a soft gasp, she reached out a fingertip and traced the smooth lines of one of the combs. "Tell me you didn't sell your pocket watch," she said shakily, trying to keep it light.

"I did."

She knew he never owned a pocket watch.

"Sophia." Lucas reached across the table and took her hand. "I'm glad we're friends."

"So am I."

"I also love you."

Her heart pounded, and she found herself without words.

"I'm content to stay friends if that's all we can be. Do you know why?"

She shook her head.

"Because your happiness is more important to me than my own." He squeezed her hand, gentle and affectionate. "Your happiness is essential to my own."

She felt tears of joy springing to her eyes. "Do you know what would really make me happy?"

"What's that?"

"If you'd kiss me."

The more Alex thought about what Sister Winifred had said, the more he believed she was right. Alex was the man of the house while his father was away, and the man of the house made gingerbread pancakes on Christmas morning.

On Christmas Eve he set his alarm, and on Christmas morning it woke him well before sunrise. Without turning on the light he tiptoed downstairs, past the living room, where he paused to admire the pile of colorfully wrapped gifts that had mysteriously appeared beneath the Christmas tree overnight. Grinning, he plugged in the lights, found a box with his name on the tag, and gave it a careful shake — then remembered his mission and hurried on to the kitchen.

A few days earlier, he had found the recipe on a card in the wooden box by the toaster, and when his mom wasn't watching, he had checked the pantry and the fridge to make sure they had all the ingredients. Now it was time to fill in for his dad, like Sister Winifred said.

In a big glass bowl, he mixed together flour, baking soda, baking powder, and salt. He stirred in ginger, cinnamon, and ground cloves. In another bowl, he melted some butter in the microwave, added brown sugar and molasses, broke two eggs into the mix, picked out a few stray eggshells, and stirred it all together into a gooey mess. He added the dry stuff to the wet as he had seen his dad do and prepared the griddle.

The first batch turned out burnt on the outside, soggy on the inside, so he threw them out and adjusted the temperature. The second batch wouldn't flip right, so he ended up with a lot of crumbly half-circles and weird shapes. He could eat those, he decided, but he couldn't use up all his batter on mistakes. Resigned, he turned off the griddle, went upstairs to Charlotte's room, and shook her awake.

"What do you want?" she groaned, rolling over onto her side. "We can't open gifts until Mom gets up."

"I know that. I need your help with something else."

"What?"

"Pancakes. What do you know about them? How do you make them turn out . . . like pancakes?"

She rolled over and peered up at him. "I ask again, *what?*"

"It was supposed to be a surprise," he began, and went on to tell her about his project gone awry. "Can you tell me what to do?"

She flung off the quilt and sat up. "It would be easier if I showed you."

"Okay, if you want to." He would never admit it, but that was exactly what he had hoped she would say.

They tiptoed downstairs, and after Charlotte's eyes widened at the mess and she declared in a whisper that he was responsible for cleaning it up, she was actually helpful. Her pancakes turned out perfectly round, cooked all the way through but not dried out or burnt to a crisp.

"You're a pancake genius," Alex said, impressed.

Charlotte smiled as she expertly flipped the last one. "Thanks."

Suddenly the overhead light went on in the hallway. "Kids?"

Startled, they looked up and discovered their mother standing in the doorway, blinking in the light, mouth open, hand over her heart. Alex watched with increasing alarm as her gaze traveled around the kitchen, taking in the spilled flour on the counter, the trail of molasses on the floor, the ruined practice pancakes in the trash, the milk carton left open on the table, the fingerprints in batter on the refrigerator door, all of it.

"We're making gingerbread pancakes," Alex said weakly. "It's not Charlotte's fault. It was my idea. She was just helping me. I was going to clean everything up before you saw it, and I still will, I promise."

His mother burst into tears.

"Mom?" said Alex, horrified. "I'm so sorry. Please don't cry."

"I'm not sad," she assured him, reaching into the pocket of her robe for a tissue. "I'm crying because I'm happy."

In a tiny, bewildered voice, Charlotte said, "But we made this huge mess."

Alex felt a sudden surge of love for her for that "we."

Their mother nodded. "Yes, but you made it *together.*"

Words seemed to fail her then, so she smiled instead and held out her arms to them. Alex ran over and hugged her, and Charlotte — after removing the last perfectly

cooked pancake to a plate and turning off
the griddle — hurried over to join in.

Soon their mom put on a pot of coffee,
Alex set the table, and they all sat down to
eat. They all agreed that Alex and Charlotte's pancakes were second in delicious-
ness only to their father's, and that they
ought to seriously consider opening a
pancake restaurant.

Even though everything was happy and
good, Alex suddenly felt a surge of loneliness. "I miss Dad."

"Me too," said Charlotte, her eyes welling
up with tears.

"Can we talk with him today?" Alex
begged. "Please, Mom?"

"It's not up to her." Charlotte played with
her fork, then set it down next to her plate,
looking miserable. "It's not her fault that —
that the Internet is broken over there."

Their mother took a deep breath. "Kids,"
she said, her voice trembling, "there's
something I need to tell you."

Charlotte shot her a sharp look and
straightened in her chair.

"What?" said Alex.

She reached across the table, took his
hand in one of hers, and Charlotte's with
the other. "I need for you to be brave."

Alex nodded, suddenly afraid.

Their mother inhaled deeply. "Alex, Charlotte, the reason we haven't —"

At that moment, the phone rang.

Laurie jumped, released her children's hands, and banged her knee against the table leg. Dishes clattered and the phone rang again. "Honestly," she said, shaken, her thoughts immediately going to telemarketers and robocalls. "Who would call this early on Christmas morning?"

"Grandma," said Alex helpfully. "Aunt Susan. Uncle John —"

"Oh, right." Feeling foolish, Laurie rose and hurried over to snatch up the phone. "Hello?" she said, heart pounding from the strain of a confession narrowly averted. She could not ruin Christmas for Alex and Charlotte, not after all they had done to make the morning special for her.

"Good morning. May I speak with Mrs. Moran, please?"

"This is Mrs. Moran."

The voice was deep, crisp, and formal. "This is Lieutenant Colonel Jorge Reyes with the United States Army."

She could not breathe.

"Yes?" She finally managed. Her voice sounded as if it came from a thousand miles away. Suddenly dizzy, she stumbled back to

481

the table and sank into a chair. "Yes?"

"I'm calling to inform you that your husband has been injured, and at this time he is being transferred to the Ramstein Air Base in Germany."

"You found him?"

"Yes, ma'am. We found him."

"He's alive? He's all right?"

"Mom?" said Alex, frightened. Charlotte darted from her chair and put her arm around his shoulders.

Silent, shaking, Laurie wept while the officer anticipated her questions and answered them all. Jason had suffered injuries to the head, shoulder, and left leg in the attack, and it was believed that he had either sought shelter behind a rocky outcropping or had wandered there, dazed from the blow to his cranium. After the convoy was forced to evacuate, two children from a nearby village had found him, and under the cover of darkness, they had guided him to their home. Their family had hidden Jason in a small back room, tending his wounds, keeping him warm and fed, risking their own lives to save his. They had no means to transport him to his base, nor any way to safely send a message to the Americans or their allies. The children's mother, an educated woman who years before had taught a school for girls in her home in defiance of the Taliban, heard of a Western reporter asking around the village about the attack on the convoy. She managed to get word to him about their unexpected guest, and the reporter arranged for him to be smuggled out of the village and back to the base.

"Two children," said Laurie softly, wondering if they were a brother and a sister, if they were around the same ages as her Alex and Charlotte.

"Yes, ma'am."

"Are they safe, the children and their parents?" she asked. "There won't be any retaliation against them?"

The lieutenant colonel assured her that the operation had been completely undetected. No one except the family and the correspondent knew that an American soldier had stayed in the village.

"Your husband should be arriving at the Landstuhl Regional Medical Center within two hours," Reyes continued. "Before his flight took off, he asked us to pass on a message."

"What did he say?"

"He asked us to assure you that he's fine, and that he loves you all, and that he wishes you Merry Christmas."

Laurie closed her eyes and pressed a hand to her mouth to hold back sobs, trembling. He was alive — injured, but conscious, and well enough to send them a message.

"Mrs. Moran?"

"Yes, I'm here," she said quickly, suddenly aware that he had been speaking. "I'm sorry. What did you say?"

"Your husband will be able to phone you late tonight — later this afternoon, East Coast time. Would you be around to take his call at fifteen hundred hours?"

"Yes, of course. Of course. We'll be home. We'll be ready."

After the call ended, Laurie composed herself, assuring Alex and Charlotte — who were worried and frightened, with tears streaming down their cheeks — that their father was going to be fine, that everything was going to be fine.

Then she took their hands again, gazed at her two wonderful, precious children, and told them she had bad news, good news, and an apology.

At noon the bells rang in the steeple of St. Margaret's Church, joyful, hopeful, singing of peace on Earth and goodwill to every-one, everywhere. Sister Winifred stood in the vestibule beside Father Ryan, sending

484

the parishioners home with warm smiles and heartfelt wishes for a blessed Christmas.

Hate was strong, she knew. In some cold hearts and shadowed places, hatred ruled and wreaked havoc upon all it encountered, mocking the gentle promises of a better way to live. But wild and sweet, the bells sang of hope and salvation, of love and kindness, of the spirit of giving, of offering shelter to the lonely traveler, of light in dark hours.

"God is not dead, nor does He sleep," she murmured to herself as the last of the worshippers departed for home, for the welcoming hearths of friends and family. For each of them she wished the blessings of hearts full of goodwill and a renewed dedication to the glorious promise of peace on Earth.

# CHAPTER EIGHTEEN: CHRISTMAS 1864

When the festive season came once more, Henry decided to celebrate in the good old style, with family and friends and all the glorious sights, sounds, tastes, and fragrances that reminded him of the happiest moments of Christmases past, cherished in memory, celebrated in song. A Yule log crackled on the hearth, and a plum pudding smoked upon the sideboard. Santa had filled the little girls' stockings with his prettiest offerings, and all day long, friendly visitors brought the much-beloved children so many gifts that the drawing room table resembled a stall at a fancy fair. All who joined the Longfellows at Craigie House enjoyed music and stories, a delicious feast and excellent wine, cheerful company and news from loved ones far away.

Throughout December — a month of bitterly cold temperatures and heavy snowstorms that had followed a glorious prolonged Indian summer — Henry had observed that the people of Cambridge and Boston were anticipating the holidays with more enthusiasm than they had since before the war. The deeply packed snow had forced the horse trolleys to cease operations for a long string of days, so the people had sped about their errands in sleighs, the riders' happy shouts and the chime of harness bells ringing out joyful carols through the frosty air. Shops had been crowded with eager folk purchasing gifts for friends and family; throngs of people had jammed the markets determined to procure the fattest, tenderest goose for their Christmas feasts. Prices had been remarkably reasonable, given the constraints of wartime, and Henry was especially pleased to hear that bookstores had enjoyed brisk sales, the best in years.

It was a season of hope and joy. President Abraham Lincoln had been reelected in November, and although the war ground on as destructive and devastating as ever, General Grant's armies steadily advanced, and it began to seem that a Union victory was inevitable if not imminent. Although the Union army had endured significant losses, the North yet had more men and resources than the South, and the results of the November elections proved that the people of the North were resolved to see the war through to victory. It could not come too soon.

On Christmas Day, just as Henry, his family, and their guests sat down to their Christmas feast, word came to Craigie House that three days before, General William T. Sherman had sent President Lincoln a most extraordinary dispatch, one that he had received only that morning: "I beg to present to you, as a Christmas gift, the city of Savannah, with 150 heavy guns and plenty of ammunition, and also about 25,000 bales of cotton." Yet another of the great cities of the South had fallen, and surely the capture of Petersburg and Richmond would soon follow. With no more strongholds to retreat to, the Confederacy would be forced to capitulate.

But while the people of the North celebrated — some confidently, others with guarded optimism — Henry's heart was wistful, longing, as it had been every holiday since he had lost his beloved wife. And on that Christmas Day, no hopeful anticipation of peace could ease his yearning to be reunited with two absent loved ones: not only Fanny — his wife, his darling, his life's companion — but also his eldest son, Charley.

Charley's wounds had been frustratingly slow to heal. Two months after the bullet had torn through his son's back at New Hope Church, Henry still had to help him dress in the morning. Then, in the second week of February, the Longfellow family was astonished to read in the newspaper that on January 24, Charley had been promoted to First Lieutenant with the First Massachusetts Cavalry. Charley had received no official word of his promotion, but while Henry was investigating to confirm whether the report was true, Charley received an official letter from military headquarters informing him of his dismissal from the army due to disability.

Shocked, Charley immediately replied that he had every intention of returning to duty as soon as he was fit. On February 17 he submitted to an examination by a doctor, who provided an affidavit that he believed Charley would be "sufficiently recovered to return to his post in forty days from the date hereof." But it was to no avail. Despite the military's well-known need for officers, Charley's injuries precluded him from returning to duty. Charley was bitterly disappointed, all the more so because he had been unable to muster in at his new rank, so he was discharged as only a second lieutenant.

Henry was sorry for the sake of his son's pride, but he was greatly relieved that Charley's service to the United States Army had come to an end. For a year, Henry had begun each day with fear and trembling, his heart tight in his chest, his anxiety unrelieved until he had finished reading the long column of names in the day's casualty list. Now, at last, he could breathe easier.

It was not until April 20 that Charley's wounds had finally closed, but some pain and sensitivity had lingered, and his legs had been stiff and his feet swollen, reminding Henry of a gouty old aristocrat. As the summer passed, Charley had abandoned his plans to seek a new commission and had resigned himself to the rank of veteran. But the conclusion of his military career did not mean the end of his restlessness and hunger for adventure, and by autumn, Henry had resolved to remove his eldest son far from the temptations of the battlefield.

In October, Henry proposed that Charley tour the Mediterranean. Friends and relatives abroad would meet him at various cities along the way, and he could experience a grand adventure that would be both educational and enlightening. Charley quickly warmed to the plan, and while

Henry inquired about a suitable vessel and made the arrangements, Charley studied maps and read travel memoirs in preparation for the journey.

On the first day of November, Charley had embarked for Palermo, Italy, aboard the bark *Trajan*. He wrote home frequently as he traveled from one city to the next, brief, enthusiastic letters describing the cities he explored, the people he met, and the sights he had seen. On Christmas Eve, the family received a cheerful letter wishing them a Merry Christmas from Gibraltar. Charley was well rested and happy, had recently toured Tangiers, and was planning to travel next to Málaga, and after that, Palermo again and perhaps Grenada. Charley was not viewing as many cathedrals and libraries as Henry had done during his own tours of the Continent, but he and Charley were two very different men, and Henry accepted that his son would chart a separate course.

Henry would have preferred to have his eldest son home that Christmas Day, but he was content to know that Charley was safe and happy. Ernest, Alice, Edith, and Annie were near, so Henry did not want for company, nor did he ever doubt that he was as cherished and loved in his household as any father could ever hope to be.

He knew too that the poem he had written that strange and wondrous Christmas night the year before was as true on the eve of peace as it had been during the bleakest nights of the war. It was not in vain that Christmas bells rang out their old familiar carols, wild and sweet, of peace on Earth and goodwill to all. The unbroken song, wistful and true, filled the skies above Cambridge and Gibraltar, across North and South, over homes and upon battlefields. On Christmas Day, the promise of peace offered a soft and shining light in dark times, an eternal flame that warfare could not douse, nor hatred extinguish.

# ACKNOWLEDGMENTS

I offer my sincere thanks to Denise Roy, Maria Massie, Liza Cassity, Danielle Springer, Christine Ball, Ben Sevier, and the outstanding sales team at Dutton for their contributions to *Christmas Bells* and their ongoing support of my work. I'm grateful for the generous assistance of my first readers, Marty Chiaverini and Geraldine Neidenbach, whose comments and questions were, as always, insightful and immeasurably helpful. I also thank Nic Neidenbach, Heather Neidenbach, Marlene and Len Chiaverini, and friends near and far for their support and encouragement.

The research for my historical fiction always involves many enjoyable visits to the Wisconsin Historical Society on the University of Wisconsin campus in Madison. The sources that most informed this work include: William Appleton, *Selections from the Diaries of William Appleton, 1786–1862* (Boston: Merrymount Press, 1922); Charles C. Calhoun, *Longfellow: A Rediscovered Life* (Boston: Beacon Press, 2004); Robert Ferguson, *America During and After the War* (London: Longmans, Green, Reader, and Dyer, 1866); Andrew Hilen, "Charley Longfellow Goes to War," *Harvard Library Bulletin,* XIV, Nos. 1 and 2 (Winter and Spring 1960), 59–81, 283–303; Christoph Irmscher, *Longfellow Redux* (Urbana and Chicago: University of Illinois Press, 2006); Christoph Irmscher, *Public Poet, Private Man: Henry Wadsworth Longfellow at 200* (Amherst and Boston: University of Massachusetts Press, 2009); Henry Wadsworth Longfellow, *The Letters of Henry Wadsworth Longfellow, Volume IV,* ed. Andrew Hilen (Cambridge, MA: Belknap Press of Harvard University Press, 1972); Henry Wadsworth Longfellow, *Poems & Other Writings,* ed. J. D. McClatchy (New York: The Library of America, 2000); Samuel Longfellow, *Life of Henry Wadsworth Longfellow: With Extracts from His Journals and Correspondence* (Boston: Ticknor and Company, 1886); Thomas H. O'Connor, *Civil War Boston: Home Front and Battlefield* (Boston: Northeastern University Press, 1997); Charles Sumner, *Memoir and Letters of Charles Sum-*

*ner,* ed. Edward L. Pierce (Boston: Roberts Brothers, 1893).

I also relied upon several excellent online resource while researching and writing *Christmas Bells,* including the National Park Service's website for Longfellow House (www.nps.gov/long/index.htm), Genealogy bank.com's archive of digitized historic newspapers (www.genealogybank.com), the website of the University of Notre Dame (www.nd.edu), and the website of the Archdiocese of Washington, DC (www.dc priest.org).

Henry Wadsworth Longfellow's poem "Christmas Bells" inspired the historical elements of this novel, but the contemporary storyline I owe to Madison Youth Choirs, director Michael Ross, and conductors Randal Swiggum and Margaret Jenks. I wrote a significant portion of this book in the hallway outside the studio during rehearsals, and I thank the talented young singers of Britten and Purcell for offering me many hours of entertainment and inspiration. For more information about Madison Youth Choirs, including a schedule of upcoming performances, classes, and auditions, please visit their website at www.madisonyouthchoirs.org.

As always and most of all, I thank my

husband, Martin Chiaverini, and our sons, Nicholas and Michael, for their enduring love, tireless support, and inspiring faith in me. You make everything worthwhile, and I couldn't have written this book without you. Merry Christmas!

# ABOUT THE AUTHOR

**Jennifer Chiaverini** is the *New York Times* bestselling author of *Mrs. Lincoln's Dressmaker, The Spymistress, Mrs. Lincoln's Rival, Mrs. Grant and Madame Jule,* and the Elm Creek Quilts series. A graduate of the University of Notre Dame and the University of Chicago, she lives with her husband and two sons in Madison, Wisconsin.